COA

D1393836

THE REDEMPTION OF
ALEXANDER SEATON

THE REDEMPTION OF ALEXANDER SEATON

Shona MacLean

Quercus

First published in Great Britain in 2008 by

Quercus
21 Bloomsbury Square
London
WC1A 2NS

A CIP catalogue reference for this book is available
from the British Library

ISBN (HB): 978 1 84724 505 2
ISBN (TPB): 978 1 84724 506 9

10 9 8 7 6 5 4 3 2 1

Typeset by Deltatype Ltd, Birkenhead, Merseyside
Printed and bound in Great Britain by Clays Ltd, St Ives plc

To the memory of my parents,
Gilleasbuig MacLean
and
Margaret Jane Farquharson MacLean

There is a short glossary of Scottish words on pages 303–4.

PROLOGUE

The younger of the two whores rifled the man's pockets with expert fingers. She cursed softly. Nothing.

'Leave off, then,' said her sister. 'The baillie will be here any minute.'

Mary Dawson rolled the man back over onto his face. He groaned, then retched, and she cursed once more as he vomited bile over her foot. 'Pig,' she said, and kicked him. The wind sent a barrel careering past them down the brae to smash into a wall below. Somewhere, a dog took up a demented howling.

'Leave off,' insisted her sister.

Mary turned away from the form slumped in the overflowing gutter. Janet was right: there was nothing to be gained here tonight. A quarter hour would see them out of this tempest. She took her sister's arm, ready to make for home, and then she froze. A hand had come from the ground and held her ankle. The words came in a ghostly rasp. 'Help me,' he said.

Unable to shift her foot, Mary looked to her sister in silent, distilled fear. The other lifted a finger to her lips and came slowly towards the dying man. Mindless of her already filthy clothes, Janet knelt down in the gutter and brought her mouth to his ear. 'Say it again.'

The words came with even greater labour this time. 'Help me,' he repeated. Another convulsion took him. He gave up his grip on Mary's ankle and his face sank into the mud.

Janet Dawson looked up slowly at her sister, who began to shake her head. 'Oh, no. We cannot. There has been evil here. This is no drunk. Think who he is. The baillie will come soon; they will have us for this.'

'We cannot leave him,' said Janet.

'Please,' her sister pleaded. 'They will have us. Let's get us away.'

'He'll be dead by morning if we leave him.'

Mary looked at the still convulsing form at her feet. 'He's dead anyway.' The bell above the tolbooth clock began to toll the hour. Her voice was urgent. 'It is ten. The baillie ... Let's get us away.' But she knew her words were useless.

Janet Dawson, on hands and knees now, heaved the man's left arm about her own neck and looked up at her sister. 'Well? Am I to do this alone?'

At length the two women got him to his feet, but all strength was gone from him, the paralysis spreading through his body slowly disabling him. They half-carried, half-dragged their burden across the cobbles of the Water Path towards the old schoolhouse. The wind whipped their hair across their faces and the rain lashed into their thinly clothed backs. His head, beyond his power to lift now, lolled first onto the one and then the other. Words came, forced from his constricting throat, but were lost in the darkness as the storm took hold of the night.

The bolt on the pend gate leading to the backyard of the house gave little trouble to the sisters, and they passed through, taking the man the last few yards of his journey. A gust slammed the gate shut and the tableau was gone from view. The schoolhouse was all in darkness: no light from lantern or candle glimmered from the cracks in its shutters as it loomed three storeys over the narrow street below. No sounds came either of disturbance in the backland, of startled animals, no knocking on the door. It was not many minutes before they came out again the way they had gone in, not three this time but two.

'Do you think they will find him?' asked Mary.

'They will find him.'

'Aye, but in time?'

Janet was weary now, anxious for her rest and to be out of the storm. 'I cannot tell; we have done what we could. It is in God's hands.' They closed the pend gate behind them and went swiftly up the Water Path. As they forked to the left, Janet looked back. She had not been mistaken, then: they were watched. The figure met her eyes for a brief moment then disappeared into the darkness. She would not tell Mary whom she had seen, not until they were safe home. Perhaps it would be better not to tell her at all.

ONE

The Tempest

Banff, the same night, two hours earlier.

The old woman lifted her candle the better to observe me.

'You would not think of going out tonight?'

'Aye mistress, I would.'

She fixed me with a look I knew well. 'On a night such as this, no honest man would stir from his own hearth.'

'Indeed he would not, mistress,' I said. 'But as you have often assured me, I am no honest man.' I took down my hat and, bidding her no farewell, I went forth into the remorseless storm.

The wind, which from my attic room in the old school house had wailed through every crack and crevice like a legion of harpies, was transformed out in the night into the implacable wrath of God himself. No lantern could withstand its force and every window was shuttered against its blasts. The sea raged over the harbour walls and soaked me with its spray. There was not a single light in the town of Banff to guide a decent man on his way. As for me, I knew my way well enough. I pulled my great furred cloak more tightly round me and pressed on. All manner of ordure rushed past my feet through the open gutters towards the sea. Many foul things could be disposed of on a night like this and tomorrow the streets would be washed clean of them. I was glad of the darkness.

Some way ahead of me, perhaps only ten yards apart, lay St Mary's kirk and the Market Inn, the one offering redemption, the other damnation. Once, I had believed I knew where each lay. Once, but not now. At the kirkyard I turned right and presently pushed open the door of the inn.

Jaffray, of course, was already there. Charles Thom sat opposite him, but did not lift his head when I entered, despite the fearsome blast that followed me through the door and caused the shutters to bang on their hinges. The shore porters looked up for a moment from their gaming by the hearth, but seeing no one of interest, returned without comment to their dice. In a gloomy corner, furthest from the fire, watched James Cardno, the session clerk. My arrival prompted no greeting other than the slow smile of satisfaction which spread, ill-masked, across his lips. He was the eyes and ears of Baillie Buchan who, by some oversight on the part of Beelzebub, could not be in two places at once. I wondered what unfortunate soul the baillie was visiting himself upon on this hellish night.

Jaffray hailed me as I approached his table. 'An ill night, Alexander.'

'It is that, doctor,' I replied, taking my usual seat beside him.

Charles Thom said nothing, but continued to gaze in misery at his ale. Such misery was best left alone; I would not press him. Jaffray, however, was determined to draw him out. He addressed himself again to me.

'Charles is not in the best of spirits tonight, Alexander. I have been hard put to extract two words from him this last half-hour.' He sucked ostentatiously on his pipe. 'I have pulled more compliant teeth.'

The young master of the burgh song school looked up at this. 'What would you have me say? It is an evil night? The ale is good? My pupils sang well today? The kirk was cold yesterday and is like to be so again tomorrow? Take your pick, doctor, please.' He returned to the contemplation of his ale.

I shot Jaffray a quizzical glance. 'Marion Arbuthnott,' he replied, not quite under his breath. And louder still, 'and our good provost's nephew – an interesting fellow.'

This was enough to rouse Charles once more from his indifference. 'And what, precisely, is so interesting about him? That he has travelled? Well so have you, doctor.'

Jaffray raised a good-natured eyebrow. 'And you think I am not the more interesting for it? I assure you, I was more of a dullard than Cardno there before I left on my *peregrinatio*.'

This at least drew a smile from Charles, and I was hard put not to laugh out loud myself, aware as I was of the session clerk's scowl burning into my back. The wind continued to howl through the shutters and down the great chimney-piece of the inn, muffling the conversations rising and falling

4

in Mistress Johnston's parlour. In between occasional arguments over the roll of the dice the shore porters pondered gloomily on the likelihood of the storm abating before the week's end. No boat could drop anchor in the harbour in such weather and none could leave. With no work, there would be no wages. All along the coast it would be the same.

'The poor box will be out for them before the week's end,' said Jaffray, nodding to Anne Johnston to send them over another round of ale.

'There will be little enough in it,' said Charles, not lifting his head from his tankard.

'Oh? Who have you been asking for?'

'John Barclay,' replied Charles. 'The boy has the voice of a very angel, and not a pair of shoes to his feet. In another age and another place, he would have a stall in a cathedral choir; he would be singing masses for the rich dead. But here, in this godly commonwealth of ours ...'

'He is safe from the tentacles of the idolater, and he can rely on the Christian charity of God's people and the kirk to keep food in his belly and a coat to his back.'

Charles looked to the doctor in mute incomprehension, but Jaffray sat tight-lipped now, only with his eyes directing Charles to where the session clerk sat, storing up his every word.

'Amen to that,' said Charles, instantly understanding, his precentor's mask descending over the mischievous, amused, subversive face he reserved for myself and Jaffray and few others. As master of the song school he received no salary at all, but only the tuition fees of those of his pupils who could afford to pay him. As a perquisite of his post, however, allowing him to scrape a living, he was constrained to take up the psalm in the burgh kirk and to read the lesson there, all for the greater edification of the townspeople. The look of abject misery that settled on his person while performing these duties was born, I knew, of a profound lack of interest in the sentiments he was paid to intone and of an intense dislike of the cold. To those of Presbyterian inclination on the council and the kirk session, however, his demeanour accorded so completely with their own that John Knox himself could not have pleased them better.

My friend's ambitions were simple: to be left to himself and his music. His lack of concern for the good of his soul had given me much anguish in the days before my own fall. Yet, over this last year, Jaffray and I had remarked in him an alteration of spirit, the alteration that comes when a man realises that he no longer wishes to be alone. Edward Arbuthnott, apothecary of Banff, under whose roof Charles lodged, had a daughter, and with that daughter, as Jaffray had now convinced me, Charles was in love. But, like myself, Charles had few prospects of making his way to a more prosperous estate in life, and while Edward Arbuthnott was not an unduly ambitious man, he was as likely to give him his only daughter in marriage as James Cardno was to buy me a drink.

I swallowed some of the Rhenish Anne Johnston had brought me and asked casually, 'So you think Marion is beguiled by the new arrival?'

Charles eyed me grudgingly. 'Her mother certainly is. To that old besom Patrick Davidson is a prayer answered. Old Arbuthnott has years in him yet, but his wife cannot look at him without seeing six feet of good kirkyard earth piled over him and herself and her daughter out on the street. She'll have Marion married to Patrick Davidson the minute he's finished his apprenticeship and Arbuthnott can drop dead the next day for all she will care.'

It was not difficult to believe this of the matron in question, and indeed there was little point in arguing the point with Charles. Even Jaffray could see that. The sense of Marion Arbuthnott marrying her father's apprentice and keeping the business in the family was self-evident. The girl had no brothers, and her mother was no prize on her own. 'And Marion? What does she think?'

He was hesitant. 'Who can tell? I think, maybe, she would not mind the idea.'

'Ach, come now Charles.'

Charles looked at Jaffray. 'No, doctor. I fear I am right. Since Patrick Davidson came to lodge with the Arbuthnotts I have rarely seen her, and I have spoken to her less. At mealtimes he regales us all with tales of his travels. Of France, and the Alps, and of what's left of the Empire. He is a good storyteller, I'll grant you. And the war,' he lowered his voice, 'he tells us of the horrors of the war.'

The apothecary's apprentice had not been the first to make his way to our corner of Scotland with tales of the brutality, the starvation, the rapine and the disease that marched the length and breadth of the Holy Roman Empire. Sons, brothers, friends had left our shores to fight for the Empire or against and had never come home. The frequent call of the kirk for collections to sustain our suffering brethren abroad kept the cause in minds that might have preferred to shut it out. It was in Charles's mind, I knew, and the tales of suffering he had heard from Patrick Davidson, with whom he now shared his attic room at the apothecary's, had engraved images in his head he would not share or indeed acknowledge. He sought to change the subject.

'Anyhow, by night he plays the great hero while I can only play my tunes – the half of them banned by the minister and his godly brethren. And by day, well, by day while I spend my talent trying to wrest a tune from the urchins of this burgh or courting an early death in the freezing cold of that kirk, he trails Marion halfway across the country gathering berries and plants and the Lord alone knows what else for her father's simples and syrups and ointments.'

Jaffray put a warning hand on his arm. 'Mind what you say, Charles. It has been spoken of already at the session and Cardno's ears are strained to your every word.'

The other's expression darkened. 'What have you heard?'

'There are those who suspect the virtue of every unmarried woman, and,' the doctor added quietly, 'that is to say nothing of the witch-mongers.'

I saw the embers of an old terror flicker in Charles Thom's eyes, and he had the sense to say nothing more. He knew that Jaffray was no gossip, but the sick bed was a tremendous place for the imparting of news. The doctor missed nothing. The warning had been given and would be heeded. Through the noise of the storm, the bell over the tolbooth chimed as the town clock struck nine, and Charles drained the last of his ale. 'Anyway, gentlemen, I must leave you. This is no night for aching hearts.' He gathered up his hat and cloak and left, his face thunderous, not pausing to respond to James Cardno's scarcely audible 'Goodnight.'

The door closed behind him and I was able to observe the doctor in one of his rare moments of rest. His short-cropped grey hair gave away something of his fifty years, but his brows were still dark and his eyes alert, and to me he had the strength and vigour of a man half his age. Perhaps I saw only what I wished to see. Conscious of Cardno's interest in our conversation, we drank our wine in silence until a noisy dispute at the hearth over a suspect roll of the dice allowed us to take it up again, in low voices.

'Do they really speak of witchcraft?'

'They are ever vigilant. The new king shows less interest in it than his father once did, but it is a canker all the same and I doubt if it will ever be cut out.'

I knew it was the hunger for the witch-hunt, rather than the ancient pagan charms and potions, that Jaffray spoke of. For too many of my fellow citizens, there was not a misfortune that could not be ascribed to the diabolic agency of another. Ignorance, carelessness, folly and sloth: when their fruits could not be blamed upon a stranger, the malediction of some friendless neighbour could be looked to instead. The vulnerable and friendless were well advised not to call attention upon themselves in times of ill fortune. 'And does the session not see that the apothecary's daughter and his apprentice have good cause for their plant-gathering?' Something in the doctor's expression made me hesitate. 'Or is there more to it?'

Jaffray sighed deeply. 'In the fetid minds of the session there is always more to it. If Marion Arbuthnott be found anything less than pure and virtuous, there are souls enough in this burgh who will see that she pays for it. That a healthy young man and a pretty young woman could wander abroad on their own and not fall prey to carnal lusts is more than our good baillie and his henchmen could conceive.'

I looked long into the dregs of wine at the bottom of my pewter cup. 'Perhaps they are right. I cannot tell.'

Jaffray did not indulge me. 'This is not a way for a young man to live, Alexander. You must give it up.'

'I cannot, doctor, for it will not leave go of me.'

'Then run from it, for it will poison you. I have known other men, good men, who would not let go of such bitterness; they are old now, and dead in their souls. Run from it, Alexander.'

'I cannot. I have nowhere to go.'

We had both said our piece, and so sat in silence a while, but away from his own hearth, the doctor was not comfortable with silences. He called for more wine from the innkeeper and returned to our earlier conversation as if there had been no pause. 'Besides, I do not think Marion is completely lost to our young song schoolmaster. The more her mother presses the interests of Master Davidson, the more the girl will incline to Charles instead.' He shrugged helplessly. 'It is the way with women. My own dear wife, God rest her, only agreed to marry me because her mother could scarce tolerate the mention of my very name.'

I knew this last point to be one of Jaffray's most self-deprecating and favoured lies. When he had returned from Basel to his native burgh almost thirty years ago, clutching his medical degree in his hand, the *summa cum laude* of his laureation not yet grown dim in his ears, every mother in Banff had thrust her daughter in his path. He had had the pick of the crop, and he had chosen, as he often told me, the most beautiful and delicate flower of them all. For thirteen years, blighted though they were by the repeated tragedy of lost children, he had lived with the love of his life, until the last of the lost children took her with it. He had never tried to marry again, and I knew he never would.

'Marion's mother is a formidable woman all the same. Charles will not have it easy. I have never yet seen the apprentice – he does not come here in the evenings.'

'Greater attractions at home than you and the shore porters?'

I laughed. 'Aye, perhaps. He has no need for further schooling and I have had no cause for recourse to the apothecary since you left for the south, so we have not met.'

'And you have not been asked to sit down at the provost's dinner table?'

The question was in jest. I doubted the provost would wish to encourage a friendship between his nephew Patrick Davidson and myself, and the doctor knew quite well that he would not. He also knew that I would care little. 'I cannot believe that you have not made yourself acquainted yet though, doctor. You have been back from your season in Edinburgh almost two days now.'

'Aye and should have returned before that. The place is full of ministers, and not a smiling face amongst them. They spread their misery like a silent plague. God forbid their like should take hold in these parts. The Reverend Guild trumpets here in Banff as he might, but we may comfort ourselves that no one listens to him.' Cardno twitched and Jaffray gave me a sly smile. 'It will be many a long day before I venture there again, or for so long. As for the apothecary's apprentice – yes, I had hoped to meet him at the provost's last night, but he was not in attendance. A pity, for there is much we could have talked of.' He mused silently for a moment and then recalled himself from his reverie, an idea evidently having presented itself. 'But of course. I will invite him to his dinner tomorrow night, and you also, Alexander. With him only lately returned from the continent he is well placed to tell us how things stand. It pains me to think what you have never seen, what you may never see, the great cathedrals and cities laid waste by this insanity of war. Gaping chasms your divinity professors at Aberdeen were powerless to fill.' He nodded to himself. 'But Patrick Davidson and I shall fill them for you; we will pick the continent to the bones. And I have a very fine piece of venison for just such an occasion.'

'You have been treating the laird of Banff again, then?' Jaffray, I knew, was in regular attendance on the laird, who was no more able than were the rest of his rank hereabouts to stay out of trouble and the reach of the point of a sword.

The doctor leaned closer towards me with a conspiratorial smile and a cautious glance in the direction of the session clerk. 'Indeed, no, but his steward was remarkably grateful for my assistance in the passing of a stone not long since.' He sat back, satisfied already with the evening already taking shape in his mind. 'Yes, I have some ointments to collect from Arbuthnott tomorrow; I will engineer myself an introduction to young Davidson and he shall be sitting across from you at my table by seven tomorrow night. You'll be well rid of your charges by then?'

'Well rid.' In the summer months it pleased the burgh council and almost everyone else in Banff that my scholars and I should be in attendance upon one another at the grammar school from seven in the morning until six in the evening. When the winter nights began to draw in, some human pity and common sense impressed itself on our good magistrates, and they allowed that the children might arrive at eight and go home at five. Even so, I knew that in the coldest months of the year, many of my pupils had to stumble a good half of their journey home in the dark without a coat to their back or proper shoes to their feet. If it were not for Jaffray and the few like him there would be many more. My doctor friend practised what others preached. His wealth, he said, was held in stewardship only, and in life he returned to God that which was God's. He had told me once that as the Lord had taken back into His own care all the children He had granted him, then he would care for those He had left behind. Many an orphan and a poor man's child in Banff owed their education to the intensely personal piety of James Jaffray. One of them had been Charles Thom.

'Will Charles be joining us?'

Jaffray regarded me with dismay. 'Alexander, I'll swear I never saw a more intelligent man with less good sense than yourself. What in the world is the good of me removing Patrick Davidson from Arbuthnott's table tomorrow night if not to give Charles a clear field? I shall stop at the song school on my way from the apothecary's and tell our friend the good news, so he might make his preparations. I may even give him a few words of advice myself.'

'I should start then by advising him to dispose of that scowl he sported tonight.'

Jaffray nodded vigorously. 'Indeed. On more than one occasion I was constrained to glance at Cardno by way of relief.'

Before our laughter had died down, or the session clerk had mastered his evident fury, the door to the inn burst open and Jaffray's stable boy, utterly drenched, stumbled through it. The look of urgency on his face cut our laughter dead. 'Doctor, you must come. Lady Deskford is in child-bed at Findlater. His lordship urges you to make haste.'

Jaffray drained the last of his glass as he swung his cloak around him. 'For the love of God, on a night like this.'

I put out a hand to stop him. 'James, this is madness; you will never make it out to Findlater tonight.' Findlater Castle stood impregnable, cut fifty feet into an eighty foot rock, nine miles to the east of Banff, glowering out over the Firth towards Sutherland, Caithness and beyond. So impregnable was it in fact as to be virtually uninhabitable. His lordship had built for his family a fine new house at Cullen, but his mother refused to shift, and insisted on keeping her daughter-in-law with her.

The doctor brushed my hand away as his servant handed him his still wet hat. 'If I do not make it, Alexander, neither will she. That last bairn damn near killed her. It's time Deskford took himself a mistress and let that girl alone.' And with that he strode out, with never a backward glance to the company, on whom an astonished silence had fallen, save for the unmistakable sound of James Cardno almost choking on his watery ale.

I stayed in the inn another half-hour or so, no one bothering me. With little remaining to take his interest, Cardno had left not long after the second of my companions, and I was left to my thoughts undisturbed. What I paid out on drink in the Market Inn would have been better spent on coals for the unlit fire in my own hearth. Mistress Youngson had given up telling me so – I was a cause lost. Nine months ago I would not have thought of spending my evenings drinking here. It might pass – just – for James Jaffray or Charles Thom, but it would not pass for the minister of the Kirk of Scotland that I had then aspired to be. And yet, I was as well drinking here as I would be sitting by my own hearth, for I had no calling now. And how was such a life to be lived? I ordered another glass of the Rhenish and swallowed it down quickly. If the storm still raged I would scarcely feel it.

Once out of the inn I was grateful as ever that the journey to my lodgings was a short one. Despite the hour and the undiminished severity of the elements there were other creatures abroad on High Shore as I made my way home. Even on such a night as this, the girls of the street sought to earn their living. The council and the session claimed not to tolerate 'whore-mongering' within their bounds, but Mary Dawson and her sister Janet had too much knowledge of too many of them to fall subject to any but the mildest correction. Discretion was their part of the bargain silently struck with the guardians of our burgh's stability and morals. They called to me from the shelter of the kirkyard.

'Mr Seaton, would you not like something to warm you on this awful night? That must be a cold bed you keep in the schoolhouse.'

The righteous apoplexy of Mistress Youngson should she ever find one of the town's whores, or indeed any woman, in my bed, made the prospect seem almost worthwhile. Almost. 'As ever ladies, I can't decide between you, and I wouldn't slight either of you for all the world.'

Janet's siren voice replied, 'Nobody's asking you to choose, Mr Seaton,' followed by a good-natured cackle from the sisters.

It was an offer they'd made more than once before, and one I had never yet been tempted to accept. 'You would only break me,' I returned, throw-ing them the last shilling from my pouch.

'You're the only decent man in Banff, Mr Seaton ...' and the rest of their words were lost in the wind as I pressed on, the wine and warmth from the inn piloting me home.

As I neared the schoolhouse I noticed a fellow traveller on the other side of the road, at the foot of Water Path. He raised a hand as if to hail me, but his equilibrium failed him and he stumbled to his knees. He called something to me as he tried to right himself, but I did not wait to hear. The Good Samaritan pounded on my conscience but I had seen myself home in worse condition than his more than once, and on worse nights than this. Winning to my own bed was a more pressing concern than helping a stranger to his. The good sisters would rob him, of course, if he had not spent all his money on drink that night, but they would see him to shelter before they did so. Turning into the pend at the side of the schoolhouse I locked the gate behind me and left the fellow to his fate.

As ever at this hour, the schoolhouse was all in darkness. My eyes were practised in seeing through the night gloom. I checked on my schoolroom as I passed. The worn and barren benches echoed to me the incantations of the ghosts of schoolboys past, myself included. *Amo, amas, amat . . . amo; amo; amo.* All was empty and still. The stove was cold, but I knew John Durno would remember his duty as usher and have it lit before I descended again in a few hours to resume my labours.

Thirty-seven steps in darkness to the top of the house and my small and sparsely furnished room. I found my bed without the aid of lamp or candle as I had done many times since that night last summer when I had finally returned, after much wandering, from the meeting of the brethren in Fordyce. Not a minister then, or ever, but condemned always to my schoolmaster's robe. Mistress Youngson's celebratory dinner had lain cold and uneaten on the table two floors below. The rats had it in the end. No need now to toil late at my desk on my Greek, my Hebrew, my Syriac. The midnight oil no longer required to be burnt, so my lamp remained dark. Yet still, as I had done each night since then, I prayed, trying to reach God, trying to reach to that place where faith is. But, as it had been each night, that place was empty. And still I did not know where else to go. The withdrawal of God left me no means to justify my place in this world but to start again. And that beginning was always tomorrow.

My usual sleep was sound and featureless, and I seldom had any awareness of night passing into morning. This night, though, the intermittent banging of the shutters in the storm permeated my consciousness and I pulled the bedclothes ever tighter round me. As the first stray shafts of daylight made their way through my attic window, the banging grew more insistent and I gradually became aware of my own name being called with rising urgency. It was my landlady.

'Mr Seaton, Mr Seaton, for the love of God, wake up. Patrick Davidson lies dead in your schoolroom. Mr Seaton …'

TWO

A Dead Man's Face

And it was so. The stench reached my nostrils before my foot ever reached the bottom of the stair. Mistress Youngson had waited for me as I groped for my cloak and threw it over my shoulders, and she had led the way downstairs by the light of her candle, but when we reached the door of my schoolroom she hung back, as if not wanting to attract Death's attention. I moved past her into the dimly lit room. The windows to the west that afforded some light to my scholars for the greater part of the day remained shuttered. The only candle was at the far end of the room, in the hand of her husband, Gilbert Grant, my friend and master in the grammar school of Banff. He had taught every scholar to come from the town in the last forty years, but now, in truth, I performed more and more of his duties as the weariness of age crept over him. He raised his eyes towards me and said sadly, 'The boy is dead, Alexander; he is dead.'

His wife, still keeping to the doorway added, 'I have sent the lad for Dr Jaffray.'

I shook my head slowly as I drew closer. 'Jaffray is not there. He was called out late last night, to Findlater ...' There was little point in continuing. I could see that Jaffray's skills were, for Davidson, by several hours redundant now. The lifeless form of Patrick Davidson slumped across my desk, his head to one side in a pool of his own vomit, had a strange inevitability to it. The left arm stretched, palm outwards, in front of him, in an ultimately futile effort to support his head; the right hung down to his side, a few stray blades of the same grass that swam in the vomit before him still sticking between the fingers. I had never met the apothecary's apprentice, but the agonised features of the corpse now lying not eight yards from where I stood were, I knew, also those of the man whom I had left in the gutter the night before. I had known from the moment I had

15

stumbled from my bed that they would be. God had started with me a new game.

Grant and I kept a sombre vigil over the body while we awaited the arrival of those who had to be informed of such things. The boy who had been sent for Jaffray had also been told to call up the baillie and the two town serjeants. A servant girl had been sent for the Reverend Guild. The doctor and the minister: one powerless to help in this world, the other powerless now to help in the next. The sins of Patrick Davidson would be called to his account regardless of whatever sentiments Mr Guild might intone.

'He was a good lad, you know,' said Grant. 'A good, bright lad.' He smiled at me. 'Like you yourself. And he kept much to his own company, as you yourself would have done had it not been for the Master of Hay.' There was no hurt in this; he spoke the truth. Gilbert Grant had known me as long as any other soul living, and there was no need for dissembling between us. 'My memory is failing me though, Alexander. Were you ever in the school together as boys?'

'I do not think so. I would have been gone to the college by the time he came up from the song school. My mother may have mentioned him, but in any holiday from my studies I was more often at Delgatie than I was here in Banff. And when I was home I was far too lofty a personage to bother myself with the younger boys.'

Grant's eyes twinkled in a sad smile. 'Aye, it has always been so. The young scholar returned to his native burgh is too grand to look down and see where he came from; you weren't the first to leave with no mind to return.'

He was right: others like me had gone before me and not returned for many a year. But my return had been different. Nine months ago, I had come back. I had come back the much lauded scholar, the attestations of my divinity professor glowing in the paper in my hand. I had been pro-nounced well-versed in the biblical tongues, the handling of controversies, ecclesiastical history and to be sound in matters of faith and doctrine. There remained but the sixth and final trial before the brethren, the ministers of this presbytery – to preach a sermon before them and the people that would meet with the approbation of both. And so I had preached at Boyndie kirk, whose people wanted me for their minister and I had taken as my text Micah, chapter 7, verse 9:

'I will bear the indignation of the Lord, because I have sinned against him until he plead my cause, and execute judgement for me: he will bring me forth to the light, and I shall behold his righteousness.'

How could my sermon on that text have found favour? And yet it did. I who had lived a life blessed, who did not yet know the indignation of the Lord, who covered my own sin, even from myself. The words ought to have choked me in my throat for the shame of it. And yet they did not. My sermon had found favour with the people and with the brethren too. True, the Reverend Guild of Banff had raised one or two objections, but these were of no consequence and were treated as such. And later, in presbytery, the words that would have licensed me to open my mouth to preach as a minister of the Kirk of Scotland were already on the lips of the Moderator when the sudden entry into the kirk of Sir Alexander Hay, laird of Delgatie, Archie's father and the benefactor of all my school and college days, stopped them where they were. Before the whole brethren he had declared his fervent opposition to my being accepted into the ministry and denounced me as a debauched and scandalous person unfit for so godly a calling. He further declared that my sin could not be countenanced amongst honest men and begged that the presbytery would treat no more of me as an expectant for the ministry. And on that bright, clear June afternoon in Fordyce, in that ancient and holy place, all the walls of my deception had come tumbling down around me. The Moderator, Mr Robert Dun, minister of Deskford, a just and godly man, refused to condemn me on the word of one person and I still remembered the kind pleading in his eyes as he had turned to me and offered me the floor to defend myself. Struck dumb with the realisation, at last, that the laird of Delgatie was right, I had offered no word in my own defence and stumbled from the kirk as a blind man from a burning building. Such had been the glorious homecoming of Alexander Seaton. And here before me was the homecoming of Patrick Davidson. I could not believe that he deserved his as I had done mine.

'How did he come to this, Gilbert?' I asked.

He looked down at the body, a corruption of the work of God to something abhorrent. It was not a thing that could be comprehended in his

17

universe of the schoolroom. 'I do not know,' he said. 'I truly do not know. Perhaps the doctor will tell us, or the baillie, no doubt. But it should never have come to this. I saw another life marked out for him.' He paused. 'And never such a death.'

'What was his life, Gilbert?' I asked.

The old man turned from the image before him and sought a recess of his mind. 'A life of love,' he said at length. 'His was a life of love. His father, a lawyer in Aberdeen, died while Patrick was still a baby, and he was taken then by his mother to live with her sister here in Banff. Her sister was Helen – Walter Watt's first wife – although he was not provost then, but a prospering merchant. Walter and Helen had no child of their own; she was with child often, but she never carried one a full nine months. Jaffray did all he could for her, but not one of them lived. I think she would have,' he hesitated, 'I think she would have given much for just one of them to live. But she was not blessed. It wore her out in the end. She was not thirty when she died. But the boy – this boy, Patrick Davidson, her sister's son – was the light of her life. They loved that boy as much as any parents could. He was always to be seen around Helen's skirts in the market place, at the kirk, or atop Walter's shoulders as he saw to his cargoes at the quayside or walked for pleasure along the cliff tops in his rare periods of leisure. But then the boy's mother married again, and took him with her when her new husband, a minister, was called to the charge of a kirk in Fife. Helen's heart was finally broken, and she died soon afterwards. When Patrick was about fourteen, he matriculated at the university at St Andrews. I do not think he came back here often until he returned to take up his apprenticeship at Arbuthnott's. It is a pity you could not have known him. He was a fine boy.'

I watched as he stroked the cold forehead. He uttered not another word. His thoughts were evidently of the child the man had been, mine of the staggering stranger calling for compassion, of the dying man dismissed as a drunkard. The gnawing shame in my gut might have been too much for one who did not live each day with such a sentiment. I could find no words to comfort my old friend and so said nothing. I do not know how long we sat there before the strange companionship of we three men was interrupted by the arrival of Mistress Youngson with a bowl of porridge and warm milk, which she handed to me. 'Take this up to your room and dress, Alexander. The baillie and his men will be here soon, and there will be little enough time for food and drink after that.' It was nine months since she had uttered my Christian name, and so surprised was I by the unwonted tenderness that forgetting to thank her, I ascended the stairs without a word.

I re-entered the schoolroom perhaps a quarter of an hour later, to find the officers of burgh and kirk already there. In the room, aside from Gilbert Grant, were five other living souls: Baillie William Buchan, self-appointed arbiter of all things moral or otherwise in this burgh; the two town serjeants; James Cardno the session clerk, whose report of my movements on the previous evening would still, I had no doubts, be ringing in the baillie's ears, and Mr Robert Guild, minister of Banff and brother to Geleis, the provost Walter Watt's young wife. Guild was no friend of mine – he had been none those nine months ago at Fordyce and he was none now. I was glad to see him there, nonetheless – his well-known antipathy to William Buchan promised that the baillie would not have all his own way in whatever was about to unfold.

As ever, the baillie was dressed entirely in black, save for the plain white collar at his neck. The slight stoop to his shoulders and the ever-watchful eyes gave him something of the aspect of a carrion crow watching its prey. He addressed me without turning his head. 'You have joined us at last, Mr Seaton. Evil has been at work here.' He glanced slightly in my direction. 'You were abroad late last night?'

'Late. Late enough.' I walked the length of the room to my desk.

The baillie was ever alive to the possibility – probability – of evil in the doings of his fellow townsmen, but I knew as I looked again into the face of the dead man that on this occasion at least, he was right. The eyes of Patrick Davidson were frozen in a grotesque comprehension of what was happening to him. There could be no doubt: this had been no natural death, no accidental consequence of too much bad drink. Some external human agency had been employed in the ending of this earthly existence. I spoke my thoughts. 'Poison.'

'There can be little doubt.' It was the baillie who spoke, but the others murmured their assent.

The minister, having kept silent long enough, sought to assert himself.

19

'Has Jaffray . . . ?' but he did not finish his question. Gilbert Grant shook his head. 'My good wife sent for the doctor the instant the boy – John Durno – found him. Jaffray was not at home. He was called out to Findlater late last night. My Lady Deskford . . .' His voice dropped. 'It would have made little difference.' He brushed a little hair back gently from the corpse's forehead. 'He was cold. Long cold.'

No, Jaffray could have done nothing. Patrick Davidson had called for help hours earlier as he stumbled in the shadow of death, but the man who could perhaps have saved him had passed by on the other side. I said nothing further, and found myself, for the moment, ignored. Cardno murmured something to the baillie, inaudible to the rest of us, and the baillie nodded once before turning to issue instructions to the town serjeants standing silently by the still unlit brazier. The session clerk made for the doorway, followed by the serjeants. He addressed Mistress Youngson as he passed, hands already at the keys on his belt. 'We're away for the mortcloth, mistress. Have your girl clean him up.'

The old woman looked witheringly at the clerk. 'That is no work for any girl, James Cardno. If it is beneath you and your men to do the boy this service, I'll do it myself.' And with that the schoolmaster's wife headed slowly towards the back courtyard and the well, more hunched and frail than I had ever seen her.

The minister spoke again. 'And see that it's the best cloth, Cardno. It is the provost's nephew.'

The session clerk looked towards the baillie, and only on gaining the latter's assent did he continue on his way. Guild's displeasure was as impotent as it was evident. Since the day and hour he had been appointed to the charge of Banff, Buchan had been his nemesis, a shadow who thwarted him at every turn. I knew Guild to be a man of inferior intellect, formality rather than faith and great worldly ambition. It seemed part of God's just punishment that such a one should have been amongst those to sit in judgement upon me, and pronounce me unfit to join the ranks of their ministry. To Buchan's credit, it was Guild's lack of fervency in preaching, his lassitude in prosecuting the discipline of the kirk, and his regard for rank that had earned him the enmity and mistrust of the baillie. Buchan's ascendancy on the council and constancy at the session gave him a degree of influence amongst the townspeople that the minister could never hope to wield. As the door of the schoolroom closed behind Cardno and the town serjeants, the baillie turned to the minister and spoke directly to him. 'I think there should be little mistake here, Mr Guild, before you claim kin in virtue of your sister. As you well know, it is the nephew of the provost's first wife, who lies buried in yonder kirkyard and has done these eight years past.' His point being thus made, he turned his back on us both and said nothing more.

Little more than half an hour later, I joined in the grim little procession that made its way through an unusually sombre gathering of the townsfolk from the schoolhouse up towards the Castlegate and the provost's house. Though the hour was still early, rumours of what had occurred in the night had already begun to gain currency in the town, and as our cortège emerged into the nascent daylight, we were greeted by the murmurs of the small crowd that had already gathered outside the schoolhouse.

'A great loss to the provost.'

'Aye, and Arbuthnott too.'

'It's well to be out of it.'

'A scandal on the town.'

'God's will be done.'

The storm of the previous night had completely abated, leaving little trace of itself, other than the sodden streets, which made the pace of the pallbearers necessarily slow. The usual morbid interest occasioned by the sight of the mortcloth was much increased as news spread of the identity of the murdered man. I looked back towards the town: along by Lord Airlie's lodging amongst the old Carmelite yards, derelict for seventy years now, and the great wall of the laird of Banff's palace garden, more and more of my fellow townsmen paused in their early morning labours. Many, though, had seen such things too often before, and soon continued on their way to the marketplace and the setting up of their booths, or to their workshops and backyards. Edward Arbuthnott had joined our procession; I looked for Charles Thom beside him, but Charles was not there.

*

There was no sign of life as yet at the Market Arms, and little stirred in the kirkyard opposite. Janet and Mary Dawson had little truck with the citizens of Banff in the daylight hours; indeed, they had little truck with the daylight hours at all. I could not believe that it was only last night that I had laughed here with the town whores, while Patrick Davidson staggered in agony towards his death. My sense of discomfort mounted as we progressed up the Water Path, and I was glad of the distraction afforded by the necessity of offering an arm to my elderly colleague. He took it gladly, and nodded his thanks. The force of the previous night's rain had scoured the gutters clean. No mark remained where I had seen Davidson stumble and fall the night before, stumble again and try to pick himself up. There was an echo, though, of words I hadn't heard through the ferocious wind, but which I knew had been spoken. Words I had ignored. 'Help me.'

Near the top of the Water Path, close by the entrance to the castle grounds, we passed the site of the new manse the minister had finally succeeded in persuading the council to build for him. The land, to the general astonishment of the burgesses, had been granted for the purpose by the provost himself – the toft where his own former house had stood, the house that had been his before his fortune had been made; the house he had shared with Helen. And now he had granted it for a manse for his brother-in-law. His new wife was thought to be the agent of this change. At the head of the cortège Guild allowed himself a complacent smile while Buchan stared determinedly ahead.

The great oaken doors of the provost's house stood open, awaiting our arrival. Walter Watt and his wife, Geleis Guild, the minister's younger sister, stood a little apart at the far end of the great hall of the house, on either side of the unlit hearth. Quality of craftsmanship was evident in every aspect of the room, from the carved oak panels of the ceiling to the tiling of the floor where others would have only flagstones or wood. A great Dutch side table stood against one wall, a cabinet carved by the same hand against another. Candlesticks on the mantel shelf and holders in the wall-sconces and suspended from the ceiling were fine and intricate work, better than our local craftsmen could supply. And yet it was a sombre place; only the necessary draperies, no tapestries, no painted panels to add relief and colour, only one solitary portrait hanging from the wall. Watt came forward gravely to meet the baillie who, like the rest of us, had removed his hat on passing through the doorway. The baillie inclined his head towards the provost and said something I could not hear. Watt nodded and stepped closer to the pallbearers. At a signal from Buchan, Cardno drew back the top of the mortcloth, far enough to reveal the young man's waxen, but now mercifully clean face. The provost's wife gave out a groan and then collapsed into uncontrolled grief. 'It is him,' said the provost after a long pause, staying a moment longer to gaze on the dead face before going to comfort his wife. I think I envied him that task. I had known her since we were children; her nature had always been kind, and was not belied by her beauty. She was better loved in the burgh than either her husband or brother.

'It is God's will, mistress,' said the baillie. 'We must seek out the evil in the hand that accomplished it, but we must not question His will.'

Drawing his young wife a little closer to him, the provost answered, 'You must forgive my wife, Baillie. She is young and over-tender yet. She welcomed the lad to our home, and loved him well, for my late wife's sake and for my own. And all in all, it is a bad death. A bad death,' he repeated, more to himself than to the rest of us gathered there. The baillie held the provost's gaze for a moment, but said nothing further of God's will. Geleis Guild gradually extricated herself from her husband's embrace and searched her pocket for the lace handkerchief with which she wiped her eyes. The provost held her a little away from him and said, 'Go you to the children now. Do not let them be upset by this. I doubt the girl Arbuthnott will not be here to help you today. Now go.' Eventually comprehending, she nodded slowly and left the room, without having uttered a word.

The provost turned to face the rest of us, and it was clear that his tender manner had departed with his wife. A large and imposing man, he was well over six feet tall with thick dark hair down to his shoulders, and eyes set wide in a broad brow. His clothes gave the appearance of being simple, but their cut was good and the plain dark material of high quality; the fine Dutch lace at his cuffs gave some hint of the wealth his strong hands had garnered. I felt the full force of his personality as he again strode the length of the room to where the body had been laid. He pulled back the mortcloth again and touched the cold cheek. I heard him murmur quietly, 'Oh Helen, that it has come to this.'

'May God preserve us all from such a judgement,' intoned the minister.

'You would do well to see to your sister, sir,' responded the provost, not quite mastering an evident contempt for his brother-in-law. The minister left reluctantly, and much to the satisfaction of the baillie. The latter was the next to feel the provost's ire. 'And you think it God's will, do you, William Buchan, that a boy such as this should die choking in the gutter on his own vomit, like any common vagabond?' As the baillie opened his mouth to reply, Walter Watt raised a prohibiting hand. 'Spare me your sermon, man; we have ministers enough. As to your proper concerns, tell me what you know. Are the reports I hear correct? He was found in the schoolroom, covered in filth and vomit?'

It was Gilbert Grant who replied. 'It is true, alas, true. The boy John Durno found him at about a quarter to six, when he came to light the brazier in Mr Seaton's schoolroom.'

The provost turned a suspicious eye on me. It was seldom nowadays that I found myself worthy of his notice, and of that I was glad.

'You were with him last night? Drinking? When were you with him?'

'I was not with him. I never ... we never met.'

'And how did he come to be in your schoolroom, in such a condition and at such an hour? How did it come to be, Mr Seaton?'

'That I cannot tell.' The half-lie almost stuck in my throat, for I suspected some involvement of the Dawson sisters, but I was at a loss for any idea of its nature or how it was managed. 'I returned from the inn a little before the hour had struck ten. I locked the schoolhouse door – the mistress is very particular about that.' At this Grant murmured his sympathetic agreement; he had heard me harangued loud and long on more than one occasion on the hazards of leaving one's back door unlocked at night. To Mistress Youngson, it was little less than an invitation to the Devil himself to come take what he would. 'The house was quiet, and dark. The master and mistress always retire to bed before nine in the winter, and the serving girl rarely much later. There was no one in the schoolroom as I passed.' And what had made me look in? I wondered. I did not know.

'And you saw nothing of my nephew in the house at that time? You know not whether he was there then?'

24

'He was not there,' I said, my voice dull.

'And you had had no dealings with him in the evening?' The provost seemed determined to have me Davidson's companion on his last night on this earth.

'None,' I answered emphatically. A vague chill began to creep over me as I realised there would be some in the burgh who would suspect me of having a guiding hand in the death of Patrick Davidson. The provost, thank God, pursued the point no further. He strode again the length of the room and back.

'And the doctor? Where is he? What does Jaffray say? Was my nephew dead many hours when he was found? What does Jaffray say to the manner of death? Was the boy drunk?'

So again, this time for the provost's benefit, the story of my lady Deskford and Jaffray's summons to Findlater was relayed. Arbuthnott had not yet heard it. 'What? Then Jaffray is a madman, on such a night.'

'But Jaffray has always been a madman in matters of the child-bed. It is as if by saving one woman or child he will one day expiate the sufferings of his wife.' The provost spoke only as one who knew and who had endured what Jaffray had endured, could speak. I had seldom glimpsed the private man that lay beneath the veneer, but I thought I glimpsed him now. Cardno and Buchan, however, looked up sharply at this. Such talk, in their ears, lay somewhere in the morass of sin that led from Popery to witchcraft, and I doubted whether it would be long before the provost's name was raised at the session in the same breath as one or the other of these manifestations of evil.

Gilbert Grant hastened to turn the conversation again to the matter in hand. 'I would say the boy had been dead a good while before he was found. And,' and he breathed deeply here, 'and I believe he died in that schoolroom.'

Arbuthnott nodded. 'Aye, for the dead do not vomit.' He looked at me directly. 'If the lad was found in the state that I have heard it, he died at your desk.' Of course, it could not have been otherwise. But I would have given much to have been able to believe that Patrick Davidson had not died his filthy and abandoned death at my desk as I slept only thirty-seven steps above him.

'Was Davidson at home last night?' The question was addressed to Arbuthnott. It was understood that the 'home' the baillie spoke of referred to the apothecary's house rather than the provost's. An apprentice lived in his master's home, over his master's workshop, regardless of who or where his own family was.

'For a while.' Arbuthnott was running the previous evening through his mind. 'He took his dinner with us, but ate little. My wife chided him for it. I left them at around seven – I had work in hand in the workshop. The lad would often help me in the evenings, but I had no need of him last night. He did not seem in his usual good humour – for in general he was as pleasant as Charles Thom was gloomy – his company was often a tonic for my wife and daughter on the dark nights while I worked.' The baillie's eyes narrowed on Edward Arbuthnott, and again the session clerk's face registered his malicious satisfaction. The apothecary was not to be cowed. 'Let the sin be in your mind, James Cardno – for there is no blemish on my daughter's name.'

'Have a care that there is not.'

The provost had no interest in such fencing. 'This is hardly the matter in hand, James Cardno. Keep your imaginings for the session. Go on, Arbuthnott. Did you see the lad go out?'

'No, I did not. I was in my workshop till after nine. And heard nothing of the comings and goings in the house. I heard nothing but howling wind and the crash of the sea.'

The baillie looked at him with some suspicion. 'Surely you would have seen anyone pass out into the street?' Arbuthnott's workroom gave directly onto his shop and thence onto the market place.

'The household knows not to disturb me at my work at night. Anyone going out would have gone by the outer stair, into the back yard.'

The session clerk's voice was alive with anticipation. 'And what night work have you on hand that must be carried out in such secrecy, apothecary?'

Arbuthnott did not disguise his disdain. 'Calm yourself, Cardno. You know nothing of my trade. It is quiet I work in, not secrecy. You will have to look elsewhere for the black arts you crave.'

The session clerk's breathing grew agitated, but he could not master

26

his tongue to respond before the provost intervened once more. 'What of your wife and daughter? What do they say of his movements?'

'My wife and daughter?' The apothecary's voice dropped. 'There is such a mourning in my house this day, sir, that I have had not a word that can be understood from either of them since my neighbour woke us with this terrible news.'

There was a moment of silence and then the session clerk spoke. 'And where is Charles Thom?' The suddenness of Cardno's question struck me like a cold knife. All of last night's conversation with Charles and the doctor came back to me. And through it all James Cardno had listened.

Arbuthnott was hesitant now, answering slowly. 'I do not know.'

'What do you mean, man?'

'I mean what I say. I do not know where he is. I have not seen him since we sat at table last night. He was morose, as has been the case with him for some time now. I supposed he had taken early to his bed.' At this the session clerk snorted, but Arbuthnott paid him no heed. 'My neighbour arrived with this news at about our normal time of rising. Charles is often tardy in the mornings and I did not think it strange not to see him then.' I smiled to myself as I thought of the regular sight of my friend flying past my window to the song school long after my own scholars were well settled. 'I wonder that he has not joined us yet, though. Perhaps he is comforting the women . . .' But his voice trailed off, and even I, who was probably Charles Thom's greatest defender in that room, did not believe it.

Cardno murmured something in the baillie's ear, and Buchan nodded. I had no doubt that the baillie had already been well appraised of Charles Thom's conversation and demeanour in the inn the night before, and of the time at which he had left it. Buchan turned to the two town serjeants who had been waiting all this time at the doorway. 'Find Charles Thom and bring him here. Look first at the apothecary's, and if you do not find him go to the song school, though I doubt he will be there. There were urchins enough on the road as we came here.' He turned accusing eyes on me. 'There will be much wickedness in the streets of Banff this day with neither song nor grammar school at its work.'

I looked at the body of Patrick Davidson, still lying on the provost's great hall table where it had been laid. 'There has been much wickedness on the streets of Banff already,' I said quietly. Even at a time such as this, when a young man of good family and great promise lay murdered by some unknown hand, the authorities of the burgh thought of nothing before they thought of public order.

When the serjeants had left, the provost sat down wearily on a settle near the fire. He called for a servant and asked for the fire to be lit and for refreshments to be brought. I noticed for the first time how tired he was. Dark circles beneath his eyes spoke of many a disturbed night and the effort of standing up to the news of the last hour had taken the strength almost entirely from him. His usual demeanour was one of great strength and assured purpose. The son of a successful merchant burgess of Banff, he was not of humble origins, but it was clear, and no one doubted of it, that he intended to end life at a higher rank than he had begun. He was the first of his family to attain to the position of provost, the foremost citizen of the town. And indeed, he was the first provost in several generations not to have sprung from the Ogilvies, lairds of Banff and of many surrounding strongholds and estates besides. Walter Watt was the coming man, and those of sense could see it. Forthright, and with little warmth or humour, he was not a man to my own tastes, and I doubted whether, regardless of my own disgrace, we would ever have been friends.

Above the great stone hearth by which he sat was the portrait by George Jamesone which I had heard of before, but never seen. I knew little about painting, and suspected the provost knew scarcely more, but I understood the portrait of Walter Watt and his first wife, Helen, to be a signal of intent. It had been painted not long before Helen's death, and well before her husband had attained to the heights of the provostship. Walter Watt *would* be somebody. No portrait of Walter Watt and his present wife, or their four children, the seedlings of his dynasty, adorned the walls. He loved Geleis Guild well enough, that was clear. Perhaps, though, no matter how many strong and healthy sons she bore him, she could never take the place of the pale young woman who stood silent by his side above us, in her hand a bunch of delicate flowers, of which several had already fallen to the floor.

The baillie took up his stance in front of the provost and with his back to me. The provost indicated a seat and, to my surprise, the baillie took it. It

28

was his custom, when on public duties – and I had never seen him employed on any other – to stand towering over those with whom he had to deal. Spare of build – his very frame declaring the asceticism of his life – William Buchan was nonetheless a tall man, and he used his height to give force to his words. That he and the provost, constrained though they were to have daily dealings with one another on the business of the burgh, had little enough to say to one another at other times, was well known. It was not an antipathy such as existed between Buchan and Robert Guild, the minister, where one would gladly have seen the other ousted from his position; it was rather a discreet avoidance. Whatever he might think of the provost's life, Baillie Buchan well knew he could never oust him – I doubted indeed whether he would even want to. For his part, the provost well knew he would never be usurped by William Buchan. Yet there existed between the two men a palpable and mutually understood dislike. It was as if the understanding of this was the very basis upon which they could continue to function together. Having made himself as comfortable as his principles would allow him to be, the baillie continued with his investigation.

'When did you last see the boy?'

The provost considered a moment. 'It was on Sunday night, after the evening service. He was here a little after six – he was to dine with myself and Jaffray. The doctor is ever anxious for news of the continent, and the war.'

At this Gilbert Grant nodded, having said little since our arrival at the provost's house. 'Aye, poor Jaffray. I sometimes think he only took part of his heart home with him when he returned to Banff. He is here with us, yet I believe in his mind, somewhere, he is still in Helmstedt, or Basel or Montpellier, with those dear friends of his youth, now so far dispersed.' I knew what Gilbert Grant said to be true. Jaffray's greatest recreation was to read and re-read the letters of those companions of his student days. Some of course had pre-deceased him, but only a few. Now, though, he hardly knew who lived still and who was dead. The ravages of this infernal war, tearing the Empire to shreds these last eight years, had distorted the old lines of communication to the extent that many no longer existed.

The baillie had no interest in this diversion. 'You say "was to dine". Did he not wait on his dinner?'

'No. Patrick drank a little wine with me but would not stay to eat. He said he had business at Arbuthnott's – I took it to mean the preparation of medicines or some such work. He left after perhaps half an hour, before Jaffray arrived. The doctor was greatly disappointed.'

Arbuthnott, who had thought his part over, looked up. 'He had no work to do in my workshop at that hour. Whatever his appointment, it was not with me.'

'Perhaps, then,' suggested the session clerk, by whom no opportunity for malevolence was allowed to pass, 'he had business with another of your household "at that hour".'

It was I who eventually pulled the apothecary from the throat of the session clerk. Gilbert Grant was too old and too disgusted, the provost too lost in his own concerns, and the baillie ... he watched as a vagabond boy will watch a cat play with a mouse – with a morbid curiosity to see what will happen.

Safe at a distance of about five yards from the apothecary, Cardno continued with his tack. 'You cannot deny that your daughter has been much in company with Mr Davidson since his return to this burgh. It is known and remarked upon throughout the town.'

The apothecary mastered his anger and I loosened my grip. 'The town might remark what it likes. She is my daughter and he my apprentice. He lived under my roof and dined at my table. How should they have been anything but in one another's company? You might as well suspect my wife.'

I exchanged a covert smile with Gilbert Grant. The charms of the apothecary's wife were considered limited to say the least.

'The point remains: Marion has been much in Davidson's company outwith your house and shop. They have been seen together at the Greenbanks, on the Hill of Doune and at the Elf Kirk. It is not fitting that a young unmarried woman should keep company out of doors, in such places, with any man. You should look to your daughter, Arbuthnott. It is not fitting.' This from the baillie, who in truth was more moderate on the matter than I would have expected him to be.

Despite his earlier fury, the apothecary acknowledged the point. 'Aye. You are right. But I thought no harm would come of it. No more did her mother. She said Marion would be able to tell him where he might find the best plants, seeds, herbs and other things I needed in my work, for the girl knows these things almost as well as I do myself. And ... well.' He hesitated.

'Well?' insisted the baillie.

'I thought Marion and Charles Thom, the music master ...'

The baillie nodded slowly and Cardno could not contain his pleasure. 'Another young man lodging under your roof, Arbuthnott, who finds his diversion not far from home.'

'There is no dishonour in what Charles feels for that girl. If there is any shame on that score, it is in your own thoughts, James Cardno.' The session clerk's astonishment at my words can scarcely have been greater than my own, but I felt the first stirrings of a long forgotten freedom as I uttered them.

Baillie Buchan responded before his henchman recovered himself. 'It is not of feelings, but deeds we treat here, Mr Seaton. And as for shame and honour – those are not matters for one such as you to judge.'

At this Gilbert Grant rose heavily to his feet. 'If there be a blemish on Mr Seaton's name you will name it now, William Buchan. He has paid his penalties. He has endured nine months of such dark rumblings. He will endure them no longer. Mark me, it will not go on.'

The baillie bowed his head and, his tone conciliatory said, 'I merely meant that it was for the session, not any individual, to judge of such matters.'

The provost rose to his feet and turned on the baillie. 'Might I remind you, William Buchan, this is not the kirk session. I am provost of this burgh, you a baillie of this burgh. Be about your duties. It is of my nephew I would know, not the petty doings of the schoolmaster here.' Turning to the apothecary he continued. 'Arbuthnott, how stood things between my nephew and the music master? Was there an enmity between them over your daughter?'

The apothecary considered. 'I cannot say I marked it if there was. Charles was perhaps a little gloomier than his wont – but he has never been a young man of high spirits. They were friendly enough together, but each was much taken up with his own work. I would not think them natural companions, but neither were they enemies. As for my daughter, you will find no scandal, look as you might.' He lowered his voice. 'Her heart, I think, is broken.'

Baillie Buchan had heard as much as he needed to regarding the music master. Any further questioning on that matter could wait. His interest now was in Patrick Davidson himself.

'Tell me, provost,' he said, 'and with all due respect to yourself, Arbuthnott, and to your calling – God given and honourable in that – how was it that a young man of your nephew's family and education came to apprentice himself to an apothecary?'

The provost, even more it appeared than the apothecary, was discomfited by this question. But it was a good question. After graduating from St Andrews University Patrick Davidson had, not unusually, set forth across the sea to the Low Countries and then travelled to the great centres of learning of France and Switzerland. I had had this all from Jaffray, though I had paid him little heed at the time. Patrick Davidson's was an academic journey that should have ended with a higher degree, in medicine perhaps, rather than an apprenticeship in an apothecary's shop in a small northern Scottish burgh.

Walter Watt shifted a little in his chair, but could not get himself comfortable and eventually stood with his back to us, leaning against the mantel of the now lit fire. For a man whose life was an endless pursuit for self-betterment, his nephew's career choice, and its realisation in this burgh, can have given him little pleasure. 'Who is to say what fancies take a young man's mind? He was, as Mr Grant there will doubtless tell you, a lad of great promise. His mind was quick and agile, able. From his youngest boyhood my late wife had him marked out for a lawyer, although his mother would have had him a minister.' This last he said rather contemptuously, no doubt for the benefit of the Reverend Mr Guild, who had somehow found his way back into the room.

'The year of his graduation from St Andrews, he came to visit me here in Banff, and here met Geleis for the first time. It is a memory that I have treasured – that I will treasure. I had not seen him since the year of Helen's death, and I was proud of the fine young man he had become. His intention was to make for Leiden and prosecute his legal studies there. I myself arranged for his passage on a boat from Aberdeen, in whose cargo I had some trading interest. He did not tarry long at Leiden however – he found the lectures dull and his tutor duller. The place was awash with medics and he fell in with some medical students from Edinburgh, headed for Basel and Montpellier. He had heard much of these places at this very hearth, from the mouth of Doctor Cargill himself.'

James Cargill's name was well known to me, although I had never met him. He had been an Aberdeen physician who had gone as a poor student to Basel to study medicine. There he had become fascinated by botany, and on his return to Aberdeen he had maintained an active correspondence with the foremost minds of the day on the subject. He was one of Jaffray's most dearly missed companions, and his nephew, William, had been one of the closest friends of my own student days. The provost paused in silent reminiscence before bringing himself back to the matter in hand. 'Anyhow, Patrick made for Basel with those fellows, and though he matriculated in medicine, he had nothing in his mind but botany. From his letters it became ever more evident to me that he would never graduate. As the situation in the Empire became more grave, I wrote more than once beseeching him to return to Scotland and pursue his interests here. I promised to find him a place with Arbuthnott, for I knew he loved the country hereabouts, and that he would find plenty material for his studies. He turned around and gestured towards the bier. 'And look what has come of it now!'

Gilbert Grant went across and laid a hand on his shoulder. 'Come, my friend. You cannot undo what is done. It is God's will.'

The provost's wife returned, followed into the room by a servant bearing trays of dates, nuts, bread and cheese, and another with wine and goblets. Geleis Guild took the wine herself and poured generous measures for those who would take it. Then she took the trays from the servant, set them on a trestle near the fire, and urged us to eat. It was early in the morning for wine, but I suspected the provost kept a good cellar and accepted a goblet gratefully. I was not disappointed. The others all ate and drank sparingly, save the minister, whose enthusiasm for sating his appetite was, I thought, misplaced. We were thus engaged when the sound of some commotion in the street reached us from the doorway. I turned towards it in time to see my drenched and mud-splattered friend, the master of the music school, thrust through it by the two town serjeants, who hastily shut and barred it against the jeering mob. Though thick, the door could not keep out the repeated cries of 'murderer' and the shrill sound of one voice screaming, 'You will hang, Charles Thom, you will hang.'

THREE

The Tolbooth

Jaffray said nothing for a few moments. He dropped heavily into his chair and clenched his eyes tight shut. He was a man beyond exhaustion. The boy who had knelt down to remove his boots waited awkwardly and looked at me for guidance. I motioned towards the door and he got up and walked silently from the room.

'I cannot believe it, Alexander. Their folly, my God, their folly.' I crouched before him and started to remove the boots myself. The old familiar face was etched with lines of despair he usually masked in the face of the worst of human suffering. Whether from the great fatigue of his night and morning's journeying, or his love for the young man who now lay bound in irons in the tolbooth, he could mask it no longer. I persuaded him to have some of the wine the girl had brought in, but he would eat nothing. He had had little sleep or sustenance since leaving the inn last night, and only the blank refusal of the town serjeants to allow him access to Charles in the tolbooth had forced him home now.

'And you also think it was poison, then?'

'I am near certain of it. I shall know more by tomorrow. My examination should reveal something of the nature of the compound or the manner of its administration. I would with all my heart that I were more knowledgeable in these matters, Alexander, but my skill is with the living, not the dead.' He swallowed some wine and a determination came upon his face. 'I must rise to it, though, and Arbuthnott will assist me, for there is no one else. There is no one else who can do this work for the boy.' I did not know if it was Charles Thom or Patrick Davidson he spoke of. It scarcely mattered which. No one in Banff had a greater knowledge of medicines than did James Jaffray, nor of simples and compounds than Edward Arbuthnott – no one, apart perhaps from Patrick Davidson himself, and what he knew he now must rely on these two men to tell.

Jaffray's initial examination of the body had been necessarily cursory. The watch at the West Port had been alerted to stop him and sent him directly to the provost's house on his return to the burgh from Findlater. He knew the whole story – or as much as anyone did – by the time he alighted from his exhausted horse at the Castlegate. Charles, in a state of utter distraction, had already been marched down to the tolbooth by the baillie and the two town serjeants. The corpse remained in the great hall of the provost's house. The discolouration of the mouth and tongue and of the fingers had been enough to tell Jaffray the young man had been poisoned. At length, the provost and the minister had reluctantly agreed that the corpse of Patrick Davidson should be removed from its present resting place and taken to the doctor's home, where he, with the assistance of the town's apothecary and one of the burgh barbers, should perform the necessary autopsy. Even as we spoke, I could hear the servant boy preparing the instruments the doctor would need for the operation. The barber would bring his own. In a little over two hours, these three men would commence their gruesome task.

Jaffray stood up in some agitation. 'Damn them, Alexander. Damn them! What in all of creation has made them think Charles could have done this thing? What are the fools thinking? They have an innocent man in the wardhouse while a murderer laughs in the shadows. If only I had been here.'

'You could have done nothing, here or no. I tried my best but it availed me nothing. It availed him nothing.'

'Aye but you . . .' Jaffray stopped himself and a silence hung in the room; he was sorry for what he had been about to say. He need not have been sorry, for I knew it to be the truth. I was not a man whose word could save another. The pledge of one such as I was worthless. Jaffray had standing and respect. Jaffray was trusted and well-liked. If any man could choose one between us to vouch for him, no man would choose me. Yet not even James Jaffray could have prevented Charles Thom being warded in the tolbooth of Banff. And in the tolbooth Charles would stay, to await the decision of the magistrates' court and then the assizes, on a charge of having murdered Patrick Davidson.

'Not even you could have helped him, James. They had him condemned before he ever opened his mouth. In truth, the case against him is strong and he says nothing in his own defence. It was only last night that you and I joked with him over it. Cardno, as you know, noted our every word. The whole town knows Charles is besotted with the girl, but that she was casting her eye elsewhere.'

Jaffray knew too well the way of burgh gossip to discount this argument. 'They are in the wrong, I am sure of it. He cannot suffer this injustice. We must see to it that he is brought to liberty.'

I had expected no less, but Jaffray's belief would have to be tempered by an appreciation of just how bad things were. 'Much stands against him, James. He does himself no favours. When the news was brought to Arbuthnott's this morning, Charles was found not at the apothecary's, or the song school, but in the kirk. Praying.'

I could see that this revelation shook Jaffray as it had startled me. The formality of Charles Thom's religious observance had once been a great matter of debate between him and myself. I knew that to him the incantations he was paid to perform in the kirk were but empty ramblings, and that he had little real faith. Then it had been a matter of concern to me. Now though, we no longer spoke of such things. For now I knew too well how a man might exist in that state, although the notion of happiness was not relevant. It was to Charles's credit that he had never once gloated over my new understanding. I knew he pitied in me the loss of what he had never had. That Charles Thom should have been found praying desperately in the kirk the morning after Patrick Davidson's murder was a greater cause for concern to me than anything else that had happened in the last twelve hours. Jaffray was the only other man in Banff who would understand this.

'Then he is in desperation.'

'Yes, James. I fear he is.'

He sat down again and passed these things over in his mind. At length he looked up. 'And he offers no defence? No explanation?'

I shook my head. 'None. All he would tell the baillie was that he had gone directly to Arbuthnott's after leaving the inn last night. The apothecary looked somewhat surprised at this, and I have to say that I do not altogether believe it myself. He claimed to have risen early this morning to attend to matters in his school, but again that is something of which I have doubts – as did the others who heard it.'

'And the praying?'

'They do not know him as we do, James. Not the minister, nor yet the baillie, the provost nor the session clerk. Not one of them asked him about the praying.'

'And to you, Alexander? He would say nothing to you?'

I shook my head. 'There was no opportunity for private speech between us. He was at the provost's but a very short time before he was ordered to be warded in the tolbooth.' I dropped my voice. 'They would not let me go with him.' But I had gone with him. In my mind, in my soul, I had gone with him. For as they had dragged him out through the great oaken doors of the provost's house he had called to me just as the dying man last night had called to me. He had called to me over his shoulder as they dragged him away, desperation in his eyes, 'Help me, Alexander. For the love of God, help me!' This time, I would not walk by on the other side.

'And you will help him, Alexander. And I with you. For I promised his mother on her death-bed that I would watch over that boy, and my promise is not over yet.' I had never guessed it, never wondered at it before. James Jaffray had watched over and provided for the orphaned Charles Thom through his boyhood and into early manhood simply because a dying mother had asked him to. Of all the souls I had encountered in my twenty-six years upon this earth there were few who could compare with Dr James Jaffray.

When the servant girl came in with more coals for the fire, Jaffray instructed her to prepare a basket of food – bread, cheese, some of whatever broth was to be had from the kitchen – with some ale to be ready for me to take with me when I left. I was to take it to Charles in the tolbooth and to insist on being allowed to see him. From a cabinet in his workroom, the doctor also brought a syrup of balm. 'Tell him to take it; it will cheer his heart and chase away his melancholy.' I assured the doctor that I would not leave until Charles had swallowed some of the medicine. A thick rug, too, was thrust into my arms as I prepared to leave.

'You are a good girl, Ishbel,' said Jaffray. 'I had not thought of the cold.'

The girl replied quietly, 'He is always complaining of the cold, doctor.'

38

I took it from her. 'He shall know that it comes from you, Ishbel.' She might have said something more, but I was not sure, for she had turned away to leave the room.

'You will tell him Alexander, that we will move heaven and earth, you and I, to have him out of that place.'

Thus laden with provisions and instructions, I made to leave the doctor's house, but almost at the door I remembered something that had lain half-forgotten in my mind all day.

'Doctor,' I said, 'how went your mission to Findlater? You were not too late?'

'Only by two days.'

'Two days? I do not understand.'

'No more do I my boy, no more do I. But I tell you this, the Devil was in it, for her ladyship was not. No more was the old lady or any other of the family. The gate-keeper told me they had all shifted to Cullen two days since, his lordship having at last got the better of his mother. I did not proceed to Cullen, for I know they consult Reid when they are there – age prevents him going out to Findlater. It suited someone's purpose that I should not be in Banff last night.'

'Who brought the message?' I asked.

Jaffray sighed. 'I do not know. All the long way back from Findlater I seethed and raged and vowed I would get to the bottom of it.' He went to the door leading into the kitchen hallway and called for the stable boy. He looked frightened when questioned, fearing he would be blamed for the doctor's wild goose chase. 'Who brought the message from Findlater last night, boy? Was it someone you knew to be from the castle?'

The boy stuttered. 'I do not know, sir. I have never been that far out of the burgh. I don't know the folk at the castle.'

'But it was not anyone from the town? Think now.'

The boy was almost on the verge of tears. His words came out in a rush. 'I'm sorry sir; all I could see was someone in the darkness, with a cloak all blowing around them, and a hood nearly down over their face against the storm. They shouted across the yard that you were needed at Findlater. You were to lose no time, for her ladyship was in child-bed and had need of you. That was all; I don't know who it was.' He looked at me, pleading.

'But they did say Findlater, sir, I know that, for I asked them twice, it being such a night.'

'You did the right thing, Adam. But did you know the voice? Was it a man or a woman?'

Again the boy looked hopeless. 'I do not know. A boy I think, but no one I know.'

I handed the boy a coin. 'Go and see to the horse now. You have done no wrong.' It was with great relief that he returned to the courtyard.

'Who can it have been, James?' I asked.

He shrugged, at a loss. 'I do not know. A servant? A vagrant paid to perform the task and forget that they had done so? It little matters. The effect has been the same: someone saw to it that I was not here, and the boy is dead.' He was not to be comforted, but his response would not be to indulge himself. 'We must seek out this messenger and find out who sent him.'

A watch was being kept night and day at every entrance to the burgh, for fear of the plague that had been rumoured to be in the south. Anyone entering the burgh would have to state their identity, their place of origin and their business. I myself had taken my turn on the watch at the Sandyhills gate the night before last. I promised Jaffray that I would enquire at every port to the town whether there had been a messenger coming in with business for him last night.

I did not go directly to the tolbooth, for the baillie had warned me that no one would be permitted to see Charles until after the council had met, and that would be an hour or more yet. It was now a clear, brisk spring day. The sea rolled determinedly into the shore, but with no sense of the previous night's vehemence. Everything looked clean and new, a contrast to the formless canker at work in the heart of the town itself. I was filled with a desire to get away from it for a time, to be on my own.

I left my burden at the schoolhouse and set out along the coast, towards the west. I pulled my hat down low and ignored the greetings and enquiries of the burgesses and of my fellow townsfolk as I strode along Low Shore, beneath the Rose Craig and past the new harbour works at Guthrie's Haven. I would have stopped a while to watch the cormorants and sand pipers at Meavie Point, holding out to the last moment to their jagged perch until it was claimed at last by the irresistible sea, but I was not yet far enough from the town, and so pressed on. I passed by the fishermen's huts at the Seatoun. They would not bother me; in fact, they took pains to avoid me. With them at least I knew it was no particular aversion to my person, but to my position, or at least that which I had aspired to. It was as bad luck, they said, for them to meet a minister as it was for them to cross the path of a woman on the way to their boats. The unforgiving sea had claimed too many of their number for their caution to be questioned. I had not become a minister. I had failed at the last hurdle – almost indeed at the last moment – but I had come close enough that the fishermen would avoid my person and avoid my eye on any day when they planned to put out their boats.

As I passed by their row of miserable huts, I cast my gaze upwards, towards the great rocky promontory known from ancient times as the Elf Kirk. It was a place held deeply suspect by the kirk session, and mothers warned their children against going there. Some, no doubt, respected the feeling of the session; others had greater fear of the deep gully and jagged rocks jutting from the swirling waters below. Whatever their reasons, few of the townsfolk would be seen there. It could be a place of great beauty too, as spring gave way to early summer and the rocks were clothed in cascading green velvet with pockets of yellow primroses and soft sea pinks clinging to its folds. There were no flowers today though; it was something of flowing white, fluttering slightly in the breeze that caught my eye. The folds of a woman's cloak. Her head was uncovered and her long red hair, usually marshalled in a thick plait, hung loose down her back. Even at this distance I recognised Marion Arbuthnott. I would have called out to her, but she would not have heard me. I stood watching and in time she looked away from the ravine and out towards the sea. I lifted my arm and she saw me, but did not return my greeting. She looked at me for a long moment and then, pulling the hood of her white cloak up about her, she turned back towards the town. She had the air of a creature further from the living than the dead: I had within me a foreboding that she had had it in mind to harm herself, and I was thankful that Providence had allowed me to prevent that at least.

I pressed on, past the Seatoun and along the links to the shore of Boyndie Bay. I had often taken my scholars here, but the place was deserted today.

I sat down on a large flat rock beneath a dune and looked out towards the horizon, remembering. I remembered my own schooldays, and the joy when the master had announced at the end of the morning lesson, if we had repeated our lesson to his satisfaction, that we would go to Boyndie Bay. I had not walked then, but run, run the whole way to the beach. We all ran, laughing and shouting, like the wind. And always, at the head of us all, was Archie. Archibald Hay, Master of Delgatie and heir to the castle and lands thereof. Archie, companion of my boyhood, the friend of my life. Closer than a brother and loved beyond measure. I would have given every grain of sand on the shore, every day of life that lay before me, to have Archie sitting beside me now.

The escapades of the Master of Hay were a legend in the North long before his schooldays were over. Our schoolfellows were too far in awe of him to demur at any scheme he might have, but I knew Archie from the depths of his heart, and I – I alone –could talk him out of his wild schemes. His parents knew this, and often enough before me, child that I was, thanked God for our friendship, for Archie was all their hope, the light of their life, and even their Katharine walked in his shadow.

Katharine, Archie's younger sister, the quiet, watchful little girl, who had grown into a quiet, watchful young woman. She had taken the time to try to understand the world, whereas her brother had simply launched himself upon it. So delicate she was, and slender and pale, like the willow; I do not know when I first realised that I loved her. Sometime, it must have been, between leaving my boyhood games behind me and entering upon the world of men.

Over the years, when Archie and I had studied at the King's College in Old Aberdeen, his parents had come often to their house in the Castlegate of the New Town, and they always took Katharine with them. At first, in the nature of boys, I paid her little heed, but as time got on and Archie quested after ever-wilder escapades, I began to notice her. There came a time when I began to speak to her of things other than all the commonplaces of our shared childhood, of her brother, of Banff, of Delgatie, of the characters who peopled her sphere and mine. We began to talk of the state of the kingdom, of the confusions in religion, of the world and its beauties and its perils. Her knowledge of languages, philosophy, poetry and history far outstripped her brother's, and it was not long before I would call at the Hays' town house whether Archie were with me or no. Her parents were indulgent, amused even. They gave little thought to Katharine, save to love her. Archie was all their hopes, and Katharine's life was her own. To learn that Katharine felt for me as I did for her had been the most wondrous moment I had known.

But I had no Katharine now, and there was no Archie beside me, nor ever would be. There would be no storming of the tolbooth, no mockery of the outrage of the dignitaries of burgh and Kirk. I must look to my own reserves to help Charles and hope that I would not be found wanting. I rose from my makeshift seat and began to make back towards the burgh, as the clouds rolled in from the west.

At the schoolhouse I collected the provisions from the back pantry where I had left them. I was not greatly surprised to find the broth warmed and the basket a good deal heavier now. I looked at Mistress Youngson, searching for some new tone of address, because words of kindness were so out of use between us, but they would not come. 'His mother was a good Christian woman,' she said. 'And I was always fond of the boy.'

I did not slow my pace to speak to anyone as I passed by the marketplace and the old place of the Carmelites until I came to the tolbooth at the foot of Strait Path. The guard at the bottom doorway let me pass without comment or enquiry – it would be little mystery to any in the town what business I had there today. I seldom set foot in here unless it was to pay some new tax the crown or burgh had discovered a need for. This not being a day of taxation, the place was near silent, immovable. Another guard, having asked my business, opened for me the small doorway off to the right, giving onto the wardhouse and the stairway that would take me up to the jail itself. I had been through that door only once before in my life, when the burgh council had seen fit to instruct Gilbert Grant to take his charges on a visit of the tolbooth, that the sight of the fate of wrongdoers might discourage them from any such path in future. We boys from the town were used to all manner of smells, of damp, food, coal, peat, beasts and bodily wastes. We were used to the stink of the tanner's yard and the soap-maker, of cheap tallow candles and sometimes wax, of yeast and malt brewing, of fish gut, seal blubber and seaweed. But the tolbooth was different: few of my schoolfellows could have known such a stench as greeted us on ascending the stairs to the burgh prison. All the bodily odours we had ever encountered were compressed and magnified within those thick, stone, near windowless walls. The damp and the cold and the vermin vied for precedence in a stinking cavern of God-forsaken despair. I, and many others, had had nightmares for weeks after about what we had seen there, and I had vowed that I would never again set foot in such a place.

I ascended the narrow and twisting stone stairs warily, for the light was very poor. Two-thirds of the way up, I heard footsteps begin to descend towards me. I stood still a moment and soon, emerging from the near-darkness, was the form of Baillie Buchan. 'Mr Seaton. I had thought to see you here sooner.' If the ambiguity of his words pleased him, he gave no sign of it.

'And I would have been here sooner, had the door not been barred to me. On your instructions.'

'The prohibition applied to more than yourself, but you would do well to think further on it. These are not fit matters for you to meddle in.'

'It is not meddling to give succour to a friend, or to wish to see justice done.'

'I pray God that you might, Mr Seaton, and that soon. The magistrates have committed the music schoolmaster to an assize before the sheriff, to stand trial for the murder of Mr Patrick Davidson.'

Already. My throat went dry. My words can scarcely have been audible. 'In the name of God, man.'

'We all do our work in the name of God.'

I shook my head slowly. 'This is no work of God you do here. On what grounds do you charge him?'

Buchan eyed me clearly. 'I do not charge him, Mr Seaton. It is the whole body of magistrates sitting in council that charges him. He is, by common repute – and you will not deny this for you and Jaffray spoke of it only last night – he is by common repute infatuated with the girl Arbuthnott. She, as all the town knows, has wandered like a wanton through half the country after her father's apprentice. Charles Thom gives no account of his movements last night after he left the inn, none at least that have an ounce of truth in them. His bed was never slept in at the apothecary's – Edward

44

Arbuthnott's wife will vouch for that – and do not think I did not mark the question of his praying. Do you think me a hypocrite, that I cannot tell when one is void of faith? Your friend is lost, Mr Seaton, whatever the assize might say of him. Mind that you are not!' With this he continued down past me, his last words repeating in my head.

The guard on the door at the top of the stair searched my basket. 'There are no weapons there.' He disregarded my words and continued with his search until it was complete. His hand closed on the small package of dried fruit Mistress Youngson had slipped into the basket. 'Leave it, or the bail-lie shall hear of it and you'll be in here yourself soon enough,' I warned him. He returned the package grudgingly and stood aside for me to stoop through the narrow doorway to the cells.

The place – I will not call it a room – was but very dimly lit, only some glimmer of yellow light coming through the iron grill in the door. As my eyes became more accustomed to the near darkness, I discerned the figure of my friend Charles Thom, sitting with his back against the wall and his head resting over crossed arms on his knees. An iron gad ran the length of the centre of the room, and to this he was bound. He looked up as I stepped closer to him and forgetting his shackles tried to stand up to grasp my arm. The chain by which he was tethered brought him sharply back to the floor, but still he smiled. 'Alexander, you are here.'

'I would have been here sooner if they had allowed it. And Jaffray – it was with no little difficulty that they kept our good friend the doctor from storming their walls. He will be with you tomorrow morning at the latest, if his examination of the body keeps him too late.' I had not wished to talk so soon of the death of Patrick Davidson, but perhaps this was not the place for pleasantries in any case.

'They tell me he was poisoned.' Charles's voice had dropped to a low murmur and he did not look at me.

I cleared some straw out of the way and sat down beside him on the rotting wooden floor. 'Jaffray will know more by the morning of the nature of the substance itself, and the manner of its administration. Arbuthnott will assist him. We must pray God they will meet with success.'

He smiled sadly. 'It is a long time since you exhorted me to prayer, my friend, but I prayed today.'

45

'I had heard you were found in the kirk. What brought you there, Charles?'

He shook his head and his shoulders dropped a little lower. He began to speak slowly, unsure of himself. 'I think I wanted forgiveness.' I waited, and at length he continued. 'I did not wish Patrick Davidson well, Alexander. I wished him no harm, but I did not wish him well. I wished him little success in all his endeavours here, and I wished him away from Banff.'

'Because of Marion?'

'What else? Only Marion. In fact, there was no other reason why I should have disliked him. He brought to the apothecary's table and hearth a liveliness, an interest which had been absent before. He brought with him whole new vistas for conversation. He could converse on herbs and simples and compounds as well as Arbuthnott – and I suspect it was only diplomacy on his part that prevented him showing how much more he knew than his master. But he spoke on many things – places and people he had come to know on the continent, our own universities and their varying merits. And he knew something of music, too. He was no expert, but he had a good ear and was more knowledgeable than most of our fellow burgesses. What I would have given to have been where he had been and heard what he had heard.'

'What do you mean, Charles?'

'I mean the music, the masses in the great cathedrals of France and the Low Countries which have not been reduced to hollow chanting boxes as our churches here have been.'

'You mean the music of the papists.' Only Charles could have spoken even here so freely and with such contempt of our Church. I feared for him.

'If you like,' he said, 'the music of the papists. But Alexander, you have no idea what we have lost.'

'The great human vanities of their ceremonies? Formality and splendours that took no notice of the common man? This is no loss, I think.'

He smiled at me. 'Oh, but you are wrong, Alexander. While our poor psalms are for the edification of man, these masses aspire to the ear of God himself. I have seen them in my mind, rising from the pages of those few fragments of choirbooks that escaped the torches of our iconoclasts, but what I would have given to have heard them sung, seen them in their proper places, as Patrick Davidson had done.' I began then to understand that my friend's formality in his kirk duties was not from a lack of faith, as I had always believed, but from a different understanding of it, and while I thought him still to be wrong, I loved him the more for it.

'Was Patrick Davidson a papist, Charles?' I asked.

He looked surprised. 'I do not know. We never spoke of it in that way. He spoke to me – when we were in our chamber – of the music and the beauty of the churches. And I played for him. In all, I had begun to think him a friend. And like yourself it is not an accolade I bestow lightly or often.' He took a heavy breath and continued. 'But then, of course, when I realised that Marion was lost to me I spurned every further attempt at friendship, and I gave up all hope of Marion. I doubt if she even noticed, but he ... he did. And for that I am sorry, Alexander. For that I was praying this morning.'

I knew now that he was telling me the truth. I wished I could have done something to give him comfort, but the words would not come.

'And did you tell this to the baillie?'

'What? William Buchan? Our blameless baillie cares nothing for feelings and regrets. Sin, crime, punishment and the wrath of the Lord upon such as me are what the baillie busies himself about. No, I told him nothing of this. James Cardno's report of my conversation and conduct in the inn last night told him all he required to know of my feelings. What the baillie would know of me is where I was last night and in the early hours of this morning.' He looked at me and waited. I waited a moment too, reluctant to take the role of inquisitor.

'And where were you, Charles?'

He sighed deeply, then looked me straight in the eye. 'I was with Marion Arbuthnott.'

'I do not understand.'

He lowered his voice even further, so that it was scarcely audible. 'You must tell no one, Alexander, no one.'

'But ...'

'Give me your word, or we will speak nothing further of this.'

With the greatest reluctance, I gave him my word. I wish to God I had not: another murder might have been prevented.

Reassured by my promise, he continued. 'When I left the inn, I did as I had intended to do – I made directly for Arbuthnott's house. I had no wish to be out in that storm a moment longer than it would take me to get from the inn to the apothecary's. I had gone round to the back yard and just had my foot on the bottom step of the outer stair when the door at the top of it opened above me. I assumed it must be Davidson – for neither Arbuthnott nor his wife venture out at night, and for Marion it would have caused scandal. But Marion it was. She was startled, but when she saw it was me she came down the steps and bade me tell no one I had seen her. Well, I could think of nothing that would have brought her out in such an evil storm but an assignation with Patrick Davidson, and indeed, fired by the ale I had drunk in the inn, I accused her of as much.'

'Which she denied?'

He looked at me wearily. 'No, Alexander, she did not deny it. That is to say, there was no assignation, but she was going out to search for him. She would not tell me why, or where he had gone, but only that she feared for him and would not rest until he returned home. She would not listen to my protests about the storm and the darkness, and the scandal if she were seen wandering out on such a night. When I insisted that I would not let her go alone, she begged me to go into the house and not to go with her.'

'She wished to be alone when she found him?'

'No, she insisted it was not so. She would not let me go with her because, she said, to do so would place me in some terrible danger – not from the storm – but from some genuine evil of which she was truly afraid.'

'And what did you do?'

'I went up the stair and into the house as she had bid me. I waited a few moments – not long, but long enough – and then I went out after her; I am not the great coward most would have me.'

'I know you are not,' I said. 'Where did she go?'

'She went first of all towards the kirkyard, but I think she must have caught sight of Janet and Mary Dawson, for she turned sharply away all of a sudden and made in the direction of the Rose Craig. She climbed the steep path up to the back of the castle grounds, and here I lost her for a few minutes. It was so dark, and yet I feared discovery, for she would have easily seen me if she had looked back. When I thought it safe to ascend the path myself, I did so. I could not see her, and I had left it too long to even hazard a reasonable guess as to which direction she might have gone. A gate in the castle wall was banging. At first I thought nothing of it, thinking it was only the wind. But then I noticed a little rag of plaiding snagged on a splinter in the wood. I went through the gate and still I could not see her, and I resolved to spend some time searching the grounds.

'I must have been there half an hour or more, searching behind every wall, under every tree. Eventually I knew it was fruitless to search any further – if she had been in the castle grounds, she was not there now. There was no way I was going to venture down the path from the Rose Craig again – how either of us had made it up there in that wind and rain I do not know. I was heading for the gate in the wall that leads to the Water Path when it swung open and there stepping through it towards me was Marion. She was soaked to the very skin, and her hair blown all about her, and I could get no sense from her at all. She called out his name when she first realised there was someone on the path, and when I could make her understand that it was not Patrick Davidson but I myself who stood there, she all but collapsed. All she could say was, 'I cannot find him, he will not be found.' I think I must have half-carried her down the Water Path to High Shore. Thank God we were not seen – well, by any other than the Dawson sisters, that is. I managed eventually to get Marion back to her father's house. Her mother takes a sleeping draught at night, and as we made little commotion I do not think her father was disturbed by us.'

'At what hour did you reach the apothecary's?'

He considered a moment. 'It was something after ten, I think. Not long after.'

My heart sank within me. They had missed him by a few minutes, if that. Five minutes or less earlier down the Water Path and they would have met Patrick Davidson himself, and they would not have abandoned him to the gutter and his fate as I did. I thought I could guess the rest. 'And you went back out searching for him early this morning, when you found he had not returned?'

He shook his head. 'No, I went back out last night. Marion was in such a state it was the only thing that would stop her going out herself.'

He related to me then how he had walked the burgh boundaries, avoiding the entry ports on a plea by Marion. She had been almost as concerned that no one should know Charles Thom was searching for Patrick Davidson as she had been that Davidson should be found. He had been down every street, every vennel, every wynd in his search for the apothecary's apprentice. He had searched relentlessly through the night until, feverish and exhausted, stumbling homewards in the early hours of the next morning, he had heard that Patrick Davidson was lying dead in my schoolroom. And all the while I had slumbered.

A question had been forming in my mind. 'Charles, why do you think Marion was so fearful that anyone should know you were looking for Patrick Davidson?'

He reflected a moment. 'I think she believed that whatever danger attended Patrick Davidson would also threaten whoever might *know* he was in danger. She had a foreknowledge that he was in danger last night, and very likely from whom and why, though she would not tell me. I truly believe that her foreknowledge of what happened last night puts her in danger of her life, Alexander. If anyone should learn of it, I am determined that they shall not make the connection to her through me.'

I could see the sense in what he said, and that there was little point in trying to dissuade him from his resolve. 'What have you told the baillie, then?'

He gave a low laugh. 'Nothing that he believes. I have told him that I returned to my bed at the apothecary's, but having consumed so much ale in the inn was forced to get up again and go out into the air two hours or so later, as I was in fear of vomiting. I said I walked down to the Greenbanks and towards the sandbar at the river mouth to let the storm blast away my nausea and in the hope that it might render me sober. Once there, I began to realise my folly in setting out in such a tempest and sought shelter in the ferryman's hut, the ferrymen being stranded at the other side of the river with their boats. There, I fell asleep, and did not wake until the first essays of daylight.' He smiled. 'I always feel it is a good thing to give Baillie Buchan and James Cardno and their like a little of what they want. So firm is their belief in the debauchery of others that they are scarce likely to question it when presented with an admission. Certainly, Cardno nodded delightedly when I proffered that explanation.'

'But not the baillie.'

He let out a sigh. 'No, not the baillie. William Buchan, I think, has more knowledge of his fellow man than many might think, and he is no fool. His questions come back time and again to Marion. He suspects she was in some way involved last night. He intends to question her as soon as he has the results of the examination from Jaffray. I fear it will not go well for her if she is left alone with him.'

I thought of the lost girl I had seen this morning, staring into the depths from the Elf Kirk and I promised him I would do what I could, but in truth I had no idea where to begin. I was not indifferent to Marion Arbuthnott's fate, but I did not feel certain that she was as innocent in this whole sad story as Charles Thom believed her to be. She was a person of secrets, and now he found himself entrapped by one of them. It was for him that my anxiety increased. I made one last assault on his resolve. 'But what of yourself? You must do something to help yourself.'

'There is nothing I can do, Alexander.' He took my hand. 'I must rely on my friends, and on the mercy of God.'

How the wheel had turned with us – I who had been abandoned by faith at the first real testing, and he who had had no faith until the troubles of others' lives had crashed in on him. At length I stood up, exasperated at his obstinacy and my own inadequacy. 'But you cannot stay in this place,' I said. 'It is scarcely fit for beasts. Jaffray and I will do everything in our power to have you out of this place. And more,' I paused and breathed deep, aware that the promise I was about to give would involve me in things I had no knowledge of: 'I will do all I can to discover who did kill Patrick Davidson, for I know you did not.'

He closed his eyes tight and opened them again, pushing his head back against the wall. 'No, I did not kill him. I thought Marion was all the world to me, but she made her choice. In life or death I know that he was her choice. To kill him would have availed me nothing. And anyway,' he looked up with a rare twinkle in his eye, 'if I were the murdering kind, there are a good few in Banff whose names would be on my list before that of Patrick Davidson.'

As I descended the steps of the tolbooth I could hear the clear and plaintive strains of some highland air. I had never tried to master the Gaelic tongue as Charles had done, but the words that penetrated to my very core spoke of loss, some irredeemable loss, whose pain it was beyond the power of our Scots tongue to render.

Once out again into the damp light of the afternoon I had no inclination to return to the schoolhouse. I decided instead to seek out the truth behind Jaffray's call out to Findlater. The large as well as the smaller ferry boat had been tied up last night, for fear of loss in the tempestuous sea, but a stranger might have entered Banff at some landward port. I set out on a tour of all the gateways to the burgh, starting at Sandyhill and making my way via the Gallowhill and Boyndie Street to Caldhame and the Seatoun, but my enquiries availed me nothing. There had been no report of any stranger – or burgess indeed – attempting to enter the burgh from the outside last night, and only Jaffray and his manservant were known to have left it. I had not been the first to ask these questions, for the baillie had been there before me. And now he would be assured, as I was myself, that Patrick Davidson's killer had not been a stranger to Banff, but an inhabitant of the town itself.

I returned to town the long way, by way of the Gallowhill. And there I came upon the hanging tree. I stood beneath the gibbet and determined that Charles would not swing from it. If I accomplished nothing else in my now Godless existence, I would accomplish that. I spent a moment looking down over the town and out to the sea beyond, asking myself whether the truth was to be found there, or whether it had already been washed away. Washed away like the river Deveron endlessly running out to the sea. I recalled to myself the lines of Alexander Craig, the poet, who had built his house on the Rose Craig, looking imperiously out over the town. Charles Thom, Marion Arbuthnott, perhaps even Patrick Davidson himself had played out their last tragic act together beneath his walls last night. His words took on for me a meaning that I doubt he had meant to give them.

> Come my love and live with me
> And we shall see the rivers run
> With delicate and daintie din
> And how my Dovern night and day

With sweet meanders glides away
To pay her debts unto the sea.

I believe I stood a long time there, beneath the gibbet, meditating on those lines, but I have no notion of how long it might have been. I was aware of feeling colder as the haar drifted in from the sea and obscured some of the burgh from my view. Slowly, the sound of a drum brought me from my reverie. The drum that preceded the hangman. I waited, my eyes closed, and the drum came nearer. A hand reached out and touched my neck, a human hand. For a moment, a brief moment, my heart stopped beating in my breast.

'Oh, Mr Seaton, a mercy, Mr Seaton, please God.' Before I had opened my eyes and located the voice in my memory, a rougher hand pulled the first away. A rougher voice called out – one of the town serjeants.

'Janet Dawson. Do not lay your filthy fingers upon any citizen of this burgh. You have been told the judgement of the magistrates – do not pretend ignorance!'

And then the other serjeant began to intone, with evident pleasure, 'You are to be banished furth of these bounds. A lewd and licentious liver, a whore, a keeper of codroche houses. You and your sister also. You are to be scourged by the hangman from this place hence, and never to return within the freedom of this burgh, on pain of death.' He turned to the burgh hangman, whose was the rough hand that had pulled Janet Dawson's pleading fingers from their touch, a gentle touch, on my neck. 'Strip her to the waist.'

I turned my face away, unable to watch as Janet Dawson, who had had her whore's dignity, was deprived of the dignity of a woman. I heard the hangman raise his whip and the hurling whoosh as the knotted leather swept towards her bare flesh. It was the punishment, all too readily used, meted out by the burgh fathers to any woman whose honour was questioned and who could not prove herself beyond doubt. But the Dawson sisters' whoredom was as established as it was notorious. That Janet was now being scourged from the burgh on pain of death should she ever return I could not comprehend. Again I heard the demented whoosh of the scourge. And I heard a voice call out, my own voice; it shouted 'No!' The whip crashed down on the woman's side but was not raised a third time. The town's officer looked at me. 'I take no pleasure in it, Mr Seaton.'

'Then dress her again, and leave her be to quit this place unmolested. You have done the magistrates' bidding.' I looked at Janet as, cowering, she pulled her torn bodice over herself and scrabbled in the dirt for her shawl. 'I will testify to that.'

The officer uttered a harsh 'Leave her,' to the hangman, who looked disappointed of his prey. Janet rushed at me all of a sudden, grabbing my collar. The officer made to grab her but I held him away. She spoke desperately to me. 'A word, a kind word Mr Seaton. A coin. Any coin. To help a poor woman, a kind word Mr Seaton.' I fumbled in my pocket and drew out two pennies – of little use to her as they were. She grabbed them and raised her face to mine, as if she would kiss me. But she did not kiss me. She whispered in haste in my ear, just as they came to drag her off me. '"James and the flowers", Mr Seaton. The last words he ever spoke.'

I stood and watched, as they recommenced the scourging and drove her from the burgh bounds at the beat of their drum.

FOUR

The Maps

The grammar school was held again the next day, after its macabre holiday. Sounds of high spirits and excitement came from Gilbert Grant's classroom, but my own scholars were more subdued than I had expected them to be. A little before midday, one of Gilbert Grant's scholars came bursting into my room. He was breathless, and his words tumbled over each other. 'Mr Seaton, Mr Seaton. You are to go at once to the tolbooth. You and the master, for you are both wanted there. You are to lose no time.' In the room next door, Gilbert Grant had already replaced his robe with a good thick cloak and confirmed somewhat breathlessly that we had been sent for. The sense of apprehension that had been my constant companion since the previous day grew. I gathered my own hat and cloak and we set off for the tolbooth, leaving word with Mistress Youngson that there would be no school that afternoon.

At the tolbooth, we were allowed to pass without question, and were soon shown with little ceremony through the great timber door of the council chamber. I had entered this room only once before – on the same occasion that Gilbert Grant had taken us boys to the tolbooth jail two floors above, he had also been allowed to bring us into this hallowed place. I could still remember the words of the old provost, whose name I had now forgotten – another Ogilvie, no doubt – as we stood in awe in the oak panelled room with its huge, finely polished table and its ornately carved chairs. 'The room above, boys, you must ever strive to avoid. This, this,' he had repeated with a proprietorial sweep of his hand, 'is what you should aspire to.' I never had.

Waiting for us in the room were not only the provost and the baillie, but also Edward Arbuthnott and Thomas Stewart, notary public of the burgh of Banff. For the notary, unlike for Baillie Buchan and James Cardno, the world did not begin and end with the kirk. He was not ungodly, but he was a man of the world, a measured man who understood the needs and failings of his fellow creatures without seeing sin at the root of them all. Where he had been yesterday I did not know, but I was heartily glad to see him today. Stewart did not look up when Grant and I entered the room, engaged as he was on the removal of some papers from the open chest at the far end of the room. The apothecary looked somewhat shaken, ill at ease, but it was the demeanour of the provost that I marked most. His complexion was of a greater pallor than I had ever seen it, and his hand shook so that he had to steady himself by leaning on the back of a chair. He never once took his eyes off Thomas Stewart and the papers.

My companion was the first to speak. 'We have come, provost, as we were sent for. What business here requires us?'

Walter Watt, scarcely hearing, I think, made no response. It was the baillie who replied. 'We require your assistance, and that also of Mr Seaton there,' he nodded towards me in a perfunctory manner, 'in the examination of these papers.' He indicated the chest over which Thomas Stewart was again bent. 'The notary and I went to Arbuthnott's this morning with the purpose of examining Charles Thom's belongings in the hope of finding some evidence of evil intent against Patrick Davidson, since he denies involvement in the crime. I am glad to say – and I pray you would mark this, Mr Seaton – that we could find nothing amongst the belongings of Charles Thom to suggest anything other than a blameless life on the part of that young man.' The involuntary relaxation of my shoulders and hands must have been noticed, for he continued, emphasis on his next words, 'However, the absence of evident guilt is not the same as the proof of innocence, and that we have not found.'

'Nor will find,' I responded, 'unless Patrick Davidson arises and tells you the name of the one who slew him.'

The Baillie probed me with his long, unflinching gaze. 'Charles Thom is at liberty to talk for himself, but chooses not to. If his reasons are known to you, you would do well to divulge them. It would go the better for you both.' His eyes searched mine for a moment, but he returned to the matter in hand. 'It is not in the case of Charles Thom we require help from yourself and Mr Grant. The papers we wish you to examine belong to Mr Patrick Davidson.'

Now I thought I understood something of the provost's pallor.

'What are these papers?' I asked.

Stewart turned the first of the piles and passed it across the table. 'That is what we would like you to tell us, although we know, broadly, what they are. What we would ascertain is what they mean.'

I pulled over a chair for Gilbert Grant but remained standing myself. Buchan placed a new lit candle at the older schoolmaster's elbow. My own eyesight was far better than my colleague's. At first glance I saw what the papers were. I would have to choose my words with care.

'These are maps,' I said.

'Indeed,' agreed Buchan. 'But have you ever seen such maps before, Mr Seaton?'

I looked again and shook my head. It was the truth. I had seen town sketches, and maps, in my college days. Yet, for all I had seen before, I had never seen such work as this. The maps, perhaps a dozen in all, were not printed copies but original hand-drawn sketches, showing natural coastline features such as bays, river mouths, sandbars and rocks – all annotated and named. The Collie Rocks were there, Meavie Point, the Maiden Craig, the Bow Fiddle Rock, and many more besides. The hills and cliffs that rose above them were named. But there too were the man-made features – the new harbour works at Banff, the harbour at Sandend, the fastness of Findlater above the bay at Darkwater. And roads there were, and bridges, kirks, townships, strongholds. The whole coastline from Gamrie and Troup Head to Findlater and beyond to Cullen was sketched out in a manner which, to one who knew these places, could not be mistaken. At the edge of each sketch an arrow, next to what could only be a roadway, annotated to 'Elgin', 'to Turriff', 'to Strathbogie'. It was this last that began to give me the clue, if I had needed it, to the possible significance of the discovery of these documents, and the unrest they caused to those in the room, not least the provost. Gilbert Grant passed me paper after paper. 'These are astonishing; I have never seen such work.' He looked towards Thomas Stewart. 'I had not thought the coastline here to be mapped.'

'It is – or rather was – not,' replied the notary. 'The fishermen have their charts of course, but these are rudimentary and obscure, and can only be understood by those with great knowledge of the sea hereabouts.'

Grant shook his head in wonder. 'Then where did he get them? Whose work are they?'

'His own.' Baillie Buchan's voice was dry and deliberate.

'You cannot be sure.' Again the provost was in a rash of panic. The baillie lost patience and almost spat.

'Arbuthnott confirms it.' He thrust a paper towards the provost. 'Do you deny yourself that it is his hand?' And then another, and another. 'Or this? Or this?' The provost nodded slowly then sat down on a chair, his head in his hands. I picked up the papers he had let fall to the floor. Not maps these, but notes, numbered notes and symbols with their meaning. A symbol for a bridge, for a well, for a mill, for a farmstead, a ferry, a ford. Notes on strongholds and the names of those who held them – Findlater, Inchgower, Carnousie, Delgatie, Rothiemay, Frendraucht – all and many more were there. To my surprise, Buchan seemed to address himself to me rather than to Gilbert Grant. 'What do you make of these documents?'

I chose my words with care. 'I have some little knowledge of mapping, but I do not claim great expertise.'

'And it is taught at neither of the colleges in Aberdeen?'

I considered. 'No. There is some talk of a mathematics professor at Marischal College, but no man has yet been found to take the post.'

The baillie nodded, satisfied. 'Mr Grant?'

My elder colleague sighed. 'I can add little to what Alexander has said. The craftsmanship, the penmanship is of a high quality – but as to cartography, I know near to nothing of that.'

'And why should you?' asked the baillie, 'for maps are scarce the business of honest men.'

Notary Stewart cleared his throat and the provost roused himself. 'Have a care, Buchan. You might not slander the dead, but you risk great slander of the living. Robert Gordon of Straloch is known to have an interest in the matter of maps.'

Buchan was unbowed. 'A Gordon is not above suspicion. Straloch may well have a hand in this. Did the boy speak of any commission, any patron in this work?'

Arbuthnott, to whom the question was chiefly addressed, asserted, with some vehemence, that Davidson had not spoken of this work at any time.

The provost also denied ever having heard mention that his nephew was engaged on such an enterprise.

The baillie returned to me. His view that maps were not the business of honest men did not, it appeared, preclude a conviction that I knew all about them. 'What would you say, Mr Seaton, is the purpose of these maps?'

'I cannot answer that, baillie. Only Patrick Davidson and whoever sponsored him can answer that.'

'You guess at more than you will admit, Mr Seaton, or you would not talk of "sponsors".'

The baillie was correct, loath though I was to admit it. I knew more of maps and mapping and their cause and their uses than I wished to say, for Archie Hay had written to me of them. Archie, who had never looked at a map in his life, had never needed to for the whole of the terrain of the north was written into his very soul, had discovered his great God-given gift when he had left the shores of Scotland for the great wars of the Empire. He had discovered the value, the necessity to the foreign soldier and the foreign army, of maps. It had been with the greatest of difficulty, and relying almost completely on me and my powers of dissuasion, that Archie's parents had prevented him from throwing up his studies in Aberdeen and going to the war in Bohemia as soon as he heard of the defeat of the Bohemian forces at the White Mountain. The Elector Frederick, newly chosen king of Bohemia, the Winter King, champion of Protestantism against the papist Habsburgs, had suffered ignominious defeat. As Archie had told me, indiscreetly and on more than one occasion, he cared not a jot for the Bohemians or the Protestant cause, but he would die in the defence of Frederick's queen, Elizabeth Stewart, daughter of King James and sister of our present King, Charles. In 1622, four years ago, Archie had left home, family and country to fight to the death, as he said, in the defence of the Winter Queen.

When he could, Archie wrote to me, a small handful of letters I kept with me still. He wrote of the fighting, of the filth, the privations, the brutality of the Habsburgs and the suffering of the peasants. And he wrote of maps. Archie, who had been hard put to attend one lecture in three in our college days, fell upon the art of cartography with a passion. He learnt the art and its uses from students of the new French and German military schools. He used spies and eventually went himself, under cover of disguise, into enemy territory to chart and learn the lay of the land. At the time I had marvelled at the letters, at Archie's enthusiasm for this new type of knowledge, and I had marvelled at the knowledge itself. And I knew what the documents Baillie Buchan was holding out towards me very probably meant. The baillie knew it too, but would have it from my mouth.

'Why do you think Patrick Davidson drew these maps, Mr Seaton?'

The room fell silent. There could be but one answer that made any sense. What Davidson had drawn was a plan for an invasionary force, landing on the Moray coast and marching – marching where else but southwards – to Aberdeen, to Edinburgh, to London itself, but first by way of Strathbogie. Strathbogie, the centre of Gordon power, the heartland of the Marquises of Huntly, commanding the North East, and ever ready to rise, in concert with their sovereign or against, in the name of Rome. Forfeiture, banishment, death on the battlefield or by the executioner's axe had failed to slake the thirst of the Gordons for a return of Scotland to the thrall of the papacy. And Strathbogie lay not twenty miles from where we stood. But I would not lay that charge at one I had never met, whom I had already so wronged, and who could no longer answer in his own defence.

It mattered little: the words that stuck in my throat came soon enough from the baillie's mouth. 'I think it is evident, is it not, Mr Seaton, that Patrick Davidson was a papist spy?'

He had dropped the words into a silent room and opened the door to a tempest. As I tried to frame some response, Gilbert Grant stood up, rage and dismay contending in him for the ascendancy. 'That is an outrage, Buchan, that the boy should stand accused of such a deed. He had a thirst for knowledge, for that you would condemn him as a papist and a spy?' He turned imploring eyes on me. 'Alexander, tell them, tell them what nonsense they speak …' But my old colleague's voice fell away, drowned out by the silence of the certainty that now filled the room.

The notary was the first to speak. 'I think it well that these papers be kept in a place of security. I propose, Provost, that after we have made more particular examination of these documents, the chest be placed under lock and key in the charter room here in the tolbooth.'

The provost assented, having come to himself somewhat. Thomas Stewart and I lifted the chest to the table, away from the fire, which Walter Watt called to have lit. The baillie told the apothecary he might leave us, with a strict admonition that he should spread no word of this conference. He also spoke a word, an unaccustomed kindly word, to Gilbert Grant, that he need not tarry with us longer if he did not wish to. My elderly colleague rose stiffly. 'I will go gladly, for I have not the stomach for this. He was a fine boy, a fine boy.'

The provost clasped his hand firmly. 'Thank you, Gilbert. You do him justice.' As Grant and Arbuthnott were leaving, the serjeant was told to have the minister fetched. This again was the suggestion of Thomas Stewart, and although the baillie and the provost, I was sure, would have objected if they could, we all assented that it was right that the minister should be informed of what had been found. The provost then took his accustomed seat at the head of the table and invited the rest of us to be seated also.

It was not long before the minister appeared. As Mr Guild somewhat breathlessly removed his hat and cloak, the notary commenced on an abbreviated account of what had transpired at the search of Patrick Davidson's room.

The minister looked truly astonished. 'A spy? A papist, I will not believe it!' No mention of papist had been made by Thomas Stewart, for none was needed. What other enemy could our country have? The minister looked to his brother-in-law. 'Provost, this cannot be true, man: he was your nephew.'

The provost, who had sat silently throughout Thomas Stewart's narrative, maintained his composure. 'I would rather lose my own life than believe it. Never has there been such a taint on my family name. Never. No hint of Romanism, of disloyalty to Church or Crown has ever attached itself to me or mine. I pray to God that it be not true, for the boy's sake and for the memory of his aunt that is dead, for she loved the child to distraction, and he her.'

To my surprise, the baillie, who was not much given to sentiment, added his voice in agreement. 'It is known and well remembered that she did. And never did a child have a more Christian example before his eyes. If it be found that the boy did stray into the path of Rome, no blame will attach itself to her memory.'

The minister, ever ready to set himself at odds with Buchan, did not altogether like this. 'Nor yet to that of the provost, Baillie Buchan. Or to his family.' In all this, as in all else, the Reverend Mr Guild's concern was for himself. He was never slow to recall to all who listened that his own sister was now the provost's wife, but any hint of dabbling with Rome by that family might leave its mark on himself. For Walter Watt, perhaps, the risk was greater. He had worked his whole life to garner position, influence, wealth and power, and aimed higher still than the provostship of Banff. What of all he had gained in this great life's work would be left to him if his family name should be tainted with the odour of treachery? He could not even approximate to the position of the Marquises of Huntly, forgiven again and again by their indulgent monarchs. The king did not know Walter Watt, Provost of Banff, from any other middling creature in his kingdoms. Both for Watt and for his brother-in-law the minister, the revelation of Patrick Davidson as a papist spy would be a personal disaster.

The baillie seemed unconvinced, uninterested even, in the minister's assertion in defence of the provost. 'Whether any blame attaches itself to the provost, his present family or indeed to any other indweller of this burgh remains to be seen, Mr Guild. When our community is threatened by the blackest of evils, as it is now, vigilance, vigilance in the Lord, is all.'

The provost leaned forwards, his eyes cold and hard. 'There is none more vigilant for the good name of this burgh than am I, baillie, as well you must know.'

Buchan was unperturbed. 'And the good of its soul, provost? For make no mistake, what we deal with today is the good of its soul.'

The notary, used to the endless shifting for position between baillie and provost, waited silently while they spoke out their piece. When the natural pause came, as he had known it would, he took charge once more of our discussion. 'I hope it will be understood and agreed amongst us that we must take great care how this business is handled. Any suspicion of inhabitants of the town having truck with foreign enemies will cause poisonous division in the burgh. Accusation will be hurled against accusation, suspicion grow like a fungus in the hearts of the indwellers. Trade, and the security of the burgh will be disrupted.' How quickly Stewart had cut to the heart of the matter. While some, like the minister and provost, might fear first of all for their own position and others, like the baillie, might have genuine fears for the immortal souls of the inhabitants of Banff, in the end, the real concern was not for Kirk or king, but for the security and trade of our town. 'This business must be addressed with the utmost secrecy.'

'But how can that be?' spluttered the minister. 'If some higher authority should come to know of it from other mouths than ours, then we might all be held guilty of apostasy and treason.'

Thomas Stewart sought to assuage the Reverend Mr Guild's concerns. 'Great care will be taken over the security of these papers, minister, and as soon as we have some better knowledge of their true import, they will be delivered to the sheriff. On this you have my word.'

The minister was still not satisfied. 'I am not assured that this secret can be kept. I would call into question, for instance, the presence in this room of Mr Alexander Seaton. Neither by position or repute is it fitting that he should be one of our number and privy to this knowledge.'

To my surprise, Baillie Buchan spoke in my defence.

'Mr Seaton is here as one who has particular knowledge of the matter before us. You will be aware, I am sure, of the great friendship that existed from boyhood between him and the Master of Hay?' The minister was bursting to interrupt, but Buchan would not permit it. 'Sir Archibald Hay died in the cause of our faith and the defence of our Church against the idolatrous forces of the Empire. In the course of that service, as you will recall from the funeral oration given by the Earl Marischal, he became expert in the drawing and using of maps. Also in the course of that service, he wrote many letters from the lands of Germany and the Low Countries to his childhood friend, Mr Seaton.' He looked towards me as if awaiting some protestation. 'It is known, Mr Seaton. Few letters enter this town without my knowledge. What I know of their contents depends upon the gravity of the times. I believe it likely that Sir Archibald would have revealed to you at least some of his new knowledge and his practice of it.' I knew, as did everyone, what were the centres of power in our community, and yet I had not understood until that moment the true extent of Buchan's control of knowledge in the town, and would never have foreseen his frankness on the matter. There was little point in protesting a desire for privacy or outrage that it had been infringed; such protestation would be taken as little less than an admission of complicity in some act of treachery or private vice. I simply agreed that he was correct in his belief, and that Archie had written to me a good deal on his new passion for the cartographer's art. Buchan nodded, satisfied. 'I thought as much. And it is fortunate indeed that he did, for I could think of no other in the town who would have been able to advise us with any sure knowledge of the matter.'

This was not enough for Mr Guild. 'To cite Mr Seaton's old friendship with the Master of Hay in his support – when it is known throughout the country that the laird will no longer have him in the house, that he it was who barred Mr Seaton's way to the ministry – is beyond endurance.' The minister could scarcely contain his impotent outrage. 'You should have consulted a higher authority before taking such a step.'

'He did,' interrupted the provost. 'Mr Seaton's position in the burgh may well be lowly, but he is acknowledged a man of great learning and I know of no other in this town with any understanding of maps. As for his repute – I know little and care less for your tittle-tattle, but I know there has never yet been any suggestion of heresy or collusion with the forces of idolatry in his carriage, public or private.'

'But his mother, the Irishwoman—'

'Is dead,' I said. 'My mother is long dead.'

The minister thus chastened said no more of my unfitness for this trust, but simmered silently at the double-edged affront to his dignity and his person.

It had been many months since any save my closest friends in the burgh had treated me with anything other than either wary suspicion or open contempt. There were those of course like the Dawson sisters, the shore porters, the journeymen labourers – those on the margins of our com-munity – who had been little impressed by my college learning and my progression towards the ministry and so were little shaken by my fall. Most of the rest found it expedient to avoid me now. All save my closest friends. I had never cared to claim friendship of casual acquaintances, and in the first few months after my rejection by the Presbytery at Fordyce, I had eschewed the company of even my few good friends – the doctor, Charles Thom and Gilbert Grant in Banff, and the two or three companions of my student days who still lived in Aberdeen. They, a wonder to me now, had persevered with me throughout my darkest days of self-loathing.

My astonishment at understanding, at last, that I really was not fit to be a minister had, for a while, almost robbed me of my senses. Days of wandering wildly along the cliffs and shoreline, eastwards then westwards with little consciousness of where I was had ended, not with my death on the rocks as might well have been expected, but with an exhausted collapse on the shore below Findlater. I had been found there by a local wise woman who many accounted a witch, but I did not believe she was. She dragged me – God alone knows how – the length of the beach to the cave in which she dwelt, summer and winter, and nursed me there. When my delirium was finally broken, she sent word to Jaffray of where I was to be found. The fact that I still lived was a matter of joy to him as well as to Gilbert Grant and, even then, to Mistress Youngson. It was not a matter of joy to myself. I drank, I wallowed in self pity, I drank more, I railed in bitterness at my fate, in anger at all who came near me; I went with women and hardly knew their names. Three times I had been brought before the session, three times forced to sit in front of the whole kirk and proclaim a repentance I did not feel.

For nearly six months it had lasted, until all who were left were James Jaffray, Gilbert Grant, and Charles Thom. No one else of any decency or standing would look me in the eye, and from my scholars I had little respect and deserved less. Mistress Youngson, the childless Mistress Youngson, who had taken me to her home and loved me as if I were her husband's son, could scarce bear to look at me. Six months, until at last I stood on the precipice between existence and death. I was not dead, and though I did not live, I might exist. At first I relied almost entirely on Jaffray: he had persevered belligerently and relentlessly with me regardless of my assertions that I did not need him; Charles Thom in his own passive and morose way had done the same. Gilbert Grant had simply waited, waited patiently for me to rediscover at least some civility, as he had known I would. My shame at my carriage towards him, when I eventually dragged myself out of the trough of aggressive despondence, was profound. His forgiveness was quiet and complete. But his wife could never forgive me; she could never forgive the hurt I had caused her husband – and even herself – and as she once told me, she had now seen the dark side of my soul. And here now, in this chamber, in the provost's defence of me, a door had opened slightly offering a passage back towards the world of men. And there might be respect in that world, and it mattered all the more because the hand that had pushed open the door was not that of a friend.

I nodded my head a little towards the provost in a gesture of thanks. 'I will be of what assistance I can in this business. I can make no claim for great knowledge of the art of mapping, but what I was given to understand from Sir Archie you will know entirely. As to my discretion, Mr Guild need not fear: what is spoken of here will not be noised abroad by me.' In enforced retreat, the minister favoured me with a look of practised contempt.

The baillie, paying him no heed, strode towards the chest. 'Then let us bend our necks to the task, for enough time has been wasted already.' For the next three hours, until the light began to fade and other duties called the attention of the notary, baillie, provost and minister, we pored over the maps. As our examination progressed, the question arose as to what military uses they might be put to. One or two suggestions were somewhat fantastical – the minister claimed to fear the burning and desecration of the marked churches by the idolatrous horde. I believed it more likely that the churches were indicated as landmarks, and that an invading force landing many miles from the centres of power would be unlikely to tarry in the presbyteries of Fordyce or Turriff to burn churches. Of greater concern were the great lengths to which Davidson had gone in describing the boun-teous contents of the laird of Banff's gardens and orchards, as well as the nature and times of the fleshmarket in the burgh and the location of the great barnyards of Delgatie and Rothiemay – brimful of corn and barley. An invasionary force coming by sea and with a long march ahead could provision itself well with such information. There was little doubt in any of our minds that the enemy would be papist – the question was simply from where. The minister and the baillie, united for once, suspected France. I, along with Thomas Stewart the notary, inclined towards Spain.

The baillie was in little doubt. 'The French – long a godless people and ever the enemy of Scotland. France would have had us in her snare sixty years ago, when we had scarce yet freed ourselves from thraldom to Rome. The late king's mother was but a pawn in their schemes. It grieves me greatly that her grandson should have fallen in with yet another French marriage, for no good will come of it.' King Charles had only succeeded a year ago, yet within two months he had married himself a French bride. This 'dabbling with Rome' had made many uneasy, myself included.

The provost turned to Thomas Stewart. 'You think Spain the more likely foe. What is your reasoning?'

The notary pushed one of the maps across the table to the provost. 'We are agreed that a substantial landing force could be disembarked here or here?' The provost nodded, and the notary traced a line with his finger slightly north and eastwards of the sea at Banff. 'Any invasionary fleet would be most likely to come in here. A journey up the west of Scotland and around Cape Wrath or even the Orkneys would be fraught with navigational perils and could not hope to escape detection for long enough to surprise us. But that is the way the French would have to come, for they could scarce sail up the English Channel and hope to progress up the eastern coastline of England without attracting notice. But think of the Spaniards. Think of the Netherlands.' What he said was true; since the revolt of the Dutch twenty years ago, Spain no longer held the northern Netherlands, gathered now into a republic under the auspices of their States-General. But they still held the south, and soldiers and ducats flowed from Madrid to Antwerp and Brussels, sustaining a network of Spanish spies and intrigue on a seem- ingly limitless supply of gold from the Americas. Perhaps Patrick Davidson had simply been one more cog in the great Spanish wheel that drove the Habsburgs' will through Europe and beyond.

The provost began to nod his head slowly, evidently thinking the thing out for himself. 'A fleet – armada they call it? – could set sail from Flanders and possibly avoid detection sailing north. A favourable wind would bring them to our shores in little enough time. But why here? Why so far north?'

The minister could hold his tongue no longer. 'In God's name, do we tremble to say it? There is not one among us who does not suspect the hand of Huntly in all of this.'

Walter Watt would have restrained him. 'Have a care—' but for once the minister would not be cowed by his brother-in-law.

'No, provost, I will not. How long must we live in fear of the papist Gordon backsliders, who would sell our nation into Roman whoredom for the price of a mass?' What he said was true. It was common knowledge that the Gordons had never accepted the Reformation of religion in our country, and were ever striving for a return to Rome. They did not blanch at treachery or civil war in their efforts. And now, with the king in England and the whole continent of Europe at war, might they not well intrigue with Spain as they had done before? The provost addressed me.

'And have you anything to add, Mr Seaton? How seems the Spanish answer to you?'

I worded my reply with caution. 'I believe that if our country is to suffer an assault from the Spaniard, it will be because the king himself has brought them to it.' These were dangerous words, I knew. Dangerous words to use in the company of men with no reason to wish me well. The provost, whom I did not like but was coming to believe I could trust, spoke first.

'On what grounds do you hold this view?'

'On the grounds that are known to us all: that after his accession, King Charles lost little time in abandoning his father's policy and showing himself the enemy of Spain. England will always be the prize for Spain, but they might reason soundly that much might be achieved in England by striking our king first in his Scottish kingdom, and where else would the Spaniards find so firm and well-placed a friend as the Marquis of Huntly?'

Thomas Stewart seemed somewhat ill at ease. 'I feel we are all of one agreement: that if our nation is under threat from a foreign force, then that force will come from Spain, and that if Patrick Davidson was spying for anyone, it was at the behest of Madrid. And yet—'

'And yet,' interrupted the provost, 'we have no proof whatsoever that my nephew was engaged on any such activity; these maps may be the fruits of a blameless pursuit.'

I felt somewhat as a fly might do when led into a trap by a spider. The provost had allowed us to entangle ourselves more and more in a web of speculation of our own making, and now he was ready to pounce upon us in his dead nephew's defence. I felt that I was as responsible as anyone, in my failure to speak up for him when Gilbert Grant had asked me to.

'I am no expert in these maps, provost, and I have no interest in calumniating an innocent man.'

The baillie was swift. 'Even to save your friend?'

'Even for that.'

He nodded. 'Good. It is as I thought.'

I did not know what to make of the baillie's words, but I had little time to pursue the enquiry in my mind. Thomas Stewart eyed me levelly. 'Whatever we do will not be lain at your door, Alexander; you have done no more than we asked of you, and that well, yet I believe we should not proceed further in this matter without first taking further counsel.'

The minister was wearied of listening to the views of others when his own were so clear to him. 'And to what reprobate must we now turn before we may proceed as any group of godly and honest magistrates?'

The slur on me was let pass as the notary responded in a steady voice. 'Robert Gordon of Straloch.'

The minister snorted derisively and the baillie rose from his seat in some alarm. 'The risk is too great.'

'Straloch is no papist,' asserted the notary.

The Reverend Guild snorted again. 'No papist? He is a Gordon! They drink in incense with their mother's milk.'

The notary repeated himself, an edge to his voice being sharpened by his growing impatience. 'Robert Gordon of Straloch is no papist. He is a Justice of the Peace and one of the best-respected men in the kingdom. The king himself does not scruple to seek his counsel.'

'Aye,' retorted the minister, 'and Huntly does not blow his nose without consulting him first.'

'Perhaps so. But many's the time it has been the restraining hand, the measured counsel of Straloch, which has held the Marquis back, when his own impetuous nature would have precipitated us all into disaster.'

When the baillie spoke his words were slow and deliberate. 'And what say you, provost? Should we consult Robert Gordon of Straloch on the matter of these maps?' He was watching the provost closely, as if hoping something in the man's reaction would reveal complicity or innocence in his nephew's doings.

It was a moment before Walter Watt began his reply, and as he spoke, I understood what it was that had set him apart from his peers. Walter Watt, when he chose, could speak and reason with a degree of authority that silenced other men. 'I too am uneasy about approaching so close to the centre of Gordon power on a matter so potentially dangerous for us all. Nevertheless, we cannot proceed on an investigation relating to these maps without expert opinion of their nature. It is known that there is not a man in the whole of Scotland who has a greater understanding than Straloch of the art of cartography. That he is a Gordon and a confidant of the marquis cannot be denied, but what the notary says is true. He is respected as much as any man, and may oftimes have been the one voice that counselled against catastrophe. We should consult Straloch. We should ask him for his opinion on the basis of one map – only one. For if my nephew had fallen into such a blasphemous treachery as he may have done, I am resolved that these papers should burn to ashes and never another eye look on them.'

Minister, baillie, and notary were all, at length and to varying degrees brought into agreement with the provost as to the way to proceed. There remained the question of how the chosen document should be transferred safely to Straloch. Under the present circumstances, with a murderer either walking abroad in the burgh or lying untried in the tolbooth, neither the notary nor the baillie could be spared. The minister declared that it was not his intention to break bread with the idolatrous Gordons, and the provost was no message boy. The gaze of the baillie fell upon me. He must have known what I myself in the maelstrom of the past two days had almost forgotten – that I was committed to travel to Aberdeen the very next day. He himself would have signed the authority to release me from my duties for a few days. His gaze began to weigh heavy on me and I cleared my throat. 'I am bound to journey to the town tomorrow. Two of Dr Liddell's scholarships at Marischal College have fallen vacant and one of my most promising scholars could make something of a claim to compete for one of them. I am travelling to Aberdeen to ascertain what I can of what will be required of the boy in his trial for the bursary, and to purchase some books required by the grammar school here. My journey will take me within two miles of Straloch.' And so, after much protest from the minister, silenced by the provost, and no further comment from myself, it was resolved that it should be I who carried the map to Robert Gordon. I was to tell him as much of its tale as we knew and were prepared to apprise him of, and ask him for his opinion on its nature and import. I had never met the laird of Straloch, but I knew him by repute to be a man of great learning and wide experience. I did not fear, as did the Reverend Guild, that I would be infected with popery simply from dining at the table of a Gordon. I was distant, very distant from my God, but I knew without question that mine was still the God of Calvin and Knox, whatever the Reverend Guild might fear I had learned at my mother's knee. The light was dull now, and the sea pulled the clouds in from the west as the town bellman marked the hour as five. It was agreed that I should return here at seven the next morning. The provost would meet me and release into my care one – only one – of the maps drawn by his nephew.

I made not to my lodgings and the promise of Mistress Youngson's meagre but wholesome supper, but to Jaffray's. With all the broken links of my life these past few months, the doctor had become the only tonic that I knew.

FIVE

Post-mortem

The girl's eyes were alive with questions.

'Let me in, Ishbel, and I'll tell you.'

Jaffray's servant looked a little abashed as she held the door open wider for me and helped me off with my cloak. 'The doctor's in his study, Mr Seaton. I'll get you your supper.'

'But I haven't come for my supper.'

She was unmoved. 'The doctor said you would come when you finished your work at the tolbooth. He said you'd be wanting your supper.' She turned and headed for the kitchen. Further protestation on my part was useless and I made my way down the long hallway towards Jaffray's study at the back of the house. Here James Jaffray used to watch his wife in her garden, through the little study window, and here I believed he watched her still. More than once I had walked into the room to find him gazing out into the darkness, his hand on the page of an open book he could not have told me the title of. I knocked gently on the door. A slight shuffle and then the familiar hearty voice.

'Aye, Ishbel, that's all right, come in.'

I entered. 'It's not Ishbel, I'm sorry to say. Are you waiting on your supper?'

He started, then laughed heartily. 'Well, you could make a minister yet, with yon creeping step and that knock of a girl.' Then his face registered regret, but there had been no malice in his joke. 'You have been much busied with this business today, Alexander. I spent the morning going through the shelves at the apothecary's, checking he kept only the licensed poisons. When I had finished I learnt from Arbuthnott that you were at the tollbooth. For a moment I feared that Charles Thom's fate had befallen you also. It was some time before the serjeant was able to persuade me that you were detained in the council chamber and not above in the jail.'

'If I ever suffer that misfortune I doubt that I would show myself the stoic that Charles does.'

A light came into the doctor's eyes. 'They have not broken him, then. Thanks be to God. He is better than all they can do to him. But his body is not strong.'

'No,' I said, 'and that is a hellish place that they have him.'

'I know it, for I have been called there often enough to salve the sores of poor souls rotting in there.'

'And did they permit you access to the tolbooth today?'

He snorted contemptuously. 'The baillie has left instructions that I am not to be in commune with Charles. The confines of his narrow mind have expanded themselves to imagine that I have no other object in visiting the boy than to pass on details of what my examination has found, that Charles might be all the better placed to deny complicity.' Then he asked in a low-ered voice, 'You have been to him, Alexander. What is he hiding? He surely has no part in this business, but he is keeping some secret, is he not?'

I hesitated. Charles had made me promise to tell no one of his night searching with Marion for Patrick Davidson, yet the bond of honour and friendship that bound us had been all but forged by James Jaffray. The secrets Charles would keep from Jaffray were those that a son would keep from his father, but Charles's silence before Baillie Buchan was of a quite other nature – it was for fear of imperilling the life of Marion Arbuthnott. I told him what I knew. He listened carefully, and when I came to the end of my short monologue, he nodded slowly. 'It is as I suspected. Charles will say nothing in his own defence for fear of endangering Marion.' He stoked the fire absent-mindedly. 'Then you and I must prove his innocence, Alexander. Have you had the opportunity of speech with Marion yet?'

I shook my head. 'None has, as far as I can gather. The baillie has tried, I believe, but has had even less from her lips than he has from Charles's. I do not know if she would speak any more freely to me than she does to Buchan. And it is a pity, for there are other matters that I would ask her of.'

'What matters are these?'

I filled my glass with some of the wine Ishbel had left out for us and began to tell him of the maps. He listened with great interest and, to my surprise, no little knowledge, interrupting every now and again to seek clarification of some point or to ask about the reactions of the others engaged in the examination of the drawings and their notes. Before I had got halfway through my narrative he advised a visit to Straloch. Then he raised the question of espionage, and, like me, he suspected the hand of Spain, and of course, of Huntly.

'And how does the provost take the news? Does he defend the boy?'

I reflected. 'When Gilbert Grant and I first arrived at the tolbooth, the provost was shaken, very shaken. He was as a man who can scarce follow events, still less control them. I have never seen him in such a way before.'

Jaffray was remembering. 'I have. Once,' he said.

I waited for further explanation, but he waved his hand dismissively. 'It is unimportant. Go on.'

'In time, he mastered himself. His defence of his nephew became more – reasoned. Had his authority not been added to Thomas Stewart's caution and good sense, we would be there yet.'

Jaffray smiled. 'Listening while the minister piled up a pyre for heretics then managed to set himself atop it.'

'I wish I had your facility with words, doctor, for that is just exactly what would have happened.' And who then in Banff would be safe? I could have written there and then the names of twenty papists who did not flaunt their faith but did not hide it sufficiently. If Patrick Davidson was indeed shown to have been a papist spy, God alone knew what would happen in our town. Jaffray's mind was clearly working along the same lines.

'Did they question the provost as to his nephew's time abroad, whether he fell in with papists there – was he in the region of Douai, or Paris even?'

'You think he might have been to one of the Scots seminaries there?'

'Well, when did ever you hear of a new-trained priest, returned from France to declare himself as such? They all come by clandestine roads, disguised as students, teachers, doctors, even.'

'I do not think he was a priest. The subject was not raised in that way. No mention was made of Douai, or indeed of Paris. And yet ...'

'And yet?' prompted the doctor.

'When I spoke to Charles, he told me of Davidson's love of the music, the masses, the great cathedrals he saw on his travels. I think he may well have had papist leanings.' If this had been the case, he could have made common cause with many – prominent Gordons among them – within easy reach of Banff.

'If Davidson was in clandestine meetings with papists, they must have taken place, as must his map-drawing, on his gathering expeditions.'

'With Marion,' I said.

'Yes, we are back once more to Marion, and I would be more than astonished if the baillie had not come to the same reasoning. He will question her closely on it if he suspects she has any knowledge at all that might be useful to him. She may have held out against him so far, but I doubt she has the strength of will to do so indefinitely.'

I thought about the girl as I had seen her the day before, peering into the depths and then looking through me when I hailed her at the Elf Kirk. I was not as sure as Jaffray that even Baillie Buchan could reach to what she knew. The doctor, however, was not to be reassured.

'It is necessary that we should know what she hides if we are to help Charles.' He closed his eyes, the better to concentrate on the problem. 'I will see her, tomorrow.' He called for Ishbel and handed her a hastily scribbled note, addressed to Arbuthnott. 'Have the boy take that to the apothecary's. Tell him he must give it only into the hand of Arbuthnott and that he must see to it that he reads it immediately. He is to lose no time.' Ishbel, who had been given many stranger commissions before, went immediately without question. I looked to my friend for an explanation. 'I have told him that Buchan will come looking for his daughter tonight and that he is to give the girl a sleeping draught and see to it that she takes it. I have told him that I will come and see to her in the morning, and that no one else is to be admitted to see her until I have done so.'

'Will he do it?'

'He will do it. The man is in a state of near terror – a murder and now perhaps treason – all emanating from his house. If Baillie Buchan comes looking for his daughter, Arbuthnott will know it is for no good purpose to Marion or her family. He must know as well as you and I do that the girl is implicated up to her neck.'

It was, in the circumstances, a chilling assessment of Marion Arbuthnott's situation. Her graceful neck might yet be circled round with the executioner's rope, she not being high born enough to lay it beneath his axe. The knowledge that Charles's fate rested in hers added to my already mounting sense of apprehension. In the alleyways and vennels, the backlands and the courtyards of Banff, evil was waiting. Watching. And it would not watch for ever. It was only ten days now till the sheriff returned to hold the assize. Ten days perhaps, to save our friend.

'Will she talk to you, doctor?'

'Aye, she will. I have known her since she drew her first breath. She will know her friends from those she cannot trust, or those who cannot help her.'

'With Davidson dead, and Charles in the tolbooth, what friends are left to her?'

'You and I, Alexander. You and I, and she must know that soon. I am certain that whatever the nature of her burden, she cannot carry it alone much longer.'

And then a thought struck me, and I wondered that it had not done him also. 'The minister's sister, though. Geleis Guild.' The provost's wife. 'They are friends, are they not, she and Marion? And Marion helps with the children. Might she not unburden herself to her?'

Jaffray reflected. 'I had not thought of that. Aye, she might, when she comes to herself a bit. But those would be women's things. We can do nothing for a murdered heart, but perhaps we can help dispel her more immediate fears. I will talk to her, tomorrow,' Jaffray repeated, and I did not see the need for further questions on the matter.

The candles on the mantelpiece were burning low. The church bell had struck seven, but it was still light outside the window. The usual caw of the gulls trying their luck at the shore and the town middens was joined now by the twilight songs of the spring birds. At last, as April approached, we were hauling ourselves out of the last dregs of winter and towards the light and freedom of the spring and summer. It was as if the storm of two nights ago had blown the darkness further back across the northern seas. The doctor went over to his desk and picked up a sheet of paper, which he handed to me.

'These are the findings of my examination of the corpse of Patrick Davidson.' I waited. 'He was poisoned.' A matter-of-fact statement; a piece of common knowledge. He took the paper back out of my hand, crumpled it, and threw it in the fire. 'Patrick Davidson was one of the healthiest specimens it has ever been my duty to examine. And yet he is dead. Dead because someone took the root of a small and beautiful flower and fed it to him. So lethal was it that it started to kill him before it ever reached his stomach, for there was little trace of it there. He was lost to this world from the moment he swallowed it.'

I did not understand. 'A flower? But ... if there was no trace, how do you know—'

'I know because we found it in the vomit, Arbuthnott and I, before we ever had the barber help us open him up. We found elements of the root, pieces and two whole slices, in the vomit congealed on his hair and his clothes. Mistress Youngson is a woman of experience and wisdom – she knows what to clean away and what to leave. It was the apothecary who spotted it. The man has an eagle's eye, and a knowledge of botany far in advance of my own. And yet, when he pointed it out and voiced his sup-position, I knew him to be right.'

'What is it?'

'*Colchicum mortis* – the colchicum of death.'

A flower. 'James and the flowers.' The words of Janet Dawson, whispered so urgently only yesterday, came back to me now. But Jaffray was warming to his theme, and did not notice my abstraction.

'You will not have heard of it. Indeed, why would you have? I have never come across a case myself before. Other varieties of *colchicum*, of course, are of use in medicine and cooking.'

'In cooking?' I knew that poisons were often used in the preparation of medicines, but that they were put into food was something new to me. 'Is that not dangerous?'

Jaffray laughed. 'Saffron, Alexander, saffron. Many women will use it for its colour and its flavouring. It is obtained from the stamen of the *colchicum* and Arbuthnott stocks it openly on his shelves. I have often myself prescribed it for the treatment of gout and arthritis. However, a high dose can be dangerous, giving rise to palsies and fits. Arbuthnott, like any good

77

apothecary, will measure his doses carefully.'

'So someone has been storing it up, with a murderous intent.'

Jaffray shook his head. 'No. It was the root, remember, the sliced root that we found. Almost like a small, discoloured onion – by the look of it he had eaten it in a stew. There are many varieties of *colchicum* that, wrongly used, will harm a man, but only one that will kill him, and with such speed. The *colchicum mortis*; to judge from Patrick Davidson's face, and the set of his corpse when he was discovered, he had suffered convulsions and paralysis before his death.'

I remembered the contorted features and the grotesque arrangement of the body I had seen dead at my desk, and I did not argue with the doctor. He continued. 'The plant is grown and its properties well known in the Alps where, despite its beauty, none will touch it. I have seen it only once and at a distance, at a lecture at Montpellier nearly thirty years ago. I cannot pretend I remember it clearly or could describe it accurately. Later, though, I did see some sketches of the flower.'

I was as ignorant of botany as it had been possible for a student of divinity to be. I had always been so taken up with the internal world of man that the external, with all its seasonally changing beauties, had in many ways remained a mystery to me. And yet I was doubtful. 'And with this knowledge you can identify the root of one small plant?'

Jaffray reached again for his pipe. 'I cannot be certain I would even have thought of it had not Arbuthnott drawn my attention to the residue in the hair. The root – bulb, in fact – could be from one of several plants, but none with such lethal effect as the *colchicum mortis*.' He paused for a moment in thought, sombre. 'Poisoning is an act of veiled and contemptible cowardice, born in the blackest region of a man's heart. It admits of no possibility of the victim fighting back. And yet,' he hesitated.

'Yet what?'

'I do not think, in the end, that the murderer was able to fully conceal his crime from the boy. The colchicum should have no taste, but I believe that in his last minutes, Patrick Davidson knew he had been poisoned. Death did not come quickly enough for either of them.'

There came a searing flash in my mind again of a man calling out to me, a man falling, trying to get up, calling to me for help. A wave of nausea ran through me. Mine had been the second face that night to condemn him to death. I did not want this to be true.

'Why do you think so, James?'

'The grass. A dog eats grass to make itself sick. There is no briony to be had at this time of year, for that would have done the trick, so in his last conscious moments in this world, Patrick Davidson resorted to the behaviour of a dog in an attempt to save his own life. He tried to make himself vomit because he knew he had been poisoned.'

'How long would he have suffered?' My voice could barely hold the question.

'Longer than he should have done. Fifteen, perhaps twenty minutes.'

And when, in those fifteen or twenty minutes, had I seen him? How near to death or to the possibility of salvation had Patrick Davidson been when he had made his desperate, hopeless appeal to me? 'And Arbuthnott is of your view?'

'I did not discuss that point with the apothecary. I trust him implicitly on the matter of plants and compounds, but the human psyche is beyond his expertise.' He smiled mischievously. 'Else he would not have married him such a wife.'

I could not help but smile myself, grave though the present matter was. The doctor had seen greater tragedies and greater evil before, no doubt, and it was only his humour that allowed him to bear it day after day. He called his humour a gift of faith, a grace. It was a gift greatly misunderstood by some of the narrower minds in our community, those whose chief delight in life was to cast withering glances and utter words of reproach. Those such as Baillie Buchan, James Cardno and even, I sometimes thought, my landlady, Mistress Youngson. 'What does Arbuthnott have to say about the provenance of the root? Was it taken from his shop?'

Jaffray shook his head. 'He has never had nor would ever have it. There is, he claims – and I do not disbelieve him, for I know of none myself – no use in medicine or hygiene for the root of that variety of the species. I checked every shelf and every drawer in that shop today – there is no poison under the apothecary's roof that is not on the permitted list.'

'Then was it grown here?' I knew that many plants native to the Alps had become favourites in the gardens of landed and professional people who had returned to our shores after study abroad. Some grew them for further study, but many, I knew, simply for the joy of it.

Again Jaffray was doubtful. 'That was my own next thought. I know little enough about the cultivation of flowers myself – it is Ishbel who tends to Elizabeth's garden – so I went and inquired of Gilbert Jack.' As ever, the doctor had seen to the heart of the matter: if any man in Banff knew of the flower, it would be the laird of Banff's gardener. The laird's palace gardens ran down opposite the kirkyard and towards the Greenbanks, taking in much of what had once formed the yards and gardens of the Carmelites in the burgh. Three generations of gardeners – Gilbert Jack's father and grandfather before him – had redeemed what was best in those gardens: the herbarium, the kitchen garden, the orchard with its many types of apple, plum and pear, and had created a garden that was the glory of the north. If Gilbert Jack could not grow something in Banff, it probably could not be grown here at all.

'And?'

'And it cannot be grown here. The winds and the salt air are too harsh. He knows because he tried once, many years ago, with bulbs the laird had brought from the continent, and failed. So that should have been an end to the matter.'

'But it has not been.'

'No, it has not.' He went to light another candle against the failing light. 'I fear that my examination is next to worthless. It has done nothing to bring us any nearer to discovering the identity of Patrick Davidson's killer. And so it does nothing to open the locks of the tolbooth for Charles.' He returned heavily to his chair.

'It may yet do something.'

'I do not see how.'

'"James and the flowers".' I murmured it quietly to myself and then repeated it to him, more clearly this time. '"James and the flowers".'

Jaffray's face was a study in incomprehension.

'They were the last words Patrick Davidson ever spoke: "James and the flowers".'

He looked at me, unable to understand something. 'But Alexander, how do you know?'

I had forgotten, completely, to tell him of my encounters with the Dawson sisters – either on the night of the murder or with Janet Dawson yesterday. And, I now acknowledged, with a sinking heart, that I had utterly neglected to tell him of my own sighting of Patrick Davidson on the night of his death. And so I told him it all. Throughout the narrative he said nothing, but his eyes, when I told him of my abandonment of my fellow creature calling for help, spoke much of what was in his heart. I saw in him a deep and sincere sorrow and a disappointment he could not mask – the one for Patrick Davidson, the other for me. I made no excuses for I knew there were none. I finished my piece and he sat in silent contemplation of what I had told him. After a time, he spoke.

'And you say it was a little before ten? Where was he heading to, or coming from?'

I shook my head. 'That I cannot tell you. He was,' I cleared my throat, 'he was slumped against the wall of the Castle grounds, before he fell. He may have fallen before that – I do not know. I did not,' and my voice fell, 'I did not linger long enough to see a second time if he righted himself, or where he tried to go.'

'And in those ten, fifteen minutes from where he'd parted from his killer, he might have travelled far enough.' He sighed deeply, 'No, it does not help us.' He paused, and then roused himself again. 'But what do you think it means, "James and the flowers"?'

I confessed that I had little idea – the matter had been put almost entirely from my mind by the discovery of the maps, and the explanations that did suggest themselves to me I did not like.

Jaffray packed his pipe again and reached another spill from the fire to light it.

'Evidently,' he said, 'the flowers refers to the *colchicum*: the boy knew exactly what he had been poisoned with. And as for the "James" – well, I fear there can only be one conclusion.'

I hesitated to say it; I had been avoiding the thought. 'The murderer?'

'Indeed, what else?'

'Then it does not help us greatly. For every ten men in Banff, two will be named James.'

Jaffray smiled. 'And one of them is myself.'

81

I looked at the loved old face. 'And you, my friend, I discount. But as for the rest – how can we tell who had dealings with Patrick Davidson and who did not?'

'We ask anyone who knew him. At the same time we must see where any other evidence may point, and if that also points to James, then so much the better.' Jaffray was animated, for he had a scheme, a plan. He was not a man who liked to wait upon events.

I set my mind to work. The killer of Patrick Davidson must have a minute knowledge of plants and their properties – better even than a physician and as good as an apothecary. Not only of native plants, but also of the more exotic alpine species that could not be found or grown on our harsh and windblown scrap of God's earth. And to know of this *colchicum mortis* they must have travelled or have been in close commune with someone who had. As the doctor sat looking sadly into the fire, I went through the burgh in my mind, in search of the most likely poisoner. There was the apothecary himself, Edward Arbuthnott. There was only his word to say that he did not have access to a stock of the *colchicum* roots. But then, why would he have pointed them out to Jaffray, and what possible motive might he have for murdering his apprentice? The doctor himself? I could not countenance such a thing. There was Marion Arbuthnott – might she have managed to obtain the plant without her father's knowledge? Again, I could see no possible reason she might want Davidson dead. By all appearances she had loved him. Her mother? No. According to Charles, Marion's marriage to Patrick Davidson had been her mother's goal. And if there had been some scandal? Betrothal, not murder, was the answer to that type of scandal – for such as Marion and Davidson, at least. I was certain Charles had no knowledge of or interest in botany. True, he would have access to Arbuthnott's stores, but if Arbuthnott did not store the poison – again, I was going around in a circle, and arriving where I had begun. I was tired and my head was beginning to ache at the temples. 'I must go, James. The light is fading and I rise early tomorrow.'

'Tomorrow?'

'Yes, I had almost forgotten myself. I must go into Aberdeen, about the business of the bursaries.'

Jaffray was interested. 'Indeed? The bursaries? But yes, I recall now. And will you find lodging in the college, or in the town?'

'The town. I will lodge with my old friend William Cargill—'

'James Cargill's nephew?' The doctor interrupted.

'Yes. William is married now and has his own home in the Green quarter. He has been building up a lucrative lawyer's business since his return from Leiden. He'll be the town's advocate in Edinburgh before long.'

Jaffray was unimpressed. 'A great pity that he did not follow his uncle into medicine. The young–' He was about to launch himself into one of his well-rehearsed diatribes on the laziness and thanklessness of my generation – not a word of which he meant – when he stopped suddenly. 'Of course. James Cargill. Cargill's notebooks – that is where I saw the sketch of the flower! If anyone in the north of Scotland ever knew that flower it would have been James Cargill.'

'But the doctor has been dead these ten years and more,' I protested.

He brushed this aside. 'It matters little. His notebooks were the most exact I ever saw. He was an excellent physician yet his great pleasure, passion even, was the study of botany. He told me once that he was never happier than the summer he spent at Montbéliard with Jean Bauhin in the gathering and study of flowers. These troubles in the Empire would break his heart, if he lived today. Yes, I must see James Cargill's notebooks. If his nephew has them, I trust you will manage to persuade him to lend us them awhile.'

'I have no doubt. But how might they help?'

Jaffray muttered at my idiocy. 'They will show us the flower. Arbuthnott has but a very hazy memory of its appearance, and I none. If we at least know what the plant from which these noxious bulbs are harvested looks like, then it may avail us something. Gilbert Jack may yet be proved wrong – perhaps it has been grown here, but we will never discover it if we do not know what it looks like.' I felt Jaffray and I were leading each other farther and farther on the same wild goose chase, but we had nowhere else to go if we were to help our friend. I assured the doctor I would do my best to secure James Cargill's notebooks.

'Good, good,' he said. 'But this business of the maps, Alexander, I doubt it will avail Charles Thom anything. If Davidson were spying for every papist from here to Madrid, what good does the discovery of it do Charles Thom?'

This was a question I had asked myself as I'd walked down towards the doctor's from the tolbooth. 'If Davidson was a papist spy, then that would at least allow of a motive for his murder other than this nonsense of jealousy over a woman. It may be that his activities had been found out – that he was murdered to prevent his maps falling into the hands of his sponsors. Yet in such a case, why not accuse and try him openly?'

'Because it would cause panic, my boy. And it might expose others whom the authorities might not wish to have exposed.'

The pain in my head was now throbbing relentlessly. The faces of Patrick Davidson, the provost, Marion Arbuthnott, Baillie Buchan, Charles Thom, the unseen Gordon of Straloch were all crowding in on me.

For his part, on my mission, Jaffray took it upon himself to enquire into Patrick Davidson's connections in the burgh and its hinterland – be they Gordons, papists or simply 'Jameses' while I was away. My headache receded after I swallowed a draft of laudanum he had given me from his own store, and he and I talked much later into the night than I had planned, of other things. Finally, having promised that I would leave fresh provisions from Ishbel for Charles at the tolbooth before I left Banff early the following morning, I bade the doctor's household farewell until I should return from Aberdeen.

SIX

A Journey

There was already much business at the shore as I passed on my way to the tolbooth early next morning. The first boats since the great storm of Monday had put into port, and their wares had already been unloaded to make way for salmon, grain and woolfells destined for their entrepôt at Aberdeen. The shore porters who had spent Monday night gaming in the inn were now busily engaged on their proper labours. Traders and merchants' boys ferried goods from the harbour to the market place in small carts or on their backs. The gulls were circling and cawing round the gutting station where the women cleaned the fish just landed for salting. Everything was as it had always been, as if the murder had been but a pedlar's tale. The slight haar brought a smell of stagnant seaweed up from the shore; I had never liked it. I was glad that much of today's journey would take me many miles away from the coast, almost till I reached Aberdeen itself.

The provost was not yet there when I arrived at the tolbooth, and I was directed instead to his house on the Castlegate. I had hoped to see Charles before I left, but the town serjeant was under strict instruction that no one – and something in his manner implied that it was myself in particular who was meant – was to be permitted access to the jail. It was becoming clear that Charles was to be kept from any communication with his friends.

As I drew near to the provost's house I saw him waiting for me in the open doorway. He hailed me from a distance of ten yards. 'Mr Seaton. I am glad you are about your business early. You will reach Aberdeen in daylight?' There was no apology for his lateness and I had expected none.

'Easily. I have Gilbert Grant's horse, and I will change mounts at Turriff.'

He cast a practised eye over the animal. It was no thoroughbred, but it was a sturdy and dependable beast. 'Keep a watchful eye around you as you go. There are vagabonds aplenty on the roads who would not scruple to attack a schoolmaster. The map must not fall into the wrong hands.'

'I can take care of myself well enough.' There was nothing Walter Watt could tell me about vagabonds on the highways. Three times in four years Archie and I had been set upon as we returned from the college to his father's stronghold of Delgatie. But Archie had been taught to manage a sword before he could manage a pen and, from the very beginning of our friendship when, small boys though we were, he had realised what a hopeless knight I was, what he knew he had taught to me. From each assault we had come away with our purses and our pride intact.

The provost seemed satisfied. He handed me a leather pouch with the chosen map inside. 'You know what you are to ask Straloch. And remember that – you are to ask him. Our business here in this burgh is none of his.'

'I know little of this burgh's business, provost; only that on which I am sent.'

'I'd wager you know more than that. I did not entirely speak the truth yesterday, when I told the minister I knew little of your ill repute. I know it all, Mr Seaton: the drinking, the whoring, the attempts at self-harm. You have had a wild time of it, six months or more.'

'All that is past.'

'Perhaps. The baillie for one is of a mind that it may be so, and that is something in your favour. I care little for the censure of the Kirk, but I have seen you in sack-cloth on the stool of repentance. I know nothing of the state of your soul or the extent of your repentance, but I know of your humiliation before the whole town. Better men have been banished from this town for little worse than you have done.'

'I know as well as any man what I have been and what I am, provost. For the state of my soul I cannot answer, but my repentance is complete. If I had the choice, I would not still be here. But I have no other place in this world.'

He looked at me, but said nothing. As well as the map, and a private letter of his for delivery in Aberdeen, he held a written authority to Straloch to treat me as the representative of the burgh of Banff. He handed me them all with a final instruction. 'You must tell no one of the purpose of your visit to Straloch. There will be bloodshed and dissent in this town should the fear of a popish plot become generally known. You have been entrusted with a matter of great importance. Do not disgrace this burgh. Or yourself.'

He turned away into the darkness of his doorway and I bade my farewell to his back. As I left the house, early in the day though it was, I heard the sound of a child crying from over the garden wall. I took a step towards the gate and stopped: a little girl, the provost's daughter, perhaps three or four years of age, was lying on the stony path where she had just fallen, her chubby arm grazed and bleeding. I would have gone to lift her up, but Marion Arbuthnott, unnoticed by me until now, was there before me. She lifted the child tenderly then gently examined the injury. Murmuring some words of comfort she softly kissed the curly head and carried the girl in to her mother. As she was about to step through the door she turned to me and nodded, briefly, in acknowledgement. She had not taken the sleeping draught then; she had not hidden herself away. All would be well with the girl I had had such fears for but two days ago at the Elf Kirk.

When I reached the sandbar at the mouth of the Deveron the larger of the two town ferries was waiting. The tide was high, unlike the day twelve years ago or more when Archie and I had been riding from Banff to Delgatie. He had insisted that the water was low enough and the sandbar wide enough for our horses to ford the river with ease. The horses had made it, just, but only the diligence of Paul Black, the ferryman, had saved their two young riders from drowning. The tongue-lashing he had given each of us once he had pulled us both to safety at the end of his boatman's hook was as nothing to the leathering we both received at the hands of the laird's stable master for risking the horses. Eight years later, that same stable master had sent his only son to the Bohemian wars to serve the young Master of Hay, and the two fathers, master and servant, had wept together when they received the news that neither would return. Yet here was I still: on a borrowed horse, little more than a messenger, of no great worth to those who thought themselves my friends and of none to myself.

Paul Black still held the tack of the ferry. He hailed me from a distance, an identical boat hook in his hand. 'Bring him round this way, Mr Seaton.' He helped me settle and tie the animal. Having seen to the other travellers he did not cast off, but instead came over to talk with me. 'I am sorry Mr Seaton, you will be inconvenienced today. The smaller boat is not out.'

'I have no need of the smaller boat,' I said, not comprehending.

'No, but it means we will have to wait for Sarah Forbes.' He nodded back in the direction of the town and I followed the line of his vision. The name Sarah Forbes was something familiar to me, but I did not know why. Then, as I looked towards the town, I remembered, and the bleakness of it filled me. A crowd, not large but notable none the less, was making its way past the Greenbanks towards the ferry landing. At its head was the town drummer who struck out a relentless beat. The image in my mind was of George Burnett, master mason. He had sat in the kirk last Sunday on the stool of repentance, as I myself before the whole congregation had often done. His public shaming was in recompense for his having been found guilty of the sin of fornication, adulterous fornication, with one of his servants, which he had denied until Sarah Forbes's six-month swollen belly gave him the lie. He would sit on the stool another two weeks, for the good of his soul and the edification of his neighbours, and he would pay a six shilling fine which would be put into the hand of the presbytery divinity bursar such as I had once been. As for Sarah Forbes, who could take her punishment but not pay her fine, she and her unborn child had been condemned to banishment from the burgh, never to be found again within its bounds, on pain of death. Such was justice in our godly commonwealth.

At the sound of the drum I had thought immediately of Mary Dawson. I had not seen her since Monday night, and had not heard of her about the town since her sister Janet's banishment. I wondered what fate had befallen her.

As the procession came to a halt, the town's officer read out the terms of Sarah Forbes's banishment one more time. A woman spat; another hurled a stone that missed the girl but caught the drummer on the cheek. Some filthy names were called and then the performance was over. Paul Black helped the girl and her meagre belongings onto the boat and the crowd turned away, the mundane business of the day calling their attention once more. Once aboard, the girl reached in a small leather pouch and brought out a coin which she held out to Paul Black. He shook his head and closed her fingers back over it. She settled herself at the end of a bench opposite me and looked directly ahead of her out to sea. She spoke to no one and no one spoke to her on the short crossing to the other side of the Deveron.

As we landed on the east bank of the river, I had to wait for Paul Black to help me off with the horse, and stood back as he reached for the girl's bundle and then her hand to steady her as she stepped warily down the gangplank.

'You are a good man, Paul,' I said, as he untied Gilbert Grant's horse for me.

'"Whosoever shall receive this child in my name receiveth me."' There being no travellers waiting for passage back over the river to Banff, he set to the oars with his three sons and soon the boat was pulling away towards the opposite side of the river.

Sarah Forbes was walking away in the direction of the parish of King Edward. I myself had a call to pay there with packages from Mistress Youngson to the minister's wife, who was her sister. She had given me to understand that the non-delivery of these packages safely into her sister's own hands would place in jeopardy my continued residence in the schoolhouse, protest her husband however much he might. Still on foot and leading my horse by the head, I had caught up with the banished girl in less than a minute. I could not just get up on the beast's back and ride past her. 'It is Sarah, is it not?'

She glanced at me and then looked ahead of her, blankly. 'Yes. I think that is well known, today anyway.' She continued on her way.

'You are Ishbel's friend, Ishbel MacGillivray?'

Her face had lightened a little when she turned it towards me again. 'Yes. Ishbel is my friend. I doubt I will ever see her again, though. And the doctor too, he was good to me. He tried—' She paused, unsure how to proceed.

'You must know the doctor is my friend. You are free to speak with me. My name is Alexander Seaton.'

Now at last she smiled, a smile that lifted her face from the ordinary and took something of the wariness from her eyes. 'I know who you are, sir. Your name is also known.' She looked down as if she regretted being so open, then said, 'But Ishbel says you are a good man, and that the doctor thinks well of you.'

'The doctor thinks better of me than I deserve. He tried to help you, then?'

She nodded. 'He guessed at my condition two months ago. He spoke up

89

for me before the session and at the council, but it did not sway them. Why should it? I am a fallen woman.'

'Where will you go now?'

'I have nowhere to go but my uncle's house – on the far side of King Edward. If he will take me.'

'Are you afraid he will not?'

She gave me a dubious smile and then looked down at her belly. 'He had little enough opinion of me before he sent me to work in Banff, and he will have less now. Anyway, I must get on. The haar is coming in. Goodbye, Mr Seaton.'

I remained motionless by my obedient mount as she walked away and up the track. 'Wait,' I called. 'Please wait.'

She turned around and lowered her head.

'Sarah ...'

'What do you want from me?'

'I ...' I did not know the answer. 'It is a long walk to King Edward. Six miles, maybe.'

'Not so long. Two hours, or a little more, will take me there. Anyway, I am in no great hurry.'

That I could believe well enough. The condemnation of the citizens of Banff would hardly have faded in her ears before that of her aunt and uncle started.

'It will be hot when the haar lifts. Much of your journey will be uphill. I am going by King Edward myself.' I indicated the saddle, broad and worn by many years in the old schoolmaster's service. 'If I moved these bags a little, and doubled this blanket, there would be room ...'

She looked at me, perplexed, and then laughed out loud, a true laugh of delighted mirth. 'Mr Seaton, where are your eyes? Have you seen the size of me? The poor beast's back would break with me up there as well, and you would have to sit on his ears just to make room for me.'

I stood aside from the horse and stepped a little closer to her. 'You do not understand, Sarah. If you can make yourself comfortable up there, I will walk.'

She parted her lips slightly and drew in her breath as if she was about to say something. She looked up at me for a moment and then looked away as the pale green eyes that had looked blankly out to sea on the ferry threatened to give way to her feelings. She took the hand that I held out and let me lift her up onto the horse.

We passed only one or two people on the road, and they took little notice of us. I thought of her former master George Burnett, the father of her child. I had never liked the man, and neither had my father before me. I remembered my father coming home from meetings of the craft guild and talking of the swagger and the coarseness of George Burnett. But the stonemasons were a powerful guild in Banff, and Burnett the most skilled amongst them.

'Will George Burnett care for his child?' It was not unknown for a father to raise a natural son with those of his marriage.

Again she laughed, a different laugh this time. 'Care for his child? George Burnett is too busy to concern himself with anything so profitless. These last storms have cost him many days' work, and the fine the session forced from him is more than he thinks me or my baby worth. He should have been much further on with the building of the minister's new house by now, but the weather has held him up so badly he still has much of the garden ground to clear before he can even complete the foundations. The longer it takes him, the longer he will wait on his payment. My fate is of little interest to him, other than that I should be out of his wife's sight and cease to cause him inconvenience. He will not acknowledge the child. But I would have it no other way.' I waited for her to continue, and she did. 'I arrived in Banff a maiden and no whore. I have left it a maiden no longer, but I am no whore either. While there is breath in my body he will never set a hand on my baby.' She placed her hand over her belly, and in that moment I knew she would kill to protect her child if she had to. I began to fear a little less for Sarah Forbes.

The rest of our journey passed quietly and we arrived in King Edward without incident. Sarah's uncle lived on the far side of the parish, where the road dipped then rose again towards Turriff. Mistress Youngson's sister lived, of course, in the manse beside her husband's kirk. As we approached the kirkyard gate I sensed the young woman shifting uneasily on the horse's back.

'Is there something the matter?'

91

She smiled, too bright a smile. 'I am fine, thank you, just fine. But I think maybe it would be better if I walked from here. It would do your name no good to be seen here with me, and you do not deserve to be calumniated for your kindness.'

'Nor you for your condition. I think, perhaps ...' I hesitated, but she was looking at me intently. 'I think perhaps, it was not your will that George Burnett should have—' This was none of my business, but I was too far on now to go back.

She looked away. 'No, it was not my will.'

'I am sorry,' I said.

I reached up to help her down from the beast's back, but as I set her gently on the ground I – without knowing what I did – let my hands rest a moment at her waist. From the warmth under my fingers I felt the full force of a small kick, a touch from another world. I pulled my hand away as if burnt, then placed it back in wonder. She smiled, a little confused, as I was. I had not known such an intensity of human touch, different, and yet greater than that I had known in my passion for Katharine Hay. I think I would have stood like that a lifetime. The sound of the byre door opening startled me from my reverie, and I managed to step back a pace or two from Sarah Forbes before Mistress Youngson's sister emerged carrying a pail of freshly taken milk.

Esther Youngson, wife of the minister of King Edward, knew me immediately. Carrying the pail carefully, she walked towards us, smiling, as her sister seldom allowed herself to do. 'It is Mr Seaton, is it not? And,' she looked beyond me and put down her pail, 'Sarah Forbes. Oh, Sarah, my child, so it is true, then.' Sarah, who had held her head high as she had walked away from the jeers and stones of the mob at Banff could not withstand the tenderness of an old woman who had known her from childhood. She hung her head and wept. Mistress Youngson made her way past me and held the girl for a moment until the crisis subsided. There would be no going to her uncle's just yet. Carrying the milk and the packages that had brought me here, I followed the two women into the manse.

Hamish MacLennan, a formidable preacher and fervent for the discipline of the kirk, was not at home. His wife insisted that Sarah lie down on the serving girl's bed set into the kitchen wall. Despite her protests that she was not tired, it was scarcely ten minutes before the level rise and fall of her breathing told us she was asleep. In sleep she looked younger than her eighteen or nineteen years, almost childlike. Mistress Youngson laid another blanket over her and came across to where I sat on the window seat.

There was bread baking in the oven and its aroma filled the room. The warmth of the kitchen enveloped me so that I too felt I might sleep. In childhood I had often sought out the kitchen and the window seat. From there I would watch my mother at her work and listen to her stories of her Ulster homeland. There were many legends, of kings and princes and giants, and of the fairy folk, tales that would have had my mother up before the session, just for the telling of them, had it been known. To me the saddest story was not of princesses, or sea-folk or fairies, but of a young woman, a wealthy burgess's daughter of Carrickfergus. The girl had fallen in love with a Scottish soldier returning to his homeland by way of Ireland from exile in France with his master. The young woman's father had been opposed to any match between them; his daughter had not been brought up to be the wife of a mere soldier, a hammerman to trade. She had been educated in the ways of a lady to be the wife of a lawyer or civil servant or wealthy merchant. He forbade his daughter to see any more of the soldier. Three weeks later, the laird of Delgatie set sail in the night with his men up Belfast Lough and away towards Scotland, far away from his lovely daughter. But when the maidservant went to wake the girl in the morning she found the girl was gone, gone sailing to Scotland with the laird of Delgatie and his armourer, Andrew Seaton, my father.

I never tired of hearing the story as I sat silent in the window seat, watching as my mother kneaded bread and plucked birds and gutted fish; I watched as she rubbed the ointments Jaffray had prescribed from the apothecary into the sore and calloused hands that had been meant for sewing and drawing up household accounts and playing the lute. Or I would sit there working at my Latin and Greek until the light faded or my father found me and called me instead to the smithy, where he and his apprentice toiled before the roaring furnace over axes and hunting spears and swords of every description.

'The girl is exhausted.' It was Mistress Youngson's voice that broke into my daydream. 'Did she ride with you all the way from Banff, or did you meet with her on the road?'

'I saw her on the ferry. She took a good deal of persuading before she would consent to get up on the horse. She had been of a mind to walk.' A thought crossed my mind as Mistress Youngson's question repeated itself in my head. 'The child is not mine,' I said. 'I never spoke to her until this day. I—'

The old woman smiled. 'Calm yourself, boy. I know whose child it is. The girl should never have been sent to work in that man's house. My own sister, your master's wife, told me what manner of man he was, and I warned her uncle and aunt not to put her there.'

'And they did it anyway?'

She nodded.

I wondered what sort of home the girl was returning to, what kind of place in this world she was bringing her child into. 'Will they take her in?'

'Aye, they will. But she'll have a hard time of it.' She went wearily over to the hearth and stirred the pot from which the smell of mutton stew drifted over to me. I remembered my commission from her sister, forgotten in all the business of Sarah, and handed her the packages.

Mistress Youngson's eyes lit up. She had a child's delight in receiving a gift. There was hardly a mystery about the first package – four fresh herring, bought before it was light at the shore of Banff. The second package revealed a pot of honey, a gift from the hives in the laird of Banff's great garden. There was a letter, which the old woman set up high on the mantel, for when she could take her time and read it on her own. Last was a soft, bulky parcel, wrapped in a muslin cloth and tied with hemp. A note was stitched to the cloth. Across the table I could read the words as the minister's wife unfolded a knitted woollen shawl, the colour of oatmeal, with a tiny silken bow stitched at the corner: *for Sarah Forbes's bairn.* How had I ever reached such a pass, to have lost the affection and respect of a woman of so stern demeanour and yet so replete with quiet kindness?

The minister's wife insisted I take some of the mutton stew she had made for her husband's dinner. 'In any case, Mr MacLennan will have no notion of mutton stew when he catches sight of these herring.' She ladled me out a huge bowl from her steaming pot and went to the kist for oatmeal to coat the fish in.

By the time I had finished my meal, Sarah Forbes still slept soundly. There was no reason I could find words or voice for to stay until she woke, yet I was reluctant to leave. Mistress Youngson had assured me that she herself would go with Sarah to her uncle's house, once she was awake and had taken a good hot meal. She assured me also that she would make it known in very clear terms that she and her husband would keep an eye on how the girl was treated. Yet I could see that she still had fears for Sarah's welfare and that of her child. I walked out of the manse door and then I turned back to Mistress Youngson with my hand at my pouch. I pressed the coins into her hand. Five pounds Scots – the price of some books I had been going to buy for myself in Aberdeen. 'Give it to them. Tell them it is from friends in Banff. It is for her food, and she must not be made to work beyond noon. Tell them there will be more when the child comes, if her friends are satisfied that she is not mistreated.'

She closed her hand over the coins and I could see tears in her eyes. 'You are a good man, for all … for all else that might have happened.' Further explanation was unnecessary. I thanked her for her kindness and rode away from King Edward.

The road became busier over the last few miles to Turriff with country people returning from the morning market in the town. Some of them might have known me, but I kept my hat pulled down low and, avoiding their eyes, kept my gaze fixed directly ahead of me. I did not turn to the left where the road branched off for Delgatie. I could count on the fingers of one hand the number of times I had reached this crossing and continued directly ahead rather than turning towards that great stronghold. I can have been little more than five years old when I first rode up with my father. Every step of the horse took me further into this strange, unimagined world. And then I had seen the castle. Only an ogre, I thought, a giant such as held sway in my mother's stories, could live in such a place as that. Try as he might my father could not make me believe that the lord of that castle was the same jovial man who would arrive at the foundry with a great retinue of men, ordering arms for fighting and weapons for the hunt. He would joke with my father about my long slim fingers and my pale boy's hands, and ask me to show him where were my hammerman's muscles. I remembered my mother coming out on one such occasion and fixing his lordship with what I knew to be her most dangerous look and saying to him, 'This child will be no hammerman,' before taking my arm from his hand and bringing me back into her kitchen. My father was so ashamed it was days before I heard him address a word to her. But the laird of Delgatie never made sport of me again.

But that was over twenty years ago, that first of many visits, that first time I had met Archie, the laird's boisterous bear cub of a son, who even at five years old transfixed and overwhelmed me with his intoxicating spirit. And then too I had met Katharine, the serious three-year-old Katharine, who even then watched her brother with a quiet wariness far beyond her years. But now Archie was dead, and Katharine was here no longer, gone far, far away from her home and her family because of me, and their father would have thrown me from the castle's ramparts rather than welcome me within its walls once more.

The horse travelled steadily on, and I was soon in Turriff. I had no need to tarry in the town beyond changing my horse and delivering a letter from Jaffray to one of the doctors there. I refused the doctor's offer of refreshment, and with the wind at my back left Turriff and rode hard towards Aberdeen.

The first time Archie and I had taken this road together we had been little more than fifteen, boys still, setting out for our studies at the King's College in Aberdeen. We had ridden from the gates of Delgatie as his mother and sister watched from an upper window, my head full of Latin and Greek and Archie's full of fighting and women. At the head of us, his lordship himself had ridden.

My own father no longer rode with Lord Hay. He was a burgess of Banff now, and owed his allegiance first to the town and then to the king. The laird would have given me a horse that almost matched Archie's, but my father would not allow it, the first time in his life that he had ever spoken against Lord Hay. And the laird, understanding my father better then than I did, had not pressed the point but had had his stable master bring me round a roan cob – a respectable mount for one of my station. My father had by then stopped believing that I would ever be apprenticed to his trade. I was as tall and strong and able as any son he might have wished for, but I had my eye on other prizes and had little regard for the craft at which he excelled. I think he would gladly have burned the books my mother gave me in his hottest furnace, if he had thought she might ever forgive him. She would not have done, and he knew that well enough. But there had been bitter words between them on the eve of my leaving Banff for the college.

The evening had started well enough. Gilbert Grant was there, and Jaffray had come round too and brought the young Charles Thom with his fiddle to give us some music. In his bag the doctor had also brought a jar of the *uisge beatha* distilled by the mountain people, the people of Glenlivet to whom he journeyed every year in the summer. It was forbidden and fulminated against from every pulpit, but the doctor cared little for such fulmination when he was amongst friends. My mother made a small show of protest before going to fetch beakers for the men, and when she had her back turned, my father let the doctor pour a small measure into my own cup. 'Be sure to sip it, boy. A taste. You will not need to swallow.' I had never tasted anything like it. It numbed my lips and set fire to my tongue before melting, sweeter and more mellow than the finest of honey, on the roof of my mouth.

As the evening wore on, I noticed my father become more and more silent. At last he stood up and bade Charles Thom hold off from his playing. He pushed the food and drink away from him and then he addressed himself to me. If any had expected some final parting words of love or advice or paternal pride, they were disappointed. Before my mother and my friends, my father told me to remember that the one and only cause of my going to the King's College was to serve the Master of Hay. Whatever vanities I might indulge in, whatever foolishness others might fill my head with, I was to remember I owed it all to the family of Delgatie, whose servant I was. Having said his piece, he called the dog from the hearth and strode out of the door. In the sudden silence of the room, I looked at my mother's face and saw a death in it. For years she had quietly, secretly as she thought, nurtured my mind, brought me books, talked to me of everything she knew of the world, of philosophy and poetry and religion. She had made me into the son she would always have had, wherever Providence might have led her, and in her struggle to do it she had trampled on the man she knew my father to be and rendered him something else. In making me so completely hers, she had taken me from him, and I never saw it until that night. I do not know if my mother ever uttered a word to my father again.

And yet, my father had been right. My Latin and Greek would have availed me nothing had it not been for my connection to Archie. Of the few bursaries then available for poor scholars at King's College, I was not eligible for any. All the available resources of the Kirk were focused on helping the divinity bursar of the presbytery survive his studies without starving or freezing. My father was not poor, but by no means could he keep me four years at the college while training up the apprentice he would not otherwise have needed. So, like a handful of other fortunate young men, I would undertake my studies, my fees paid and living full board in the college, as the servant of a nobleman friend. Archie. I had to rouse him twice in the morning, after the bursar had come past with his bell; I had to find ways of getting him past the janitor after the night curfew had fallen and the college gates were shut, holding him as straight as I could to try to mask the extent of his intoxication; more than once I had to travel in the other direction with him, concealing between our two cloaks some pretty girl who should have been at home in bed in her father's house many hours before; I had to get him to the college kirk in the hours of divine service and do my best to keep him awake while he was there. In all, I did what I could to keep him out of trouble, and most of all, out of fights. It would not matter where a fight was, what it was over or whom it involved; if Archie got the merest whiff of it he would be in the thick of it in minutes, or, often enough, he would start a fight where there had been no fight at all. 'Mind him well, Alexander,' Archie's mother had said as she bade me farewell, 'and for the love of God, keep him safe.'

I had kept him safe as long as I could, then he had taken his path and I mine. Now he was dead and I was not. There had been a point in his dying. I rode on. Turriff was soon behind me, and then Old Meldrum. I passed close by Straloch in the mid-afternoon, my hand going instinctively to my saddlebag where the map was hidden. I traversed the barren lands to the north and west of Aberdeen, only the horse sparing me complete isolation. Then I turned the beast's head towards the Don and followed the river's course as it made its last few miles towards the sea, until at last I saw the twin spires of St Machar's Cathedral on their sturdy towers, challenging the godless to approach Aberdeen. Godless or not, my heart warmed to the sight. The Irish saint's seat, rising above the great river where it curved in the shape of a bishop's crook, had always been for me the gateway to a place that was home. It was not long before the hooves of my mount were clattering over the cobbles of the Brig o' Balgownie, and I was nodding to carters and other country people on horseback or foot, making for home after their business in the two towns. The road swept out past the Bishop's Ward and over the marshland towards the sea, the east coast, looking out towards Norway, Denmark and then the Baltic, unseen, but full of possibilities, and then it turned back towards the town. I passed the port to the Bishop's Green and the Chaplain's Court. The Machar kirk was behind me now, to my right, and, for the first time in almost a year, I was back in Old Aberdeen.

I headed down Don Street towards the Market Cross, where the Chanonry met the High Street. I could not see beyond the frontages, but I knew that behind the houses blossom would be forming on the trees in the orchards and gardens of College Bounds. The market was finished now, and the stallholders had cleared away their booths and gone home. Dogs and gulls occupied themselves with clearing whatever unwanted wares and produce might have fallen to the ground. The pigeons of the bishop's old doocot always fed well on market days. As I passed the majestic crown tower of the college chapel, my heart nearly gave within me. I was a part of those stones, a century old and more; I belonged to that place, with all the others who had gone before me and with those still to come. Yet at this moment, this hour and day of my life, I had no place there.

I passed out of College Bounds and made my way up the Spittal hill, past the ruins of the Snow kirk to my left and then the Spittal kirk to my right. What a desecration of churches there had been these past sixty years, all in the name of God. Further down, as the road descended towards the town of New Aberdeen, I passed the old Leper House. Unwelcome as they were within the burgh, there had been here a place of some compassion where they might rest. A light breeze stirred the arms of the windmill on Windmill Hill, overlooking the cornfields where they bordered the town. It was not long before I reached the Calsey Port, emblazoned with the royal arms to give weight to its authority, and, having answered for my name, place of origin, business in the burgh and lodgings when staying there, was riding down the Gallowgate towards the heart of New Aberdeen.

The houses rose on either side of me, three and four storeys high. Some were divided into tenements, the apartments on the upper floors being reached by wooden flights of outside stairs. Other dwellings were grander, the houses of wealthy merchants, professionals and landed men with business in the town. I turned down into the Upperkirkgate. The houses here were not so grand as those of the Gallowgate, the rents cheaper, but here too, many had aspirations, with brightly painted porches giving onto the street. Halfway down I reined in the horse outside a modest two-storey house with the legend *E. P. 1624. W. C.* engraved in fine gold lettering above the lintel. Elizabeth Philip and William Cargill. Tying the beast to a post in the road, I knocked on the door. There seemed to be a great commotion and rustling of skirts inside until at length the door was answered. My friend's wife stood there in the doorway, her eyes alight and her cheeks glowing, filled, *mirabile dictu*, with happiness to find me there.

'Alexander, oh, Alexander. How we have missed you.' She held her hand out toward me and I took a step closer, removing my hat as I did so. She looked again in my face, my eyes. Her arm fell to her side. 'In the name of God, Alexander, what has befallen you?'

SEVEN

Destination

I awoke the next morning to a bright clear Aberdeen morning such as I had known nowhere else. As I lay, hands behind my head, looking up at the curved ceiling, the bell of St Nicholas kirk began to strike the hour: one, two, three ... it tolled nine times. Nine o'clock. I could not remember the last time I had slept until this hour. I would have been about my labours in my schoolroom in Banff over two hours by now, ready to send the town boys home for their breakfasts. A pitcher of fresh water had been set by the Delft wash bowl in my room. Someone must have come in with it in the hours since dawn, but I had heard nothing.

My body had been weary after the long ride and its strange meeting, but I had not seen William in nearly a year and there had been an unburdening at my destination, which had left my mind and heart something clearer than they had been for many months. Even as I had entered Aberdeen, with its narrow winding streets of tall houses and its busy lanes of people, dogs and beasts, the stifling feeling that had oppressed me in Banff had begun to lift. And then, once Elizabeth had been finally persuaded that I was not actually ill, and had brought us a fine dinner of roasted capons and cold ham pie, she had left us to the talk of men and of friends, and I had told William my story.

When I had finished, he hesitated. 'It is,' he began, 'something of what I had imagined, although I could not have guessed at all. And you have heard nothing of Katharine since?'

'Nothing since that last meeting on the road from Fordyce, though for a time I could scarcely remember even that. Now, though, the words are burned on my very soul, every one of them, hers and mine.'

'You must not dwell on it, Alexander.'

'That is what Jaffray says, too, in his many different ways that he thinks so subtle.'

William smiled. 'The doctor's heart is on his sleeve, and for all his learning and experience of the world he cannot hide it. And yet I think his counsel is good.'

I shrugged. 'Oh, it is good, but it is counsel easier to offer than to act upon. I have tried with all my strength not to dwell on it. I have tried to drink it out of my mind, my body. I have, in my worst of days, disgraced myself with other women, but in the end the knowledge of it finds me out again.'

I had told him everything, even the last part, that part without which it might have been easier to face myself.

William had guessed, long before Archie himself had, what were my feelings for Katharine. Archie and I had spoken of it for the first and only time on the eve of his departure for the Bohemian Wars. There had been a great feasting and speech-making that night in the town house of the Hays. The great and the good of Aberdeen to burgh and to land had toasted Archie's family, his valour, his honour and his health, and then toasted them again. Archie and I had been party to many such nights together, but on this occasion I noticed that while he smiled and laughed and joined the toasts, in reality he ate little and drank less, and the smile faded as soon as its re-cipient turned his or her attention elsewhere. I often wonder now whether Archie knew then that he was going to his death, and that he would not see these faces or the sun set on this town again. The noise of the drinking, the laughing, and the music rose, and the light of the fire made faces dance in and out of fleeting shadows. As the company was roaring at a lewd tale of an Edinburgh minister and the wife of a rich Leith merchant, I felt Archie's hand on my shoulder and he leant towards my ear. 'Come, Alexander, let us away.' I do not think anyone noticed us slip out, save Katharine, whose eyes kept count of all I did.

We made our way down the servants' stairs and out through the kitchen to the backland. Light from the upper windows kept our feet from mis-adventure in the courtyard, and we slipped through a side gate into the vennel leading to the Broadgate, away from the house. I did not need to ask Archie where we were going – we had used this route often, to escape the eyes first of his parents, then his tutor, and occasionally of any of the town's officers who might have come to look for him. In a few moments we were out on Broadgate and headed towards Guestrow in the direction of Maisie Johnston's house. Maisie Johnston had brewed ale in the burgh for forty years, and there was but a handful of burgesses on the council or the session who could deny in truth that they had ever been carried home, incapable, from her parlour or spirited, half dressed, out her back door when the session on its rounds knocked at the front.

The cur in the yard scarcely stirred as Archie knocked on the back door of the house. It knew of old who was permitted to be here and who was not. The mistress herself opened the door to us, and nodding to me, she led the way up the stairs to an apartment I had never been in before. I had not Archie's taste for whoring, and my previous visits to Maisie's house had always stopped at the drinking parlour at the foot of the stairs. It was with some relief, then, that I saw the room she opened to us was unoccupied, and that a table had been set with food and drink and two places. Maisie took a coin from Archie, nodded again and left the room without having uttered a word.

Archie sank down on a settle and let out a huge sigh as the door closed behind her. 'Thank God, some peace at last.' This was not his usual style of talking.

'And since when have you sought peace?' I asked.

He was silent a long moment. 'I crave – a kind of peace, an end to the hunting and the dancing and the days of no consequence. I crave a peace that comes when a man finds his place, when he ...' He was searching for the words.

'When he meets his calling?'

'Yes,' he said, as if he had only just now realised it. 'When he meets his calling.'

'And that is what, in truth, you are sailing to tomorrow? To meet your calling?'

He unbuckled his cloak and let his hat fall to the floor. 'Well, it is not here that I will meet it. I cannot play the fool all my life. One day I will have to return here, return to Delgatie, take my father's place, have charge of the lands, the tenants, the family debt. I will have to fight my neighbours as they will me. I will have my honour slighted and trample on that of others. I will marry me a wife I do not love and father as many bairns on her as she can bring forth into the world. I will die and I will leave my son my debt and my lands and my quarrels, and so it will go on. But, Alexander, do not tell me that is my calling. I cannot believe that God in his heaven does not ask something else of me on this earth.'

I had known always that there was more to my friend, to the foster brother that he had declared himself to be, than the laughing, drinking, dangerous, adored noble son, but it was a part of himself that he took pains not to reveal, even to me. Tonight though, there was to be no dissembling, for either of us. There would be no mysteries, no unanswered questions, no lack of understanding to carry down the years to our deaths, should we never meet again.

'And do you think, Archie, that in these foreign wars you can do something that you could not do at home? You have no need to prove your honour or your courage here.'

He poured wine into the glasses, finer work they were than I would have thought to find in this house, and handed one to me. 'What passes for courage here is but a case of me doing what it is known I shall do, what those who went before me did. It will change nothing. But the wars on the continent have greater stakes than our petty doings on these shores. I have a choice. I do not have to go there, but I choose to go; I wish to play in that great game, and to make a difference.'

I was silent for a moment, searching for the right words that he would carry with him. 'I think you are wrong,' I said.

'How so?'

'I think there is a difference to be made here. Changes in the world need not always proceed from kings and their causes. A change in one man, howsoever lowly he be in the beginning, can affect many in the end.'

His eyes twinkled and a smile played about his mouth, just as it did when he knew he had a better hand of cards than I, or when I had made a careless move on the chessboard. 'And there you have it, Zander. I could not have put it better myself. As ever, you give yourself away without knowing that you do.'

'I do not understand.'

'It is in your words, Alexander, in your words. You speak of a change *in* one man. That is your calling, not mine. Your mission is to change what men are. Mine is to change what men must face, to put right by force the damage done when those of your vocation have failed. Mine is to seek to alter the destinies of kingdoms from the top, yours from the very smallest component in them. Neither of us will succeed alone, but we may one day come close to one another in our paths.' He drained his glass and refilled it. 'Until then, though, there is food, there is drink, and there are women, by God, there are women.' His face, his mood had reverted to their old selves. His well-accustomed mask was in place; he had told me what he had to and we would not need to touch on the subject again.

'Archie ...'

He looked up briefly from the chicken leg he was gnawing at with some gusto.

'Archie, there is something I have wanted to tell you, to talk to you about before you leave. I ...'

Again the twinkling eyes, the playful smile. 'You are in love with my little sister.'

I felt the breath go out of me, and could say nothing for a moment.

He shook his head and laughed. 'Oh, Zander, you think me a dullard after all. How many years now? One, two? Half the pretty girls in Aberdeen and Banff have thrown themselves at your feet, while I have had to make do with the wanton ones, and you have shunned them. Twelve months or more ago, my friend, I realised that you were in love. It did not take a great casting about to find the object of your affections. At first I was bemused, I will confess. The idea that my sister could be seen by any man as other women are seen by me had not occurred to me. And then for a while I reasoned that it was simply that she talked more sense than I that led you to seek out her company, but in the end I could not deny what to others had been long obvious.'

'To others?'

'Why, aye. To my mother and to yours.'

This was horrible; I felt I would vomit.

'Och, Alexander. You have the colour of a dead fish, and much the same expression. Bear up, man. It is not so bad. My mother is a little pleased, your own delighted, and of course your father does not know.'

'God be thanked. And yours?'

Archie shrugged and reached for a mutton chop. 'My father knows, but he trusts my mother in these matters, and Katharine can put her heart where it pleases her.'

'That is your father's view?'

He nodded. 'In as far as he takes a view. He knows you are a good man, and the son of the best of men. He loves his daughter and would see her happy. Trust in me, Zander. I will return from these wars covered in glory. I will marry me that fertile, rich bride of my parents' choosing. Katharine will be of less consequence than a brood hen. They'll let her marry whom she wants.'

'I hope to God you're right.'

He tossed a mutton bone to his dog, lying between us on the floor. 'Of course I'm right, Zander. Am I not always right? Besides,' he sighed as he got up and went to the window, looking out over the blackness that was the burgh at night, 'my parents love me well, too well. I shall ask them, and she will be yours.'

As ever, he had run on to a thing decided, leaving little space or time for reason. 'But what of Katharine? Will she have me?'

He looked at me, astonished. 'You do not know? You have never tried her on it?'

'I have never ... I did not think ... No.'

He shook his head in amused exasperation. 'Well, Alexander, on that score I cannot help you. On that you must shift for yourself. But I think you will find a willing listener to your pleas. And then we would be truly brothers, and there would be nothing dearer to my own heart.' He smiled at the thought and presently his smile took on a look of mischief. 'And you shall have the kirk at Turriff, or King Edward or Banff, and thunder from the pulpit at my wicked and wanton ways.' And thus he tried to make light of our parting, thanking God that he would soon be relieved of my 'lang dreep' of a face. 'If ever there was a minister born it's you, Zander. You will sermonise the life out of them.'

We laughed, and as the rumble of our laughter receded, we remained in companionable silence a few minutes, he kicking at a log with the toe of his boot, I watching the candle flicker and splutter in the draft. I wondered when next I would see that loved, arrogant, noble face, hear that roaring laugh. I wondered how war would change him, how living out in the world, away from our charmed college life would change me, how my practice of the word of God would measure against my knowledge of it.

He broke into my reverie by throwing his unbuckled sword at my feet. 'Enough of this lovesick nonsense, Mr Seaton. Tonight you will accompany me on my farewells to the "ladies" of Aberdeen. You must not be completely out of practice when you get my poor deluded sister to your bed and I ... I must not disappoint the ladies, for tomorrow I sail from our safe harbour, and how they will weep for the Master of Hay!'

And that night with Archie had been the last of my wild nights. For two years after that, I had immersed myself in my divinity studies. My mother had died in the second winter after my graduation Master of Arts. She had been ill a long time by then, too ill to travel. My father had not come to hear me present my theses – he had no Latin anyway. For those two years my head was buried so deep in my books, and she and her mother came so rarely into town, that I hardly saw Katharine above a dozen times. I do not recollect what nonsense I spoke to her the first few times. The harder I struggled to say something that would imprint my image on her soul, the worse the nonsense became. But one day, nearly two years after Archie had left, I walked from Old Aberdeen to the house in the New Town. The Hays were preparing to journey back to their fastness for the winter, and I would not see them again for several months. I went to bid them safe journey and farewell, as Lady Hay had asked me to do. We ate a cold dinner and drank the good wine that his lordship did not wish to leave in the house. Lady Hay busied herself with many questions about my studies and my progress and the comfort of my college room. His lordship, wary now of too close a familiarity with matters of religion, plied me for the college gossip. And through it all, as I held my conversations with her parents, my thought, my mind, was all on Katharine. She was a child no longer – had not been these last three years – and the knowledge of her proximity engulfed me.

The meal ended all too soon. The parting was over quickly. But as Katharine passed me at the entrance, just as she was about to step out onto the Castlegate, a huge careless hound bounded past her to join his master's train, and toppled her into my arms. I felt the softness of her through her winter furs, and the warmth of her breath against my neck. The heat of it ran through my whole body, and I held her a moment longer than was needed. She steadied herself, and I could see the flush of confusion on her cheeks. She left, with no spoken farewell.

I did not see her again until the Yuletide festivities at Delgatie. The kirk session might fulminate as it liked, but the laird of Delgatie would have his Christmas feasting, and all his adherents would know his hospitality as if there had never been a reformation of religion in our country. The dancing and the music and the storytelling, more raucous with every new teller, went on for three days, and by the end of the first I had danced, spoken, laughed, sung with Katharine more than I had in the previous two years. At first, in the dancing, the thrill of being able to touch her in full view of all the company without attracting notice or censure almost paralysed me. Her red silk gown, embroidered with golden flowers and tendrils, and the sparkling jewels set in her pale blonde hair, made her seem like a visitor from some winter world of fable. By the end of the evening I did not want to relinquish my hold on her. I could not sleep that night; I could not eat the next morning. I could not pray; I could scarcely read the lesson in the castle chapel. My lord would hunt after breakfast, but I, a student of divinity, was spared the obligation to attend him on his hunt. Katharine's mother was overseeing the work of the kitchens, in preparation for the night's feasting to come.

And so it was that I came upon her on the stairs. No great work of chance, really. In truth, I know I had been looking for her, as I think she had for me. The great turnpike stairway of Delgatie was broad enough for us to pass with ease, but not so broad that we could not somehow contrive between us a slight stumble, a touch. A brush of her shoulder against my chest. 'Alexander.' She said my name and called to every part of me. I pulled her close into me and held her as if my very breath depended upon it. We were there a long time. How it was that no one in the castle came upon us I do not know. I feared that if once I should let her go she would be gone for ever, that I would never recapture that moment, that feeling of pure existence, a complete engrafting of my whole self upon the world. But loosen her I did, eventually. She did not run, or evanesce, but took my hand and led me further up the stairs then down the three steps to her own chamber. I had not set foot in the room for years, not since as boys Archie and I had crept in there to steal a doll, which we then set on a stack in the castle yard and burned as a witch. From that day her mother had forbidden us to cross the threshold.

The room I stepped into had lost many of its childish trappings – it was a lady's chamber. The wall hangings and bedding were of rich damask. A tapestry showed a knot of berries and flowers. A Venetian looking glass of the finest quality hung on the wall. Katharine took my hand and led me to a settle by the fire. She took rugs from the chest beneath the window seat and cushions from the high, heavily canopied bed. On a table was a box of the deepest ebony, inlaid with mother-of-pearl. I had been with Archie when he had bought it for her, the last gift he gave her. I knew it to be filled with her grandmother's gold and jewels, kept for great occasions; at other times she preferred to wear but a single cream pearl at her neck. Outside, although it was not yet midday, the sky was darkening to a heavy and deep grey, and snow began to fall. A candle flickered under a copper burner, filling the room with a warm incense of winter. She bade me build up the fire and went down to the great hall to fetch wine, cold meat, cheese, nuts and pastries from the side table laid out for those who would take a midday meal. Two or three times she went back and forth between her chamber and the hall, and was remarked by no one. We spent the remainder of the day together, with the rugs wrapped around us by the fire, holding each other and talking of how long we had loved until now, and how we should manage our secret until Archie came home. We could not marry until I had completed my divinity studies, until I had a man's station in the world. Until Archie came home to plead the case of the friend who was not worthy of Katharine's hand. We would not speak our love to any other until Archie came home.

The months passed, the yuletide festivities were long over, I passed my course in divinity to the approbation of all my teachers, and still Archie did not come home. I took up my teaching post in the grammar school of Banff while waiting for a kirk to fall vacant. The kirk of Boyndie in my own presbytery, not four miles from the town of Banff fell vacant, and I was invited to preach there, to commence on my trials for the ministry. Still Archie did not come home.

And then the news arrived that he was dead. 'They will weep for the

Master of Hay!' he had said. And they did weep. The whole of the North wept, a torrent of unceasing grief for the heir to Delgatie. The best and bravest of our youth, the hope and pride of his family, slaughtered in the German mud. I had been with him seventeen years, different as black and white and closer than brothers. I should have been with him then. I should have walked beside his horse through the mud; I should have put my body between his heart and the bayonet that killed him; I should have cradled his head in my lap as he died, leaving me worthless and alone.

Archie's family was not to be consoled. His mother cried as if her very heart had been ripped out. His father looked into the long tunnel of death with no light behind him. They wanted me with them every hour of their blackest days. For I was of Archie, no substitute, no second or third best, but of their boy. They looked at me and they saw us climbing trees at seven. They saw us diving into waterfalls at twelve, fishing, hawking, laughing. They saw us ride through the castle gates at fifteen, to King's College and all the delights of Aberdeen, riding to manhood and to our future. In my eyes they still saw their son's brilliant smile. In my hearing, my Lord Delgatie begged forgiveness of God for grieving so deeply for his son. The God of Scotland gave children and He took them and His will was not to be questioned. I watched the old man's heart break.

As for Katharine, Katharine was all but forgotten in those first weeks. She was left, frozen in her own grief, a loved younger child but no compensation for the heir that was lost. So engulfed was I during those early weeks in the maelstrom of grieving at Delgatie that I did not see it at first, but Katharine did. Katharine, the sole heir to Delgatie, must marry now, and marry well. No minister, nor bishop even, but land and family. The heirs of Delgatie would spring not from the son but from his sister, and all my hopes lay with Archie where he had fallen.

There was no one to speak for us. A relative was found, an old, wealthy, childless relative. Katharine would be despatched to his Borders tower-house to marry him and bear him children and return one day, or send her son, to hold Delgatie for the Hays. She understood; I understood. There was no pleading, no begging not to be sent to the cold bed of a man so old he might have been her father, no protest that one day I would be a man whom their daughter might, with no dishonour, marry. All that was gone.

Fate, in all her wilful cruelty, or helped along perhaps by Katharine's now fearful and watchful parents, decreed that the day of my final trials at Fordyce should be the day of Katharine's departure for her Borders jail. We had four weeks, a month of warning, but in that month I could only see her once. My preparations for the final trial, my work in the school, and Katharine's farewell progress round the ladies and castles of Banff, Moray and the Garioch gave us but one day, and one night. Wary as she was by now, Archie's mother could not refuse me that last hospitality. His lordship was away from home, but she watched us; we were scarcely left alone together two minutes in the day.

And then, in the darkness of the night, I stole to Katharine's chamber and for the first and only time I took her as my wife, and told her she would always be my wife and mine only. And we slept, naked under the cover, entwined in each other's arms. I had not meant to fall asleep. I should not have fallen asleep and slumbered with her those long hours till dawn. The light of the early May morning and the singing of the birds gradually began to play upon my eyes and ears. The perfect warmth and comfort of waking with Katharine still in my arms was slowly replaced by a dawning horror that I should not still be here. And as I opened my eyes, Katharine's head and loosened hair across my bare chest, her pale arm on my shoulder, I was met by the horror of Lady Hay's face. Her skin was drained of all colour save grey. She moved her mouth but no words would come. Her eyes were filled with the cold disaster of the scene before her. And then she spoke. Slowly, quietly. 'Get out. You are filth. Get out.' And then the woman who had loved me as a son staggered from the room and vomited.

And that had been my parting from Katharine, less than three weeks before my final trial for the ministry. I do not know how I kept my senses. A lie. I know how I kept my senses. I had lost the man who would have called himself my brother; I had lost the woman who should have been my wife. I had betrayed my childhood. Everything of my heart, what I had understood as my kin, was closed to me. Yet I still had my calling; I had always had my calling. Even in my one night with Katharine I had told myself there was no sin, because I had meant her for my wife. I did not acknowledge my wrong. Parted from her, I might have been convulsed with grief. Yet I had my calling and my trials were before me. I threw myself still deeper into my books. In those three weeks, less, I turned the Bible on its head and turned it back again. I composed the sermon of my life. There could be no chance of failure, of rejection. I would live for and through my calling. And this I believed until the words were in the mouth of the Moderator of the Presbytery of Fordyce that would have licensed me to preach as a minister of the Kirk of Scotland. And in that moment all tranquillity, all that I still understood in the world was shattered by the cry of my Lord Hay of Delgatie. His wife had finally broken and told him that very morning what I had done, and he had ridden to Fordyce with all the devils in Hell at his heels. He would die before he would see me a minister. He would throw in my face my betrayal of himself and of his family and every single thing they had done for me through all the years of my life. He laid not a finger on me, but before the brethren I was as a man beaten into a stupor. The moderator, aghast, pleading in his eyes, asked me to defend myself. But I could not utter a word. I had no answer for my accuser, for there was none left to give. My dignity lost, I stumbled from the kirk of Fordyce.

This much, or the gist of it, William Cargill had known, or guessed. Knowing of old of my feelings for Katharine, he had known what Archie's death would mean for us. The whole of the North knew of my humbling, my great fall, at Fordyce. But if my humiliation had been public, Katharine's was worse. What was not known was guessed at, and whispered on the roads, in the inns, in the great halls of castles and at the firesides of hovels. Her name was bartered by those who were not worthy even to look on her face. Many wild theories abounded, until the people had some new scandal to keep their tongues active and their spirits content, but I had destroyed what I most loved, and Katharine, banished to that cold marriage bed, could never come back to Delgatie again.

William and I had never spoken of it before last night. 'And for this, for what many men have done, ministers among them indeed, you were cast out from your brethren and they will never let you become a minister? Alexander, it is hypocrisy, and you should not bend to it. Why, Delgatie himself was a notorious adulterer in his younger days.'

I had heard this argument before, from Charles Thom, who had also guessed aright at the heart of the scandal. Jaffray had not argued in such a way, for he knew me better. 'No, the hypocrisy has been mine, William.

My Lord Hay is the head of a family, a magnate, a soldier, a leader of men. What he does in his bed or any other is of no consequence. Yet I sought to be a minister in God's Kirk, to lead people from the path of damnation to the blessed assurance of righteousness. I knew what I did was wrong. And such was my arrogance in the face of God that I thought it did not matter because it was I who did it. And ...'

'And what?'

'It was a betrayal. And my every memory of my whole life up to that point is coloured now by the knowledge of that betrayal. There is nothing in me that is not rotten.'

William would not allow this. 'No, I will not have it. You did what other men, worse men have done. You loved the girl and she you. God in his Providence decreed she should not be your wife. In that at least, you may be wretched, but you are not rotten, for it was no work of yours that killed Archie and took Katharine from you.'

If this had only been so, I might have found myself a more tolerable being. But it was not so. William did not know it; no one knew it, save myself and Katharine. I had had a chance, only a chance, to hold onto the shreds of my life and to make of it something new. But I had rejected it, left it in the gutter. For, on the day of my fall at Fordyce, Katharine too had ridden from Delgatie. She had taken the finest horse left in the stables and she had ridden as no woman before her could have ridden. It availed her nothing. She could not catch her father's party; she could not overtake him or plead my cause before the brethren as she had sworn to her mother she would do. By the time she arrived at Fordyce the kirk and kirkyard were empty and the brethren gone. She asked all about, but no one could tell her where I was or which way I had gone. Eventually, she came across a pedlar who had seen me on the road to Sandend. It did not take her long to find me then. I was on foot, and my form as well known to her as her own. We had not seen each other since that early morning in her chamber at Delgatie. How often since then I had meditated on the words, taken from the book of Proverbs and painted on the beams of that room's ceiling: 'If thou does labour in honesty, the labour goes, the honour bides with thee. If thou does any vice allo, the shame remains when pleasure is ago.' The shame was burning now into me, burning my eyes so I could scarcely see.

And the shame engendered in me a kind of madness, I think. There on the road she slid from her mount and took a step towards me.

'Stay,' I said.

'Alexander ...'

'Come no closer. Do not come near to me.'

'But Alexander——'

'You know what has happened. You must know it. It is lost, all lost.'

'But no, Alexander. No. All that is nothing to me. I love you more than life itself. I would defy God, my father, my mother, and all the legions of Hell to be with you. Alexander, I will not go. I will not marry him. I am yours. I will be yours. Alexander. We can marry and we can live, somehow.'

I was shaking my head at her, stepping back as she took another step forwards. 'You have lost your mind.'

'No, Alexander, but I have found my will. I will not leave you.'

She was before me, in all her pale and distracted beauty, and a troop of demons was taking hold of my mind. 'You must leave me, Katharine, for I will not have you. You say it means nothing to you? Well it means everything to me, and you have cost me all. All.' All? What 'all' did I think there was without her? What ministry, what life did I think I would have led that did not have her in it? There was none, I knew that now. But I think, truly, in that moment I had been out of my senses, for I had turned from her and strode away, leaving her collapsed and crying in the road, the woman I had sworn to love until the day I died. Sometimes at night, when all the schoolhouse was silent save the noise of the sea at the shore, I would be kept awake by the sound of Katharine Hay's desperate cries, as she lay weeping where I had left her, lying in the dirt on the road to Sandend. A hundred times on those nights I would have gone back to her, but she was no longer there.

And that I had told last night to William Cargill, the first living soul to hear from my lips how I had rejected the woman who had humbled and dishonoured herself for me. I wanted someone to know me for what I was. The bitterness Jaffray was always counselling me to let go of was at the root of my soul, and my soul knew what I had done.

William had sat silently for a long time after I had finished. He stoked the fire and stared into the flames. Finally he turned to me and said, 'And yet I know you for a good man, Alexander. And this will pass. All pain will pass.' We had said nothing further of the matter and had retired to our beds soon after, before the bell of St Nicholas struck midnight. If he could, I knew that William would take the great burden from my shoulder, and tell me I need carry it no longer, and I loved him for it. But William would never understand that should I once put down that rock, the man I had once believed myself to be would be destroyed for ever.

EIGHT

Much Business in Town

And thus I had slept through the early morning bells. I opened the window shutters and looked out. Elizabeth was in the backland, gathering eggs from her chickens and trying, with little success, to keep the pig from trampling on the vegetable patch. She was much too small and slight for such a task, and soon the old manservant was out in the yard, bidding his mistress leave off such work, before the master should hear of it. She smiled at the chastisement and returned to her eggs.

I washed and dressed quickly, but William was long gone by the time I descended to the warmth of the kitchen. Elizabeth's eyes were full of kindness – I saw William had told her my story – but she masked it as she could. William was a fortunate man. He had loved Elizabeth from the day he met her. He, a scholar, the son of a schoolmaster, she, a kitchen maid, the daughter of a cooper burgess. They had been promised to each other six years, while he completed his course in philosophy at the Marischal College in New Aberdeen and through all his absence at Leiden in the study of law. Neither had strayed. They had married within three months of his return from the Netherlands and now, as he had told me last night, she was carrying his child.

She regarded me with a mischievous glint in her eye. 'You slept well, I trust, Mr Seaton. Or is this the accustomed hour of rising for the burgesses of Banff? I had heard of your slovenly ways in those parts, but would scarce have credited them.'

I laughed in return. 'Mistress, it is the unaccustomed luxury of your linen kist that kept me at my slumbers. We simple fisher folk know but coarse blankets and howling gales in our desolate dwellings. I dreamt I had fallen amongst the luxuries of Babylon, and was loath to extricate myself from their embrace.'

116

Elizabeth wagged an admonishing finger at me. 'Mistress Youngson shall know of this loose talk, and then we will see how coarse are the blankets she will find you.' It had been in the kitchen of the old schoolhouse in Banff that William had first met the girl who would become his wife.

She bade me sit down at the table and ladled steaming porridge into a bowl before me. 'And then you will have eggs. My hens give the finest eggs in all the town. I sing to them.'

I made to protest that the porridge would do me fine enough, and she had better need of the eggs herself. She would not hear of it. 'You need restoring. You have got so thin and gaunt, Alexander. Please, let me care for you a little. To see you better will do me more good than all the eggs in Scotland.'

Humbled, I did not know how to respond. The kindness in her was almost more than I could face. She saw my discomfort and made light. 'Besides, if I consume many more eggs, my child will be born with feathers.' She chattered on about what a fat wife she would be to William, who made her eat while she was not lying down and lie down while she did not eat. But I knew how worried he was. She had always been a pale girl, and slight, and while her pregnancy had brought a joy to her eyes, her cheeks were faded and those eyes tired. The weariness of her body, with five months of her burden yet to carry, was already evident. I thought of my friend, who had all of the promises life could afford a man in his hand, and prayed God that, if He still listened to me, He would not take them from him.

With a full stomach and a warmth of heart I had not felt in a long time, I set out on my morning's business. My first call would be at the bookseller's. David Melville's shop on the Castlegate had been to me a place of greater delight than all the taverns of Aberdeen, and light though my purse now was, I set off along the street with the anticipation of a child on a holiday morning. The day was sunny and already warm. I decided to take the shorter route to the Castlegate, and avoid the noxious smells of the crafts already rising from the direction of the Netherkirkgate and Putachieside, where the tanners and dyers had been at their work several hours now. I glanced to my left at St Nicholas kirk. It rose, magnificent, dominating the skyline of the town. I had aspired, in the quiet, honest moments when ambition overtook calling, to a pulpit in that kirk. The building had been sectioned into two to allow a more fitting form of worship, now we had severed ourselves from the blandishments of Rome. But I would never preach in either kirk, East or West, now. I passed by a cobbler's shop; through the open shutter I could see him working at the last, a fine piece of leather turning and moving in his hands. I coveted that leather – my feet were sore and my shoes almost beyond the power of the cobblers of Banff to mend again. I had meant to buy new boots, but the money to pay for them and much else was now in the greedy hand of Sarah Forbes's uncle in King Edward. Perhaps, before I left town, I would try one of the cheaper cobblers who worked beside the tanners near Putachieside, at the Green.

At the Castlegate, I found the door of David Melville's bookshop open. I could smell the piles of new books and the rows of well-bound older ones before I was fully in the shop. The bookseller had his back to me, a piece of paper in his hand as he checked a row of Latin grammars on the shelf. Affixed to the inside of the shop door were lists of books for the use of the town's schools, which all clustered around the back of St Nicholas Kirk on the Schoolhill. I ran my eye down the list for the grammar school. Editions of Cicero, Virgil, Ovid, better and newer editions than Gilbert Grant knew of or I could afford. Melville finished counting off his catechisms and turned to greet me with a furrowed brow and then a broad smile. 'Well, if it is not Mr Seaton. I have been expecting you these last few days. You said you would be here before the end of March.'

I shook his hand. 'We have been much busied at the grammar school. The presbytery and council make their visitation at the end of April, and Mr Grant is determined that they will have no cause for fault-finding on this occasion.'

The bookseller gave a weary sigh. 'The presbytery and council will always find fault. That is what they are for. But they will have little cause for complaint over your books. I have here the Cicero you wanted, and the Buchanan, and this Greek grammar.'

Melville tied up my books then turned a page in his ledger to check the rest of my order. He went to the back wall of the shop, stacked from floor to ceiling with Bibles, and ran his finger along the shelf until he found what he was looking for. He carefully eased out a book bound in soft red leather, almost twice the size of those near it. 'Here it is. Your good Master, Mr Gilbert Grant, asked me many months ago to find him a Bible printed large enough for his failing eyesight. And I think I have found it. I scoured the country,' then he smiled, a little sheepish. 'Well, at least I sent to Edinburgh, and here it is.' I looked at the imposing volume he held out to me, the print large enough for my friend to read indeed, although I suspected every word of it was already imprinted on the old man's heart. The bookseller was proud to have managed what he had been asked, but I was a little discomfited.

'Mr Grant made no mention—'

Melville held up a conciliatory hand. 'It was many months ago he asked me. He can send payment down from Banff with another courier, once he has the book in his hand. Now, for Dr Jaffray.' I looked at the mounting pile of books on the counter and began to pity the horse that would carry me home. The bookseller went to another shelf and selected two medical textbooks which he brought over and untied for my examination. I paid Melville what he was owed for the doctor's books and my own, and sadly declined to look at the most recent works of theology he had from Antwerp. Similarly, I shook my head to the offer of the latest tracts and pamphlets to have landed in Aberdeen from the Low Countries and the North of England. Arguments over the correct form of worship, of kneeling in kirk, of vestments and prayer books were of little interest to me now, although I did not judge it wise to confide that to the bookseller. He pointed to the ceiling above him, to where Raban, the burgh printer, plied his trade.

'Raban is near worn out with the thing. Dr Forbes and Dr Baron and the other ministers do not let their pens lie idle on the matter. And I fear there will be much more of it to be heard yet. Anyhow, if I cannot tempt you to join in the pamphlet war, perhaps there is something more pleasant I can show you, if you do not have it already.' From a shelf behind him he passed me a slim volume in quarto, printed here by Raban only three years ago. *Poetical recreations of Mr Alexander Craig of Rosecraig.* I thought of Charles Thom in the darkness and squalor of the tolbooth in Banff. What good might it do him to have the volume of Craig in his hand, summoning images of clear rivers, and freedom and love to his mind? The price of the volume was reasonable. My boots could be mended one more time. I arranged with the bookseller for the delivery of my purchases to William Cargill's house.

It was only midday, and I was not to meet with Principal Dun at the university until tomorrow. I had one more errand to perform and then the day would be mine to fill as I wished until William returned from his business. I had a letter from the provost in my pocket. It was addressed to George Jamesone, artist, New Aberdeen. I did not need to ask for directions to Jamesone's house. It was on the Schoolhill, not five minutes from Cargill's place on the Upperkirkgate. I retraced my route of the morning and in a short time was presenting myself at the street door of the artist's imposing house.

I knocked loudly on the door and waited. A pretty face appeared in the turret window two floors above me and then disappeared back into the darkness. I was still looking up when the door in front of me was opened inwards and a stern-faced old man asked me my business. He eyed me with some suspicion – I was not dressed in the usual manner of one who had business with his master, and he did not know me. He said he would fetch the mistress, and made to close the door.

'Willie Park, will you let the gentleman in. Do you not know Mr Seaton?'

Willie looked me in the eye, and that thoroughly. 'Indeed I do not. No more does the master, either, I'll tell you that.'

'Oh, Willie, away and fetch some wine.'

Willie went shuffling away, grumbling that it was changed days in this house, and what need had the master for a wife?

'And do you not know me, Alexander?'

My eyes were only slowly becoming accustomed to the dimmer light of the interior. The pretty face that had looked down on me from the turret now emerged, still smiling, from the stairway in front of me. The young woman held in her arms a bundle of swaddling from which emanated a mewling sound. She came right to me and stood, beaming, almost as tall as myself, and glowing with happiness and pride at her bundle.

'I am sorry I do not ... and yet ...' and yet something tugged at a memory in my head. A forgotten recess, unlocked by that smile. I looked into the woman's face and saw the face of a twelve-year-old girl, six or seven years ago, running with her brothers around the garden of the Hays' town house, throwing chestnuts at myself and Archie until, roaring, we got up to chase them. 'Isabel? Little Isabel Tosh?'

She nodded triumphantly. 'The very same. How are you, Mr Seaton? I am pleased to have you in our home. I had heard you were not ... I had not heard of you here in Aberdeen for a long time.'

'No, I have been away a good while. So you are mistress here? You have married George Jamesone.'

'I have, and I have borne him a son, the first of many, pray God.'

'May you always be blessed. I am glad to see you.'

'You remember the gay times with the Hays? Those were good days. Before this awful German war robbed them of their light. And you of your friend. I was as sorry for Archie's loss as I would be for my own brother. He had such a heart, such a life in him.' She paused in reflection a moment. 'And you have business with George. Well, come away in. I will take you to him, and then I'll get to the cellar myself. The wine will have turned before Willie ever brings it.'

She led me up the turnpike stair, chattering away and pointing out features of the house. On the third landing she knocked on a door and went before me into the room. I waited a moment until she reappeared and told me her husband would be glad to see me.

I had never met George Jamesone before, but I had known the painter well by sight in the latter days of my divinity studies in Aberdeen. From his time at Antwerp he dressed very much in the Dutch fashion, and affected a broad-brimmed black hat at all times – I now saw that the rumour that he wore it even while he painted was true. He greeted me with a wave of the hand as he finished some detail of the portrait he was working on, indicating that I should take a seat. I looked around me and settled for a stool by the door – I knew from my father that no craftsman likes to be disturbed in the middle of a piece of work. The room was remarkably large and airy, suffused with a northern light through the great window overlooking the long garden at the back of the house, and beyond that a stretch of woodland to the loch. Jamesone worked near the window, on a large canvas depicting a noblewoman and her two young daughters. I recognised her from gatherings at Delgatie – Anne Erskine, Countess of Rothes. He had her likeness well. Around the room were the tools and props of his trade, several I had no notion of the use of. In a small antechamber to my left I could discern pots, tubs, glass jars of myriad colours. Stacked to the right of the door were frames and parts of frames of various sizes, most black but some gilt, awaiting the fruit of the painter's labours. There were other canvases too, some mere line drawings, others near completion.

Eventually Jamesone left off his work. Still with his back to me he stretched his arms wide and yawned, and then removed and hung up the smock he had been wearing. He turned and afforded me a broad smile. I liked him instantly – it was a smile of genuine fellowship in a face alive with humour and intelligence. 'Mr Seaton, I am glad to see you. As you know, we have never met, but my wife tells me you are friends of old. Come, sit here by the window – you will be more comfortable and I can better see your face – I have an interest in faces.' Had I not already known that he had travelled to learn his trade, his manners and way of speech would have given him away. He did not have the air of a man who had spent all his years within the confines of one society.

I did as he asked and moved to a seat near the window. He continued to move about the room, cleaning and tidying his brushes and paints and cloths. The old manservant came in with a tray of wine and a dish of nuts and raisins, which he set down grudgingly before me at his master's request. 'Now, Mr Seaton, you have business with me.'

I brought the letter from the pouch at my side. 'Not I, but Walter Watt, provost of Banff.' I held out the letter.

Jamesone took the letter that I held out to him. 'So Watt has had himself made provost now, has he? Well, I cannot own myself surprised. He sat for me several years ago – he and his wife. He was a man who would not wait long on destiny, I think.'

I adjudged it better not to add my thoughts to those of the artist. He left that subject, and turned his attention to the letter, whose seal he had now broken.

'Your provost wishes me to come to Banff once more to paint him and his family.' He looked up. 'I am glad they have had children. I think their lack was a great sadness to his wife.'

'It is not the same wife. The first died some years ago.'

'I am sorry to hear it. There was a great beauty and kindness in her. She should have been better blessed.' He sighed. 'But the provost has little notion of the press of patrons on me in these days. Those I paint now usually come to sit for me here. But I was glad enough of his business once and should not scorn him now. Besides, it would be interesting to paint the same face once again, and see how the years have marked it.' He gestured towards the work he had just been engaged upon. 'I am to travel with this portrait to Rothes at the end of the month. I will return home by way of Banff and see the provost and his family then. I cannot promise him that I can do any more than a sketch of them there – I think it likely they must come sit for me here. You can pass on this message for me?'

I assented, although I did not anticipate with any great pleasure telling the provost of Banff that, risen in the world though he was, he was of less consequence to George Jamesone than once he had been. The painter and I talked for a while of Banff and the country around and people he knew there. He avoided mention of Delgatie, and I suspected news of my disgrace had reached to Aberdeen and to the ears of those who hardly knew me. But here was a man who did not hold it to my account. He had travelled in the world and, as he told me, 'A painter sees many things in the lives of men that others do not see.'

'I am not sure of your meaning,' I said.

He moved across the room to stand beside his canvas of the Countess of Rothes. 'What do you see here?'

I scanned the portrait for a moment but could divine no great secret in it. 'I see Anne Erskine and her two daughters.'

He quizzed me. 'Is that all you see?'

I looked again and shrugged. 'Well, no. I see a window, some heavy, rich draperies, a table, some artefacts. There is a box on the table with a necklace hanging out of it. There are some portraits on the wall behind the countess, and there is a chess board with some pieces on the table.' He continued to eye me expectantly. I lifted my hands in resignation. 'I am sorry. That is it.'

He smiled and took a clean brush in his hand and used it as a pointer. 'You look, but you do not properly see. You see the Countess of Rothes and her two daughters. Yes. You see a window – is it simply for light? I am not a painter of windows. Look again – the arms of the family are stained in the glass – there is nobility there. And should you doubt it, regard the portraits behind her – there is lineage, too. The jewel box on the table; has she been careless, and not put things in their place before the painter should arrive? I think not. There is wealth, opulence in the world displayed for all to see. And the chess board – again untidy. A game shortly played by the countess and her children – why no doll, nor rattle nor spinning top? Because these are no childish games this woman and her children play – theirs is a game of strategy; these are girls of good wit and learning. Yet there remains one feature you have not mentioned.' I looked again. The painter studied me as I did his picture.

'The cherries?'

He nodded. 'Indeed, the cherries. Did you think they were just an affectation of colour, a painter's indulgence?'

I had to confess that I had not thought much about them at all – they were simply there, as fruit often is in such portraits.

'You see a portrait of the Countess of Rothes and her daughters, no sons – for there are none. The fortunes of the family may rest with these two little girls. So see displayed their lineage, their nobility, their wit, their learning and their wealth. But more than all that, one thing is required of them – fertility. And look, look again, Mr Seaton. See how fertile, see how ripe they will be.' He turned away and walked back to the window, where he stood looking out at his wooded garden and its delicate blossoms.

I said nothing, being now a little discomfited by the picture. He turned round and indicated a set of shelves behind me and, as I cast my eye over them, several things that had puzzled me on first entering the room now made a little more sense. He came across to me and picked up the human skull that grinned horribly from the bottom shelf. 'I am not, as you know, a medical man. I have no interest in this skull other than its use to me in the depiction of death, the certainty of death. These shells you see here were, indeed, gathered on a happy walk along the shore on a summer's day with my wife, and are to me a memento of things pleasant, but in a painting they would become the symbols of wealth. If you look at these books here, you will see by their titles that they are of no great consequence. Those books of true interest to me are downstairs, in my library. These books here are again mere props, but they have been used many, many times to symbolise the learning of some of my illustrious sitters.'

I began to understand. 'And this lute?'

He picked up the instrument that had been left leaning against a chair. 'The lute – as many musical instruments – is a symbol of human love, even lust.'

'So that is why you have not had the broken string mended, because it is never played?'

'No, I wish that that were the case. Not all affairs between men and women are as happy as the union by which I am blessed. The broken string is for disharmony.' He was silent a moment and then smiled and said briskly, 'So now you are an expert, Mr Seaton. When you look, you will see.'

'I wonder. I doubt if I will ever see what is truly there.'

'I think you speak of more than paintings.'

'Perhaps.'

He replaced the lute by the wall. 'For all my draughtsman's tricks I am no expert on the nature of men. I think there is perhaps more of a story to be told in their faces, if I could but unlock it. That is why I am of a mind to take this commission from your provost, to see what story the lines in his face will tell me of his life since I painted him last.'

I laughed a little. I did not want to be drawn too far into this line of conversation. 'I think you might have better luck were you to study the fine cut of his clothing, the size of his house, the number of his adherents.'

The painter was not convinced. 'Such things might tell me much about his fortunes these last few years, but it is his face that will tell me of the man.' He regarded me for a moment, his head tilted slightly to the side. 'I think there are things your face can tell me.'

Vanity overtook me and I was aware of a strong need in myself to know what others saw when they looked upon me.

'What things?'

He motioned me to come closer to him and I sat before him at the window seat. 'I know from my wife that you are a schoolteacher, an under-master in a burgh grammar school. There is intensity, earnestness in your eyes, yet you say little. I think – though I may be wrong – that you are a man of great learning. If so, you seem too old for your current station in life. What age are you? Thirty-four, thirty-five?'

'I am in my twenty-seventh year.'

He nodded, biting his upper lip. 'Then you are younger than you look. And you are not of Banffshire stock – too tall and spare of build, although the gauntness, I think, comes from self-neglect and not nature; and your eyes ... they have a quality in their grey – almost green, in this light – that is not found hereabouts. And your hair is too dark – like an islander, or some of the Irish. Am I close to the truth or have I covered myself in folly?'

'I am of Banffshire stock, for my father and his father and back for many generations hale from that part of the country, but my mother was an Irishwoman, of native Irish lineage. You are right also in that I am too old to be an undermaster in a school – I had hoped to do other things with my learning, but that was not to be my fate, and—'

He shrugged. 'And you do not wish to speak of it to a man who but twenty minutes ago was a stranger.' The painter saw more than he would own. I waited another five minutes while he penned a reply to the provost, then took my leave of him. As I was about to descend the stair he said, 'Mr Seaton. I hope to see you again in Banff. If you would permit it, I would gladly paint your likeness – as a study. Yours is not a blank canvas.'

I had planned to spend the afternoon studying more closely the list I had got from David Melville, the bookseller, of books he was commanded by the council to supply to the grammar school. I did not want the scholars of Banff to be disadvantaged in their trial for a bursary. My mistake, once back at William's house, was to lay myself down on my bed to work, rather than sitting at the table. I was soon asleep. I was awoken in the late afternoon by a familiar voice in my ear.

'Oh, Alexander, Alexander, make haste; you are late for the lecture.' I jumped out of bed, scattering books and papers around me as I did so, and it took me near a full minute to understand it was now 1626, and not 1618, and that I was no longer a student in the King's College, in peril of the ire of my professors. As I came, with little dignity, to my feet, I was greeted by the broad smile of William Cargill. 'You have grown lazy in your old age, Alexander. You were never one for backsliding. Do you teach your scholars in the afternoon at all – or do you have them plump your pillows instead?'

I stooped to pick up the fallen papers. 'In the mornings I teach them their grammar and to fear God; in the afternoons I teach them to mistrust lawyers with soft linen.'

He laughed and sat down on the crumpled bed. Then he looked at me in seriousness. 'You are a man exhausted, Alexander. Must you really return to Banff so soon? Can you not stay here with us a while longer? We can make you well – give you food, rest and friendship.'

I avoided his searching gaze and busied myself with tying the strings on my book covers. 'You are kind, William, but I do not starve in Banff, and a man, even a fallen man, must work. And,' I looked up at him now, 'there is also friendship there, different from ours, I suppose, but it sustains me.'

'I do not pretend to be a Jaffray, Alexander. I know he has kept you where you might have fallen further – he has been a rock to you. But you are a young man still, and he no longer young, and you need to look at the world again with the eyes of a young man, I think. There are other pathways ahead of you; there are still choices for you to make.'

'My choices have proved poor ones, and the arrogance and folly with which I disported myself as a young man have brought me great shame. I must accept the judgement on me.'

'That day is not in this world. There is life yet in this world, and it is not condemned by God.'

I gripped his hand. 'I do not know how to find it, William. It is not here, not yet, if it is to be at all. I must be penitent and, you know me for no papist, but I must do my penance as it has been given to me. Besides,' I said, wishing to draw the subject to a close now and for all, 'if I am not in Banff in four days' time, the provost will have me slung in chains in the tolbooth.'

William took me to be in jest at first, but gradually I made him understand that I was not. I had told him nothing of the murderous business of Banff, or the commission to Straloch that I carried in my pocket. I had not even asked him yet for his uncle's notebooks – having told him nothing of the cause of my request. But I told him all now – I told him of Charles Thom and Marion Arbuthnott, and of the blow Charles's infatuation had been dealt by the return of the provost's nephew. I held nothing back – not my own shame at ignoring, wilfully mishearing the pleas of the dying man in the storm, nor the grotesque sight that greeted me at my desk the next morning. I told him of the firm belief of Jaffray and the apothecary Arbuthnott as to the manner of the poisoning that procured Patrick Davidson's death, and William promised me immediately that I should have the notebooks or any other thing I wished of his uncle's to take back to the doctor in Banff. And I told him of the speed with which the finger of accusation had been pointed at Charles, on the basis of little but innuendo and gossip. William listened to all without interruption. 'And when does the sheriff sit?' he asked.

'A week from tomorrow. There is but a week to save Charles from a dance on the Gallow Hill.'

William looked at me hesitantly. 'You are not suspected yourself, though?'

'No, thank God, it appears I am not.'

William was troubled, his lawyer's mind not satisfied. 'It is odd though, is it not, when it was your schoolroom Davidson was found in?'

I considered. In my determination to be the means of releasing Charles from the tolbooth, the question had not entered my head. I thought on it now. I had no motive, of course, but in a town such as Banff one could always be found. I had no knowledge of poisons – but then Charles Thom had no knowledge of poisons either. I felt a kind of dread begin to seep through me, and my mind go blank in a sudden white wave of fear, as though I was trapped in a room without window or door. For one who claimed to value his life so little, I found myself confronted with the terror of death.

'William, I do not know why I am not suspected. Had you been there, would you have suspected me?'

He looked at me straight, unflinching. 'We have been friends many years, and I would swear on my life that you would kill no man in cold blood, but had I been there, and had I not known you as I do, I would not have discounted you.'

'But William, I never knew him. What reason could I have for killing the apothecary's apprentice?'

His answer offered little by way of comfort. 'Whoever killed Patrick Davidson had a reason that has not yet been guessed at.' The bell of St Nicholas Kirk tolled five times. The silence that followed was broken by the sound of Elizabeth's voice calling to us from below.

128

'Are you both asleep up there? Is there no one in this house to do work but me? William, you have two letters to write before the post leaves for Edinburgh tonight, and I told Bella Watson you would be in her parlour ready to sup by six. William, are you there?'

My friend called to his wife that he would be down in a minute. 'Alexander, I must go and see to these letters. But we must talk more this evening. Elizabeth has arranged for us, just you and I, to go out for our dinner. She worries that I am too much at my work or by her side, and that I see nothing of my friends. You do not mind going to Bella Watson's?'

'Not at all,' I smiled. 'She always kept a good table.'

Little over an hour later we were seated by a fine fire, supping Bella Watson's ale, which William declared to be the best to be had in Aberdeen, and waiting for the girl to bring us our dinners from the kitchen. It would be a good meal, for Bella cooked as well as she brewed. I had little stomach for eating or drinking, though. We were fortunate that no one else had yet come into the small back parlour, and we had peace to talk, without prying eyes or sharp ears. Bella's daughter brought in a platter of two perfect, full-grown crabs, fresh from the pot, where they had so recently died their scalding death. There was no dressing, no adornment, just the two conquered beasts of the seabed, ferocious-looking still in all their armour. William leaned over towards the one nearest him and broke off a large claw. 'Have you thought more on what we were talking about this afternoon?'

I took a claw myself. 'I have thought of nothing else.'

'And can you think of any reason yet why they have not turned an accusing finger on you?'

'I can think of nothing. And it is all the stranger because I have few friends in Banff and am not well trusted.'

'And yet you walk free, unaccused. Is Charles misliked in the burgh? Does he have enemies?'

'Who could be an enemy to Charles? You know him well, William; what is there to mislike in him? He is a loyal friend and would, I imagine, be a foe of little consequence, so little effort would he make. He shields his contempt for the session and the burgh fathers well. He offends no man, trespasses on no man's rights, is not a greedy or harsh schoolmaster and calls little attention to himself. He does not seek out much company, is not always looking for friends – those that do him do him well enough. Of course, he is morose and difficult to draw out, and yet, when you can get beyond that, there is a warmth and humour in him that draws your heart to him. He has more friends than enemies, if he would but lift his head to look.'

William smiled sadly. 'A hard thing to do from his present position.'

I remembered Charles as I had last seen him, chained in the tolbooth, and the plaintive Gaelic air he had sung as I'd left. 'I saw him only on the first day of his imprisonment. It will be the worse for him now, and I do not know how his spirits can be lifted.'

William drew off another claw from the platter. 'There can be but one way, I think. With yourself and Jaffray working in his favour, he need not be lost. But, Alexander, if Charles has no enemies, I think you must have friends, whether you know it or not.'

This, too, I had wondered about in the last hour. 'I have no friend in the minister – Robert Guild is a small, self-seeking man, of poor wit and little godliness.'

'A dangerous enemy.'

'Enemy or friend, he is not a man to put trust in. And then the baillie – I think the baillie and all his retainers would gladly see me hounded from the town, if not hanging from the Gallow Hill. I sometimes fear he might be playing some game of cat and mouse with me.'

'How so?'

'He it was who invited me into the debate about the maps, for he knew I had knowledge of them. He openly admitted he knew of my letters from Archie. At the tolbooth too, when I went to visit Charles Thom, I felt the baillie had been waiting for me. I think he wants something of me. And he watches me.'

'Were you seen, do you think, the night you passed Davidson, the night of his death?'

'By none but the town whores, if even by them. Certainly not by the baillie or session clerk, if they were abroad at that hour, for they would have had me for it by now.'

'And are there others you do not trust?'

I laughed. 'William, how many hours have we got? There is not one man on the kirk session, save Gilbert Grant himself, who would not forget them-selves and dance a devilish jig to see me fall further in the eyes of God and man. My mother's alien ways and airs, my friendship with one so far above me as Archie Hay, and the enmity, at his death, of my own father have all seen to that, to say nothing of what I once had the pretension to aspire to.'

'And for friends – I mean amongst those in power?'

'I believe I have a friend in Thomas Stewart, our burgh advocate.'

William nodded, pleased. 'Then you are fortunate – I know him well. He is a just man. But go on.'

'I think it may be that Walter Watt, the provost, at least wishes me no ill. He has spoken up for me before the baillie and the minister, though he has few illusions about me, as he took pains to make clear. He it is who has entrusted me with this commission.' I took the map from my pocket and passed it over the table to him. He wiped his hands on the cloth the girl had brought us, and opened the package. He carefully unfolded the paper and smoothed out the map. He studied it silently for a few moments and then looked up. 'Whose work is this?'

'It is the work of Patrick Davidson.'

His brow furrowed. 'But you tell me he was an apothecary – indeed an apprentice.'

'He was. But he also, it would appear, had an interest in the drawing of maps. This is but one of several – the rest are under lock and key in the tolbooth of Banff.'

William's thoughts moved quickly to the point. 'And the magistrates suspect espionage?' I nodded, and he passed the map back to me, not liking the feel of it now. I folded it back into its package and returned it to my pocket. 'What is your commission?' asked William.

'I am to take it to Robert Gordon of Straloch and ask for his assessment of it. It may well be that it is simply the fruit of an innocent pastime.'

'Let us hope so. But Alexander, you have shown this to no one else in Aberdeen?'

I snorted. 'If it were known that I had shown it even to you I would be rotting in irons in Banff by morning.'

'Aye, but in truth, Alexander, when you were at Jamesone's today, you told him nothing of this?'

131

I could not comprehend the direction of his anxiety. 'Nothing. Nothing of any connection with it. But why Jamesone?'

He swallowed a draught of his wine and poured himself and me some more. 'What do you know of George Jamesone?'

I shrugged. 'About as much as I do of any painter – no, that is not right; I know a little more of him from today. I had been aware that he painted many of our foremost countrymen hereabouts. Many of the nobility and some of the more middling sort. I would not wager against him painting yourself and Elizabeth and your brood one day.'

'May God grant that it might be.' He waited then for me to say more.

'I know also that he is married to Isabel Tosh, whom I am astonished to find grown up and out of the habit of hurling missiles at young men of good quality, and that she has borne him a son. He lives in a fine house and is an interesting companion and a student of the nature of men.'

William pushed the platter away from him and leant forward, his elbows on the table. 'You know that he studied mainly in Edinburgh, but spent some time also at Antwerp?'

'Yes, but many of our countrymen continue to travel and study in the Spanish Netherlands. Is it to be imputed to them all as a crime?'

'Of course not. But while at Antwerp he studied at the studio of Pieter Paul Rubens. You have heard of Rubens?'

'Art is not much talked of in Banff, but yes, in my days here, even I heard of Rubens.'

'But you will not know – indeed why would you? – of Rubens' diplomatic activities. When I am in Edinburgh on business, I am often in company at the dinner tables of the advocates with the wealthy merchants of Leith. They have a better knowledge of the doings of folk in the Low Countries and the Baltic than they do of ours here. Rubens is well known as an agent of Madrid – nothing passes in Antwerp but he posts his own account of it to his masters. It is no secret. But more also, he is in the pay of the Medicis – the dowager of France. Little intrigue passes between the exalted heads of Romism that Rubens does not know of; little occurs in the Netherlands that he is not able to inform his Spanish masters of.'

Less than a week ago I would have thought my friend lost to the puffed up gossips of our capital and its sea port. What relevance could such nonsense have for the burgesses of Banff, for Charles Thom, for myself? But the death of Patrick Davidson and the discovery of his practice of cartography had changed that. 'Is Jamesone suspected for a Spanish spy?'

William shook his head. 'No, he is not – at least I have never heard rumour of such a thing and,' here he smiled, a little shamefaced, 'there are few rumours that pass me by.'

'But do you think it is possible?'

'I think many things are possible, and that most men have their price. Jamesone moves freely in the circles of the great and the powerful. But as he is a painter, he provokes little jealousy or suspicion. In fact, I would be hard put to think of an occupation better fitted to the business of espionage. But no, on balance, I do not think it likely he is a traitor.' He rang the bell for the girl to come and take the carcass of crab away, and bring us our meat. I could see he was still troubled. After the girl had gone he did not immediately touch the food, but returned to our conversation. 'But what were you doing there, Alexander? What business did you have with him?'

I felt my mouth go a little dry. 'I had a letter to deliver to him from the provost of Banff.'

'Did you see the contents of the letter?'

I shook my head. 'He, Jamesone, told me what the gist of it was, but no, I did not read it myself. It was – he said – to do with a commission to paint the provost's family. I have in my room in your house the artist's reply.'

I thought I saw my friend flinch, but only for a moment. 'You have not read this letter?'

'It is sealed.'

He pushed his fingers to his temples in thought. 'Then you must deliver it. You must go to Straloch as soon as you are able and fulfil your commission there and then you must return to Banff, deliver this letter and hope to keep yourself from the provost's further notice.' At that moment I felt I would gladly never have seen the provost, or the town of Banff again. But duties and promises called me back there, and there I would go. We resolved that I would leave Aberdeen a day early, as soon as the Sunday sermon was over. The laird of Straloch would forgive my Sabbath intrusion when he learnt the purport of my business.

We talked late, and when we finally left Bella Watson's house it was with little greater ambition than to lie down and rest our heads as soon as we might. As we walked we kept our voices low and kept ourselves to the main arteries of the town – all manner of creatures might wait in the darkness of vennels and winding lanes for unsuspecting night travellers. The near-full moon carved out the houses looming over the Castlegate, but gave us less guidance on the narrower, more winding streets, whose tenements tottered three storeys above us. Shadows lurked under forestairs and beyond pends. A snarling dog drew its owner to a window and was silenced with a curse as we passed. We kept as far as we could to the middle of the street to avoid the muck and ordure in the gutters. As we turned onto the Flourmill Lane, some movement at an upper storey caught William's eye and he put his hand on my arm to stay me. I followed the direction of his gaze and saw a flicker of light at the top of the backland stairway of a house I knew well – Maisie Johnston's, forever in my mind as the place where Archie and I had had that last evening together. A crook in the wall obscured us from view, and we were able to watch the dumb-show at the top of the stairs. It was Maisie herself, and although her face was obscured by a shawl, the other was certainly a young woman. Maisie was casting her eye about her, and speaking to the younger woman in low but urgent tones. William whispered to me, 'This is not like Maisie. She takes a great care not to draw attention to her establishment, and to avoid the wrath of the session.'

'But everyone knows what manner of house Maisie's is.'

'Everyone knows, but Maisie does not flaunt it. She does not give room to vagrants to ply their trade. Her girls are never to be found abroad at night, and that is the way Maisie and the council and the session like it.'

Maisie gave one final sweep of the street with her eyes, then handed the young woman a pouch before embracing her briefly and ushering her down the stair. As the young woman took her leave, her shawl slipped a little and I had to stop myself from calling out. The pend gate opened and I was face to face with Mary Dawson. 'Mary,' I began. The girl opened her mouth as if to reply, but her momentary recognition had been replaced by a look of sheer terror. Almost losing her bundle, and with her shawl now trailing behind her, she pushed past me and ran. William had a hold of my arm and it was several seconds before I was able to shake him off.

'Alexander, for the love of God – the woman is a whore. Is she known to you?'

I gasped a brief reply then made after her, with William soon at my heels. I could not see initially where Mary had gone, but the sound of her running feet on the cobbles directed me to a vennel behind the lane and towards the kirkyard. Two or three times I almost stumbled, being less accustomed to this night running than was Mary, who had often had to take to her heels to avoid being caught in the performance of her nocturnal trade. William caught up with me as I reached the kirkyard. 'I will explain later,' I told him breathlessly, 'but I must talk to this woman.' I scanned the jutting slabs that gave memory to generations of indwellers past and long dead, and the mounds and humps of earth where the poor lay scarcely noted, but could see nothing of Mary Dawson. Bats swooped and whirled from the steeple of the church and amongst the trees in the kirkyard. An owl hooted and I imagined I could feel and hear every scuttling thing about my feet. She could have been hiding anywhere amongst the graves, for I was sure she could not have left without being seen. I gambled and started to make for the kirk itself. As I did so I caught sight of a swift movement out of the corner of my eye and then saw Mary Dawson running out towards the Netherkirkgate, as if all the creatures in Hell were after her. I checked my path and ran after her, William still with me, although comprehending no more than he had at the start of my pursuit. Mary was clearly no stranger to Aberdeen, for she knew the lanes and vennels of the town better than I myself could remember. From the Netherkirkgate she headed down west of St Katharine's Hill by Putachieside towards the Green. The smell of the tanners' and the litsters' work still hung in the night air, although they had long since gone to their weary beds. I almost lost her at the Green, a cat having darted out from behind a midden, nearly sending me into the Putachie Burn. As I righted myself I could see no sign of her, but a movement ahead had me starting off again in the direction of the ruined Carmelite friary. William, bent double with so much running after such a dinner, grabbed at my cloak, gasping.

'No. She went this way.' He was indicating the line of the burn as it went to meet the mouth of the Dee and, recovering, he pulled me after him in the direction of Shore Brae: she was headed for the harbour.

The harbour was never silent, never at rest – it was the heart and lungs of the burgh. Whereas before our running had sent noise ricocheting into the silent hum of the night-time town, our falling steps – and those of Mary Dawson ahead of us – fell into a rhythm already gently approaching from the sea. The putrid smell of the trades was now being lost, overwhelmed, by the sheer salt and seaweed smell of the quay head. There were lanterns lit along the quayside, and the shore porters were busy at their work. A huddle of merchants deep in conference with the ship's master was animated by the lantern light. The group looked up at our approach.

'It seems you have some tardy passengers, captain. They are all out winded to get here in time.'

Another merchant peered at us. 'Is it not William Cargill? What are you doing here at this hour of the night, Mr Cargill? Are you making ship for the Baltic, then? Will you not be needing my bill after all?'

William laughed and responded as casually as he could, 'No, it is since my wife has been with child it is safer for me to walk abroad at night than to venture to my own bed. The humour that is on her brings tears the one minute and scolding the next.'

The men laughed. William went over to the captain and drew him aside a moment for some private speech. I envied him his facility of going through the world without causing offence. The merchants went to see to the loading of their goods and I remained in the shadows, watching for a sight of Mary Dawson. William came back over to me presently. 'The captain takes six passengers as well as his cargo tonight, in less than an hour. They sail for Danzig. He has two students, two merchants, a master mason and a woman who calls herself a widow. He says she is no widow such as he has seen before and he is certain her testimonials are forged, but her money is not and he will let her aboard without over much questioning. He says she is a young woman, of medium height, shapely, with hair the colour of burnished copper, and eyes the same shade. Is this the woman you seek?'

I nodded slowly. 'Her name is Mary Dawson. She and her sister are – were – whores of Banff. I would swear they were the last faces Patrick Davidson saw before he departed this world. Their occupation has been long known in Banff, but tolerated – they were discreet enough. Yet two days ago Janet

136

Dawson was driven from the bounds at the end of the hangman's scourge, not to return on pain of death. I saw it with my own eyes. Before the town serjeant pulled her away, she repeated to me the words she said were the last spoken on this earth by Patrick Davidson: "James and the flowers". I am certain it was the sisters who put Patrick Davidson in my schoolroom to die, and I can make very little of Janet's report of his last words. I must talk with Mary Dawson before she leaves these shores. I cannot believe that this and her sister's banishment from Banff do not have their cause in the murder of the apothecary's apprentice.'

William took some coins from his pouch and bade me follow him. He walked to where the shore porters were and went to talk quietly to one of them, then another. It was the third man who finally showed some sign of knowing what he was being asked, and taking the coin from William motioned to us to follow him. Behind a large stack of English coals I found my quarry, cowering like a frightened dog. She tried to bolt again when she saw me, but this time I was too fast for her: I caught her by the arms and forced her back down.

'Mary, you know me. Why do you run?' Still she struggled, but I held her firm. 'Mary, it is Alexander Seaton. You know me.'

At length, when she realised she could not release herself from my grip, she stopped struggling. She looked directly at me through defiant, and yet fearful eyes. 'I know you, Mr Seaton, and I know you to have goodness in you, but you have not fallen far enough in this world for me to trust you. Let me go, for you will have nothing of me.'

'A few words, Mary, that is all I ask, a few words.'

She looked suspiciously at William. 'Who is he?'

'A friend, no more.'

'He has not been sent after me with you?'

I slowly loosened my grip on her arm. 'What do you mean? Mary, I have not been sent after you. I never knew you were here until this night, not half an hour ago as you left Maisie Johnston's house. You think I was sent here after you, to bring you back to Banff?'

She was rubbing her arm where I had gripped her, and let out a hollow laugh. 'Back to Banff? I will never see Banff again all the days of this life, unless it is to hang from the gibbet or be drowned at the shore. You nor anyone else to come will ever be sent to bring me back, but I fear one might be sent to see to it that I do not.'

Now I understood her terror; it was some of that same creeping terror that had been coming over me these last hours, but in Mary Dawson it had taken such a hold that no one could reason with her, such was her certainty of some awful retribution. For what, I began to guess, but from whom I did not know. 'Tell me what you know, Mary.'

She shook her head fiercely, like a madwoman lost in herself.

'You have nothing to fear from me. I swear before God, I am not one of them.' I had no earthly notion who this 'them' might be, but my oath seemed to calm her a little, although her lips remained tightly shut. I had to try another tack. 'There is something your sister told me ...'

Her eyes flashed up at me. 'Janet? Where is she? Is she here in Aberdeen?'

I put my hand out to calm her, to let her down as gently as I might. 'No. She is not here. I do not know where she is now. I last saw her three days ago. The hangman and the town serjeant were beating her from the bounds. They drove her out to the west, on the Cullen road.'

Mary's eyes were still eager. 'Then they do not have her? She is safe?'

'As far as I can tell you, she is safe. I do not know where she is gone, but I know,' I hesitated, but there was no good in keeping it from her, 'I know she was bound never to return to Banff, on pain of death.'

These tidings did not seem to trouble Mary as I had expected them to. She was nodding slowly, smiling to herself. 'Then she is safe. She will go to our cousin in Strathspey. She will be safe.'

'Strathspey is a long journey, over hard terrain.'

Mary was not concerned. 'She knows the country well. The last frosts are almost gone. She will make her way. She will be safe. May God keep her.' I realised then that Mary Dawson had no expectation of ever seeing her sister again. She was silent in her thoughts and I let her be for a while, but I knew time was passing and that neither tide nor captain would wait, so neither could I.

'What is it that drove you from Banff in such a way?'

She looked at me curiously. 'You truly do not know?'

'How could I know? I am not privy to the magistrates' council.'

She almost snorted with contempt. 'The magistrates' council!' And then, more softly, she said, 'It was not the magistrates' council, but the beggar chief that warned us to leave Banff. His warning is not to be taken lightly.'

'The beggar chief? Lang Geordie? But why?'

She answered, and I knew I had guessed the thing right. 'The apothecary's apprentice – I never knew his name. We found him, Janet and I, at the bottom of Water Path. He was sick, near to death. It was us who set him at your desk.' She looked up. 'And they say you never saw him until he was gone?'

I sat down beside her and took off my hat. William watched at a distance. 'I was not called until he had been found, long dead.'

She smiled a sad smile. 'It was a chance we took. It was a slim hope, but a hope all the same. We knew he was dying – I have seen dying men before. We had seen you pass only a few moments before, and we doubted you would be yet sleeping. We hoped you might hear him and find him, find him in time to help him.'

'I heard nothing.' For the tenth, twentieth time I cast my mind back to that night and tried to listen again, tried to hear what I had not heard then. There was nothing, nothing but the noise of the storm, drowning out whatever else there might have been.

'Neither you, nor Mistress Youngson?'

'Not even she.'

She pulled her shawl closer around her shoulders. 'Ah, well. It was not to be. It was his lot to die.' Then she looked up sharply. 'He was not drunk, though, Mr Seaton, whatever they might say. It was not a natural death.'

I knew this already, and was anxious to get on. 'He spoke to you though, did he not?'

She showed surprise that I knew this. 'Janet?' I nodded. 'Aye, he did. He babbled two or three times about "James and the flowers". We could not make head nor tail of it, but he was very anxious about it.'

'And he said nothing else?'

'Nothing. His senses were beyond him by the time we got him to the schoolhouse.'

Something in this was troubling me. 'But how did you get beyond the pend and into the house, for I know I locked both door and gate.'

She looked a little proud at the memory. 'We grew up at the smiddy at

Fordyce, Mister Seaton. There is not a lock or bolt we do not know how to turn. And as for getting over the gate to open it, well,' and here there was a trace, just a trace, of the old sly smile, 'my sister and I are famed for our agility.'

These little mysteries were of no great consequence at this moment, though. 'But what is this to Lang Geordie that he should tell you to run? Why, after all this time, was your sister driven from the town and why do you flee?'

'Because we were seen. And it was made known to us that we had been seen. Geordie beds down at the same house as my sister and I. The message came through him to us that we were to be gone from the town before daybreak, or face our own fates.'

'What, for helping a dying man?'

'For seeing who it was that killed him. Someone was watching. They watched us and I would stake much that they had watched you before us. Someone was watching, to make sure that he would die; I would stake all that I have on it.' All that Mary Dawson had amounted to very little, but I did not doubt the sincerity of her vow. And I, too, had been seen. But I had not yet had my warning.

At that moment a shout went up from the captain that all who were going aboard should be aboard now or lose their passage. Mary gathered up her bundle and scrambled to her feet. I grabbed at her arm. 'Mary, wait, who was it? Tell me who it was.'

She pulled away from me. 'You'll not have it from my lips. It will not be laid at my door that anyone had it from my lips.' She was running now towards the ship.

'Mary, wait, please. How will you live?'

'By my trade and by my wits. But I shall live, have no fear of that. I will never see Scotland again. Farewell, Mr Seaton. Be careful who you trust.' I tried to go after her but the sail was already up and the anchor weighed – less than a moment from her embarkation the vessel was pulling away from the quayside. I made to leap the distance but a strong arm was pulling me back. It was William.

'Leave her be, Alexander. I have seen fear in many witnesses; you will have nothing more from her.'

We stood and watched as the ship carrying Mary Dawson from her homeland pulled away into the distance, the moonlight illuminating the white of its sails in the night. I uttered a prayer for her under my breath. 'Amen,' said my friend William Cargill. We turned our backs to the departing vessel and began our weary trudge homewards to William's house.

NINE

The King's College

My sleep was fitful and filled with nightmares. Several times through the night I found myself awake, listening in the darkness to sounds of the sleeping house. Each time I slipped back into the realm of sleep only to find myself in some new place of terror, with an unseen assailant awaiting me. Always I was in chains – under the altar of a ruined church; in a vault filled with the dead, my own dead; at my desk in Banff, with the cold hands of Patrick Davidson clasped to my wrist. In each dream the terror came closer till I could almost smell the warmth of human flesh. At the last, I thought I caught a sight, a glimpse only, of the face of my assailant. When I awoke I could not tell who it had been. I did not sleep again after that, but lay in the darkness for long hours, while the town bell tolled the stages of the night. Before six, I rose and threw some water over my face. I looked out over the garden but little stirred: the animals were at their rest; the cock had not yet crowed.

I took a spill to the still glowing embers in the hearth and lit the candle by my bedside. From the small kist at the foot of my bed I took out the letter and turned it over in my hands. It was addressed to Walter Watt, Provost of Banff, and sealed by the ring of George Jamesone. Turn it a hundred or a thousand times, yet nothing could be seen of what was written inside. This pastime of espionage was new to me, but I was certain that no great intrigues and treacheries could be drawn up in so short a time, no message of any great import given in the few lines I had seen Jamesone scribble.

I put the letter back in the kist and threw on my outer clothing. Down in the kitchen all was warm and busy. Elizabeth was not yet up, but William was already at his breakfast and giving his instructions for the day, principally that the mistress should not be allowed to over-work and should be made to rest.

'Have no fear, master, she'll not get the better of me.' The old man-servant had due respect for his master, and love too. The mistress that had once been a kitchen maid was no match for his benign dictatorship of the house.

When William looked up to greet me I saw at once that he had slept little better than I had. 'I see we have been dreaming the same dreams,' he said.

'May God forbid that you or any other should have the dreams that I had last night.' I sat down and accepted the bowl of hot porridge that the serving girl offered me. William bade the girl go see to the goats, but to his houseman he said nothing.

'Have you found any answers, after the events of last night?'

I shook my head. 'I have questions, more questions, but few answers.'

He broke a piece of bread from the loaf on the table and smeared some butter on it. 'You have no idea who it might have been that the women saw as they carried Patrick Davidson to the schoolhouse?'

'None. Well, no. That is a lie. I am over-laden with ideas. By the time the clock had struck four this morning there was not a soul in Banff I did not suspect.'

William smiled. 'Aye. For all my exhortation of you to tell her nothing of all this, I was hard put myself not to waken Elizabeth and ask her her views on the matter. For the whores to be tolerated so long and only now to be banished, forced to flee for fear of their lives, can have little to do with the nature of their profession. They must indeed have seen the murderer – and been seen by him. But who could take the risk of sending a warning message to them by a known vagrant?'

'I do not know, but I suspect it may have been Lang Geordie, or one of his band, who was used to call Jaffray away to Findlater on the night of the murder.'

'I think you are right,' said William. 'Unless it was the beggar man himself who killed the apprentice?' He said this more in hope than expectation, and offered no argument when I disagreed with the idea.

'Poison would not be Lang Geordie's style. A knife in the back in a dark alleyway, and then being left to bleed in the gutter – that would have been Patrick Davidson's fate at the hands of Lang Geordie or his men.'

'Aye,' said William, 'the poison is the thing. And then the maps, and Marion Arbuthnott's prescience of some evil to befall her father's apprentice.' He rubbed the heels of his hands into his eyes, as if to gouge the confusion from them. 'What sense is to be made of it all?'

I swallowed the last spoonful of my porridge. 'I do not know. These questions and others have been troubling me the whole night. But I mean to make sense of them, to make a start at least. You have business this morning?'

He nodded. 'Yes, but I shall be here before twelve, and then we can walk up to the King's College to take our dinner with John and Matthew before you must go to your appointment with Principal Dun.' He paused. 'You are still happy to meet with our friends again?'

When William had first received my letter telling him of my plans to make this trip to Aberdeen, and asking if I might lodge with him, he had taken it as a sign that I had emerged from the great black tunnel of despair that I had hidden myself in since my disgrace. He had written back to me almost instantly, suggesting that we should seek out some old friends of our student days who were to be in the Old Town at the time of my visit. My first impulse had been to say no, I could not face it, but Jaffray had dissuaded me from being so hasty. Now the meeting no longer filled me with dread. Indeed, the thought of seeing those friends again gave me some pleasure. 'I will be glad to see them,' I said. 'But as for the morning, I mean to use it to examine your uncle's notebooks. Jaffray is sure that if the flower used to poison Patrick Davidson is to be found, it will be found there.'

'Then you must use my study. The light there is the best in the house, and it is the room furthest from the kitchen, so you will have peace. What these women find to gossip and cackle about the whole day long, I do not know. I am sure old Duncan only pretends at deafness to save himself having to listen to them. Is that not right, Duncan?'

'I could not tell you, master. I have the deafness in one ear,' said the old man, with a sly smile. 'I'll have the girl set a fire in your study for Mr Seaton here. The room will be cold at this hour of the morning.' And he went off in search of the kitchen girl, who was still out at the goats.

'You are a good master, William,' I said to my friend. 'Your servants are fond of you, and would do much for you, I think.'

'I am very fortunate. But it is beyond even Duncan's power to keep Elizabeth at rest. He and the girl do all they can, but the time is soon coming when she will need more help, and I fear she will not take it.'

'Do you really fear so much for her?'

He sighed and put down his bread. 'Aye, and with cause. She was ill, early this winter past, very ill, with a fever. She hardly swallowed a morsel – a bit of thin soup, little more – for nigh on three weeks. Sometimes she was so far in the fever she hardly knew my face. Dun had done all he could for her and I was on the point of sending for Jaffray when, thank God, she started to mend.'

'But she is well now?'

He gestured helplessly. 'She was never strong, and she has not the strength even that she had before her illness. The pregnancy is hard on her. I pray God morning and night that she will survive the birth.'

'And the child, too.'

He looked at me sharply. 'Oh, do not mistake me, Alexander. I love that child in her belly already, but at what price might I become a father? And then she insists she will feed the bairn herself. She will not listen to sense on the matter, Alexander; but she will not have the strength or the milk to nurse her own child. I am at a loss to know what to do with her.'

But I was not. An inspiration came to me; a gift from God in my mind: Sarah Forbes. 'William. I think I may have an answer. We will talk on the road to the Old Town.'

He looked at me with curiosity but little optimism. 'All right then, Alexander. I will see you after noon.' And still with furrowed brow he took his hat and left on his morning's business.

I spent the next few hours lost in wonder at the notebooks of James Cargill, William's uncle. I had fancied – and I think Jaffray had too in the throes of his enthusiasm – that I would carry a small, neatly bound book back to Banff with me for the study of the doctor and the apothecary. The moment I stepped into William's study I was disavowed of this notion. On the desk, Duncan had placed an old leather kist with a curved lid; beside it was a key. Duncan had been Dr Cargill's servant before he had been William's. I knew by the reverence with which he turned the key in the lock that these papers were to him a treasure more valuable than jewels. He opened the lid and let his hand rest briefly on a book on top, then moved aside for me.

'The doctor's most valuable books are in the Marischal College library now, but these papers have not been touched these thirteen years. Have a care of them.'

'I will,' I promised the old man, and, satisfied, he left.

I set to work immediately, lifting books or bundles out one at a time and trying to put them in order. There was no index, no catalogue, and indeed no apparent order in which the items had been set in the chest. At length I fixed on chronology as my best means of arranging the items and after some little time had the notebooks and bundles of letters and papers set out before me in the order they had been written. Jaffray had suggested that the *colchicum* would be most likely to have been sketched at the time of Cargill's residence at Montbéliard. Consequently, I began with the first of his notebooks from 1596. The work was meticulous – the hand a fine italic and the abbreviations precise. The drawings were as detailed and careful and exact as any artist might have done, the colours rendered in words as well as Jamesone could have rendered them in paint. Not all was in Latin – true, the scientific and geographical detail was in clear and exact academic language – but much of what accompanied it was written in the Scots tongue. Had I not been engaged on such pressing and impor-tant work, I could have spent many contented hours reading through the journals of the student days abroad of James Cargill. I resolved that once I had found what I was looking for, I would ask William to allow me to take three or four of the notebooks back to Banff.

It was towards the end of the third book that I found it at last: *colchicum mortis*, the plant that brought death. Cargill had sketched and labelled every aspect of it from seed to petal. Every detail of every part of the plant was drawn with what could only have been a very great effort at accuracy, and the moment I saw the sketch, colourless though it was, of the plant in flower, I knew I had seen it before. I had seen its globe-like head, large and yet delicate above its narrow, dark, strap-like leaves. The description in Scots given by Cargill of its colour was perfect. 'The petals of the plant in flower,' he wrote, 'are like the pale grey blue of the winter sky over the northern sea after it has snowed.' It was just that, exactly. And he wrote too of the terrible properties of this exquisite flower, the poison from its seeds that would send a man into convulsions before paralysing him; the certainty of death. He finished his account with, 'Found only in the mountain passes between Basel and Montbéliard. Not known to be transported or to endure elsewhere. *Dei Gratia.*' But Cargill's God, like mine, had been minded to change his blessing, and the awful, beautiful plant had found a Scottish sanctuary and was growing somewhere in Banff. I knew, for I had seen it. I had seen it in the hand of a woman. But where, in whose hands, should every beat of my heart depend on it, I could not remember.

I breathed deep and screwed my eyes tight shut, trying to force the memory from the recesses of my mind. It would not come. I got up and began to pace about the room, to look out of the window at the business of the street outside, to stare into the flames of the fire, but still it would not come. I pictured every woman I knew, put the flowers into her hand, but every time the face went blank and I could see nothing, discern nothing. I searched my awful dreams of the last night for assistance, but none would come. I prayed aloud, but my words echoed unanswered in the empty room. The face was blank, and the hand began to fade away. The case was presently hopeless, and would not be mended here, at this hour, in this room. Frustration, then fatigue crept over me. It wanted two hours yet till William was to return from his morning's business. I returned all but the one, special journal to the leather kist, and returned to my room to sleep the sleep that had eluded me in the night.

William had been glad of the walk up to the King's College, glad of the chance to leave the confines of town for a while, if only for the neighbouring burgh not two miles up the road. It was a fine afternoon, and the schoolchildren of Aberdeen had taken gladly to their afternoon's play at the links and on the King's Meadows. I waited until we were beyond the Gallowgate port and past Mounthooly before I told William of my idea that Sarah Forbes might alleviate the coming burdens on Elizabeth's strength. He listened carefully, quietly, without making the objections I had halfexpected, even from him. For a moment after I had finished he said nothing, deep in thought, and then, 'I think it may be possible that it would work, Alexander. I think it just possible that she would agree to it.' He continued walking and then stopped. 'You can obtain the relevant testimonials?' I assured him that I could. 'Then I shall clear the way here. I doubt there will be many objections from council or session. I will win the day.'

'If Elizabeth will allow it.'

William affected a look of mock indignation. 'Do you suggest that I am not master in my own home, Mr Seaton? I wish it and it will be so!' We both laughed, and I think for each of us, the rest of the journey was made with a lighter heart. The burden of concern for his wife weighed less heavy on him, and I had a feeling within me of having done good.

We were still laughing as we walked through the door of the inn. Matthew Lumsden and John Innes were already there, at our favoured table between the front window and the side door of the inn. It had been a useful spot for Archie to watch and escape from, should anyone he did not wish to encounter be spied coming up the High Street. First Matthew, and then John got up and embraced me. 'It has been too long, Alexander, too long.'

I took off my hat and sat down on my old seat by the door. 'It has indeed, and the fault is all mine.'

'Old friends need not speak of fault. Who amongst us is blameless?'

I studied the kind, open face. 'You will never fall as I have done, John. You will never feel such shame you cannot look your friends in the eye.'

He laid his hand over mine. '"And thou mayest remember, and be confounded and never open thy mouth any more because of thy shame, when I am pacified toward thee for all that thou hast done, saith the Lord God."'

'Ezekiel chapter six, verse nine,' I said. Matthew sighed audibly and slurped his beer.

John smiled. 'I knew you could not have forgotten. That you have felt such shame is testament to God's grace in you, his forgiveness.'

'I see you are still too good, John,' I said.

'Too good by half,' said Matthew as he beckoned the serving girl over to us. 'They will make a bishop of him yet, if he is not careful.'

'Hold your tongue, Matthew,' said John, blushing a deeper red than was the hair on his head.

'You still regent in the college here, then?'

John nodded as he took another draught of his ale. 'Aye. I have the second class now, but the competition from the Marischal College in the New Town threatens our numbers.'

'Pah,' snorted Matthew contemptuously.

John put down his tankard. 'Pah! Will not do, Matthew. What is your objection?'

Matthew had never been one for thinking before he spoke, but now he took a moment before his reply. 'My objection is that the very place was founded as an affront to the Gordons. The Earl Marischal gave church land that was not his to give—'

'Matthew,' cautioned William.

'That was not his to give,' continued the Marquis of Huntly's man, 'to the burgh of Aberdeen in order to curry favour with the magistrates and wrest influence in the town from the marquis's family. But worse than that, he planned to set it up as a seminary more narrow and joyless than Geneva. Thank God the old devil was too mean to match his endowment to his schemes.'

'The earl's intentions were nothing darker than to promote necessary learning in our corner of Scotland, where this college here had taken so long to throw off the slough of Rome. And there were many here who refused to take up the new methods of learning brought in from France by Andrew Melville.'

The very mention of Melville's name was, I knew, guaranteed in itself to provoke an outburst of fury from Matthew. I was not to be disappointed. 'Melville! Presbyterian upstart! Impertinent, disloyal—'

I feared for him, so evident to any who cared to listen was his sympathy with Rome.

'And yet we are all friends,' said William, 'and will always be so, I hope, for all our differences. Let us pray God that matters of politics and religion may never come between us.'

'Amen to that,' chorused my friends. Our conversation had been drifting into dangerous waters, and I had learned in Banff that there were unseen currents in such waters. Looking around the inn, no Baillie Buchan, certainly, no rabid session clerk came into view, but who was to say that others were not to be similarly feared? I steered the conversation to safer ground, concerned suddenly that my friendship with Matthew might be used against us both. It had been agreed between William and myself that nothing should be said before the other two about the troubles in Banff, and especially that no mention should be made to Matthew of my commission to Straloch. His loyalty to Huntly had always made him rash.

The remainder of our meal passed in merry reminiscence of past deeds and some contemplation of future hopes. For my own part I would have been happy to listen to them all – William knew this and I think John saw it too, but Matthew would not have it. He was determined to draw from me some optimism, some plan for myself. He had never had much time for the ideas of the predestinarians. He had fallen himself many times, and confession before a mass priest in one of their many safe houses in Strathbogie had salved him of further conscience about it. He would not allow that my fall in the eyes of God and my disgrace before men had been inevitable, that the evil was inherent to me. Thus fallen, I knew I was counted amongst the damned.

'It is nonsense, Alexander, and you must know it is. What? Because you took a girl to bed – and I have no doubt that is what is at the heart of the matter, but I will not press you on who she was – you have revealed yourself to be of the eternally damned? Well, if that be the case my friend, you will find yourself the most feared man in the country, for why should you not now revel in your damnation? You are free now to murder, rape and rob without fear of further punishment in the afterlife since your course is already set.'

There was no disputing with Matthew when he was in this humour, so I did not attempt to. I only said, 'I still have a conscience though, Matthew. I still know the law of God, and it binds me not to treat my fellow man with contempt in this life.' Even as the words were in my mouth, the image of Patrick Davidson came again to my mind. 'I shall try to do what I can in this world, come what might in the next.'

Matthew put down his tankard, pleased. 'That is all I wanted to hear, Alexander. A lot of wailing and gnashing of teeth is a waste of an able man. Be mortified in your conscience if you must, but do not throw away the gifts God gave you because of it. There is a passage in Joel, is there not?'

John came to his assistance, '"And rend your heart, and not your garments, and turn unto the Lord your God: for he is gracious and merciful,

slow to anger and of great kindness, and repenteth him of the evil.'"
Sometimes it was too easy to forget that beneath Matthew's bluster lay a
simple but firm humanity. How could I ever have hoped to be a minister,
when I was such a poor judge of even my own old friends?

A little before two our party broke up. A group of Huntly's men arrived,
bound for the South, and Matthew was to ride with them on the marquis's
business. William was returning home to Elizabeth for the afternoon. John
and I walked over to the college together. He, who had always been gentle
and diligent, knew he would never be a bishop. He had been a hard-working
student and was a competent teacher, but he did not have the sharpness of
mind needed to distinguish him from so many others. Yet John was not
ambitious, and was content to study and to teach within the safety of the
college. I had used to wonder at his lack of ambition, but now I believe I
envied it.

We were soon at the entrance to the college, beneath the chapel's great
crown tower, symbol of our nation's now slumbering imperial hopes. We
went in under the gateway and John pointed out to me a door across the
quadrangle where Dr Dun could be found. He embraced me again, and I
promised that it would not be so long until we saw each other once more,
then he hurried off to take his afternoon class.

I found myself a little nervous as I approached Dr Dun's door. He
would know little of me, I hoped, but I knew much of him. Principal of
the Marischal College, he was Mediciner here at King's as well, a friend
and support to the bishop in his efforts to reform the college and stamp
out abuses where they might be found. In addition to these already heavy
responsibilities, he carried out a busy medical practice amongst the wealthy
landed families in the countryside about. He was all that Jaffray might have
been, had my old friend not been content to fight his daily fight against
pain, malnourishment and disease in our own small town.

A student showed me to Dr Dun's room, where I was greeted by a tall
and spare-looking man of little more than forty. He dismissed the student
and bade me sit down while he finished off the piece of work he was engaged upon. After a few moments he looked up. 'Now, Mr Seaton, you are
here on the matter of the bursaries?'

Thankful for the lack of preliminaries, I launched gratefully into my well-rehearsed speech. 'I have a young scholar of great promise in Banff, who, through his mother, has a claim to one of Dr Liddel's bursaries at the Marischal College. I know there may well be several boys competing for the benefit. I am anxious that he should not be disadvantaged through some want on my part. In particular, I would like to know the standard of Greek that is required of petitioners for the bursaries. My own scholars are at an elementary stage in their Greek studies, but I am confident that with extra tuition I might be able to make up any deficiency.'

Dun smiled broadly and put down the pipe he had been turning over in his hands. 'Mr Seaton, if your scholars have any Greek at all, then they will be at no disadvantage against the town boys. We have, of course, excellent masters, but they have a great press of duties upon them and do not always attend to the school as much as might be required. Yet schooling is the most important work our kingdom has to offer. If we are to build the godly Commonwealth here in Scotland, schooling must be our foundation.' I had heard this before, in many quarters, but Dun spoke with true conviction. If there were more such men the great project of our reformers might have a chance. He got up and lit his pipe from the fire. 'Tell me, do you have another occupation, or aspirations, as well as your schoolmastering in Banff?'

'I have no other occupation,' I said, with, I hoped, sufficient finality that he should not press me further.

Dun, however, was not to be put off. 'And aspiration?'

I shifted in my seat. 'Whatever aspirations I might once have had are finished with.'

Still he persisted. 'You had some other calling?'

There was little point now in further prevarication; he should have what he was asking for. 'I had hopes once of being a minister. At my final trials I was accused of a wrongdoing I could not deny. The passage of time will not right that wrong. I will not recommence on my trials for the ministry.'

He returned to his desk, the tips of his fingers pressed against one another. 'And you have found another calling now, as a schoolteacher?'

It would perhaps have been politic to have obliged him, but I was resolved to be done with such dishonesty. 'Schoolmastering will never be a calling to me, but it is what I did before, while I was a divinity student on my trials, and it is something I can do; a man must eat. And I know, as you will tell me, that it performs a necessary role in society, and for that, and for the affection I bear my scholars, I do it as well as I am able, but for myself I have no great love for the task and derive no great satisfaction from it.'

'I am sorry to hear that, Mr Seaton, for I think that a schoolmaster who will travel fifty miles for the sake of one pupil, who takes the time to teach Greek to the sons of a small burgh such as Banff, and of whose proficiency in many disciplines I had already heard, has much to offer. If, as you say, you will never return to the pursuit of your first calling, it is a great pity that you derive little comfort from your second. For myself, I do not believe that God gives a man such gifts as you have been given only to condemn him to repeated failures.' He did not call for his servant to show me out, but rose and accompanied me out into the quadrangle himself. 'The trials for the bursary take place at the end of June, when I trust we will meet again. May God go with you until then.' He turned away and I watched him disappear beyond the cloister into the darkness of the college. I walked over to the well and drew up some water. It was cool and clear, and the taste of it brought me back to this place several years ago, when the future had been a realm of possibility, and the past a thing not considered.

I finished the ladle of water I had drawn from the bucket and was about to move on when I heard footsteps coming towards me from the college gateway. I knew those footsteps. Had I not stopped to indulge my thirst I could have been away out of this place by now – the college gateway was not ten yards from the road. Instead I was here, in the centre of my gilded past, with no means of avoiding the eye of the one man in the whole of Aberdeen, new town and old, whom I had most wished not to meet. I looked up, waiting for the reckoning to come. The face coming towards me broke into a smile of genuine joy; a hand reached out and grasped mine.

'Alexander Seaton, it is truly you? I had not thought to see you here again, though I have often wished and prayed for it. What has brought you back to us? Why did you not tell me you were coming? Have you been waiting on me long? I have been kept busy the whole morning on college business with my father.' Dr John Forbes of Corse, son of the bishop and Professor of Divinity in the King's College of Aberdeen, the most learned man I knew, stood before me, his face filled with affection. He was a man of the deepest spirituality and had had greater hopes for me than even I had ever done. There can have been few teachers more disappointed by the failure of a pupil than he had been by mine.

So shocked was I at the sight of him there that, for a few moments, I could find no words to answer him. Nevertheless, I think my face told him my thoughts, for his hand fell away and his smile faded. 'Alexander, you have not come to see me, have you?'

'No,' I replied, my voice dry. 'I had business with Dr Dun, about the bursaries, and had to come and meet him here.' I registered the hurt in his eyes and cursed my pride. 'I am sorry; I should have told you I was coming, but I was ...' There was little point in lying to this man who for four years had been my spiritual guide and who had kept the fervour of my calling burning within me. He deserved at least my honesty. 'I was ashamed,' I said.

Dr Forbes well knew the cause of my shame. Astonishment at my failure to secure the approval of the Presbytery of Fordyce had given way to fury, and he and his father had both written to the brethren, demanding an explanation. The brethren had responded obliquely – for they had not the information to do otherwise, and had directed both the bishop and his son to myself and to my Lord Hay of Delgatie. Bishop Forbes had written then to Delgatie, his son to me. His lordship, I was given to understand, had given a plain and truthful account of the grounds of his objection to my person and to my candidature for the ministry. I had written that whatever the family of Hay should accuse me of, of that was I guilty, before God and man. Urgent letters of friendship and entreaty to turn to him for spiritual counsel had flown from the divinity professor's rooms at the King's College of Old Aberdeen to my attic room in the schoolhouse of Banff. None had been answered. Now here we stood, face to face, no hiding behind silence.

Dr Forbes stood squarely before me. 'There is a time for shame, and a time for repentance.' His voice was measured, calm. 'You were right to feel shame for your deeds, but to hold fast to that shame at the expense of all else is an indulgence. You were carnal – who among us has not been tempted, has not fallen? You betrayed the trust of a friend and patron. Ungrateful and graceless indeed, but who amongst us has not been guilty of ingratitude, of gracelessness in our behaviour?'

I looked at the man. How was I to believe that he might ever have been led into such behaviour, such immorality as I had? He leant against the wall of the well, tired-looking now, his eyes searching mine for an understanding I was struggling to find. 'You may have sinned, Alexander, but remember the words of the prophet: He waits to be gracious.'

I felt the resilience seeping from me. 'I have tried, believe me, doctor, I have tried. I have looked for God, called on God, but found myself only in a wilderness.'

He spoke gently, quoting Ezekiel. '"For my gracious Lord was pleased to let me see, that, by leading me into this wilderness, and pleading with me there, would he bring me into the bond of the Covenant." In all your years here, Alexander, you grappled with and mastered the most abstruse theological propositions. You could argue any point almost as well as I could myself. For all that though, God's greatest gift in you was the pure faith with which He graced you. It was that above all that I thought would make you the finest of ministers. I have no doubt that you could still argue with insight and exactitude whichever point I might throw your way, but I fear you have forgotten the most important lesson of all, the promise of that Covenant.'

I looked at him, expectantly. He answered my unasked question. 'The Son of God came into this world to save sinners such as you and me. That is the great Covenant. Do not ask me ever to believe, Alexander, that you have grown so arrogant as to think your sin greater than His sacrifice.'

I could not look at him. 'Take thought on this,' he said. 'For friendship's sake promise me that you will. Come back and see me soon. We will work on this together. Never be ashamed to call me friend.' He clasped my hand and then left me.

My last night with William and Elizabeth was an evening of quiet content- ment. Elizabeth had, to our great relief, at length agreed to my suggestion for easing her present and coming burdens. She asked many questions, and I felt that only the whole truth, as far as I knew it, would be worth telling to her, so I did. Anger and compassion vied within her as I told her Sarah Forbes's tale, and at the end of it it was all that William and I could do to prevent her from setting out there and then to put the matter to rights.

'Alexander will see to it all on Monday,' William assured her. 'All will be well; only have patience.'

I had much to prepare for the following day's journey, and was glad, for once, of an excuse to retire early. As I lay in my bed in William's house, my candle snuffed out and the shutters still open, I looked up at the northern stars, at the majesty of the works of God. They challenged me, as Matthew and Dr Forbes had challenged me, to leave off from my self-imposed indulgence of penitence and sloth, and to set forth once again with purpose on this earthly life. My last thought, before I was finally conquered by sleep, was that I was looking forward to the day to come.

TEN

Straloch

I left Aberdeen the next day in the early afternoon. The service in the West Kirk of St Nicholas had lasted from ten until noon, and I had shared a hasty meal of broth and bread with William and Elizabeth before taking my leave of them. When I rode out from Aberdeen that afternoon it was with a new determination to be whatever it might be given to me to be. The need to free Charles from his prison was as strong as it had been from the first, not just for his sake now, though, but for my own, for I felt that I had been chosen for the task. I felt no great sorrow at leaving Aberdeen, as I had feared only two days previously that I might, and no sense of dread at the prospect of making my way back to Banff. I had not failed myself, not shamed myself or my burgh since leaving, and I had come to understand, in my few days with old friends and new acquaintances, that it was not universally expected of me that I should hang my head in shame and achieve nothing.

As I crossed the Don at the Brig o' Balgownie, and left the two towns behind me once more, my hand went to the saddlebag and I checked the clasp once again, fearful that it might have been interfered with. My commission from Banff, the precious map, with its accompanying letter from the provost were still there, still sealed, but now they were accompanied by not one but two other, sealed documents, whose contents remained a tantalising secret to me. There was the letter, written before my eyes, by the artist George Jamesone to the provost of Banff, and there was another, by the same hand, which had arrived by a servant at William's door late last night, addressed to Robert Gordon of Straloch himself. Jamesone's servant had relayed that his master very kindly asked that I might deliver this letter into the laird of Straloch's own hand. As I had assured William, I had told the artist nothing of my business at Straloch, other than that I would bed there on my homeward journey. William was uneasy that I had said anything at all. I could scarcely refuse, but I did not like the commission.

Not only letters, but voices too, accompanied me as I left the two towns behind and took the road north-west. Voices of encouragement, voices of warning, voices of fear. As the horse, not yet wearying under its extra burden of newly bought books, trampled out the road and the spires and coastline of Aberdeen faded further into the distance until at last they disappeared, so too did the encouraging voices of Matthew Lumsden, Dr Dun and Dr Forbes recede. Their place was taken by the ever more insistent voice of caution of my friend William Cargill, and the determined terror of the departing Mary Dawson. 'Why you, Alexander? Why your schoolroom? Why you with this commission? Have a care, Alexander.' The horse's hooves beat out the rhythm of William's warnings and every so often they found a reply on the wind from Mary Dawson, 'I will never see Banff again.'

The sky was darkening as I approached Straloch in the late afternoon, and the storm broke just as I turned into the broad sweep of the drive. Thunder and lightning ripped from overhead and I forced the horse into a gallop for the last few hundred yards. Nevertheless, I was drenched, a poor specimen of a visitor, by the time we reached the courtyard at the front of the house. A servant answered my banging on the door and called for a stable boy to take my horse. He heard my hurried commission in the front hall and then, evidently deciding I might be who I said I was, allowed me into the body of the house. A young woman emerged into the light from the darkness of the east wing, watching for the visitor to arrive. She came forward, her flowing silk skirts rustling almost in time with the rain which poured down from the gutters outside. Her hair was dark, and she did not wear it up, but long and loose, brushed back from her face to show cheekbones that looked to be the work of some master sculptor and not formed by God. Her eyes were grey crystal. She was too young to be Straloch's wife, but a little too old, I thought, to be one of his daughters.

'It is a messenger from Banff,' said the servant, 'for the master. He says he has a letter from the provost.' The man's bearing implied that he was not entirely convinced that what I said was the truth, but the young woman seemed satisfied and dismissed him.

'I am sorry, sir,' she said. 'The laird is not in the house at this minute. He is still out, hunting. He should return within the hour, or sooner, if this storm does not pass. The mistress is resting, but will be up for dinner. Can I be of any help?'

I looked at her, unsure as to how to proceed. She had a bright and open manner, and her face spoke of intellect, yet the provost's dire warnings were ringing in my ears, and I knew I must wait on an answer from Straloch himself. 'I'm sorry, I am not ...'

She made a gesture of awkwardness. 'Oh, I am sorry. I have not said who I am. My name is Isabella Irvine; my aunt is the lady of this house.' She waited.

'I am Alexander Seaton,' I said. 'I have come to see the laird of Straloch on the business of the burgh of Banff. I am sorry, but I am under authority to place my commission only into the hands of Robert Gordon himself.' Although her feet had not taken a step, she looked as if her whole body had shrunk backwards, and not at my rebuttal of her offer of help, but at the mention of my name. She recovered herself quickly enough, but that she had been shaken, and that her manner towards me was now somewhat changed, was unmistakable.

She indicated a large, high-backed chair beside the fire. 'If you wish to wait until the laird returns, you may sit there. I will have some refreshment sent.' Then, with little more conversation or ceremony, she excused herself and departed up the stairs and out of my sight. I took the chair with gladness and, since it appeared no one would be around to see it, I removed my boots and let my feet dry by the fire. A servant brought ale and warm bannocks. As I took my rest and my refreshment I tried to think what might have occasioned the change in Isabella Irvine's manner towards me. Could it really be that the mention of my very name, bad as it was in Banff but surely not notorious here, was enough to put fear or contempt into young women in lairdly houses all over the north? I did not think so. And yet it was my name that had marked the change in her, as if borne in on a cold wind from the North. I pondered it, as the rain beating down outside contended with the roar of the fire within: I knew the name Isabella Irvine, but I could not think how or from where.

I had not too long for reflection, for within the quarter hour I could hear

a commotion of horses and riders out the front, and servants started busy-
ing themselves from one room to another, crossing the hall and back again
like busy ants. As the great oaken front door was opened, a whole troupe
of children – at least six or seven of varying sizes – rumbled down the
stairs from an upper gallery, followed by their cousin, Isabella. 'Children,
give your father a minute to get his breath. Boys! Come back in here this
minute.' Two of the smaller boys had rushed through the door as a weary
huntsman had come in it, and out into the courtyard, calling for their
father. They returned a moment later, utterly drenched, one in each arm of
Robert Gordon of Straloch. The others rushed at him with questions about
the hunt, and complaints about not being allowed out by their overzealous
jailer, their cousin Isabella. Three older boys and a girl followed their father
in from the hunt, the girl calling out orders behind her as to what was to be
taken to the kitchens, and what hung in the stores. There was arguing and
boasting about the size of the kill, and laughter about the escape of a wild
pig. Only the hounds noticed me, as they contended with each other for
proximity to the fire. It was once the initial excitement of the homecoming
died down and Straloch had been helped from his soaking hunting coat by a
servant, that Isabella Irvine announced me to her uncle. Her voice was low
and her eyes filled with a quiet anger; she watched me as she talked.

The laird of Straloch turned towards where I now stood, between his
dogs and with my back to his hearth. 'Mr Seaton? You are here on business
from Banff?'

'I am, sir. I have a letter from the provost, Walter Watt, which he bids
me wait for a reply to.'

He nodded and said briskly, 'Then let us see to it in my library. Robert,
give instructions to Hugh about the gutting, and see that the birds are hung.
Margaret, go with your cousin and see if she cannot turn you back into a
lady. I will hear over much about it from your mother if she cannot.' The
smaller children were also ushered away, and I followed the laird down
into his library in the west wing of the house. It was a long, high-ceilinged
room with large windows to the west, affording the best possible light.
William Cargill's small and tidy lawyer's study bore no comparison to this
workroom of the laird of Straloch. There were more books in this room
than I had seen in the room of any other individual, even of Dr Forbes.

From where I stood I could see books of every size, colour and description. Huge charts were spread out on tables near the windows, tables that were also piled high with books and sheaves of script. I had not much time for scanning the shelves, for the laird was a man with little time to waste.

'You have a letter for me, then, Mr Seaton.' I handed him first the letter from Walter Watt, without the map; Jamesone's missive would also keep. He broke the seal and took the letter over to the window, leaving me little chance of ascertaining its contents. I watched him as he read. He had been transformed from huntsman into learned scholar by little more than the changing of the room and the light. Poorly governed locks of hair receded from a high, intelligent, brow, and the fingers that held the letter were long and slim, fitted for the great cartographer that he was. His eyes were kind, tired almost. After he had read some way down the first page he glanced up at me. His mind too, like his niece's, had some knowledge of my name. He did not pause for long though, and continued to the end without any word. When he had finished reading, he folded the pages once again and walked to his desk, placing the letter in a small wooden case that he then locked. He looked at me directly. 'You know the contents of this letter?'

For a brief moment I considered pretending that I had no notion of what was in it, in the hope that Straloch might reveal something – what? – to me. But that was a dangerous game, and I had always come last or too late in games of strategy. 'I have an idea of its message, but I have not read it, nor has the provost given me any detailed account of what he has written.'

Straloch nodded. 'And the map?' I held it out to him, but he would not take it in his hand. Rainwater was running down his sleeves and every other part of his clothing, and he would not risk damage to the document. He asked instead that I should place it on his desk next to the cachet box. 'I take it you have no other business elsewhere tonight, Mr Seaton?'

I affirmed that I had none.

'Good, then you are free to spend tonight here? I am much interested in this business, and the assessment of a map cannot be made in a moment. Your provost makes clear his desire that the matter should not be noised abroad, and I fear we will have no privacy at the dinner table here, but if you will stay the night we can talk at more length of the matter, and I can examine the map. You can stay?'

I had not expected an instant answer from Straloch on the map or its import, and had made no arrangements to spend the night elsewhere. I was not entirely glad, though, at the prospect of facing down the cold dislike of Isabella Irvine throughout the meal. I accepted the offer of his hospitality with something of a heavy heart.

'My niece will have a room made up for you. My wife is still recovering from her latest childbed, and is not yet ready to take charge of the house again.' He smiled. 'As you will see, we have been many times blessed. I will have Isabella fetch you some dry boots, too, or you will die of a fever before the night is out, as will I if I do not go and change soon out of the rest of these sodden hunting rags.' Our interview presently over, he opened the door and called for his niece to be fetched. Within two minutes, the girl appeared and accepted her instructions without demur, although not without registering her distaste for the task in her ice-grey eyes.

I had scarcely had time to dry myself and change my clothing before a gong in the hall below beat out the call to assemble and eat. I followed the echoing noise and the stream of people spilling from the upper floors down the great stairway and on to the dining hall of Straloch. The room was brightly lit, with candles burning in every sconce, and in two chande-liers suspended from the ceiling. Family portraits lined the panelled walls, and vases and ornaments of the finest German porcelain decorated a side table. Heavy black velvet drapes, trimmed with gold brocade, were shut against the darkness of the night. The glassware must have been the work of the finest Venetian craftsmen. I had not seen such a room since I had last set foot in Delgatie. The long refectory table was seated for twenty, the younger children having already been fed by their nurses. Robert Gordon was seated at one end of the table and his wife, indeed tired and pale, yet with a welcoming smile, at the other. At least four of the older children were there, and a gaggle of cousins, friends and kin whom I could scarcely distinguish one from the other.

There was little conversation to begin with. The hunters were all too ravenous for talk and those who had stayed at home showed little enthusiasm for conversing without them. I was seated across from Isabella Irvine. She had exchanged her day dress for a gown of deep green velvet, the sleeves shot through with silk and the wrists and bosom trimmed with the most delicate white lace. At her throat was an emerald set in gold. I looked over at her several times, in a vain attempt to remember her, to find that passage of my mind through which she had already walked; she contrived to look at me not at all. As dishes were disposed of and more brought in, the hunger was gradually sated and conversations began to rise at the table. There was talk, inevitably, of the day's hunt, of the pursuits, the triumphs and the near misses, the prowess of the horses, the courage of the dogs and the cunning of the prey. The lady of the house could be assured that her larder was well-stocked. In time, conversation turned to talk of other hunts, in other places and then to those places themselves, and the families and peoples and history thereof. And soon, as often in such cases, there was talk of slights and offences, and scandals and outrages and foes. The laird, who had sat throughout at his meat with an air of benevolent contentment began to look less at his ease as his sons and their cousins began to speak hotly of slanders encountered and how they should be met. He knew too well how such things must end, of the fights and the fires and the deaths and the mournings. The ballads would be no comfort to their mother once they were gone, and he counselled them to speak no more of such things in front of her. There was a lull, a pause, before other things began to be spoken of; mention was made of dissatisfactions in the South and of rumours heard in the North, but again these were quickly silenced, this time with reference to me.

'Mr Seaton here can have no interest in these matters, I am sure; he is a man of learning, not politics. There will be politics aplenty in the town of Banff to satisfy him, no doubt, without we should force him to listen to our concerns.' The warning had been given, and it was the laird himself who had given it: I was not one of their own, and was not to be made privy to the affairs of the Gordons. As this registered, there was an alteration in the atmosphere round the table; I recognised it well as attention shifted now to me. Robert Gordon's wife, Catherine Irvine, came to my aid.

'You are a schoolmaster, Mr Seaton.'

'I am, madam. I am undermaster in the grammar school of Banff.'

'I have heard it is a good school.'

'I have many able pupils, and the master, Gilbert Grant, is a fine man of great learning and good discipline. He has affection and respect in the town as well as the schoolroom.'

'Respect in the young is a rare and precious commodity,' interjected Straloch. 'Without it there can be no good schooling, and without that the state is in peril.'

The younger men around the table had, I saw by their faces, heard this many times before, but had the good sense not to respond.

'And were you a scholar there yourself, Mr Seaton?' It was the lady this time.

I did not like this narrowing in on me. 'Yes, I had all my grammar schooling there, under Mr Grant.'

'Well, then,' said the lady, a sad but warm smile coming on to her face, 'you must surely have known Archibald Hay, the heir to Delgatie.'

'Who did not know Archie?' It was one of Straloch's nephews, discarding a chop and reaching for another one. 'There was never a fight nor a feast in the North that Archie Hay was not at the heart of. Do you remember that time at Rothiemay—'

But he was interrupted by his brother, who was looking at me now with narrowed eyes. 'But surely, are you not that fellow, the minister fellow who was always with him? Was that not you?'

I had not had the chance to answer before another joined in. 'Why, yes. Alexander Seaton! Always at Archie's side. Heavens! I remember that time at Slains when he lost his boots at a game of dice and you carried him on your back through the mud to his horse! That is why I thought I knew you; it was not from here at all.' The fellow was well pleased with the memory. Others joined in with their reminiscences of Archie, but I heard little of what was said. Nothing reached me through the wall of ice now risen between me and Isabella Irvine. She had avoided my gaze throughout the meal, but now she fixed me with cold, unflinching eyes. With a rising feeling of nausea, I began to remember how I knew her name. I would have got up from the table then, pleading illness, or fatigue, or God knows what other excuse, but there was to be no retreat for me.

'So you were the young fellow Delgatie had such hopes of, that you might calm his heir? Well, there are some colts that will not be broken: they are better left to run free. I am heart sorry for the loss of your friend, Mr Seaton. He died in a noble cause.' The laird's words were echoed round the table, and toasts were drunk to the memory of Archie, and to Queen

Elizabeth of Bohemia, and to her brother, our own king. The laird had carried on talking directly to me, about the family of Delgatie, and the tragedy of Archie's loss to the family and to the country, and then of Katharine. 'And why they sent that lassie away to the South, banished to that old man, I do not know. A brood of fine grandchildren near to hand would have eased their grief and their old age.'

'Robert,' his wife began, but he did not hear her.

'And as for the lassie herself, to send her so far from her own friends when a good marriage could have been made hereabouts, if they had only consented to the name of Hay going into abeyance for a generation or so. Why, Isabella here was – is – her friend, but is constrained to travel for days on end on bad roads just to see her. And it is a cold harsh place she is in, is it not, Isabella?'

'She does not complain,' said the young woman, still gazing steadily at me.

The laird's wife intervened before her husband could say any more. 'My niece is not long returned from visiting Katharine Hay in the borders. They had not seen each other since Katharine's marriage to her father's cousin.' She looked uncomfortable, as if she wished that could be an end to the subject, but I could not leave it there. I spoke directly to Isabella Irvine.

'And how is she. Is she – well?'

'She is well, sir.'

'And happy?'

'She is well. She does not complain. She knows her duty.' Now she stood up. 'Please excuse me, aunt. I would like to look in on the little ones before they go to sleep.' Her aunt nodded and she left without further word or look to me. Gordon looked perplexed, but his wife cut him short.

'You have an early start, Robert. Perhaps you and Mr Seaton should discuss your business before the hour is too late. You can leave the young ones here to their drinking and their storytelling; you will not be missed.' She called for a steward to show me back through to the laird's library, and to bring wine and fruit there for us also. She asked her husband to wait a moment as she had a matter touching the household to discuss with him. I was taken to the library alone.

The room that I had seen earlier in the fading light of day was transformed now into a cavern of flickering light and shadows. A fire roared in the great hearth and candles had been lit in the sconces, but none were yet set on the tables. A draught, a careless servant bumping into a table on which one was lit, could have destroyed in moments the work of a lifetime, for Straloch's notes and charts covered every table. I was too cautious now about the matter of maps even to wish to look at any of them. I went over to a recess by the fire, where the light now was best, and peered at the titles on the shelves as they glowed in and out of shadow with the light. The shelf my eye lingered on was filled with histories, histories of our country and our people. Spottiswood, Boece, Buchanan and Knox I knew well, but I eased another volume from the shelf: I had heard of Robert Johnston's work, but never come across it before. I untied the laces of the binding and opened the book; inside the cover, in a neat hand was an inscription, in Latin, 'To my dear friend Robert Gordon, in memory of happy Paris days in the springtime of our youth, Robert Johnston.' The book was still in my hand when the door handle turned and Straloch entered the room. I moved to put it back, but I had not tied the bindings and so was left with it, helpless, in my hands. Gordon came over and looked more closely at the volume.

'A fine choice, Mr Seaton. You may borrow it tonight if you wish, and return it to its place here before you leave tomorrow.'

I thanked him, but declined. 'The study of the past is something I have found little profit or comfort in.'

'Then you have been unfortunate. Those who do not know their history do not know themselves, and therefore act for the future, as it were, like a blinkered steed.'

I passed the book to him, and he retied the bindings before returning it, carefully, to the shelf. When he turned back to face me, I could see he was about to address a subject he did not much care for. He asked me to sit and then waited for the servant to finish lighting the room before proceeding. He cleared his throat. 'In the course of my time, in my work, and due, in some measure, to my position in this world, I am obliged to conduct myself with all manner of men. I believe, though perhaps not all do, that God has given it to me to do this without offence to my fellow man. You are a guest in my house, Mr Seaton, and yet I believe tonight that I have – albeit unwittingly – been a cause of discomfort to you and to others at my table.'

My heart pounded hard within me, and I felt my breathing grow deeper. I did not like the confidences of strangers, and what the essence of this was, I could guess. I wished myself anywhere else but this library.

'I am sorry; I do not know what you speak of. I have been,' I paused, thinking of Isabella Irvine – I was not going to claim some experience of warmth, 'I have been treated with civility and hospitality. I can ask no more in the house of a stranger.'

'And yet you should, in this house.' He pushed back his chair and went to the window, looking out into the darkness. 'My wife has told me, briefly, of your former closeness and your present estrangement from the family of Hay. She has told me what the enmity of the earl has cost you in the world. She has also told me – and I do not play with my words here – that the girl was sent from Delgatie to sever an attachment she had formed with you. This latter part she had from my niece, and I have no cause to doubt it, for she is an honest girl with no malice or thirst to slander. I suspect there has been much women's talk between the pair over this whole business, long before you ever set foot in this house. You must excuse my niece's coldness – and I did mark it at dinner – she has all the passionate notions of one who has not yet lived in the world. As for myself, I would never have talked on as I did had I known any of this.'

The warmth of the wine and the fire were working through me, and I felt a desire to meet the laird's honesty with an honesty of my own. 'The conversation gave me no discomfort that is not with me in any case. I do not like the study of history because it cannot be changed – my history cannot be changed. I do not look for your sympathy. The family of Hay deserved better at my hands.'

He shuttered the window and turned back towards me. 'Maybe so. But there must be a limit to retribution, or our society will never prosper; our godly commonwealth will wither and die before it ever bears fruit. The laird of Delgatie can be the warmest and most loyal of friends, but he is also a very dangerous enemy. I would counsel you to be careful of such an enemy, Mr Seaton.' There was nothing for me to say in response.

Straloch seemed pleased to have got that business – that women's business – over with. He strode over to his desk and poured us each a drink of wine. His manner was brisk now, no longer hesitant. 'Well, then, let us get down to the matter in hand. Your good provost writes that the map he has sent you with was found amongst the belongings of a visitor to your town, and that he would have my advice on its nature. He asks that I should speak to no one but yourself about this business.' He took a key from a chain in his pocket and unlocked the box I had seen him put the map next to that afternoon. I experienced some little relief to be fulfilling my commission at last, and sat back to wait.

The laird opened out the sheet and took an eye glass from his desk. He began at the top left corner and worked very slowly with the glass over the entire sheet. As he did so, I studied the arras hangings on the panelled wall behind him – a well-worked suite depicting the journey of the Egyptian Princess Scota, daughter of the Pharaoh, and progenitrix of our race, to our cold shores. The myth had been used three hundred years ago to argue the rights of our nation against the overlordship of an English king. What did Straloch think of those rights, now that the king in England was our own? I looked at my host; no word escaped him. At length he put the glass down, and sat heavily back into his chair. He looked up at me.

'Have you seen this work, Mr Seaton?'

I affirmed that I had.

'And what is your assessment of it?'

I had not expected this again, and had no intention this time either of making accusations against a man who was not able to answer for himself. My only course was to lie.

'I have no assessment of it – none of any significance. It is a map, it is of the coast near Banff, and it is a tidy and detailed bit of work.'

I did not meet Straloch's eye; I knew he did not believe me.

'Come now, Mr Seaton, you are a man of some intelligence. This document gives rise to no curiosity, no conjecture, in your mind?'

I met his gaze now. 'Only a fool would not be curious,' I said. 'I am as curious as our provost and the rest concerned in this business to know what this map signifies. As to conjecture, though, I have learnt that it is a habit best indulged in solitude.'

Straloch nodded. 'I believe you may well be right. If more of our country-men were of the same opinion, this would be a more peaceable land.' He laid the map on a table near the fire, and motioned for me to join him at it. 'But as to this map, we must deal in specifics, and I cannot believe that you have not formed any view as to why it might have been drawn. The authorities in Banff would never have sent it to me for examination had they no notion at all of what it might be used for. And you must be of their counsel, since you have been entrusted with the document itself, and with my reply – should I choose to make one.'

There might have been some hostility in the laird's tone; I could not tell, for I did not know him well enough. I could not blame him for it: if I would not be frank with him, why should he be so with me? What did I owe to the town of Banff, or to those who had sent me on this commission, that I should lie for them? Straloch returned to the map. 'I will tell you straightly. This is fine work, amongst the finest I have seen. Whose is it? Who is this mysterious visitor to the burgh who has such a thing in his possession?' The provost had warned me that I was not to answer the laird's questions, but I was a guest in the laird's house, and the provost was not here.

'It is the work of the provost's nephew, apprentice to Edward Arbuthnott, apothecary of Banff.'

Straloch set down the document. The expression on his face did not allow of further dissembling. 'Do you tell me that this map was drawn by the man lately found murdered in Banff?' He saw my awkwardness but waved it away. 'Do your minister and baillie really think such matters can be kept within the bounds of your burgh like a tethered cow? The whole country is alive with the news, and that the music master is in jail, suspected, all over the love of a woman. But what you bring me today is no lover's trick. I think you fear you have the wrong man in jail, and perhaps for the wrong crime.'

'I know that the wrong man is in jail. Charles Thom is no more capable of murder than I am, over a woman or anything else. And as to the crime – I speak for myself here, you understand, and not for those who sent me?'

He acquiesced.

'That there has been a crime is not in doubt; that there has been a murder, is not in doubt. The reason for the murder – that is in doubt. If once that can be established, the rest should follow. But in truth,' and here I knew I was departing completely from the commission given to me, 'I think those in whose place I have come – the provost, baillie, minister and notary public of Banff – have forgotten there ever was a murder, so aroused are their fears by the discovery of the document before you.'

Straloch looked up and spoke slowly. 'And are there others?'

'There are,' I said. 'In sequence they cover the entire coastline from Troup Head to Cullen, and inland towards Rothiemay and Strathbogie. There are pointers southwards for Turriff, Oldmeldrum, and Aberdeen.'

Straloch straightened and regarded me directly, no longer looking at the map. 'And so the authorities of Banff fear their burgh is to be the first staging post for an invasion force, and you have been sent to ask me whether the Marquis of Huntly intends to head the invasion in person.' A smile played upon his lips now, but his eyes were in deadly earnest.

'They fear a Catholic invasion. That much it would be pointless to deny, but they mean no insult to you or to your noble patron, the marquis. It is in virtue of your learning and expertise in the matter of cartography that you are consulted. We,' and now I revealed that I was of the inner counsel, 'thought it might be possible that Patrick Davidson was acting on commission – a legitimate scholarly commission, and we could think of no one other than yourself who might be in any way placed to know about such things.'

Straloch seemed to accept that there was some sense in this. But he knew also that I might well have worded it differently. I might have said, 'The authorities in Banff do not trust you, and they trust your master less, but we have no choice other than to seek your advice.' My host stood up and walked to a table on the other side of the room. It was covered in charts and sheaves of notes. 'What you see here is the fruit – the bud, more rightly – of many years' labour, my own and others. You have heard of Timothy Pont?'

I confessed that I had not. My ignorance seemed to surprise him, but he continued. 'Pont spent many years involved in the mapping of our country. On his death a few years ago, the task remained uncompleted. As you know, I have long had an interest in the subject, and it is an interest shared, I am glad to say, by my son James. Our researches go further than this work of your apothecary's apprentice – we have a great interest in genealogy, in our local history and antiquities, but our cartography is not as fine as this. This is the work of a strategist, as is evident from the detail he chooses to include. One might well suspect that an invading army could put a document such as this to much use. I am certain that no legitimate commission was issued for the doing of this work – I would have been sure to hear of it. You must believe that it is experience, and not vanity, that make me confident in this.'

'I would not have thought otherwise,' I said.

'I can assure you, in consequence, that I know of no project, other than that which I myself am engaged upon, to map this part of the country. I can also assure you, and you and your masters may believe this as you wish, that there is no plot that I know of for the invasion of our country from the coastline of the firth of Moray.'

I was embarrassed to be the receiver of such an assurance from a man so learned and so worthy of respect as Robert Gordon of Straloch. My discomfort was all the greater in knowing that he knew my own history, and that I had proven myself unworthy of trust and undeserving of respect. He should never have had to make such a declaration to me. I was conscious now not only of the grandness of the room, of the hundreds of books that lined the shelves, but of the portrait of Robert Gordon himself that hung over the fireplace – Jamesone's work, by the look of it – the smell of sandalwood, the painted mural on the far wall. This was a man of wealth, family and standing, and he had felt constrained to defend himself to me. I began to see now why I, rather than someone who mattered, had been sent here on the business of the burgh of Banff, and I did not like it. I assumed our interview was over and got up to leave, but he put out a hand to stay me. 'Tarry a while, Mr Seaton. The hour is not yet late and I will not keep you long. I would know more of this bad business in Banff, if you are willing to tell me.'

In my head I again I heard the provost's words of warning: 'our business here is none of his,' but again I reasoned that the provost was not here and I was, and, with William Cargill's admonitions still fresh in my mind, I was no longer sure that I trusted Walter Watt or any others in Banff who had sent me on this mission. 'There is little enough to tell – little that I can understand, at any rate. What is it you wish to know?'

Straloch indicated the map. 'Tell me about the murdered man. What was a man capable of such work as this doing apprenticed to an apothecary?'

So again, for the laird of Straloch's benefit, I rehearsed the tale of Patrick Davidson's childhood, his years of study at home and abroad, his return to Banff under the roof of Edward Arbuthnott and the talk of his relationship with Arbuthnott's daughter. The laird interjected once or twice in the course of the tale with 'a good college', 'a wonderful city', 'a wise choice', but said little more until I got to the end of it. Laughter and music were reaching us from the dining hall; it was at once comforting and yet incongruous as an accompaniment to our conversation. When I was finished the laird got up and raked at the fire.

'It does not make sense, Mr Seaton. No, it does not make sense.' He leant against the mantel in thought and then turned around to look at me. 'Why did he come back to Banff? Why? When his love of botany had been strong enough to steer him away from the study of the law, and even medicine?'

'He came to study the apothecary's craft,' I said, unsure what it was about this that so bothered the laird. It was plain enough to me that Patrick Davidson had returned to the town of his childhood because his connections of influence – his uncle – were able to secure him a place to train with a good master. But this did not satisfy Straloch.

'No,' he said. 'When one has a passion such as this – or a calling even, it overrides all other considerations. If advancement in the study of botany and the usage of plants was his guiding desire, he would not have come to Banff. He would have stayed on the continent of Europe, war or no, where he would have learnt much. What is there in the flora of our corner of Scotland that could engage the heart and the mind of one who already knew it from childhood? Nothing, I would wager, to what the Alps, the Pyrenees, the warm lands to the South have to offer, to say nothing of the exotic riches of the East or the undisturbed forests and swamps of the New World. No, one with a true passion for the understanding of plants would not cast all aside in order to play out his youth in the town of Banff.'

I conceded that there was some sense in what the laird reasoned, but it seemed to me that he deliberately did not mention the maps; that he was drawing me to his point instead. I held the document up. 'You think he came to do this?' I asked.

His voice was low and he spoke slowly, not looking at me. 'I think he may have done,' he said, 'and that if he did, he was killed for it.' His words hung in the air a moment, and then he changed his tack. 'But tell me also, Mr Seaton; where was the body found?'

I swallowed and looked at him directly. 'The body was found in my schoolroom, sprawled across my desk.'

He nodded, and seemed satisfied. It was as I had thought: I had been asked the question as a test of my honesty and trustworthiness. Robert Gordon had known exactly where the body of Patrick Davidson had been found. I wondered what else he knew. The singing and laughter from the dining hall was becoming louder. A voice called out 'Gray Steel' and the sounds of clapping and the stamping of feet was followed by the dragging noise of furniture being cleared from the floor for dancing. Straloch crossed the room and shut tight the door, which until then had been left a little ajar. 'How did he come to be there?'

I swallowed. 'He was brought there.'

He was watching me closely now. 'By whom?'

I had no reason that I knew to distrust the laird of Straloch, but neither was I content to tell him all I knew. 'For their own protection, I cannot tell you.'

'The killer?'

I shook my head. 'No, I am certain of that. Those who found him saw the state he was in and sought to help him. They had seen me entering the schoolhouse shortly before, and thought I would not yet have been abed, or at least asleep. They left him there. I knew nothing of it till morning. He was dead then.'

'Why did they not call for you?'

'They did not wish to be discovered themselves.' I had given away too much already. Mary Dawson was out of the country, and safe now, but her sister Janet might not yet have gained a sanctuary. The laird, sensing my reluctance, did not press me further. He changed his line of questioning a little.

'They tell me he was murdered on the night of the great storm. We were battered here for many hours, and lost some trees in the park there. On such a night there cannot have been many abroad. These Samaritans of yours, they saw no one else?'

Since he would not leave it I would lie. 'No.'

'And there is nothing, in your past or his, nothing in these maps, that links you in some way to Patrick Davidson or his fate?'

The sensation of fear began to creep through me, and I could feel a coldness under my skin. 'I know of nothing.'

Straloch was grave. 'But he was laid in your schoolroom to die. And yet it is your friend, the music schoolmaster, who lies in the tolbooth of Banff, while you walk free.' He looked at me in silence for a moment before proceeding. 'I fear there is some great game of evil afoot in Banff, a game that will not end at the one death. You must take great care, Mr Seaton, great care.' We had neither of us finished our wine. I sat and sipped the warm red liquid while the laird's words resonated in my head.

I drained my cup and stood up. 'I must go to my bed now, I think.'

Straloch came towards me and offered me his hand. 'I myself have an early start. I ride out tomorrow at seven. I am bound for Edinburgh. I doubt if we will meet again before I leave. As you can see, I am much surrounded by young men and in their company often, but it is not so often that I find one whose conversation is of interest to me. I hope we may meet again some day.' We shook hands and I gave him the letter from Jamesone that I had almost forgotten, and made for the door. I had my hand on the handle when he suddenly called me. 'The map!' How quickly it had been forgotten in the talk of its maker's murder. 'I will write a line for you to take back to the provost tomorrow. I can be of little help to allay his fears. It is the finest piece of cartography I have seen, and would serve any army well, if the others you spoke of are of anything like the quality. But I tell you again, I know of no intended invasion, and if there be any, the hand of the Marquis of Huntly is not in it.'

I believed him; whether or not Baillie Buchan, the Reverend Guild and the rest would was another question. Assuring the laird I could find my way myself to my bedchamber, I took the candle he offered me and made my way back along through the west wing to the great central stairway. The sound of a raucous ballad and much laughter filled the whole ground floor of the house. How many times I had been party to such evenings, such gatherings of friends and kin, the storytelling, the music, the catches and rounds, that went on into the small hours of the night. I longed to go in, just to listen, to be one of them again, for a moment. The ballad came to an end as I stood at the foot of the stairs. And then, when the laughter and cheering had died down, a woman's voice, clear and alone, rose in a lament. All around was silence. Isabella Irvine. I ascended the stairs.

I had reached my small chamber at the very top of the house before I remembered the boots that a servant had taken in the afternoon to dry for me. Wearily I turned and began to make my way down again. I used my knowledge of such houses to guess where the kitchens might be. I turned to the right at the foot of the stairs and knew that something had gone wrong. I looked around the great entrance hall of the house and saw nothing or no one to give cause for alarm, and yet something was not as it should be. I stood still and listened. I heard nothing. And that was it: where before there had been music, and voices singing, and laughter, now no sound came from the dining hall. Yet, I had heard no one come up the stairs after me. I followed the corridor past the dining hall towards the kitchens, and was met by the steward coming the other way. He was carrying my clothing and riding boots. I thanked him and took them from him. As I did so, a bell was rung in the dining hall and he hastened to answer it. As he stood in the open doorway I could see beyond him into the room. Straloch stood with his back to the fireplace, talking in a low but authoritative voice to his older sons and two or three of the young men who had been at table earlier. Of the women I saw nothing. The steward closed the door behind him, and in the darkening silence of the house I climbed the stairway once again and made for my bed.

Sleep was not long in coming, but it was not sound. At the top of the house though I was, I was conscious of much movement and low voices on the floors beneath me. Once, someone with a candle paused outside my door. The flicker of light seeped beneath the doorway for a moment and then withdrew. The footsteps were light and soon I could not hear them at all. And then somewhere, deep into the long night, I was brought to full wakefulness by the sounds of horses gathering in the yard below. Conscious of the patrol that had earlier passed my door, I crept from my bed and peered through a gap in the window shutters. Gradually, I prised them further open. In the light of a full moon I could see, far below me, five men on horseback: the young men to whom Straloch had been talking in the dining hall. He was not there now, but I could see Isabella Irvine,

175

her night-clothes a startling, ghost-like white in the moonlight, bidding her cousins and their kinsmen farewell. Quietly, they set off away from the house, only picking up speed once they were far enough away not to disturb those in the sleeping house. Isabella watched after them until they disappeared from sight, before turning back to the house. As she did so she looked up, directly, at my window. I could not tell whether she saw me or not. I returned to my bed, the window shutters still open, and watched the night sky until the first shafts of sunlight appeared from the east.

The laird had also departed by the time I appeared in the dining hall for my breakfast. The room was a noisy babble of the younger children of the house and their nurses. Bowls of porridge with warmed milk and scones spread with sweet confits were played with, spilt, dropped for the hounds or left, all to the indignation of the nurses. I took a good meal, as I had no plan to tarry long at any of my staging posts on the road home. Just after the chapel clock struck eight, I rose from the table and returned to my room to gather my few belongings. As I descended the stairs, relief that I would soon be leaving the strange house of night-time partings turned to apprehension: Isabella Irvine stood at the bottom, watching and clearly waiting for me. I held her gaze until, at the last step, she looked away.

'Good morning,' I said.

She did not respond to the civility and for a moment seemed at a loss for how to proceed at all. In the end she held out a small package and a sealed letter. 'My uncle asked that I should give you these. The letter is to be delivered to your provost; the packet is for yourself.' I took them from her and thanked her. She merely nodded briskly and turned to walk away.

'Wait,' I said, touching her arm with my hand. She looked down upon it as if it were an object infected. I let it drop. 'Please spare me a moment.'

She faced me impassively, waiting.

'Katharine Hay,' I began.

She sighed impatiently and made to turn again.

'No, please,' I persisted. 'I only wish to know how she really fares, how life is for her ... so far from home.'

Her eyes blazed at me. 'How do you think it is for her?' she asked. 'He is a man of near sixty. You had as well drawn your sword and ended her misery.'

My stomach lurched. In the early days and weeks after she had gone south, my imagination had filled with images of Katharine and her husband, images that I had fought, through drink, into some sort of oblivion, and now, here they were, being thrown in my face. And how could I tell this girl that there was nothing she could say to me, no words of condemnation, that I had not already said to myself? What could I say to make her understand that whatever the depths of her revulsion, I knew they were not deep enough? I swallowed hard. The words I wished for would not come: there was little point in continuing this interview. I turned away from Isabella Irvine and walked towards the door. Perhaps, though, I could somehow reach to Katharine all the same; perhaps this was one last chance I had not expected. At the entrance portal I turned to face her again. 'One thing more.'

Her head tilted upwards a little and her nostrils widened. 'Yes?'

'The next time you should see Katharine, will you tell her that I was wrong, and I am sorry; Alexander Seaton is sorry.'

She regarded me coldly. 'I will not. You made your choice, Mr Seaton, and you must live by it, as does she.' She bade me no farewell and was gone, vanished into the darkness of the east wing.

A light drizzle fell as I rode from Straloch. It was a house of much life, much happiness, but over which my very presence seemed to have cast a dank and dismal shadow. I might have been happy there, once, in former days, but I could not be now. I was not long in reaching the inn at New Machar, and was grateful to see there the familiar and welcoming face of William Cargill's old manservant, Duncan, who was to travel with me as far as King Edward, to fetch Sarah Forbes. He must have left Aberdeen before dawn. He assured me he had breakfasted at the inn, and was as eager as myself to get on. In no time he had fetched from the stableyard the sturdy pony and cart William had sent him with and we were on our way.

Duncan made little conversation and that suited me well. His only comment was that he had not been out on this road since he had gone to Banff with the master to fetch back his bride, and that that had turned out well enough. The pony's pace was steady but slow, and it was into the afternoon before we stopped at Fyvie to rest the beasts and take some refreshment. Elizabeth had packed two baskets – one for us, the other for Sarah. There were chicken legs and eggs and cheese and wheaten scones spread with marmalade, and flasks of good ale. Duncan, a fine Presbyterian, muttered at the excess, and at the numbers of the hungry such a feast would feed. I helped myself to two chicken legs and eyed the third enviously, wondering what poor soul met on the road would have that to his supper on the old fellow's return journey. He watched accusingly as I put a second slice of apple pie to my mouth. I pretended not to notice.

We finally reached King Edward as the late afternoon light began to lose its warmth and turn a colder grey, portending dusk. Duncan had instructions from his master to take lodgings in Turriff before dark if it could be done, and not to think of attempting to finish the journey back to Aberdeen by night. Rarely can a warning have been less needful: the old man would never have been so foolish. We went first to the manse, where to my relief I found that the minister was at home. His wife offered us food, of course, but Duncan, thanking the mistress profusely, said we had dined to our fill, and that a drink of water for ourselves and the pony was all that was needed. I had changed my horse at Turriff, and was now once again on Gilbert Grant's mount. Duncan warmed himself in a seat by the fire while I was shown through to the minister's spartan study.

Hamish MacLennan was tall and spare and learned-looking. As we entered at his call, he was standing at the window with a small book in his hands. I recognised it, for it was an identical edition to that I and all teachers used with our children: Craig's *Shorter Catechism*. His wife announced me and nodding in my direction, he invited me to sit down.

'I am sorry to have interrupted you in your work,' I said.

'I am always at my work. Here in my study, out in the parish, in the kirk, in my every solitude. My life is in my calling.'

I did not know how to respond and he saw my discomfort.

'I meant no criticism of yourself, Mr Seaton. It is the Lord who judges all.' He paused for a moment in contemplation of this thought, and I wondered how it was that the town of Banff had to endure the self-serving mediocrity that was the Reverend Guild while this poor country parish was so blessed in its minister. MacLennan might almost have forgotten I was there, but his wife, who had not yet left, called me back to his attention.

'Hamish, Mr Seaton has a favour he would ask of you. For myself, I hope that you might feel able to grant it him.' Thus having said, she left us to our business.

MacLennan smiled now, and there was warmth in his austere face. 'I am intrigued,' he said. 'My wife is not a woman who asks for favours, for herself or even others. Please tell me what it is you want.'

And so I told him of Sarah Forbes. He listened without interruption, once or twice nodding as I spoke. Occasionally, he would look up sharply, and I knew on what points I would be questioned when I had finished. When I had indeed finished, he got up and stood in front of the empty fireplace. The evening was now drawing on and the room was cold, but I had met many men of such frugal habits and self-denial, and it did not surprise me that Hamish MacLennan was one of them. Now he drew a deep breath and began slowly. 'I think, in all, what you propose is a good thing, and I will do what is in my power to have it effected, but there are one or two things I would know first.'

And so he asked me all the questions I had known he would ask. He asked first of all, although he asserted he already believed he knew what the answer was, whether I was the father of Sarah Forbes's baby. I told him I was not, and he lingered no longer on that matter. He asked next about the character of William Cargill, and of his wife, and of the soundness of their marriage and the nature of his household. I told him of William's respect-ability, of his kindness, his reliability, his firmness of purpose and his fine mind. I told him of Elizabeth's joyfulness, her loyalty and her zeal for hard work, and of the fondness she had evoked in his own good sister-in-law and in her husband, Gilbert Grant. I asked that Duncan might be called in, to give testimony as to the nature of his master's household. It was allowed, and I watched in wonder as these two godly men, one of great learning and the other of little, conversed without dissemblance on the topic, and with mutual respect. The minister shook the servant's hand and asked God's blessing on him before dismissing him. He read again the letter from William that I had brought him.

'And they will let her take the child, too. They are indeed good people, I think, and it will go better for the child that way, much better. Sarah is strong, and God willing, if she can be got away from under her uncle's roof, she and her child will remain so. She will manage the two bairns well enough.' He folded the letter. 'It was a blessing on her, the day you met her on your way to visit your friend.'

'And on me also,' I said.

'How so?'

'Because I do not remember the last time I was called to be an instrument of good and answered that call.'

He looked at me for a long moment. 'We are all sinners, but the Lord gives it to us to do good. Like Jonah, we often flee from His presence before we will submit to answering His call, and yet the Lord does not turn His face from us for ever.' He smoothed the front cover of the small book of catechism, still in his hand. 'What is taught to the bairns would be well remembered by us all.'

In little more than ten minutes, Hamish MacLennan, minister of King Edward in the Presbytery of Turriff, had written a testimonial of Sarah Forbes to the kirk session of St Nicholas in Aberdeen. He testified that she claimed her present condition to be the result of a vicious and scandalous assault at the hands of her former master in Banff, and that he, Hamish MacLennan, firmly believed this to be the truth of the matter. He asserted that she had fulfilled the penance and punishment laid upon her by the kirk session of Banff, and he enclosed with his own the letter from the kirk session of Banff to that effect. He petitioned that the session of St Nicholas and magistrates of Aberdeen might raise no objection to the employment of Sarah Forbes by Mr William Cargill, lawyer in Aberdeen, as a servant in his home.

He did not seal the letter but took it open in his hand and bade me, Duncan and his wife accompany him to the croft of Sarah Forbes's uncle. The minister's wife refused a ride on the cart that Duncan brought now ready for the journey away from King Edward, and strode purposefully at her husband's side. It was not long before worn footpaths gave way to rough ground, and eventually, a miserable effort at cultivation. We reached the mean dwelling at the outer edge of the parish which, I quickly understood, was all the home Sarah Forbes knew.

A dirty face, a woman's, looked out at what passed for a window at the approaching party and hastily withdrew, pulling fast the flimsy wooden shutter. A man, small and gaunt with roving, distrustful eyes, appeared in the doorway. He offered no greeting but waited, shifting uneasily until the minister was within ten feet of the house.

'I have done nothing, Mr MacLennan, whatever William West will tell you. I was too ill to be at the kirk yesterday in time of sermon. I could scarce stand.'

'Nothing? Your drunken roar and brawling were heard at the manse itself on the eve of the Sabbath. But that is a matter for the session; I am here concerning your wife's niece.'

The man yelled for the aunt, uttering harsh words about the girl. The minister's wife favoured him with a look of scathing contempt then turned, more gently, to the woman who had now appeared at the door. 'Where is your niece, Anna?'

The woman came forward, past her husband, pleading. 'She is not a bad girl, Mistress Youngson. Please, she has not gone beyond our toft in four days. She feared to go to the kirk yesterday for the shame ...' But the woman was interrupted as Sarah Forbes emerged behind her. To my confusion, I felt my heart beat faster at the sight of her. Her face had grown paler in the last few days, and there were circles of darkness beneath her eyes, but there was something in those eyes still that spoke to me. She appeared somewhat startled at seeing me, but recovered herself well enough and addressed herself to the minister. 'I am here, Mr MacLennan. Please tell me your business.'

And he did. He told her of William Cargill and his wife Elizabeth, of their need for a servant and their coming need for a nurse. She listened to all and then looked enquiringly at me.

'William Cargill is my friend,' I said. 'I have known him many years. He is a good and kind man. His wife was kitchen maid in the schoolhouse of Banff. She will be a good mistress.' I turned to Duncan at this point and he nodded his assent. 'And they will take the child in also. It will be a good home for you both. Will you go?'

'I will,' she said.

It did not take five minutes for Sarah Forbes to gather her belongings – the same bundle she had carried from Banff, only the precious shawl now added to it. Her aunt gave her hand a squeeze as she passed through that doorway for the last time, and Sarah bent a little to kiss the cheek of her dead mother's sister. While Duncan steadied the pony, I helped Sarah Forbes up onto the cart. William's servant looked at me suspiciously, but said nothing. Some mischief must have been in me, for just before I mounted my own horse, I whispered in his ear, 'The bairn is not mine, you know.'

He continued to busy himself about the bridle. 'Aye, well, it could have done worse, I dare say.'

Before she turned towards the road that would take her away from here for good, Sarah Forbes looked at me and her lips opened to mouth a silent 'Thank you.' The word echoed through the breeze and carried me the six miles home, to Banff.

I could feel the nearness of the sea long before I saw it, but there was something else in the air of the falling dusk too. There was fear. As I headed the brae at Doune Hill and started to descend down by the Gellymill, I saw a thick pall of smoke rising from the heart of Banff itself. I could hear nothing, nothing but the sound of God's retiring creation around me, but the wind was changing, and soon it would bring the smell of that smoke into my very nostrils.

I was in luck that the ferry had not yet put up for the night and I would not have to spend it in the ferryman's mean hut on the east bank of the Deveron. It was one of Paul Black's sons who had the watch that night. I hailed him across the river and he came slowly to his feet and stood looking at me for a while before going to untie the boat. Even at this distance across the river mouth I fancied I sensed some reluctance in him to come across for me. When he finally came to the shore on the other side he did not look at me.

'It is Martin, is it not?'

'Aye, Mr Seaton,' he replied in a low voice, still avoiding my eye.

'What is the matter? What is happening in the town tonight?'

He made no reply.

'Martin, come, you know me. Whatever they say, you need have no fear of me.'

Now he looked at me. 'It is not you, Mr Seaton it is ... the town. Everything has gone wrong in the town. I think,' he hesitated before continuing, 'I think we have been damned.'

'What has happened?'

His eyes glazed over and he seemed to look past me, at nothing. 'Marion Arbuthnott is dead, by her own hand. Her body lies at Dr Jaffray's.'

I spent some effort in persuading him to ferry me back to the other side. The coining I handed him once the beast and I had disembarked fell from his hand to the ground, but I could not tarry any longer over Martin Black. I mounted Gilbert Grant's poor horse and sped him into a gallop, books and all, towards the town. Within minutes I was at Jaffray's door. Tying the beast hastily in the stableyard I hammered on the back door, but to no avail. I ran round to the front, but was not answered there either. I pushed the door open – it was not on the bolt – and went, calling out for the doctor, to his surgical room. Ishbel came stumbling to meet me, her face streaked with tears. I pushed past her into the room. All was in disarray. Glass bottles smashed on the floor, a chair turned over and broken, instruments strewn across the work table and desk and onto the floor, and a bloodied winding sheet trailing from the table on which I knew he laid the dead. The stable boy was trying to make some order in the chaos. In the midst of it all sat the doctor, his clothing torn, an angry gash on his cheek. He stared blankly ahead of him.

My voice was hoarse. 'Jaffray. What in the name of God has happened here?'

He shook his head and slowly looked up at me. 'Hell has been here, Alexander. Hell has been here tonight. They have taken her, taken her poor dead body from this room, from that table, and burnt her for a witch.' His head sank forward. Tears of utter despair rolled down his cheeks.

ELEVEN

Concerning Witches

The ashes still blew about the early morning marketplace. All was quiet. The images and sounds that had haunted me through the night were gone now, altogether gone. Alone, at the bottom of the sodden, lifeless pyre, crouched Edward Arbuthnott. He had no cloak or hat about him, and the wind blew through his clothing without remorse. He held his head in black-streaked hands and the tears still flowed down his cheeks. I walked over to him, conscious of the sound of my footfalls amongst the pools and ashes.

'Come, Edward, she is not here. She was never here.'

The apothecary glanced up at me and slowly shook his head as if I did not understand. 'They took her; they burnt her. My own girl, my princess. They burnt her here. Black.'

I took off my cloak and wrapped it around him. 'She was gone, her soul long gone before they took her from Jaffray's. She will be buried decently in the kirkyard. They will not triumph over her.'

'In truth?'

'In truth,' I said.

'And I can take her flowers there.' He did not resist as I eased him to his feet. He shuffled uncomplainingly forward, like an old woman with no more interest in this world. I would not take him home yet: the hysterics of his wife would be no comfort, do no good to him, and the sight of him in such a condition might well finish her.

Where were the people, all the people who, on any other weekday morning would have been here? There was not a soul to be seen but myself and my broken companion, and where there was usually bustle and human warmth there was now just silence and desolation. I glanced up at the town clock as I guided Arbuthnott away from the market cross and towards the schoolhouse and Mistress Youngson's welcoming kitchen. The provost

184

could wait on our meeting, on the letters in my bag another hour or two; I doubted whether he had yet had leisure to remember me or my business in these last days. Certainly, the man I had seen last night rise above the fury of the flames would have little thought of maps or painters.

I had heard the baying of the crowd long before I had seen it. As I ran from Jaffray's door towards the marketplace, I had felt not that I was getting closer to the mob but it to me. The smell first and then the heat of it wrapped around my throat and stung my eyes as the relentless clamour for the flesh of its victim grew louder in my ears. And when I turned the corner to face the market cross the sight before me froze me where I stood. It was a vision of Hell that John Knox himself could not have conjured. The people of Banff had become one heaving mass of thick, blackened clothes, red-glowing faces, some alive with spittle and foaming at the mouth in their excitement, eyes gleaming and glinting with a desire that was not of God's sending. The mass, consumed with its own success, pressed in on itself as the eagerness for its prey rose. There was a chanting, a rising chanting, and beyond it shrieking and screaming, worse than the gulls. Through it all there pierced an inhuman wailing, issuing from the throat of Marion Arbuthnott's father. Gilbert Grant and some other decent men held him back from cleaving to his child as she burned. And she did burn. High, high above the heads of the crowd that fed upon her, her body, naked, the skin of the girl who had been so white as to be almost a ghost in life, burned to a dark and broken black, a gnarled, dry, unspeakable black, the hair on her singeing and crackling and curling and melting, the dead mouth open in a silent scream.

Disgust and horror overwhelmed me. My first instinct was to run from it, but I could not move. My feet were rooted to the ground and I could do nothing but stare, transfixed, at the terror. An arm grabbed mine and shook me from the stupor of revulsion. 'Alexander! Thank God you are returned safe. Come, man, we must end this.' Thomas Stewart, the town notary, was dragging me with him around the side of the crowd to the steps of the tolbooth. It was then that I saw Walter Watt. He was there, shouting instructions to the town serjeants and to the laird of Banff's men who had been put at his disposal. Some other burgesses I saw too there, who had not succumbed to the clamour of the witch-mongers. Of the baillie there was no sign. The town serjeant was throwing out pistols to the men of the watch as the laird's men drew their own. I, and some others, were handed swords and clubs. Thomas Stewart shouted to us that we were to circle round the crowd, no further one from the other than the length of a man's arm with outstretched sword. It was hard to hear over the noise of the fire at its sickening work and the rising hysteria of the mob, yet within a short while, the ring was in place. And then a shot rang through the air. Walter Watt stood atop the scaffold cart, the moon now at its fullest clear behind him, the smoke from his pistol rising into the yellow darkness of the night. His eyes shone through the flames and his voice was clear above the clamour. 'Get back, you curs, you filthy rabble. What court is this? I have your names, every one. You will never work another day, nor sleep another night in this burgh if you do not leave off this Devil's work!' He swung his arm, his pistol arm, towards the tolbooth. 'You will all sweat there before this night is through.'

'This is God's work, it is God's work!' screamed James Cardno. I had not noticed the session clerk until now, but he too was on a platform, at the right hand of the minister, the Reverend Robert Guild. The clerk's face was alive with the certainty of his moment; all the days he had waited, watched, taken orders, been humiliated, they had all led to this. The fervour of his certainty lent a gleam to his eyes only glimpsed at before.

The provost laughed. 'God's work? You're the Devil's whore, Cardno. Get down off there before I have you shot.' The laughter was real, and it was the laughter of derision.

The session clerk stumbled slightly as if the blow had been real. When he righted himself there was a trace of desperation on his countenance and panic in his voice. 'God is not mocked! Provost or no, you will burn for your blasphemy! She was a witch! Satan has walked and danced these streets. It will be found out! It will be hidden no more!'

Some members of the crowd had given off their own demented medley to follow the exchange between provost and session clerk, and some now took up their cries again, encouraged by Cardno's maniacal defiance. Others, though, kept a watchful silence, or started to mumble amongst themselves. I watched the minister, and others in the crowd had turned to look at him too. He had stepped back, once, and then again from Cardno, but he could step no further, for he had reached his platform's edge. He had no option but to face the crowd, and his brother-in-law. The provost now addressed him directly.

'What say you, minister? It is time to stop this madness. There are whores yet in the town who would satisfy your lusts – you and all your like – without this barbarity. Remember you were once a man of God.'

This was almost too much for the Reverend Guild, but Cardno took it as mother's milk, waiting for his master to respond in kind. Robert Guild, however, was not the man to answer such a moment. Sweat rolled from his forehead down his fleshy cheeks. His chest heaved with indignation and fury and impotence. Cardno, though, would not allow it. 'Tell him, minister, tell him what you know: of the sabbaths, the girl Arbuthnott and the provost's own nephew at the Elf Kirk, of their nakedness, their calling on the dead! Your own nephew, provost! Tell him.'

The crowd had fallen silent now. No voice was raised, and all that could be heard was the relentless burn and crackle of the fire and the corpse at its heart, with the quiet sobbing of Edward Arbuthnott. Eyes moved from the minister to the provost. Walter Watt's face was contorted in disgust. 'So this is what you have peddled, this filth. You ... you sorry excuse for a man. That I have put up with you for my wife's sake all these years. You and your perversions. And you lead these poor idiots with you. All to garner yourself a name.'

The minister was shaking his head. 'No, it is true. It is all true. There are witches abroad in this town. We none of us know which of our neighbours has lain with the Devil, has ridden the besom at his side. This town will pay, we will all pay dear, for this turning from godliness. The storm was the first sign. Beggars and famine and pestilence will be our lot. And invaders,' he said quietly, but with a sly glance at the provost. 'The witches must burn!'

I could see, through the thick smoke and above the heads of the towns-people, that the minister had little faith in the words that fell in desperation from his mouth. The provost had at last openly condemned and abandoned him, and there was no retreat so he had to go forward, although he had neither the wit nor the stomach for it. For James Cardno, though, it was enough. He took up the minister's words and fed them to the crowd, his voice rising higher and higher until at last it was a screech. 'They have danced with the Devil; they have ridden the besom. Find out the witches; the witches must burn.'

The blood within me turned cold. There was one girl, one body, lashed to the stake and aflame, but Guild and Cardno spoke of witches. They concerned themselves now not with the dead, but with the living. For the witch whose lifeless body burned before them, there were others, living, breathing, in this town, standing beside them, perhaps. Fearful looks moved from neighbour to neighbour. Each man and woman avoided the eye of any other, for to be caught would be to make oneself vulnerable. Vulnerable to the cry of 'witch!' Better to cry out than to be the one so called. I kept my own eyes straight ahead of me and stood my ground. Cardno carried some more with him now – not all, but some. There were those who took up the chant once more, and it was more menacing in its deliberateness than all the chaotic screeching of before. I feared that the provost might yet lose this battle. The chant was rising and several in the crowd were becoming more nervous. I looked to Thomas Stewart, the notary, but he was watching Walter Watt. Watt himself, however, was not looking at the crowd any more. He had turned his back three-quarters on them and was staring up the road behind him, the steep slope of Strait Path. I followed the line of his gaze, as had Thomas Stewart and saw, approaching rapidly on thunderous hooves, a party of unknown riders, at their head Baillie Buchan.

As they approached, all but the baillie's horse whinnying in panic at the flames, I began to discern that every one of the front riders was clothed from head to toe in deepest black. This meant only one thing to me, and as they drew closer and their faces were caught in the light of moon and fire, I saw that I was right. The brethren who had witnessed and countersigned my own fall were coming in force to attend the culmination of the witch-hunt of Banff, and there rallying them was Baillie William Buchan. They came charging, yelling, shouting, and I feared their horses' hooves would not stop until they had trampled us all underfoot. It was a wonder the beasts' necks did not break. And yet they did stop, and out of the snorting of exhausted beasts, their hearts near bursting, and the settling of hooves on the cobbles grew an expectant silence. It can scarcely have been a matter of seconds, but to me it seemed several long minutes. I waited, as the baillie drew in breath, to hear our doom.

'Provost, the moderator is here and most of the brethren, as at your command.' And he slid from his horse, utterly spent.

There was some confusion before I and others understood that the brethren had come not to stoke the flames but to put an end to them. In the momentary commotion the provost ordered that the baillie be carried to Jaffray's, and then the Moderator of the Presbytery of Fordyce heaved himself up on the scaffold cart beside him. The moderator, a gentle and fair man as I had known him, opened his mouth to speak and his voice was a roar.

'Douse these flames! Put out that fire, or you will all burn longer and blacker than any witch that ever rode the besom. In the name of the Kirk of Scotland, cut down that girl.' There was a great deal of movement at all sides of the crowd and I saw now that bucket upon bucket of water had been gathered ready from the nearby wells, and that a chain of men was in place from the laird of Banff's garden to as near to the market cross as they could get. The provost now ordered the way to be cleared and I, like the others in the circle, began to force pathways in the crowd for the water-bearers. As the first sloshes of water fizzled onto the pyre the moderator took up his roar again. 'And you, Robert Guild, by whose authority do you sanction this heathen orgy? In whose name, on whose behalf do you act? Slavering wretch! Get down off that podium. You will never preach in this or any other parish of the presbytery again.' Robert Guild opened his mouth to protest, but what he said I did not hear as he was dragged from his platform and onto the dirt below, without ceremony, by two of the provost's men. Cardno too was taken and he was hauled to the tolbooth, still noising out his demented accusations.

Others were brought under arms also to the town jail, ringleaders or those thought to still have trouble in mind. In time the tolbooth was full to overflowing, and the dungeon of the castle was also brought into play. There would be much work for the session, the burgh court and then the sheriff when he returned to town in five days' time, or sooner, surely.

I do not know how long it took to douse and dull the flames, or when they cut what was left of the broken body of Marion Arbuthnott down from its charred stake and carried her, covered in the town's mortcloth, to the vault of St Mary's kirk. When I saw that the provost and Thomas

Stewart, with the neighbouring ministers and the lawmakers of our town had matters under control and no longer needed my help, I stole away from the market cross. I did not go directly to the schoolhouse, but went down past the kirk and the music school towards Low Shore. It was dark now, a pitch darkness at first, after the astonishing brilliance of the bonfire, but I knew my way of old. I had to get myself clean. I walked away from the town and what lights there were and went down to the shore itself. I took off my hat, my boots and my cloak, and stepped into the glacial waters. Wave after gentle wave came to me and I continued to walk out, until the water was so deep I could walk no more. Numb to my bones with the cold, I turned and lay on my back, floating, looking up at the clear, full moon. The night sky was the same, the same as it had always been. It reigned impassive over the folly and the futility of man below. And over me. I floated as long as I could, wondering at the corruptibility of God's earthly creation, but it was no use; I would never be clean. I swam back to the shore. As I wrapped my soaking self in my cloak, I caught the smell of smoke still in my hair.

And the smell was still in my hair now, this morning, as I led the apothecary away from the scene of his daughter's last degradation to the decency of the schoolhouse. There would be no school today; Gilbert Grant had taken the authority upon himself. 'But what of the session, of the council?' his wife had asked, for once fearful and caring of the general opinion.

'Let them look to what business they have on hand and I will look to mine. There is a spiral of madness, of fear in the town and it must be brought under control; it must be stopped. The town itself must stop a moment before we all rush headlong to the abyss, shoving our neighbours before us and dragging our friends behind us in some blind folly. I will not hold the school until some sense and godly order is re-established in this town, and no mother in her senses would send her child away from her own skirts until the evil is rooted out.' But what was the evil and where did its roots lie? To root it out it must be known, and there was further to go before we knew it.

Mistress Youngson was glad to see me back. I had disturbed the house in my drenched homecoming last night and slipped away without eating this morning. The darker events in the town became, the less wicked I became in her eyes, and she now showed herself solicitous of my welfare. Once she had set water on the fire to heat for the apothecary, and called for dry blankets to clothe him in, she set two steaming bowls of porridge before us and bid us eat. The apothecary took nothing, did not even seem to notice the spoon in his hand, but I was ravenous and had emptied my plate in little time at all.

'Where did you find him?' she asked quietly.

I told her.

'He had been there all night?'

'I do not know. I think so. God help him.'

'Amen to that. He has lost his only light in this world. She was all his pride and his treasure. It is a wonder if he does not lose his mind also.' It was Gilbert Grant who spoke. He turned to call for the serving girl. 'We must send for Jaffray.'

'I have sent her for him already,' said his wife.

I had not sat like this, familiar, in the schoolhouse kitchen for a long time, but it did not seem strange to do so now. Neither Gilbert Grant nor his wife had asked anything of my business in Aberdeen; I had little interest myself in those matters for the moment. My baggage and packages from the journey lay in my chamber, brought there by Jaffray's stable boy last night before I had returned from my night swimming. We sat in silence. Even Mistress Youngson, who was seldom at rest, was still and quiet. 'How did it come to this?' I asked at length.

The schoolmaster heaved himself to his feet and took a spill from the fire to light his pipe – something the mistress would have forbidden on other days. 'How long have you been gone, Alexander? Four days, five?'

I calculated. 'I left for Aberdeen on Thursday morning, early, and returned last night. Five days.'

'And yet it might have been a lifetime. A great pestilence has crept through this town in these five days.' He thought a while, wearily. 'There was a fearfulness brewing before you left. From the time the death of Patrick Davidson was noised about. You must have marked it?'

I had not. I had been too taken up in events to realise how their consequences were infiltrating the minds of my townsfolk and feeding their ready capacity for fear.

The old man continued. 'The authorities had Charles thrown in the tolbooth soon enough, but there are more than ourselves who believe him innocent. It is of little comfort to them that an innocent man lies in chains while a murderer walks the streets.'

'And he is still there.'

'Aye,' said the mistress, 'but better there than in the hands of that mob last night. Who knows where next they might have turned?'

And if they had not been checked in their witch-hunt, who would have been safe in the cold clarity of daylight? The flames and the heat and the darkness might send madness to men's minds, but the daylight made them think themselves sane, and I knew that the witch-hunt legitimated by the light of day was a terrible thing. I did not wish to pursue this thought. 'When did they turn on Marion?' I asked. I did not much lower my voice; next to us he might have been, but Edward Arbuthnott had no notion of who was in the room with him or of what we said.

Gilbert Grant sighed. 'The ground was prepared before ever the boy was dead. There were rumours, voices raised at the session, about Marion and Patrick and their wanderings over the country. Arbuthnott gave assurances they were on plant-gathering expeditions, for his simples and compounds, but others of meaner minds saw debauchery, and finally witchcraft at the bottom of it. They were seen in places where it is best for those under suspicion not to be seen – at the Elf Kirk, by the minister himself, it was said. They were seen at Darkwater and even, it was said at Ordiquhill.'

The image of Marion Arbuthnott high above the rocks at the Elf Kirk on the day after Patrick Davidson had been found dead came back, like the ghost of the girl herself, to my mind. But for the rest, I thought of the maps. It made sense that they should have been there, at Darkwater, that hidden stretch of beach below the fastness of Findlater, or at Ordiquhill, on the road from there to Huntly's stronghold in Strathbogie. But Gilbert Grant had not been privy to the full discussion of the maps we had found, and I did not wish to endanger him or his wife by telling him more of the matter. That was a consideration for another time: for the present, Gilbert Grant was disposed to talk on.

'When the boy was killed, and Jaffray pronounced the cause to be poison, there were many who saw no need to look any further for the evildoer than the apothecary's shop, for who knew better the properties of plants than Marion Arbuthnott?' I had not been aware of this growth of suspicion in the town, so caught up had I been in events. Gilbert Grant continued, 'And it was seen, too, that those in authority also had their fears of Marion: the baillie and the doctor were at odds over her person just as the provost and the minister were last night over her soul. It was easily seen that the baillie suspected her of a hand in the deed, for he was rarely away from Arbuthnott's door. Jaffray matched him in his constancy – he was there almost as often as the baillie. The doctor is known for a softness towards young women, an indulgence of their faults. The more he was seen to be protecting Marion from the baillie, the darker became the people's guesses at what she might know. And yet,' his voice faltered, and for a moment I thought he had lost the thread of what he was saying; I was wrong, for he continued, clear and with an unwonted bitterness, 'still she managed to slip away. It is said she wandered the country in a state of distraction. People were afraid. Soon, the great storm of the night of the murder was ascribed to the conjuring of Marion Arbuthnott to cover her foul deeds. Then there were claims that she had been seen again at the Elf Kirk, conjuring black currents under the sea. On Saturday night a fishing boat from Seatoun bound for home before the Sabbath was lost on the rocks in calm seas. Only by God's grace did the men on board make it in safety to the shore.'

Mistress Youngson had got up to put more coals on the fire under the pot. She looked over at Edward Arbuthnott, almost fearfully, and spoke in a low voice. 'It is said that Marion went over again to Darkwater.'

'Hush woman; I will not have that nonsense in this house.'

I was truly astonished: I had never before heard Gilbert Grant chastise his wife, nor come anywhere near it.

'It is what they say,' she repeated determinedly.

I looked from one to the other in puzzlement. 'I do not understand,' I said. 'Why should it signify, that she has been to Darkwater?' I saw nothing very odd in her seeking solace there. The long white beach below the rock of Findlater Castle was indeed a beautiful place, and the cliffs would be coloured round with wild yellow primrose and the first pink flushes of thrift just now. I remembered my mother and Jaffray's wife taking me there once when I had been a boy.

The old couple now looked at me with equal puzzlement. 'Do you not know, Alexander? But surely you remember?'

'No,' said Mistress Youngson. 'He would have been no more than a bairn, if he was yet born indeed. In fact,' now she was thinking, hard, 'he was not even born. It was before his father had ever returned and brought his mother with him from Ireland. As well for her that it was.'

'Please,' I said. 'I have no notion of what you are talking about.'

Mistress Youngson came over to me. 'It is the wise woman of Darkwater. The one who tended to you when you, when you were ...'

'When I was in my delirium,' I finished for her. Nobody spoke to me, openly, of that time, when Jaffray had had a message from the old woman of Darkwater that she had found me, wandering, delirious, near the crag of Findlater, and had taken me safe into her home to nurse me. I had very little recollection of it myself; the days between my disgrace at Fordyce and the arrival of Jaffray to take me home to Banff were lost to my memory, and I made little effort to seek them out there.

Mistress Youngson continued. 'She lives in a sort of shack, does she not? Or a cave at the far end of the beach – I have never been myself so I could not say for sure,' she added somewhat too hurriedly. 'She is held by many to be a witch. She sets great store by the healing and holy wells, by secret pools known only to herself. It is said she consorts with the spirits, the wee folk—'

Again Gilbert Grant stopped his wife. The serving girl had returned from Jaffray's and her eyes were growing wide. 'To return to the point,' said the woman, 'in the last great scare of the witches, before you were born or the old king had gone down to England, the woman of Darkwater was lucky to escape the stake. It was said that only the fear of her great powers and great fellowship with Beelzebub stopped the others from naming her.'

I had heard something of this time, of course, but people did not care to speak much of it. To speak of it too freely might be to give life to the memory, to the fears in people's breasts, and to start it all again. There was something I had not known of before, though. I looked at the old woman. 'And what has this to do with my mother? You said it was as well for her that it was past before she ever came here.'

The old couple remained silent, uneasy, not knowing what to say. It was

Edward Arbuthnott, almost forgotten in the corner, who spoke up. 'Because she was different. Like my Marion, your mother was different.'

Mistress Youngson went and sat by him on the bench. 'Aye, she was.' She looked at me and smiled. 'Your mother was tall and beautiful, with her long dark hair, hanging loose, and those grey green eyes, like your own. She spoke differently; she had different ways. And though she was not a papist, that she was Irish was enough for many. Your father knew it, that she was different, and that it was not well-liked, but he was proud of her for it, until it broke the both of them. There were those who resented her for her marriage, who thought your father would have done better, by himself and by the town, to have taken a local girl to wife.' She looked away a moment, and I wondered if she had been one of them. 'This is not an easy place to be different. The longer she was here, the more of an outsider she became. And—'

'And she would not have fared well at the hands of the witchmongers, I fear.' I looked at Gilbert Grant, who was looking directly, honestly at me, and I felt cold to my heart.

There was little sound in the room now, save the bubbling of the water starting to boil, and the slow and heavy breathing of Edward Arbuthnott as he looked again into the flames. 'I do not know why Marion was there,' he said. 'At Darkwater. There is no good reason for a young, unmarried girl to visit such a woman. No reason for my girl to have been there. They would have burnt her alive if they could have got her, but they could not; she ended her life before they could take it from her.'

Again the image came to my mind. I spoke in a low voice to Gilbert Grant. 'Was it at the Elf Kirk? Did she jump in the end from the Elf Kirk?'

Both Grant and his wife turned puzzled frowns on me. 'At the Elf Kirk? No boy, surely you have heard. She poisoned herself on the Rose Craig. She was found there, dead, by Geleis Guild and her four children on the evening of the Sabbath; they had gone that way to pick flowers to take to Marion before the service in the kirk. But Marion already had flowers; when they found her, she was wearing a garland of henbane in her hair.'

Henbane: the wanderers awaiting their transportation across the Styx, it was said, had worn henbane in their hair. And in the wilder imaginings of the townfolk, henbane was the special flower of the diabolic, of the witches

195

and warlocks who flew in the night in their satanic ecstasies. But Marion Arbuthnott would have been in no ecstasy. I thought of the provost's lovely, delicate young wife and of her four pretty children. I remembered the sight that had greeted me across my schoolroom desk only a week ago. It was not fitting that children should see such a thing. I prayed God, sincerely, that he might take the vision of it from their minds. I had not long, I am thankful, to dwell on this, for there was the sound of a familiar commotion from the front parlour and soon James Jaffray was showing himself into the schoolhouse kitchen. With no needless greeting or ceremony he went directly to where the apothecary sat and knelt before him, taking his left hand in his own and putting the other to the man's forehead. 'You are ill, my friend. There is a fever coming on you. We must get you quickly to your bed. Your wife can prepare the simples?'

Arbuthnott tried to rally himself. 'I will take mallow; there is always some ready for the fevers.'

The doctor nodded. 'I will see to it also that she prepares you a dish of rhubarb. And a decoction of melancholy thistle in some wine. It will revive your spirits a little.'

The apothecary nodded wearily. 'For myself, I wish for nothing now other than death, but the woman cannot manage on her own. Without myself or Marion, she would be destitute. But for myself, for myself,' watery eyes now stared at some distant private vision, 'all is gone.'

'Come now,' said Jaffray kindly, 'you are still needed in the town. I have not half your knowledge of medicines and cures, and there is no one else now.'

Arbuthnott raised bitter eyes towards him. 'And do you think I would lift a hand to help any one of them, after what they have done to my beautiful girl?'

'Not all, now.'

'No,' the man conceded, 'not all.'

We left the kitchen then to the doctor and the apothecary and the mistress, who stayed to help bathe the sick man and persuade him to take a little warm broth before he should move out in the cold again. A spare suit of Gilbert Grant's clothing was found for him; my own only spare set of clothes was on my back, my other now being pummelled by the maidservant in a tub in the backyard. I should have been more thoughtful before taking to my night-swimming. It had done me little good.

The schoolmaster retired then to his study, inviting me to keep him company. It was a place of comfort and good reflection, a place of exercise for the mind, and my heart always warmed to the old man when he asked me to join him there.

'I have something for you first,' I said. 'I will be down in a minute.' I headed up the stairs as he made himself comfortable in his easy chair. The packages and luggage carried over by Jaffray's stable boy were lying by my bed. I checked all were there; none had gone amiss on my journey. The mid-morning gloom afforded very little light to my small chamber, but I found what I was looking for without much difficulty. I was down again at Gilbert Grant's door only a few moments after leaving him. He was sitting in contemplation by the room's only window, an unlit candle at his elbow. Around him was an air of sadness I had seen on him only once before, when I had finally come home and told him that what he had heard about my final trial for the ministry had been true. He was a man too ready to share in the sufferings of those dear to him, and of the innocent. In his many long years as schoolmaster in Banff, he had come to love many and had had cause to weep with them too often. His face lightened a little when he noticed me in the doorway.

'Come in, Alexander, come in. We will rest ourselves here. While we cannot be of any use, at least we can keep ourselves from getting in the way.' I smiled as I recalled how often I had heard his wife scold him for being in the way. She was always so busy, in the midst of much movement, and he preferred to be quiet and move little, but I think she knew that the reason he was always in her road was that he loved her so dearly. Before settling myself in the only other seat in the room I handed him the package.

'I have brought you this from Aberdeen, from Melville's.'

'Ah, is it really? From Melville?' He was thinking, searching in his mind, delaying the pleasure by not unbinding and opening the package straight away. 'I have not had a minute to ask you how you fared on your journey, or to quiz you for news from the town. I trust to God that there is no such business there as we have on hand here?'

'None that I have seen,' I assured him, 'although what goes on up the

197

vennels or behind the pends of other men's houses I do not know. This time last week we would not have thought such things possible here in Banff.'

He raised his eyebrows at me a little in surprise. 'Ah, would we not, do you think?' He mused quietly a moment. 'But you are young. I forget, sometimes Alexander, how young you really are; you have the air of one who has seen more of the world than he cares to. You will not remember that we have seen this sort of thing before. And yet we have learned nothing. Like the Israelites, time and time again we have turned our face from God and he has hidden his face from us.'

'You think this portends the judgement of God on us?'

'No. This is the turning from God and not the judgement. What the judgement will be I dread to live to see.' He opened now the package, knowing all the while that it was the Bible that was there. Without examination, without the careful caress of the finely bound volume that I had half expected, he opened the book and, with well-practised hands found the passage he wanted. He started to read, and although his finger ran along the lines, he did not look at them, for the words were already at his lips. 'Hosea, chapter four: "Hear the word of the Lord ye children of Israel; for the Lord hath a controversy with the inhabitants of the land, because there is no truth, nor mercy, nor knowledge of God in the land. By swearing, and lying, and killing and stealing, and committing adultery, they break out and blood touches blood. Therefore shall the land mourn, and every one that dwelleth therein shall languish.'"

I cleared my throat. 'But does the prophet not also say, "I will heal their backsliding, I will love them freely"?'

I had not spoken in this way, preached to another human being in many months, and the words came strangely unbidden from my mouth. Grant afforded me a saddened smile. 'Indeed he does, Alexander. But how shall we answer to this offer of God? How did the Israelites answer when sent the Redeemer? Was he not slain? What if this young man, Patrick Davidson, was also sent to us from God?' he looked up sharply. 'No redeemer mind, but a prophet, a messenger only, to tell us something, to get us to mend our ways. And he is slain. How now shall God deal with us?'

I myself had no notion of Patrick Davidson as a message from God. In his short time in our burgh he had gathered plants, drawn maps and courted a girl. There had been no public speeches, no preaching, no giving of admonition or warning by him. No passing on of messages. And yet I could not mock the old man's fears.

'But you, Gilbert, you have nothing to answer for, you who do only good to friend and stranger alike. Whatever has brought this visitation of darkness upon our town, it is not you.'

In less than a moment I saw that the words I had intended for comfort aroused only a sudden and real anger. 'I, nothing to answer for? Who amongst us has nothing to answer for, is without sin? It is not I. What nonsense did you hear preached in Aberdeen? We are all sinners. We are none of us capable of doing the least good thing, unless it be the Lord who ordains it. God destroyed the cities of Sodom and Gomorrah, and could find only one good man. If there is one good man here, it is not me.'

If not you, then who, I thought. Who in this town could argue our case in the face of the wrath of the creator? 'And yet it does not stop you trying,' I said.

'As we are commanded to do. And you too, I know, Alexander, you try also to do good as you are commanded to do.'

I could not answer him, and was glad when I was summoned through to the kitchen, to help the doctor bring Edward Arbuthnott back to his comfortless home.

'How will he fare?' I asked Jaffray, after we had seen Arbuthnott settled into his own bed under the care of his wife, in whom the advent of a true disaster seemed to have awoken some common sense and, what I had never remarked in her before, affection.

Jaffray pursed his lips. 'He will be as a man who waits for nothing more than the grave, I fear. Marion was all his hope and joy.'

The door to Jaffray's consulting room, the scene of last night's desolation, was shut when we arrived in the house, but I suspected all would be clean and orderly again. The doctor went first to the kitchen, to warn Ishbel that I would be coming for my dinner that night. He wanted proper news of my trip to the town, and to interrogate me in peace, and there were things I had to ask of him. He emerged from the kitchen and ushered me quietly towards his study. 'Ishbel is taking it very badly,' he said, in a low voice. 'I do not know how it was that I never saw it before, but I think, whether he realises it or not, he has taken her heart. They will let no one in to see him, and though she sends baskets of food up to the tolbooth every day, I do not know whether he gets them.'

'You have not been allowed in to him?'

'But once. It was Thomas Stewart who persuaded the provost. The baillie was near beside himself to be let in on the interview but Stewart said he would come in with me himself and that would be enough.' Jaffray paused, remembering. 'And it was enough. He has a quiet authority to him, the notary, that even the baillie cannot question. I think he will sit in the provost's seat one day.'

We had reached Jaffray's parlour by now, and mention of the provost had recalled me to my earlier appointment. 'I cannot wait long,' I said. 'I should have seen Walter Watt by now, to report on my business.'

'Then I will not keep you.'

'But tell me first,' I said. 'How was Charles when you saw him?'

Jaffray sighed deeply. 'He was ... less sanguine than I had hoped to find him. 'He sees little prospect of success in our endeavours to free him. And I fear he is getting ill.'

'Any man would get ill in that festering hole.'

'Indeed. Ishbel's clean blankets can only do so much against the cold and the damp in that place, and he has been a week now without proper exercise. Being parted from his music and, strange to say, his pupils, affects him too, I think. I fear he might take a fever and not have the will to defeat it.' Then a thought came to him that cheered him somewhat. 'You must see him today though, Alexander. They will surely let you see him?'

'Have no fear over that,' I said. 'They will let me see him or they will know nothing of my business in Aberdeen or at Straloch. But I doubt if there will be much room in the tolbooth after last night.'

'No. No more in Hell, either,' Jaffray added bitterly. He opened the door and shouted through the house for some kindling to be brought for his fire.

'Do you think there is anything in what Mistress Youngson hinted at? That if Charles had not been secure in the tolbooth they would have turned on him last night too?'

Jaffray looked up from his efforts with the fire. 'I am certain of it. You did not see them at their height, Alexander. They were like a pack of wolves. We had very little warning of it. I was carrying out the examination. Her mother insisted on it – against Arbuthnott's wishes – but his wife was certain her daughter would never have taken her own life.'

'And had she? Did you have time to discover that much?'

Jaffray looked at me. 'I did, and she had not. I am as certain as I can now ever be that she died by the same method as Patrick Davidson, and by the same hand.'

'How can you know that?'

'The vomit, the contortions in the face, the signs that paralysis had begun to take hold – they were all the same. And yet I could not get very far, to find better proof, before the baillie burst through the door. I did not understand him at first; I thought he had lost his senses.' The scene was being replayed in his mind. '"Jaffray, they are coming. Cover her up. For the love of God, man, they are coming for her!" And before I knew what he was rambling about, the minister and Cardno and a whole mob of them were through the door. They had pushed the lad aside and Ishbel was knocked to the ground. They near trampled the baillie underfoot till they got to me and stopped. They commanded me – the minister did – to leave off my examination and give them her body. I refused. I told them my work was none of their concern and to get out of my house. And then they pushed me aside too. The mob would have had their hands in her very entrails had the minister not started shrieking at them to leave off, lest they be tainted with the witch's blood. And then at last, I understood. It was the witch-hunt, and the baillie had come to warn me of it. It was over in moments. They had smashed the place up and taken her naked body from the slab and were gone, and the baillie had gone too, to take horse for Boyndie, where the presbytery was meeting, and the moderator, to try to stop them in their madness. And then you came and we were in the state that you found us in.' He was breathing hard now, and his hands were shaking. The stable boy came in with the kindling for the fire and I saw the bruise on his face from where he had been knocked aside the night before.

'Will you bring the doctor some of his port wine?' I asked him. 'And Adam?'

'Yes, Mr Seaton?'

'Are you all right yourself now?'

The boy blinked and bit his lip. 'Yes, sir. I am fine.'

'Who was it that hit you?'

'It was Lang Geordie.'

The same Lang Geordie who had warned Janet and Mary Dawson away from Banff. 'The beggar man? What had he to do with it all?'

The boy looked at me in surprise. 'It was him who was first through the door, sir. After the baillie and before the minister. They say in the town that it was Lang Geordie who first set up the cry of witch.'

After he had come with the wine and gone again, I asked Jaffray something that it shamed me to ask, but which I had to know.

'Do you think she was, James?'

'What?'

'Do you think Marion Arbuthnott was a witch?'

He got up heavily and stood looking out through the window to his garden. 'No. She was not a witch: she was a young girl with a knowledge of herbs and flowers, who was prettier, and more intelligent than most of the girls of her age and who did not care to waste her time on mixing with them. She was the companion and friend instead of the wife of the provost and she took up with a boy who had been here and left to travel to mysterious lands. And that was more than this town would allow.'

Yet still I could not leave it. 'But why then did she go to the wise woman of Darkwater? Not only with Patrick Davidson, but alone herself, after he was dead?' A silence hung where there had never before been silence between us.

'Did you get her to speak to you, James, after his death?'

'Yes,' he conceded at last. 'Just the one time, she spoke to me, but there was nothing she said that touched on our business or Charles's.'

I had never seen him like this before, and was not convinced that he was not keeping something from me. 'What did she tell you, James?'

The doctor did not turn to look at me when he replied. 'There are things that are no longer of this world – that it is only for the dead to know.'

It was with heavy steps and a heavier heart that I climbed Strait Path to the Castlegate where the provost's house was to be found. He had left word at the tolbooth that he could not wait longer on me there and had to go home to his wife. I had little inclination now to waste further time and effort on his errands, and little interest, if truth were told, in the question of his nephew's maps and papist plots. There were greater dangers, greater evils being made manifest before us as we woke and walked and slept in this very town than anything that threatened from without or in the future. And horrible as the death of Patrick Davidson had seemed to begin with, it was worse now, and perhaps there would be worse to come. What Charles had most feared had come to pass. Marion Arbuthnott was dead and that death was part of the chain that had begun with that of Patrick Davidson.

The burgh, as far as I could see, was returning to its usual state and rhythm of life, the only sign of last night's debauch being the whiff of smoked wood the wind carried with it. But perhaps, as Gilbert Grant had hinted, such perversions had always been lurking in the hearts of my fellow townsmen, never far beneath the surface of their neighbourliness and godliness. How easily the good neighbours had taken up the call of Lang Geordie, an idle beggar, a masterless man, usually feared and reviled. How ready they had been to follow the lead of one they would gladly otherwise have seen hounded from the burgh. I banged on the door of the provost's house, the noise loud and echoing in the empty street.

Walter Watt himself opened the door to me. He had a dishevelled air and his eyes were shot through with redness from lack of sleep. He also carried with him the smell of smoke from last night. I realised the man had not yet been to his bed, and I felt a little shamefaced.

'I am sorry I did not come to meet with you at the appointed time.'

He waved away my apology as he left me to shut the door behind myself. 'I would not have had the leisure to see you much earlier than now anyway. I have been busy with the baillie and the dean of guild most of the morning.'

'The baillie is recovered, then?' I asked in surprise. I had not thought to ask Jaffray about his patient of last night.

He eyed me shrewdly. 'The baillie is a man driven. Where others would have buckled and collapsed, he sustains himself on a determination not of woman born. I would have no fears for the baillie.'

'The dean of guild, last night, I did not notice ...' again my voice trailed away. I did not know which side the leader of all our burgh's craftsmen had taken.

The provost took my meaning straight away, though. 'He was with us, thank God. If he had not been, we would be in a worse case than we are already in.'

I thought of the quietly industrious burgh I had passed through that morning. 'You think the commerce of the town will suffer?' I said.

He smiled at me, but there was no humour in his eyes. 'You are a man of learning, Mr Seaton, but a craftsman's son also. You must know that nothing passes within the burgh that does not in some manner affect trade and good government. And, I would suspect, your mind was much on other matters this morning. Did you, for instance, pass the coopers' yard?'

I confessed that I had not.

'How many of the baxters were calling their wares in the marketplace this morning? And were you, by chance, out by the tannery? Can you smell them?' Sometimes, with the wind blowing from the west, the nauseating smells of the tanners' work were wafted down to the burgh itself, and could be caught in the air and in the throat. But not today. The provost was watching me and saw that I began to understand.

'Half the tanners are in the tolbooth. With three of the baxters. Master and apprentice alike. Most of the coopers, along with the chandlers and God knows how many of the domestic servants in the burgh, as well as two or three merchants whose names would surprise you, have been parcelled out between the laird of Banff's strong room and the castle dungeon. Had the moderator and his brethren been half an hour later, the back of the burgh would have broken under the strain. It was curbed with scarcely more minutes to spare.' He looked at me and spoke with a coldness that sent a shiver through my body. 'They were at the point of going after the living as well as the dead. Your friend Charles Thom would not have survived the night, had their madness been allowed to grow. And then we would have had more murderers on our hands than all the dungeons in Banff can hold. The town is quiet today, yes, but it is not at rest.'

'And how will you act?' I asked, for it was plain that no other man in Banff could guide the affairs of the town out of the morass they had fallen into.

He rubbed a wearied hand across his brow. 'Oh, the most of them will come before the baillie court in the morning. There will be fines to pay, and reparations to be made – to the doctor's house, and the marketplace and other things damaged last night – though God knows nothing can be done for Arbuthnott himself. Then they will be passed on to what remains of the kirk session, for more fines and public penance, and then they will be left to go about their work. No good will come of creating more resentments.'

I had hoped for better revenge than this for Marion Arbuthnott and her father. 'They would have got worse for stealing a pig or slandering a shrewish wife.'

The provost took little offence at this remark. 'Oh, do not misunderstand me, Mr Seaton: the ringleaders will be appropriately dealt with. According to their crime and to their place, they will be dealt with. The minister will be put out of his pulpit. He will never preach within the bounds of this presbytery again. He will answer to his brethren, and there can be no doubt but that he will be deprived.' It was evident that the thought gave him no little satisfaction.

'And the session clerk?' He gave a shallow laugh. 'James Cardno? Cardno also is finished. The doorkeeper who guarded him last night tells me he has near lost his wits.' That I could well believe: the man I had seen inflaming the mob last night had been on the very brink of insanity. 'Cardno is very like to find himself banished the burgh. Aye, and then the session will be broken,' continued the provost. 'The power of the minister and session in this burgh will not again challenge stability and order as it did last night, and as it has threatened to do many times before now.'

And that, I now understood, was what mattered to him, what had mattered to him last night. What had driven him last night was not sentiment, man-made or God-given, for Marion Arbuthnott or her father, but for the burgh of Banff itself.

'And what of the baillie?' I asked. I knew he would not be sorry to see the back of the Reverend Guild, but the provost hoped for too much if he thought this would be enough to make the baillie quiet in the matter of kirk discipline.

'The baillie is immovable, you are right; but yet his hand might be weakened long enough, the complexion of the session and council changed enough at the outcome of this business, that it will not matter.' The provost spoke these last words to himself almost as much as he did to me. I wondered how many years he had waited for this moment, for the day when he would truly wrest control of the burgh of Banff from those who claimed to be the magistrates of God.

'And what of Lang Geordie?' I asked.

The provost looked at me quizzically and repeated the name.

'The beggar. The big, bearded cripple. He is the head of all who inhabit the codroche houses at the far side of the burgh, near the Sandyhill Gate.'

'I know who he is,' said Watt. 'But what has the beggar man to do with the matter?'

I told him of Lang Geordie's part as I had heard it. The provost's expression became a little more thoughtful. 'I had not realised; I had not seen him at the burning.' I realised that I had not either, but there was no reason to doubt the truth of the stable boy's tale. The provost was nodding. 'It may well be that he was used to rouse the rabble, to add the fear of violence to whatever the minister and Cardno fermented with their words, but I think he was of little moment in last night's proceedings. He could be fined, but where would be the point in that? He has nothing to pay a fine without he steals it from another. Lang Geordie, as you said yourself, is the leader of all the shiftless, worthless, idle and debauched creatures in this burgh. He knows he – and they – are here on sufferance, and that if they come too often to the attention of the authorities they will be suffered no more. So, they go about their shiftless business with a sort of discretion, within rules that they and we understand. They are whoremongers and thieves, I grant you. But they are our whoremongers and thieves, and they will do much to protect their position and their privilege. We have no need to fear incoming hordes of sturdy beggars as long as Lang Geordie and his crew are in the town.' I saw then that there was a balance in everything, seen and unseen, in the daily life of the burgh, that there was a place for things that might seem to have no place. Still I was not satisfied, but I said no more to Walter Watt of Lang Geordie.

We were in that same hall of the provost's house that the corpse of Patrick Davidson had briefly rested in just six days ago. It had been a sombre enough place then, but it was worse now: a dead and empty place where a great man paced the floor alone. 'How is your wife?' I asked him. I had heard from Jaffray and in Mistress Youngson's kitchen also that Geleis Guild was disconsolate over the death of her friend and helper, and that the treatment meted out to the corpse of Marion Arbuthnott was feared to send her from her senses. The children had been sent already to the home of the provost's sister in Elgin for fear of what they would see or hear next in our burgh. How the young woman would have taken her brother the minister's involvement in all that had passed, none could guess. The provost's eyes were empty as he answered me.

'She is almost beyond the reach of comfort. It should not have gone thus for my wife.' And as he said so, he could not help looking up at the portrait on the wall. I wondered whether he feared being widowed a second time. I hoped for his sake and for hers that he would not be.

But then the man became the provost and asserted himself once more. 'And now, Mr Seaton, to business. You saw Straloch?'

I answered that I had and I removed the sealed letter from my pocket. He took it and walked to the window on the south side of the room, where the late morning sunlight was beginning to filter through the dense glass. His eyes moved quickly across the page. Before they had reached the end an air of relief passed over his countenance and he nodded slowly to himself. 'You have read this, Mr Seaton?' he asked briskly.

'No, provost, I have not. The letter is addressed to you. I do know the gist of Straloch's opinion of the matter, though, and I am glad for it.'

He was watching me carefully. 'And you trust the man?'

I thought about the quiet conversation in Straloch's dining hall after I had first gone up to my bed; I thought of the sounds of horsemen leaving in the night, but I had no wish for further distractions or errands for the provost. 'I trust his word on this: that if your nephew were any spy, he knew nothing about it before he saw that map.'

'Then you still think my nephew was a traitor?'

I answered him as honestly as I dared. 'I am satisfied enough with Straloch's answer. My concern is to help the living, not to speculate about the dead.' Yet in truth, it was not complete honesty. Straloch had no knowledge of any planned invasion or the commissioning of Patrick Davidson to draw these maps, but I had seen in his eyes that he was not convinced that such a commission had not been given. He may well have ridden south himself as he had told me he would do, but it was just as likely that his young retainers had ridden at night, and with some urgency, to Strathbogie and the Marquis of Huntly. I was not ready to dismiss the possibility of Patrick Davidson's treachery as easily as Walter Watt would have had me do. If there had been treachery, then there had been a motive for murder, and its discovery would bring closer the release of Charles Thom, for what interest did he have in treachery and papist plots? I did not like to dwell on the topic in this place and this company, and was glad when the provost turned the conversation to another matter.

'And did you fulfil my private commission?'

'To George Jamesone?'

'The artist. Yes. What response had you from him?'

I drew the second letter out of my cloak. There was no fire in the grate and the place was cold. The provost too still had his outer garments about him. Jamesone's letter, as I had known, was shorter and pleased Walter Watt less. 'I see he is now much in demand amongst the great ones, and cannot spare himself long to come to our mean burgh. Ach well,' he added, crumpling the letter and throwing it into the empty hearth, 'perhaps it is not yet the time for paintings, but he will come at length, and it will be there, telling its story, long after we are gone.' He came away from the window and started to head for the small door at the back of the room which led through to the back of the house. He turned and nodded towards the main door, dismissing me abruptly. 'You did your business well and with discretion, Mr Seaton. Do not trouble yourself further in the matter of my nephew. The appropriate authorities will see to their business there. Now I must wash away this pestilent smoke.'

I was glad to see myself out, and free from further obligation to those who had so recently taken me into their trust. I closed the door of the empty hall firmly behind me and stepped out into the midday light of the street. I turned down Water Path to make my way back to the schoolhouse, needing to rest and to think and perhaps even to pray before I commenced my business of the afternoon. At the edge of my vision, for a brief, deceiving moment, I thought I glimpsed a figure flit through the gate in the castle wall. Again I experienced, more strongly now, the sensation that had dogged me since my return to Banff the night before: that I was being watched.

TWELVE

A Homecoming

The ground floor of the tolbooth, usually given over to the payment of taxes and the collection of fines, was packed, heaving with armed men and overworked officials who looked as if they had been there all night. The stench from the crammed cells on the upper floors was beyond the capacity of doors and walls to contain and combined with the lingering smell of smoke that permeated from the outside to create a putrefying miasma that almost overwhelmed me. There was no appearance of anyone being in charge, and so I asked one guard and then another and then another. When the fourth finally told me I could not at first comprehend what he said. But then I understood – half the town was chained and shackled in those cells, but Charles Thom was not there; he was gone. Charles was gone from the tolbooth, and no one could tell me where he was. 'He was taken away. By order of the baillie. He was removed in the night.' This was all the man knew, he swore to it, and his fellow guards claimed to know no more than he did. Charles might be in the cellars of the laird of Banff's palace, or he might be in the dungeon of the sheriff's castle – at neither would I be given entry or have my questions answered. At worst – I hoped it was the worst – he would be out at the Ogilvy stronghold of Inchdrewer, but to ride out there would be to lose time I did not have. A messenger had ridden that morning, at dawn, to Aberdeen, to call back in person the sheriff to sit in judgement upon our burgh. There was no choice for me but to find out Baillie Buchan himself.

The baillie, I knew, lived alone on the upper floors of a mean tenement up a vennel to the west end of High Shore. He had never married, and such house-keeping as he allowed to be done for him was performed by the wizened and mute crone whose son held the feu of the tenement. I had never ventured there before. No one visited the baillie. The vennel was dank and dark, an appropriate place for William Buchan to issue from, as he went on his nightly inspections of our town. It had perhaps not always been a place of such foreboding. Two pairs of initials and a date, 1572, were engraved on the lintel above the door, a statement of hope and faith.

I banged hard on the timber and the chickens pecking in the backyard scattered, squawking at the unheard of intrusion. It was the crone who came to the door. 'I must see the baillie, urgently. He is not to be found in the town. Where will I find him?' She looked at me with pale and watery eyes and nodded, twice, before holding up a bony finger to me, presumably that I should wait, then shutting the door. Two or three minutes later, she reappeared, opened wide the door, and stood back for me to pass. Then she pointed up the stairs and went back to her cooking pot. The mixed odours of fish broth and peat smoke pursued me silently as I ascended to the baillie's quarters. There was no candle on the stairway and the few small windows of this gable house gave very little light, faced as they were by the solid houses just a few feet across the vennel. I found my way by groping the spiralling granite of the walls, and came at length to a small doorway opened onto the first landing. A dim and flickering light issued from the gap between door and jamb, and I pushed the door open quietly without knocking. Sitting in a comfortless wooden chair, by the small fire that struggled in the grate, was Baillie William Buchan. Opposite him, in an identical chair, a bowl of the broth at his hand, sat Charles Thom.

'I had expected you before now, Mr Seaton.' There was a seriousness to the baillie's voice; it was without its usual air of suspicion and accusation.

'I have been … occupied,' I said, looking at Charles while I spoke to the baillie. I do not know what kind of picture I presented to these two who seemed so much less surprised by my arrival than I was at what I found.

'As you see, the music master is here now.' The baillie indicated a bench by the small deal table against the side wall of the room. 'Will you not also sit, Mr Seaton?' I sat down and waited, still looking at Charles, who ventured a small smile and then looked down at his feet again. He was thinner; the circles beneath his hazel eyes larger and darker than when I had last seen him a week ago, and there were blemishes, the beginnings of sores, on his skin. Yet his hair was clean and brushed and hung unmatted on his shoulders. He had shaved and was in a clean white shirt and coarse but

210

warm woollen overclothes that I did not recognise as his. They could not have been the baillie's, for he was a more sparely built man than Charles. I guessed they belonged to the son of the house.

Gaunt though Charles was, he looked, in truth, in better health than the baillie, who appeared truly ill. His sallow skin, usually taut, seemed to hang from his bones. His eyes were dark shadowed sockets, and his body was hunched and wracked with a wrenching cough. I recalled his virtual collapse from his horse last night and what Jaffray had said of his ceaseless activity since the discovery of Patrick Davidson's body. I remembered, too, the provost's assertion that he had been up half the night with the baillie in setting the business of the burgh in some sort of order. The man who had been carried to the doctor's last night should have gone home to his bed and slept. It was plain that the baillie had done neither. Unlike Charles, he had evidently not yet washed or shaved – the first time I had seen him in such a condition – and the reek of smoke hung about him yet, as it had done the provost.

He opened his mouth to speak again, but was taken by a coughing fit. When he had recovered himself, he reached for a wooden beaker of water at his elbow and took a long draught. I did not like this. I did not like the voice that began to whisper to me that I should pity this man, this sick man, this gaoler, inquisitor, spy. 'I am glad to see you returned to the burgh, Mr Seaton. I had wondered, afterwards, if we had been wise to send you away to Aberdeen at such a time.'

'Did you fear I would abscond? Baillie, I have nowhere to go.'

'The town of Aberdeen has dangers enough of its own, but with all that has passed in this burgh these last few days, there is cause to fear for all men.' He leaned slightly towards me and was taken by another, briefer, coughing fit. 'You met with no trouble in Aberdeen?' I remembered Mary Dawson and her fear of being pursued by men sent from Banff, her terror that I was one of them. Perhaps I, too, had been watched in Aberdeen.

'I met with no trouble there,' I said.

'And for the other business, your commission?'

'To Straloch, you mean?'

He glanced briefly at Charles, but evidently adjudged that Charles would have little interest, and perhaps less opportunity, than any man in Banff of spreading rumours about foreign invasions and papist plots. 'Aye, to Straloch. What other commission did you have?' I decided to tell him nothing of my visit to George Jamesòne on the provost's behalf.

'None.'

He was satisfied. 'What said the laird to our business?' He was watching me eagerly, as if there was a particular answer he was anxious I should give.

'He said he knew of no such plot, no commission of cartography. He thought the work well executed. The provost has his letter.' It was evident this answer did not please him, but I intended to spend no more time on the matter of the maps. My friend, under accusation of murder, sat before me, clean-shaven in the baillie's own house in a suit of another man's clothes. I cared little now for plots and maps. 'How do you come to be here, Charles?' I asked.

He looked at the baillie, who watched him steadily. 'I was taken last night, about the hour of ten, from the tolbooth to this house under guard by Baillie Buchan and the notary, Thomas Stewart. I am told it was for fear of my life that I was brought here, fear that I would meet the same fate as Marion.' His voice was flat, and fell on the last word.

I looked to the baillie, but he was talking directly to Charles. 'Wicked and barbarous deeds were done in this town last night. Many of the guilty were brought to the tolbooth. They held her for a witch, and you had consorted with her. They held you answerable for the death of a strange visitor to our town. They wanted less, much less, to feed their frenzy. They would have torn your limbs from your body by morning.'

I had seen the mob last night. I did not dispute the baillie's point. 'And why here?'

The baillie stood up and was again taken by a fit of coughing. He steadied himself on the arm of his chair and then straightened himself to his usual dignity. 'Because there is nowhere else, Mr Seaton. Every prison in Banff is full, full to the brim, and in each one of them there are those who would gladly have the music master for their next victim. Nowhere else was safe, and there remained no guards to be spared, so I have become the guard. My landlady's son, who through the night watched over Charles Thom, must go about his lawful work today. I am but one man, and I must rest, and make my devotions. And so I prayed you would come and you have come. I ask of you one hour and a half I may cleanse myself of the stench of last night, and rest, and pray God for his guidance. One hour and a half I ask you to guard your friend well, Mr Seaton. Do I have your word that you will?'

I was astonished, and could think of no other response than to say yes. A very brief flicker of relief passed over the baillie's face and he moved towards the small door to the left of the room, to the chamber I supposed he must sleep in, in those few hours when he consented to sleep. Before the door he stopped and turned. 'Counsel your friend to pay heed to all that I have said to him, Mr Seaton. He can do nothing now for the dead, but for the living he must tell the truth; he must tell me what he knows.' He took a well-worn Bible from the shelf by the door, and without further word he went to his chamber, leaving me with my prisoner.

So here we were, Charles and I, at William Buchan's hearth. How often, how many nights, had we entertained ourselves with tales of the baillie, of his omnipresence and omniscience? How many times had we felt ourselves under the baillie's disapproving eye on his nightly check of the inns and taverns of Banff that no apprentice or servant or infamous drunkard should be served with wine or ale? Yet here we were at his fireside while he washed, and prayed, and slept next door. It was Charles who broke the silence first, his eyes crinkling in the familiar smile. 'We have surely come up in the world, Alexander, that we are guests in this house.'

I got up and took the seat opposite him, so lately vacated by the baillie. I leaned forward a little, my voice low. 'Are we guests, do you think, Charles, or are we both prisoners? I think the baillie would be pleased to have me, also, where he can keep an eye on me.'

He laughed. 'You might well be right. He was much agitated at your absence in Aberdeen. Not just myself, but Gilbert Grant also was plied for information about your plans there – what your business was, where you would lodge, who you were like to visit – I had all this from Jaffray.'

'He told me he had been allowed in to see you.'

Charles looked down at the floor. 'Aye, the once. But I would not have had it so; I would not have had him see me in that place. It was enough to know he thought of me – I would have known that without all the baskets he sent up.' There was a great sense of failure, of having disappointed, in his voice.

'Charles, Jaffray has seen and suffered much in this life. He has few illusions about what fate can do to those who do not deserve it. You surely did not expect him to rest until he had seen you? He will not rest until he has seen you free and justice done.' I hesitated, unsure how best to say what had to be said. 'Whatever justice there can be done, now.'

Charles set down his empty bowl upon the hearth, and traced his finger a moment in the ashes. 'What justice can be done? How can any justice be done in this life for Patrick Davidson or for Marion?' He gave off his tracing and lay with his head back in the chair, his eyes tight shut. When they finally opened I could see they were filled with tears. I had nothing to comfort him and he was right: there was no justice; there could only be retribution. But Charles was not a man with a stomach for retribution, and he would only turn his back further on the ways of this barbaric world.

'Do you think it is over, Charles?'

'What is over?'

'The killing,' I said.

He pushed the hair back over his forehead in a gesture I knew well. 'Killing or dying? I do not know. Patrick was murdered, no one doubts that, I know. But,' he took a deep breath and swallowed hard, 'Marion ... they tell me she died by her own hand.'

I thought of the confusion of last night. Surely Jaffray had told someone, some authority other than just myself. I lowered my voice further still, conscious as I was of the baillie's even breathing on the other side of the door. 'Charles, has no one told you? Marion did not die by her own hand, Jaffray is adamant on that. He swears before God that she died by the same hand, and in the same manner, that killed Patrick Davidson.'

What colour there was drained from Charles's face. 'Then the killing has not stopped,' he said.

I watched him intently, watched for any flicker, any sign that would tell me something. 'Charles, is the baillie right? Do you know something?'

He bit his lower lip and shook his head slowly. 'I know nothing, Alexander, nothing. I would to God that I did. Since Marion's death, the baillie has been at me night and day, as he was at Marion before it. But I know not even what manner of knowledge he seeks. He is like a dog worrying at a burrow from which the hare has only one escape. He will not let up, and I can tell him nothing.' He looked away at the slowly dying embers in the meagre fire. 'It is as if he knows very well what it is that he seeks, but he must have another say it for him.'

A thought was now becoming more formed in my mind, a thought that had been taking shape for some days now. 'Do you think it possible that what the baillie seeks to establish is not *what* you know, but *whether* you know? You remember what you told me of Marion's behaviour on the night of your search together for Patrick Davidson: she was almost as determined that no one should guess she had confided in you as she was to find Davidson. She feared as much for you as for him. She knew that the very suspicion that you had knowledge of what Davidson was about would put your life in danger. Who can say now that she was wrong? She paid that price herself.' I could see, from Charles's face, that my point was not lost on him. 'You say, and I have had it from Jaffray also, that the baillie rarely left off his questioning of her, and now, since her death, he has taken you into his own charge.' The coldness I felt was little to do with the bare and cheerless room in which we sat. 'Charles, you must continue to play the ignorant; you must continue to hold fast that you know nothing.'

He looked at me with exhaustion in his eyes, exhaustion of the soul. 'That will be no great triumph, no great achievement, for truly, Alexander, I know nothing. If you will not believe me, how should I convince the baillie? But Marion confided nothing to me but her certainty of danger itself. Had it been otherwise I would have told him by now. I have not your resolve.'

'And I have not your humanity.' I thought of Marion Arbuthnott, of the girl who had always been distant, detached, content in herself, until Charles had been able to draw from her some of the warmth of friendship. I wondered again where that might have led, had not Patrick Davidson come soon after, and with him the first experience of love.

Charles broke the silence. 'Whatever burden Marion carried after Patrick Davidson's death, she carried it alone. I could not help her, for I was never allowed to see her after they found him, and I do not think she even tried to go to the tolbooth to see me.'

'She was lost in herself by then, Charles. No one could reach her save the children, Geleis Guild's children, but she wanted no further human contact, nor comfort either, I think.'

'But that is it, of course! There is one in whom she might have confided. Not the baillie, certainly, for she feared him. No, but in Geleis Guild. I think it possible she did, for she – the provost's wife – came to see me once, in the tolbooth. The guards dared not prevent her. It was three days ago. She also was watchful, anxious to evade the baillie's surveillance, I remember that.'

'Why did she come to see you?'

'I do not know,' he said. 'I was so glad at the time to see a kind face that I did not question it. She told me she gave no credence to the notion that I could have murdered Patrick or anybody. She spoke of her anxiety to see Marion again, alone, for they were companions, and she knew how hard all these things would be on her. I think in truth that Marion was her only friend. She was anxious to see her, but she could never escape the baillie's watchful eye, still less get past him at the apothecary's door. I hope to God she did not get to see her, or she will be in danger now herself.'

'I would have little fear on that score. I think the provost's mind is bent upon protecting his wife from whatever there is yet to come.'

'I think, then, that he is a wise man,' said Charles, quietly. 'You will ask Jaffray about it, though?'

'I will,' I promised him. Charles was greatly wearied and looked ready to sleep. I would not tax or question him further. As his eyelids flickered and then closed, I moved quietly from my chair. I had never wondered about the baillie's home, never considered him as a private person, for the life of the individual was always to him a thing of wickedness and impiety, an offence to God and a threat to the commonwealth. There was little comfort in this room, and little more, I suspected, in the small chamber leading off from it where he had gone to wash and where he now slept. William Buchan was a merchant who carried out a steady trade; he must have been a man of some wealth, yet there were few – if any – signs of it here. There were no wall hangings, such as even in Banff could now be found in the homes of some of the wealthier merchants, but one simply embroidered canvas above the door to the baillie's chamber. Each corner was adorned with a small symbol of the seasons of the year – a lamb, a cornflower, a russet apple, a sprig of holly – but it was the wording in the centre that caught the eye. I knew, without the neat legend beneath it, that it was taken from Paul's first letter to the Corinthians; it was a verse I had pondered often myself: *But I would have you without carefulness. He that is unmarried careth for the things that belong to the Lord, how he may please the lord.* At the very bottom corner, in tiny lettering, were the initials *HB* and the date *1610.* I had, in my lifetime, seen many verses from the Bible rendered in thread and canvas, but I had never seen one such as this. Was this then what drove the baillie, what lay at the heart of his inhumanity? Was it that his own mother had set him on this course of coldness towards his fellow man in some supposed pursuit of godliness? I could think of no other who could have done so.

The room itself was scarcely less bare than the walls. The only furnishings were the two hard wooden chairs on which Charles Thom and I sat and the table and bench to the side of the room. A kist with a strong lock – keeping the papers of business, I assumed – was below the one small window. There was no rug or matting on the swept wooden floor, and no ornament of any sort – what bowls and plate there were were either wooden or of coarse, local work, not burnished or painted. A low bookshelf was set against one wall, and it was to this that I gave my attention. It was from here that Buchan had picked the Bible as he had gone to his rest, yet another Bible remained. I took it from the shelf and opened it. Inscribed inside, in a thin and uncertain hand were the words: *To William, walk always in the fear of the Lord and in the certainty of your mother's love, Isabella Farquhar. 1596.* The baillie could scarce have been ten years old when his mother had given him that Bible. But more, I realised that whoever had stitched those words that had condemned him to a lifetime of arid loneliness, it had not been his mother.

This was not the place to set my mind to that mystery and I resumed instead my examination of the baillie's small library. The Psalms. Some tracts and pamphlets against the Catholics, the Jesuits, the government of bishops and the perils of assuming one's own will, all in the vernacular. All as I would have expected, all save one. For William Buchan too had an edition of Craig's poetical works, identical to that I had bought for Charles so recently in Aberdeen, yet this copy was well thumbed, well used, evidently oft read. This was not a man whom I thought poetry could have touched. As I wondered at this, my foot struck against another kist, long and low, beneath the shelf. On this one there was no lock. I bent down and opened the lid as quietly as I could. Inside, bound together, were little exercise books such as I would allow the better pupils to keep, like diaries or commonplace books. I carefully unbound the pile nearest the top and took the first book in my hand. On the front was written, in the baillie's small and steady hand, 'Sermons, March 1624–June 1625', and inside there were notes and meditations on every sermon he had heard in those fifteen months. The whole pile of notebooks beneath it went back year upon year, month upon month, week upon week as far as my own childhood and beyond. A lifetime of the man was in those books, and I would have given much for the freedom to peruse them, but I was too conscious of the low, rasping breathing coming from just the other side of the door.

I could not help but open the most recent exercise book, though. The baillie had attended the kirk in Banff, mostly, but he had travelled too, all around the presbytery. He had found much to praise, many words of wisdom on which to meditate and to thank the Lord for, but he had found more to censure. Laxity in discipline, ignorance of the true meaning of the scriptures, error in the interpretation of God's plan. Most of all, though, there was near a fury, fury at the ignorance, incompetence, and hypocrisy of the Reverend Guild. I could disagree with nothing he said of Guild's preaching. Then a thought struck me. I rifled backwards through the pages and indeed it was there: *22 June, year of God one thousand six hundred and twenty-five. Mr Alexander Seaton, undermaster at Banff Grammar School, expectant for the ministry. At Boyndie Kirk.*

Yes: he had been there. As I had taken the pulpit and looked down across my last congregation, I had seen, watching me with a peculiar intensity, Baillie William Buchan. Unaccountably, I felt my breathing come heavier and my hand tremble slightly as my eye scanned the first line and then the second. At first I could not quite comprehend what I read, could not take it in, and I had to go back over the words again until I was certain of what they said. There, in my hand, in the home of a man I had long avoided, maligned and misunderstood, I read a testament to hopes dashed and faith betrayed: William Buchan had given thanks to the Lord for the gifts He had given me, as a preacher and minister to his people, for preserving me where others had been lost, as a blessing to my community and a comfort to my friends. He had thanked God that the promise he had seen in the boy I had been had been fulfilled in the man I had become. My heart was racing and I read on, disbelieving until, out of nowhere, came a most awful hammering noise, fit to wake the dead. I scarcely had time to shut the book and throw it back in the pile at the top of the kist before the baillie came stumbling from his chamber, dishevelled from sleep. He wrenched his cloak from the back of the door and lurched towards the stairs. I hastily shut the lid of the kist and went to stand by Charles, who was also drowsily coming to; I was ready to defend him if I had to.

There was some commotion downstairs as the arrival strove to make himself understood to the crone, and then to get past her to the baillie. I should have relaxed at the voice, but my heart beat faster, for it could not be good news that drove him to this place, now, and in such a manner. There was shouting, insistent shouting, and the baillie trying to assert calmness, authority. At last he made himself understood, and I heard the men ascend the stairs. Charles tried to stand up, but his time in the tolbooth had weakened him greatly and he was far from his usual strength. It was not the baillie who came first through the door but Dr James Jaffray.

'Alexander,' he said, not comprehending that I should be there, and then his face changed and his body visibly sank as he saw Charles behind me. He took a pace towards us. 'Oh, my boy, my dear boy.' The baillie helped him to a chair and Charles knelt down at his feet, taking his hands. William Buchan, unused as he must have been to such displays of human feeling, stepped back into his chamber and, without fully closing the door, began to tidy himself. I poured some water for the doctor from the pitcher on the table.

'Drink this, James; it will settle you.'

He rubbed his hand across his eyes and as the heaving of his chest subsided, he took the tumbler from me and drank. When his old friend had recovered himself, Charles allowed himself a smile.

'Well, doctor, would it be an irate husband or a desperate creditor that chased you to the baillie's in such a spin?'

The doctor also smiled and put down the tumbler. 'No, but only two daft lads that are not safe to vague the streets on their own.' He shook his head in a mock weariness. 'There is nothing for it but I must find you both a wife to keep an eye on you, for I have work aplenty to keep me busy as it is.'

'Just the one wife between us?' asked Charles.

'Aye, perhaps,' replied the doctor, 'and lucky to get that.'

A hacking cough broke into their pleasant banter. 'Perhaps,' said the baillie, 'we should come to the matter in hand.' Charles stood up and I stood aside to let the baillie pass. 'The doctor has just told me now what I believe you already know, Mr Seaton. He has told me that by his findings, Marion Arbuthnott was no suicide but died by the same hand that killed Patrick Davidson.'

I nodded. 'Yes, the doctor told me that this morning.'

'What you will not have realised,' continued the baillie, 'perhaps because you would entertain no idea of his guilt in the first place, is that this proves, in as far as the thing can be proved, the music master innocent of the first crime as well as of the second.'

I looked from the baillie to Jaffray, the realisation only gradually dawning. Neither of us had thought of it, because neither of us had believed for a minute that Charles had murdered Patrick Davidson. It had been alone, in the peace and quiet of his little back room, looking out through the window at his wife's garden, that the doctor had at last seen it. This was the proof that would, in the sight of others, free Charles from the tolbooth and from the hangman's noose. Charles sat down again and held his head in his hands.

The doctor spoke again. 'God forbid that any of us should take pleasure in such a thing. The girl should have been living and breathing and working yet in the apothecary's shop and the provost's nursery, but she is gone, and not by her own hand. We are too late now to prevent that injustice, but not another. Surely now, Buchan, the boy can go free?'

The baillie slowly nodded. His face was impassive and I could not guess what his thoughts were. 'Yes, doctor, he can go free. Or, at least, I will consent to release him into your care. I have the authority, although I will doubtless have much answering for it to do before the council. But mark me well, see that he does not wander alone about the streets, or leave the town. He is less safe now than ever he was in the tolbooth. Heed my counsel, doctor.'

The doctor stood up, fully recovered now. 'I will,' and without further address to the baillie he turned to Charles. 'Come on, boy, we're going home.'

As we descended the dark stairway, the baillie, from his narrow doorway, spoke to me. 'And you, Mr Seaton, you also should be careful what you are about.' I made no reply and was glad soon to be out into the relative light of the vennel.

The homecoming to the doctor's was a markedly different affair from our departure from the baillie's. After her initial shock, Ishbel flew about the house making everything ready. The stable boy had been despatched within minutes to collect what was needful from the apothecary's house; the rest could be got later. There was no notion that Charles would ever return to his attic room there, nor indeed, from the manner of the doctor and his housemaid, that he should ever leave their home. The contentment on the doctor's face and the mild bemusement on Charles's were as nothing to the determination of the young girl that the music master should not suffer one more moment's hunger, thirst, cold or discomfort. That I was an imposition under her feet was made very clear, to my amusement rather than hurt, and to Jaffray's too. Promising that I would indeed return to take my dinner with them that night, I left them to their moment. I had other business to attend to.

It was a steep climb to the codroche houses, along Low Street and up Back Path with its new-built houses – prosperous young craftsmen making their mark on the world for all to see, engraving their love on the lintels above the doors of their new households. My father had told me once, as we had passed such a doorway, that he had wanted to do the same when he had first brought my mother home from Ireland, to tell the world that she was his and he hers. But there was no engraving above our door, I said. 'No boy, your mother thought it not seemly. She did not want to be as the other craftsmen's wives.' And that had perhaps been it, the beginning of the crumbling of his dream, when she had started, unwittingly perhaps, to punish him, little by little, for her mistake.

I turned left where Back Path met High Street, where some of the grander ones planned their houses away from the bustle of the marketplace and town, and headed up towards the Sandyhill Gate. The wind was not in my face, as it could often be, and it was a pleasant walk. I had no need to rush – Charles was out of the tolbooth, away from the danger of the sheriff's judgement now, and those I sought would not be abroad until it grew dark. I had the time to rest a moment where the road for Strathbogie skirted the foot of the Gallowhill, and to look upon the town of my birth. At the end of its journey from the mountains of the Cairngorm, past the teeming woods of the Deerpark, the clear waters of the Deveron came straight as an arrow, an arrow of fine silver, at the sea, where it broadened out to meet the world. Under a sky that was endless, the great promontories of Tarlair and Troup Head towered over all that might come from the east, and looked to the north and west, where the long golden stretch of the links invited us to our leisure. And our town nestled there, snug back from the west bank of the river, stretching towards its new harbour works at Guthrie's Haven. Narrow winding streets, tentacles reaching up towards the castle, Caldhame, the Boyndie road and the Sandyhills, met together at the heart of the town. The kirk and the marketplace, the tolbooth and the laird of Banff's palace, its long green garden stretching almost to the Greenbanks where the scholars played on this, another unlooked-for holiday. The tall town houses of the merchants jostled with the tenements filled with the poorer folk, the lower craftsmen, the day labourers, the indwellers. A tight, sometimes meandering network of vennels and alleyways, houses, workshops and backyards locked the streets together, a maze that ran through gardens, round wells, into courtyards, pigsties, stables, kailyards, middens. Such was Banff, a place so blessed by God in harvest of land and sea, gone rotten at the heart. And at that heart, I was. A huge cloud began to pass over the sun and the air instantly cooled. I quickened my pace towards the Sandyhill Gate and the codroche houses.

They were not houses really, but shambling, windowless shacks of wood, turf and thatch of the sort the council was striving to banish from the town for fear of fire. They were set back a good bit from the road, up the hillside where a small burn ran down by the rowans and bramble bushes. No one from the town ventured to the codroche houses. The kirk session and council fulminated often against them and their inhabitants, but they were never levelled, never cleared. Filled with beggars, thieves and whores, the detritus of poverty that gave a name to all the fears of the good townspeople. The provost had told me why he tolerated them: they were weeds – weeds that we knew and could control, weeds that would prevent other, invasive weeds coming in and taking root. Weeds that could be managed. Yes, but I also suspected that up here, out of sight, the codroche houses could be, in the minds of my fellow townsmen, a place in which all the evil that was in their town could repose, a reason for them not to look in their neighbour's face, in their own heart, and see it there instead.

As I approached the huddle of shacks a trio of mangy, hungry dogs came towards me, snarling quietly. A small, filthy child, a girl perhaps, in thin rags, ran into one of the houses from the hen house where she had been gathering eggs. A young man – it might have been her father – soon emerged, a large stick in his hand. I did not know him. He did not call off the dogs. 'What do you want?' he asked.

'I am here to see Lang Geordie,' I said.

His suspicion was all the greater.

'Lang Geordie sees no one. What is your business?'

'None of yours.'

I kept my face steady but my heart was pounding and the dogs knew it. They crept closer, and at any moment, at a word from the beggar man, they would be at my throat. More figures had emerged from the houses, two or three other young men, little more than boys, a gaggle of dirty children, a young woman holding a baby, another big with child. Perhaps a dozen pairs of eyes fixed me with cold hostility. The closest dog let out a long growl and was about to spring when a low snarl in some tongue, some vagabond's cant I did not understand, came from the doorway of the main shack. The dog cowered back with a whelp, as if struck, and then slunk away with its companions. The gathering of people at the doorway parted and surveying me, as he supported himself on two crutches, was Lang Geordie.

The man must have been nearly seven feet tall, a giant almost. He had the wild hair and beard of an Old Testament prophet. The brandings on his cheek, marking him out as a 'sturdy beggar', repulsed on pain of death from some other town, only served to inspire greater fear in those who came upon him. I stood there, my chest still heaving from the encounter with the dogs, and waited.

'If it is not the Devil's apprentice,' he said at length, with a hoarse laugh. His followers also laughed, some of the hostility in their eyes being replaced by a ready mockery, but only some. The young men continued to watch me with a clear and studied intent. 'What do you want of me? Are you here for the whores? The word on the roads is that you prefer a higher class of siren in your bed.' Again a laugh, more real now, from the gathering.

So I had made Katharine the talk of the beggars and the thieves on the roads and hovels of the north. It was little wonder her friend Isabella Irvine despised me. I made no response to the jibe. 'It is yourself I am here to see.'

All jocularity was gone now from Lang Geordie's face. He was studying me carefully, weighing me up. I think he had some notion then of what my business was. He uttered something in the cant to his people and they dispersed slowly to the places from which they had come, all but two of the younger men who continued to stand near him, on either side of the only door of the hovel. Lang Geordie gave them some instruction, too and then looked at me again. 'Then come in, Mr Seaton, come in.' I went carefully past the dogs and in between the two guards, stooping low, although not as low as Lang Geordie. Once inside, my eyes could scarce make out a thing. The door had been shut behind me and the only light came from the round smokehole in the middle of the roof and from the open fire itself. As my eyes grew accustomed to the gloom I could discern figures, shapes, huddled in various parts of the one long room that constituted the whole dwelling. A young woman stirred a pot of something – some broth of seaweeds – over the fire; an older woman, coughing as she did so, sang in an alien tongue to a baby in dirty swaddling; two small children scrabbled after something in a corner – a mouse or a rat. On a trestle bed at the far end of the room lay another woman, also coughing. The floor was beaten dirt and I knew not what I would find when I set one foot in front of the other. The stench and squalor were beyond my experience: even the tolbooth jail could scarcely compare with this. Lang Geordie ordered the woman up from the bed – the dwelling's only furnishing – and as he took his seat there himself I saw that she was not a woman, but little more than a girl – fourteen, perhaps. She was wearing a tattered dress that I knew I had seen before, too large by far around the bosom and the hips. A whore's dress; Mary Dawson's dress. The vagabond chief saw me looking at the girl. 'You can have her for a price – after our business is done,' he said, very steady, with no insinuation.

'I do not go with children,' I said.

'She is a child no longer,' said the woman at the pot, bitterly. Geordie spat some reproach at her and she said no more.

The two sentries were inside the hovel now, still keeping guard of the door. I lowered my voice, for I had only business with Geordie himself, and it was business he might not like known amongst his followers. I kept my voice low. 'I have money,' I said, 'not for whores but for information.' He was sizing me up, waiting to see what the offer was, what the terms. He had played this game before and he would wait as long as he needed to. There was nothing for it but to come straight to the matter. 'Who paid you last night?' I asked.

He continued to fix me with his prophet's eyes. 'Last night? Now, what might have happened last night?'

'You roused the rabble, the witch-mongers. You led them to the doctor's door, to lay hands on the body of that poor murdered girl.'

He continued to watch me in the same manner, a little pleased with himself. 'I? I did not rouse that rabble, Mr Seaton. Your godly minister and session clerk had that well in hand; they had no need of a poor beggar man.' He held his hands out self-deprecatingly, and smiled, almost engagingly, as he said it. I would gladly have knocked the last teeth from his head.

'You led them,' I said. 'It was you who crossed the door of an honest man's house when it was barred to you, you who knocked the stable boy to the floor. You gave the beast its head. You with your crutches – all the way down into the town. A great exertion it must have been for you. Do you tell me it was not done for profit? For what else would you have done it? Since when have you concerned yourself with witches?'

The amusement, the playfulness departed from his face. The prophet's look was gone, too. His eyes were of stone, his voice a low rumble. 'Since I watched my mother burn.' He was looking into the past somewhere. 'A hen had stopped laying; a child had grown sick; the water in a burn had gone bad. My mother had called at the house before, twice, desperate for succour to feed her bairns: she was given none.' He paused and there was near silence in the dwelling. Even the children in the corner seemed to have stopped their playing. 'It was thirty years ago and I can still hear her screams.' He pulled himself suddenly to his feet, towering and cold in his anger. 'So that is my concern with witches, Mr Seaton. They had started to talk of witches in the town – the storm, the fishing boats wrecked, the poisoning. And who do you think they would have turned on first, the good burgesses of Banff? I went for them before they came for us!' He was taken by a coughing fit and the woman at the hearth brought over to him a ladle of water. She calmed him and got him to sit down on the bed again. The look I caught from her as she returned to her pot was one of covert fear. His breathing subsided and he let go his crutch, which I had thought he was going to strike me with. 'And that girl, she was dead. What did it matter? Are we not all dust? It could not hurt her, and it gave them a corpse to work out their passions on, instead of a living man or woman. Now, get out of my house, and never let me see you back here, unless it be to stay,' he added with menace.

There was little more I could do. I believed him, and I did not. He had known, I was certain, that I had come up here about the business of the murders, but he had not expected me to ask about the witch-hunt. So what had it been? He called something to the two guards. One opened the door and, giving me a look potent with threat, jerked his head towards it. The other came over and stooped down to Lang Geordie, who murmured something in the cant. I caught the last words though – Mary Dawson. The man pulled me up by my collar and pushed me through the darkness towards the doorway.

Outside the dogs were waiting for me, snarling low. I avoided their eye. My elbow was caught as I stepped forward. 'You were in Aberdeen, Seaton. Is Mary Dawson there?'

'No,' I replied with conviction, 'she is not.' So that was it; he had thought I had come to question him on the warning off of the Dawson sisters, or that I knew something of what they had known. It was with great relief that I finally reached the road leading back to the town from the Sandyhill Gate. The dogs had shadowed me all the way down from the settlement, stopping twenty yards from the roadway. I could feel them watching me for as long as the road remained in their sight. I did not look back. I was glad to win back to the schoolhouse, and glad of the few hours to myself to order my thoughts, between now and when I must appear at the doctor's door.

It was a pleasant walk to Jaffray's. At last a little warmth was being carried on the air, and the evenings were growing lighter – the sky was a mellow golden rose reaching over the firth to the mountains of Sutherland. The storm of last Monday night and its attendant horrors could almost have been a distant memory, consigned to the last throes of winter, had it not left its bitter legacy everywhere I turned.

The evening was a quieter affair than many we three had spent together. We each of us had much to reflect upon. And there was a contentment in the doctor's household. I knew the emptiness I had so often left there when I closed the door behind me would be there no more. Charles, so often taciturn, was the quietest of all, but his was a quiet contentment and wonder of a man who has started to see things he never saw before. Ishbel came in and out of the parlour with steaming dishes and plates. Pickled herring and bread still warm, a fine rabbit pie – Charles's favourite dish – peas, beans, and vegetables of whatever manner her store could provide, a rich gravy owing not a little to the contents of the doctor's cellar, a sturdy egg custard with apples stewed in all manner of sweet spices. The doctor asserted he would be bankrupt before the week was out if they were to dine like this every night. Ishbel flushed with pride and Charles offered to go sing in the streets to pay his way.

When the food was cleared and the *uisge beatha* brought out, we got up and took our accustomed seats around the fire. Jaffray's parlour was no longer the cold and empty place it had seemed on my last few visits: it had the warmth of a home again, and told his story. The Delft tiles of the fireplace, his wedding gift to his wife, had delighted me as a child and delighted me still, with their happy scenes of life in the Dutch countryside. On the walls were the German woodcuts he had so carefully carried back with him from his studies, so many years ago. It was a man's room, filled with books and the aroma of tobacco, but with echoes of the woman who had once been at its heart, in the tapestries on the wall, the pressed flowers, their colours long faded, an embroidered footstool that had been hers. Charles stretched out his feet to the hearth and looked into the slowly dancing flames. I had brought the book of poetry I had purchased for him, having meant to give it to him as a help to sustain him in his jail, and I gave it to him then. For the next half hour, as the doctor and I talked of the news from Aberdeen, Charles was lost in the book. His lips moved in silence as we spoke, and he heard nothing of our talk. At length he started to hum some parts of a tune, and asked the doctor for some paper. 'I will play this, before the week is done; I will play this for you all,' and he hummed and mused to himself as he scrawled at the paper. The snatches of song that escaped him every so often began to work their way into my mind, until I could almost have sung them too. They reminded me of something. When Ishbel came in carrying a basket of fresh coals for the fire I broke off my talk with the doctor and told her of my meeting with Sarah Forbes and where she was now. She closed her eyes and uttered a prayer in her own tongue. 'God's mercy is with her. And his grace with you, Mr Seaton.' When she left I saw that Jaffray was studying me curiously.

'Did you know the girl, when she was in the burgh?' he asked.

I considered the question, and that not for the first time. 'I cannot say that I never saw her. I knew by name and from some of your talk here that she was a friend of Ishbel's.'

Jaffray continued to study me, working as he did so at something stuck in his teeth. 'That was a good thing you did, Alexander. Neither you nor your friend Cargill will have cause to regret it. Sarah will be a good help and companion to her mistress. And,' he added, 'a good mother to her own child.'

Charles glanced up from his scrawling. 'What is this? Are you speaking of women, Alexander? Mistress Youngson will have much to say.'

I laughed. 'Mistress Youngson has always much to say. I am not convinced Gilbert Grant has not perfect hearing, but only feigns his deafness.'

'Without question he feigns it,' rejoined Jaffray.

As Charles returned to his composing, the doctor pressed me further on my trip to Aberdeen: with whom had I met? What gossip had I heard? When I mentioned George Jamesone, his interest quickened. 'You went to see George Jamesone. Now why was that?'

I told him of my commission to the painter from the provost. And then, with some trepidation, I relayed to him William Cargill's concerns about my involvement with the painter and the possibility that his time in Antwerp and connection with Rubens might have led him into a relationship with Rubens' Spanish masters. Jaffray frowned. 'I remember Jamesone. He came to the burgh, as you know, several years ago, to paint Walter Watt and his wife. He was a clever man, and good company, too. But I think your friend is being carried away with rumours if he fears Jamesone is a spy.'

Charles had put down his pen and was listening now. 'Why should a painter be feared, simply because he has travelled? What can it have to do with the trouble in our town?'

Jaffray looked at me, as the one most qualified, albeit reluctantly, to speak on the matter. 'It is to do with the maps, Charles,' I said.

'The maps,' he said slowly to himself, 'the baillie's maps.' He looked at us, some understanding dawning. 'When I was in the tolbooth, the baillie was asking me night and day about maps – what did I know of maps? Had Patrick Davidson spoken of maps? Had I seen any maps in our chamber? What had Marion to do with the maps? And yet he would not tell me anything about them. I truly did not know what he was asking me about, though after dwelling on it a while – I had much time for thinking – I supposed he must have found some maps amongst Patrick's belongings.'

'He did,' I said. 'It was not simply that Patrick Davidson possessed maps, but that they were of this part of the land, from the sea coast as far as Strathbogie, with markings for Elgin, Turriff, and Aberdeen. They were in Davidson's own hand. It is likely that they were drawn, or at least rough sketches drawn, on his gathering expeditions with Marion. Some of the further away ones may have been done – probably were, in fact – before he reached here.'

Charles looked up at me with an air of resignation. 'So that is why they were away so often and so long. I did not think it was the season for many plants, yet I know so little of flowers and their seasons I did not question it, for fear of showing my ignorance. For fear of shutting myself further out of their bond.' He looked away. 'Then Marion must have known of these maps. Do you think perhaps that is why she too was killed? But why should anyone fear a map, kill for a map?'

Jaffray shook his head. 'Oh, Charles. You are too innocent. The rest of the country sees invaders on every wave, with their books and their bells and their beads.'

'Papists?'

'Aye, papists,' the doctor answered, 'if it suits them so to be, as pretext for overrunning our country and overturning our church.'

'I had not thought you so fervent for religion, doctor.' There was no sarcasm, no sly humour in Charles's observation. Just a statement of fact, which was daily evident.

'Oh, do not mistake me, boy. I am no zealot; no James Cardno or William Buchan, but I have my faith and I know who will judge me when the Lord sees fit to lift me from my travails here. The Kirk, though, it is more than the ministers and the session and all the fulmination from the pulpits of idiots or sainted men. The Kirk is who we are: it is our freedom, and without it, we are lost.'

I had never heard him talk in this manner before, not of the Kirk. I leaned forward further in my chair. 'What do you mean, James?'

'I mean that we are servile to no man. We can look at a king and know he is, like us, only a man in the face of God. Our nation will bow and scrape to no man and to no power so long as the Kirk of Scotland is by law established in this land. And that is why I would fight for it, fight against all the Spaniards and the French the legions of Rome can send against us and against Charles Stuart himself if need be, for without it we are not men and we have no nation.' And then I understood what I had wondered at but never before realised: James Jaffray, who seemed in his mind to live still in the great universities and cities and towns of the Europe of his youth, could only ever have called one place home, and he had been drawn back to it as an eagle to its nest.

Charles spoke quietly, looking directly at no one. 'Do you think there will be an invasion?'

Jaffray came to himself a little. 'I do not know. I think it very likely though, and likely too that Walter Watt's nephew was up to his neck in the plotting of it. What did Straloch say to it, Alexander?'

'That the work was well done, extremely well done, and would have done very well for a foreign army landing at our shores. But he denied knowledge of any commission to Patrick Davidson or anyone else for such work, and denied any knowledge of any plots of the sort.'

'Then he is surely cut off from his master,' said Charles, 'for since when did the Marquis of Huntly not plot?'

'Indeed,' said Jaffray. 'But Straloch is a good, honest man. Did you not find him so, Alexander?'

It was a more difficult question than I had bargained for, or at least an honest answer was more difficult to find. 'I think ... I do not know, James. I think Huntly has some business afoot. My old friend, Matthew Lumsden, whom I met with in Old Aberdeen, is in Huntly's retinue. He was to ride that day on business for the marquis, and Matthew is not a man you would use for diplomacy. Straloch himself rode early yesterday for Aberdeen and then Edinburgh on Huntly's affairs, yet I heard horsemen leave the place in the night, and I would hazard they were bound for Strathbogie. What need could there have been for night-riding, what sudden urgency but information I had brought myself?'

'Then we must be vigilant,' said the doctor. 'Now though, did you get Cargill's notebooks? For that is the matter we must attend to here. Charles ...' But Charles Thom had fallen asleep in the chair to the right of the doctor's fire, his stomach full and his heart something less heavy. Jaffray watched him sleep for a few moments, then quietly got up and signalled me to follow him over to the table, which Ishbel had long since cleared. I laid the book out and the doctor began to examine it, turning each leaf over carefully, and marvelling in a low voice at the quality of the drawings and the insight of the annotations. We had not yet reached the page I was sure the *colchicum* was sketched upon when there came a loud knocking at the doctor's back door. Charles Thom was startled out of his sleep, and the doctor got to his feet. In a moment Ishbel was at the parlour door, Edward Arbuthnott, the apothecary close behind her.

'I am sorry, doctor,' she said, 'I—'

'I am not here for the doctor, but the music master,' he said, brushing past her with little ceremony. Charles, still not fully wakened, shambled to his feet. I took a step towards him, but Arbuthnott was in front of him before me. 'Charles Thom, for all that you owe my family, who took you in and gave you food and lodging, and for the love you bore my girl, you will sing for her, you and your scholars, at her lykewake, will you not?'

THE REDEMPTION OF ALEXANDER SEATON

Charles blinked stupidly, not yet come to. 'Her lyikwake? Aye ... aye of course.'

The look on Jaffray's face told what was in my mind also. 'Edward,' he said, 'you cannot be thinking of—'

'Aye, but I am.' The apothecary was defiant. 'Why should my girl, my only child, be put to her rest without what others so much less worthy have had? She will have a lyikwake and all the town will know what it has lost.' He turned again to Charles. 'So you will play at it, and your scholars too?'

'Aye,' said Charles, sitting back down now, discomfited. 'I will.' The apothecary nodded briskly, satisfied, and bade us goodnight.

As the back door banged again and we heard Ishbel put the bolt up, Jaffray looked at me warily, but I said nothing. Charles looked at me, too. 'I know you do not like them, Alexander, but it is not for the money, this time, but for Marion herself.' We had argued often about it, I from the heart and he from the head. The lyikwake, the festival of watching over the dead before they should be interred, their body making its final earthly journey as its soul began its own wanderings in the afterlife. A manifestation of how far the people were still steeped in the superstition of Romanism, if not paganism, which the Kirk would have given much to have eradicated from the burgh. But the people clung tenaciously to it. The civic authorities did not like it either, but so far they tolerated it. At the lyikwake the master of the song school and his pupils would sing and play – that was where Charles made a good part of his money, and why he was loath to give it up. The council knew that if they banned their music master from performing at such gatherings, they would have to compensate him for his loss, and that they were not inclined to do.

What they did not like, and the session fulminated against also, was the lavish entertainment laid out by the family of the deceased and the consequent over-indulgence of the mourners in sweet meats and strong drink and substances that alter men's minds. As the night wore on – for these celebrations were usually at night – the singing and the music would grow louder and less godly, until, when the song schoolchildren had most of them gone home, it would become utterly profane. Dancing would grow wilder, and lascivious behaviour would increase before the very eyes of the magistrates and the session. Few would be fit for their proper work the next day. Baillie Buchan and others of his ilk had fought long and hard to have the holding of lyikwakes forbidden by the town, but to no avail, so far ingrained in the memories of the people were they. I would not argue with Charles about it tonight, though. 'You must do as you think right, Charles. And I know it will not be for the money.'

'I think I will go to my bed now,' he said. 'It has been a long and strange day.'

'Take care you do not scald your feet,' the doctor told him. 'Ishbel will have put a warming pan in your bed. If not two, indeed, for now that you are here I should not be surprised to learn that mine is in there as well. I will be left to shift as I may without one, and no doubt freeze to death. Ah, the ingratitude of the young.' The doctor was happy: all was once again as it should be in his life.

Charles looked a little bashful. Taking up his book of Craig's poetry he bade us goodnight and made his way towards the kitchen, where Ishbel would not yet have finished her night's work.

We returned now to the table, and the examination of James Cargill's notebook. The script was small and neat, the Latin perfect, but the draw-ings themselves were of an exquisite nature, beyond perfect. I looked at them in wonder for a few moments, as my older companion silently read. A bright yet distant look was in his eyes. I had seen this look on him before. He was transported to another time, another place. Alpine meadows and the valleys of the Pyrenees. A group of young men, running, climbing with all the sureness of foot of mountain goats, and stopping, every so often, to hang on the words of their teacher, as he told them of every property, pointed out every small and fine detail, of some tiny plant or flower. 'They were good times for you, James,' I said.

'Aye,' he replied, 'they were. But it is to the present that we must turn our eyes and our minds. You say you think you have come upon the flower?'

'I cannot be sure, but it is the name that you told me.' I took the book from him and then leafed through its pages until I found what I was looking for. I turned the book back towards him. 'There,' I said. 'Is that it?'

He nodded slowly, his eyes keen. 'Aye,' he said, 'it is.' He traced a finger beneath the outline of the flower, and began to read out the words. '"Petals the grey-blue of the northern sky after it has snowed. Calyx of deep purple sepals below, small, pale green bract. Stigma and anthers yellow, the colour of straw in September. The whole forming a large goblet on a slender white stem. Basal leaves, long, dark, glossy green straps, emerging after blooms. One corm will produce 6–8 blooms on 3–5 leaves. Unlike its benign relatives, flowers not in the autumn, but the spring." Aye, that is it, that is it; it is quite different from the other colchicum, you know,' he said, growing excited. He read on, using terms and talking of properties I did not understand, until his voice, slow and deliberate, with great emphasis, intoned, '"corm has the look of a small, elongated and blackened onion. Utterly and almost instantly lethal if ingested."' There was more, about where the plant was to be found, the difficulties of cultivation, the lack of any known beneficial medicinal use. Then words not in Latin, but in Cargill's own native tongue and ours. 'The Salome of all flowers: beautiful, and deadly.' Jaffray gave a short, humourless laugh. 'Little wonder he never married. Every beautiful woman must have called to mind for him some botanical instrument of death. But this is it, Alexander, this is the flower we seek. Through the vomit, the chicory scent could still be got in their hair.'

'And you have never seen it here?'

'Never. There are perhaps some like it in appearance, in the blue at least, but the purple calyx and stigma, these I have never seen here. Have you?' He asked the question absent-mindedly, little thinking that there could be any other than one answer. When I did not reply, he looked up from studying the book. 'Have you seen it, Alexander?'

I hesitated. 'I . . . I do not know. I do not think so. That is – I think I may have done.' There was something, something flitting before my eyes, in my mind. A glimpse, little more, of blue, with purple, falling, falling. I searched harder. I shut my eyes against the warm golden light of the room, for it was another type of light I sought – darker, colder, more still. I tried to clear my mind of the almost inaudible breathing of the fire, the heavier intrusion of my companion, the knowledge of the life and movement in the room and the power of the sea in the darkness outside, but I could not. The image, the memory of the image was gone, and now all I had was a construction of my own making. I opened my eyes, shaking my head in a slow frustration. 'I am sorry, James,' I said. 'It is gone. Whatever I thought I remembered, it is gone.'

The look of hopefulness faded from his face to be replaced by one of disappointment. 'Do you think it was in Banff itself, or out in the country somewhere, maybe? Was it wild, or in a garden? Do you think it might even have been in Aberdeen?' This last suggestion lit some small flicker of possibility in my memory. Had it been in Aberdeen? Somewhere in Aberdeen? There was something that seemed to make it possible, but no. I could reach no further than that into the recesses of my mind, and then the flickering light went out.

'No, doctor, I am sorry; there is nothing.'

'Ah, well,' he said, 'maybe something will bring it back to you. With these drawings at least, we know what it is that we deal with, and that is something.' He closed the book and again smoothed his hand over the front cover. 'You told your friend William Cargill why we wanted these notebooks?'

'There was no other way to explain my sudden interest in botany, and,' I added, 'in the way of friendship, I wanted to talk with him about the business.'

He smiled. 'I am glad you are allowing your friends to be friends again. And what did William Cargill think of this business here? The murder, I mean, and the imprisonment of Charles.'

I looked at him. 'He said that I should take great care. He fears for me in all this, that there are signs pointing to me, there for when people are ready to look.'

Jaffray's eyes were steady. 'He is right. I have thought it myself and never said it, though perhaps I should have done. And do you fear this, Alexander?'

A few weeks ago I would have said I had no more fear of what man – or, in the blackest of my days, God – could do to me. But that was no longer true. I had been out again in the world of men; I was not a thing damaged beyond use as I had for long believed. I had lost the respect of the world once and, as I saw it, the access to God also. 'I think I would like to keep what name I have left to me, and what future too.'

'Then you must take a great care, Alexander, that you do not lay yourself open to further danger. When you were in Aberdeen, did you tell anyone other than William Cargill of our desire to see the notebooks, or of our reason for it?'

'I told no one.'

'And you have shown no one the notebooks, until now?'

'No one,' I asserted. At Straloch I had kept them well hidden amongst the things I had taken into the house with me, having been careful not to leave them in the stables with my horse and other goods, for fear of fire. 'Does it matter so much?'

He considered. 'Perhaps not, but the fewer people who suspect you of drawing closer to the truth of this thing, the safer you will be.'

'And will you show them to Arbuthnott?' I asked.

'It would perhaps be wiser not to. I do not think it will do him good to dwell over-much on the means of Marion's death. But,' he continued, 'it may be that we have no choice, for he would have a better knowledge than either of us of the plants that grow hereabouts, and the drawings might spark some memory in him. It was Marion though, Marion who would have known more surely than anyone where it is to be found.'

'And you had only the one opportunity to speak privately with her while I was gone?'

'I did,' he said. 'For when the baillie was not about her, her mother was, and she would not talk before either of them.'

'And she really told you nothing of this business?' I pressed.

He turned away and stoked the fire. 'We spoke of other things.'

I knew of old the tenor of Jaffray's voice when he wished to close a subject, and it betrayed him now. Yet I was not ready to leave it. 'Do you think she knew about Davidson's activities – the map-drawing, and what it was for?'

'She cannot but have known about it – certainly about the drawing, for when else would he have made his sketches than when they were wandering about the countryside? As to the espionage – if there was any – Marion was not the girl to get caught up in great causes or secret plots. They would have been an unnecessary distraction for her from the essentials of life – of her life at least. She had too great an interest in her father's craft and in other science to waste her time on the politics and religion of nations. I think had Davidson been involved in those pursuits, or attempted to entangle her in them, their companionship would have come to an earlier and cleaner end.'

I thought about the girl, trying to remember the few true conversations we had had together. Jaffray was right. In her hours away from her work in the provost's nursery, she had worked steadily and with great focus on the understanding of the pharmacopoeia of her father's craft and the nature and purpose of every plant that grew around these parts. She would have cared little for Spanish invaders or popish plots, and certainly would not have lost her life in their defence. But how far might her fascination with science have taken her? 'Jaffray,' I began, 'do you truly give no credence to the idea that she was . . .'

His brow darkened and he looked at me hard. 'Go on, Alexander.'

'Do you truly give no credence to the idea that she meddled in witchcraft?'

He breathed a great sigh of exasperation. 'This again? Do you tell me you believe that pernicious nonsense?'

'No,' I answered truthfully and emphatically, 'I do not.'

'Then why . . . ?'

'Because she went to all the places, James. The Elf Kirk, Ordiquhill, where John Philp is much suspected as a witch, where the waters are said to have properties, and Darkwater.'

Instead of continuing in his anger, Jaffray broke into a smile and laughed at me, though nervously, I thought. 'Oh, Alexander, come now. Half the bairns in the town are at the Elf Kirk precisely because their mothers and the session warn them from it. And as for Ordiquhill and Darkwater, well, both are places of importance to those who would seek to land or make their way inland from our coast. Findlater guards the coast at Darkwater, and Ordiquhill is on the road from there to Strathbogie, by Fordyce. Davidson would need to know them both for his mapping.' He turned away from me and went again to stoke the fire. I knew he was hiding something from me.

'James, she went twice to Darkwater: once with Davidson, and once on her own, after he was dead. They say she went to the wise woman.'

He spun round angrily. '"They say". Who is this new "they" in whom you place such trust?'

'It was much muttered by the mob last night—'

Jaffray was incredulous. 'What? You now take the word of a rabble under the direction of a beggarman thief? Lang Geordie would have great interest in directing any accusation of witchcraft away from himself and his followers.'

'Yes, I know that. He admitted as much to me himself. But there was also Mistress Youngson. She is no idle gossip, as you know, and she wished the girl no ill.'

Jaffray's shoulders sank. 'Aye, you are right. She did not.' He went to the door and looked down the passageway. Nothing stirred in the house. 'I know that Marion went to Darkwater, with Davidson, and alone. I think I know why she went, and there was no witchcraft nor yet spying in it.' I waited, but he evidently considered himself to have finished. 'Oh, for the love of God, Alexander, you of all people must know the crone is not a witch. Who nursed you from your delirium last year? Who saved you from death on the rocks of Findlater?' I knew it, I knew it all, for Jaffray had told it to me, but I had no memory of any of it, nothing until the day Jaffray arrived on the beach below the castle rock to take me home. He continued, 'She is no witch, but a healing woman, a wise woman who was in her day a skilled midwife who brought many into this world who might otherwise have died in their struggle. But then, years ago now, I do not remember when, she took herself off, away from the world, to that cave in Darkwater to glean her living from the sea and from the cliffs and plants around her. I have not seen her since then, but they say it was because she had seen too much pain and death where there should have been joy and life. There are those who say she feared the witch-mongers, who are too ready to blame the misfortunes of life or the will of God on the agency of another. And that may be true – it would not have been long before the death of some child would have been laid at her door.'

I wondered if in different circumstances, in another life, Jaffray and Lang Geordie would have met. In this matter they had a similar view of our world, but were so circumstanced that it was unlikely either would ever know it. 'Marion and Patrick Davidson went to the wise woman for some sort of help?'

He nodded. 'I think it likely.'

'Why did she go a second time? After he was dead?'

'I do not know. Perhaps there was a something ...' his voice trailed away.

'But I do know that she was determined on going. I counselled her against it, as did Geleis Guild, who had called me to see to her, for she could see that the girl was not well. It was to no avail – I had had no great hopes that it would be, for I had got little of sense from her in all the time I spent with her after you left for Aberdeen. One thing she was adamant about was that she would free Charles, she was determined on it, for she knew he had not killed Patrick.'

'And she has freed him,' I said.

'Aye, God rest her, she has.' One of the candles in the sconce spluttered out, filling this homely room with melancholy.

'When did she go to Darkwater?' I asked.

'It was on the day before her death.'

Ideas were forming in my mind, then threatening to slip away before I could take hold of them. 'James, do you think it possible that this wise woman, this midwife, may have knowledge of the plant, the colchicum? That perhaps, indeed, she may have more to do with this business than we have guessed at?' I could feel a growing excitement as I spoke. I knew what I would do, and so did Jaffray. He looked at me a long moment and began to shake his head.

'You cannot be thinking of this. No good can come of it. Charles is freed. You must not put yourself in danger of taking his place.'

'What kind of freedom is it to hide in the safe places while a murderer walks the streets? What rest can there be for the man who glimpses the right path but takes the wrong one, for fear he will snag his coat on some thorn? I can do some good in this, James.'

Jaffray was not to be persuaded. 'You have some notion in your mind that you have been chosen to bring the killer of these two people to a reckoning – whether before God or man I cannot tell. You believe you have been called to accomplish this. But, Alexander, there are proper authorities whose place and function it is to investigate and try these matters, and you are not one of them. When Charles was falsely accused and falsely imprisoned by those authorities, it was for us, his friends, to do everything in our power to free him. But that thing is done now, and it is no business of yours to carry on in this. You trespass on the rights of those whose duty it is and in doing so may bring danger on yourself and on other innocents.'

There was a depth of sadness in his eyes that might have won me over were it not that there was something more than a grain of truth in what he said.

'You are right, doctor, I do feel called to continue in this until the murderer is brought to answer before man, and then God. It is not pride – believe what you like, but it is not pride, only an attempt to propitiate my own shame.'

'Shame?'

'Yes, shame. Shame that I ignored the cries of that man as he crawled to his death. The town whores did that good for him that I had refused to do. They brought him to what they thought to be a place of safety. And he died, alone and in wretched agonies, while I slept sound and warm in my bed above. So I do believe that God has given me this duty, that he put it in the baillie's mind to call me to the counsel about the maps, to make my mission to Straloch. I believe it was God who put me in the path of Janet Dawson as she was hounded from our burgh, and Mary Dawson when she fled from Aberdeen. Charles is free, and I thank God for that, but I believe I am called none the less to make some recompense.'

'Alexander,' he said in a low voice, 'I truly do not believe you understand what danger you may be putting yourself in by this course. You are,' he searched a moment for the right word, 'vulnerable. You could easily enough be made a target for the murder accusation yourself. You do not quite belong to this burgh – born and bred here though you have been: you are almost as different as was your mother, and there are those who yet remember her. You think last night was foul, barbarous? You are right, but it was nothing to what you in your twenty-six years have not seen. The barbarity of the witch-hunt, of the tortures, the probing for evidence, the burning stake with the screams of a living human being rising from its flames are beyond all imagining. Do not go to Darkwater, Alexander; it will avail you nothing, and, I doubt, do little to solace the living who already grieve for their dead.'

I had never before known Jaffray give up the fight. That he should do so, even partially out of fears for me, saddened me greatly. 'But James, it may well be that this murderer's killing has not finished. I cannot rest easy in myself if I believe there is a way to end this and I do not take it.'

He was not quite ready to relent. 'But why should that way lead to Darkwater?'

'I do not know. But I have a belief that it does and I must follow it. I will leave at first light and be back well before dusk, my friend. Do not fear for me.' I took up my cloak and hat and bade him goodnight.

THIRTEEN

The Wise Woman of Darkwater

Jaffray made one final effort to dissuade me from going to consult with the wise woman at Darkwater. A little after dawn on the Thursday morning, as I was washing, he appeared at the door of my chamber, and Mistress Youngson behind him. I saw at once that he had told her of my intention. The doctor watched as I put on my outer garments. I picked up my cloak with the marten collar, a gift from the Lady Hay on my laureation Master of Arts. 'You are still intent on this madness then,' said the doctor.

'It is not madness, doctor, but this thing has taken hold of me, and I fear it will lead to some madness, or despair, if I do not finish it. I do not think there is a choice.'

It was as if I had not spoken. 'Alexander, I beg of you not to go; it will do no good and may bring you harm.'

I would have made a reply, but the schoolmaster's wife was there before me. There was a coldness in her voice which, despite the hundred lectures of disapproval she had found fitting to give me, I had never heard before. 'You must not go, Alexander. You will bring down upon your head and your soul things that cannot by man be lifted.' Had I known her less well, I might have believed myself cursed.

'Have no fear, mistress. My faith may be weak and my calling lost, but the Devil shall not yet have me for his own. And as to the world of men, be assured I will have a care to bring no trouble to your door.'

Her response was softly spoken and it pierced my heart. 'My door has opened many times to your troubles, Mr Seaton. I have no fears on that count.' She turned back down the stairs. I felt shame at the sight of the old woman's retreating back. How many times could I throw my ingratitude in her face? Jaffray lingered a little longer, but soon also left, his face leaden with disappointment.

The town I passed through was quiet still, and there was menace in the quiet. So many still lay shut up in the tolbooth, or out at Inchdrewer, or in the castle dungeons, awaiting the sheriff's judgement. They would not have long to wait. Surely the sheriff must return soon. It was reported that the witch-hunt had begun again in Fife, and in Ayrshire, too. It was spreading, spreading with its own fire, and its flames left behind only the charred remains of men's souls. The loud madness of the mobs at the pyre was as nothing to the quiet madness in a man's mind as he desperately sought to save himself by damning another. The outbreak at Banff must be contained and then the burgh made safe against incursions of the hunt from outside. No one mentioned the fear, the fear of neighbour of neighbour, of accusations false or fancied, the dark twisting of the mind. To mention it would have been to call it down upon us.

The silence that had begun to weigh on me was broken by the clear tones of Thomas Stewart as I neared the top of Water Path on my way towards the Boyndie Road. 'You shall have your fee when the work is done, not a moment before.'

Reply was made in a coarser voice. It was George Burnett. 'Let the council be damned. I was to have payment at Whitsun. The work cannot be finished if I am not allowed to continue with it.'

The notary was little perturbed by the curse. 'The work should have been finished by now, and you would have had your money at Whitsun. But it is there for all to see – the ground is scarce cleared enough in places for the founds to be properly dug. The town will bear no further expense for a new manse until the matter of the minister is resolved.'

'Let him be resolved to Hell, for all I care. I have wages to pay.'

'Then have your men do their work on time,' answered the notary, 'but there is to be no more work on this land until the minister's fate is declared by the presbytery, and a new minister found.'

'Aye, and it may be long enough before another blathering half-wit is forced to bleat from our pulpit.' Having no further response, George Burnett, master mason and father of Sarah Forbes's bastard child, swung his great bulk away from the notary and strode past me down the Water Path. The acrid brute smell of him caught in my throat as he passed, and made me want to vomit. He did not notice me, and I hoped never to see him again. By the time I had recovered myself, Thomas Stewart had gone, the great front door of the provost's house shutting firmly on his shadow in the early-morning glow.

No one seemed to notice me as I made my way across the Castlegate and up Boyndie Street. The watch on the burgh gate only questioned me briefly as I sought to leave the town, and within a quarter hour of leaving the confines of the schoolhouse, I found myself again, gladly, on the open road.

I had determined that the two or three hours my walk might take me would be spent in the ordering of my mind. I would apply the Ramist principles of one of my early regents at college, distilling the essential questions, dealing with them in their parts and setting the individual conclusions into clear and consequential schemata in my mind. But my thoughts would not permit themselves to be marshalled in such a way. Where I had hoped for clarity, confusion reigned. Faces, words, phrases, came wandering, sometimes staggering, to the forefront of my mind, dragging with them suspicions of spying, witchcraft, poisoning, papists, love, fear, jealousy, hate. Strange couriers in the night, calling Jaffray out of town, riding from Straloch, on the heels of Mary Dawson, fled now across the sea because she knew – what? Frantic searches for a dead man while he still lived, because of what secret knowledge? Flowers not known but known, by myself, by the doctor, by the apothecary, in a notebook, of the dead, but in another place too, and by another. 'James and the flowers'. James Cardno? James Jaffray? James Cargill? Who?

As the miles went on, my thoughts meandered so far from where they had started, I scarcely knew what the questions were. How would Sarah Forbes and her child fare in Aberdeen? What had I brought into the lives of William Cargill and his wife and their unborn child? Would the children be natural companions, or would they grow up to dislike and envy one another? Does a man choose his friends, or are they chosen by God? What would my life have been without Archibald Hay? What would he who had such a big life, who had known the world and died in it, think of me now, and the smallness of my life that had taken me nowhere? Where was his sister now? Had she told all to Straloch's niece, who hated me so? Was Straloch to be trusted? Had Patrick Davidson truly been a spy? And so, without resolution or clarity, insight or enlightenment, I went on. By the time I came to the fork in the road where my choice was to make for Fordyce by one route or Sandend by the other, I could almost have believed that the brethren were still there, gathered at Fordyce, waiting for me to come and present myself before them, to meet my last trial, once again, for the ministry.

The damp air around me took on a chill as I left the Cullen road and turned off to my right, towards the sea once more, and the cliffs from which Findlater glowered over to the mountains of the north. By the time I crested the hill at Brankanenthum and began the descent towards Findlater on its neck of rock, the haar had begun to creep in from the sea. It crawled ashore and up the rock, enfolding all it passed in a blanket of impenetrable grey fog. Halfway up the cliff-side, forty or fifty feet or more, the castle grew straight up, a stately palace from the rock. Gradually, the haar took it too, till all that remained was a ghostly shadow of what once my eyes had seen. I grew uneasy. It might be hours, or days even, until this fog lifted, and I must not stay long from Banff. For all that I misliked and feared the superstition and the excess of the lyikwake, I was determined that Charles should not be exposed to the risks there alone. I must win back to Banff before tomorrow night, come what may.

As Findlater evanesced before my eyes, I wondered what an invading army, were it to land today, would make of its first footfall on Scotland, a grey pall of wretchedness laid over this land for which they risked their lives. And what defence should they find here, should they arrive today, to claim Scotland for their popish realm? A failed minister on his way to consult a witch. I uttered a prayer that should the day come when the Spaniard set the prow of his boat on Darkwater beach, God would send down all the haar of the oceans in his path.

I had no memory of my last visit here, save for when Jaffray had come to take me home. I had been here only once before that, many, many years ago. It had been a holiday, when my mother and Jaffray's wife, one startling summer's day, had taken me with them early in the morning from my bed, and brought me to this wonderful, secret place, to play and swim for hours. I had little memory of them or how they had passed the time that day, so taken up had I been with my own childish pleasures. What was certain was that the paths I had run down, the dunes I had tumbled on at the age of six or seven on a warm summer's day were blasted and wind-blown and so altered in this mist I was in hazard of broken limbs with almost every step. More, if I fell here, from this precipice ninety feet above the strand, I might never be found, or if found, I might never survive to tell the tale. Jaffray's pleas of the morning and of last night came to me through the mist, but it was too late now to heed them.

A few stumbling steps forward and I came to a halt. I could not see my foot in front of me; every step might bring me closer to death on the rocks. The heavy mist obscured the sounds of the sea, the birds of the air, everything but the noise of my heart thumping in my breast. All around me was an eerie, grey silence. Yet through it, through the impenetrable haar, I knew I was being watched. Further movement was not possible: I froze where I was, and it came. An arm caught me, a wizened, bony hand, coming, it seemed, from the ground and clamping itself around my wrist. 'Do not move, Alexander Seaton. If you value your life, do not move a muscle.'

I waited, scared almost to breathe. It was a voice I knew, but from where I could not tell. Another hand appeared from below, bearing an amber torch, glowing through the mist, and then hair, grizzled, grey, unkempt. Slowly the head rose towards me and I saw myself looking into the yellowed eyes of the wise woman of Darkwater. She might have been any age from forty to seventy. Her teeth were nearly all gone, and there was no humour and, I thought, little humanity in her face. Her eyes searched mine for a moment, and she seemed satisfied. 'Step backwards three paces, and then turn to your left.'

I did as she said, for want of an option. Once I had done so, she moved past me with scarcely a disturbance of the air. I saw her a little better now. Even without her stoop, she would have been little over five feet tall. Now I saw behind her, by the light of her torch, a steep drop through a crevice in the rock; I had been a few inches from falling to my death. As I struggled to master my tongue, she appraised me more fully. I felt I did not meet entirely with her approval. 'Like your mother still. I wondered when you would come.' She turned to her left. 'Follow in my footsteps – precisely, mind – and do not deviate. This is a bad path you have taken.' It took twenty minutes, twenty silent minutes apart from the occasional 'mind your foot there; keep to the right; no, not that stone,' from the crone before we had made our way safely onto the sand. Once there, she did not stop, nor turn to address or question me; she simply walked on, and I knew that I was to follow. I could hear the sea now, lapping gently onto the shore, but I could not tell how far from me it was.

We walked the length of the beach and at the end of it she started to climb again, up the dunes and towards the far headland. Then it seemed to me that she had disappeared; I followed in the direction she had gone, for a moment seeing nothing but a vague impression of the hillside. Then – though I do not know whether it was a glimpse of flame or the smell of smoking wood that drew me – I at last discerned just ahead of me the opening to a cave in the side of the headland.

'Well, come in then, and pull over that board behind you, or we will both die of the damp and the cold.'

To my left there was a double lattice screen covered in stretched hide, higher than myself and broader than the cave opening, which was wide enough to let two men pass. I pulled it along on wooden runners and lashed it by leather thongs to bolts of iron hammered into the wall. To my surprise, the cavern was warm and dry. The crone had thrown driftwood onto the fire and it blazed well. The floor was covered in rush matting and knotted rugs, which looked to be made of rags, oddments, knotted and woven together. A table, a chair, a bed and shelving had all been fashioned from what the sea had brought to the shore of Darkwater. Wrecks and rubbish from boats on the firth and further afield had served the woman well. A pulley hung overhead, suspended from huge hooks of iron chiselled into the rock, and from it hung a myriad of drying plants, only some of whose names I knew. She followed the line of my vision and lowered the pulley, taking down some specimens and setting them on the workbench behind her. She spoke almost absent-mindedly to me.

'Lesser celandine. For the piles,' she said with a grim smile. 'Sweet violet – but you, I think, have no trouble with your breathing. Common chick-weed – for the skin. You are pasty of face, but healthy enough. Coltsfoot – you will be needing that should you return to Banff in this – you will be in bed with the fever for a week. But this, perhaps, this is what you need.' She held out the long stems of a plant crowned by clustered heads of small, pale pink flowers. 'Valerian. It will relieve the insomnia, allow sleep, help with the tensions in your head.' I knew the plant well. My mother had often taken it in simples and decoctions that I had fetched her from Arbuthnott. I did not want to remember these things.

'I am not here for your medicines or healing,' I said. 'There is something I need you to tell me.'

She put down the flowers and looked at me cautiously. 'Three times in as many weeks I have had a visitor from Banff who has spoken these words to me. The first is dead, the second also. I have saved your life three times now; I would not have you the third.'

Three times? I thought the old woman wandered in her mind. 'I would be fodder for the gulls by now had you not steadied me out on the cliffs.'

She looked at me with what might almost have been contempt. 'Hmph. You would be fodder for nothing. You would not be here at all, nor anywhere else in your life gone by. Time enough for that. But tell me why you have come, what it is you think I can tell you.' I was not certain that she was speaking of last summer, but she was evidently in no humour to go into our past relationship in greater detail and I had other business in mind, so I left it. She indicated a place behind me, and I sat down on a mattress of sorts, covered by a fleece. A sheep wandering away from the flock, tumbling over the edge of the cliff as I had almost done, would have been a fine treasure trove to the old woman. I scanned what I could of the cavern, but nothing in it was familiar to me. The fruits of land and sea had not been wasted here. I wondered at the struggle some men have to gain riches in a world where God so easily will gift them. By the time I had settled myself, she had taken off the long cloak of sealskin that had protected her from the elements. Shapeless layers of unbleached wool and a tunic of rabbit skins protected her against such elements of cold as found their way into her home. She gathered a mortar and pestle from a niche in the cavern wall and continued with her work, never looking at me. 'Go on then,' she said. 'Tell me your business.'

'These visitors you had. Were they Patrick Davidson and Marion Arbuthnott?'

She paused in her work, her back still to me. All movement was stopped. 'Are you here on the baillie's business?' she asked.

'I am here on my own,' I said. 'Will you answer my question, for all that?'

She considered. 'Have you no fear of death too, then?'

It was a question I fought with now almost every night, a question that had stolen from me many hours of sleep. 'I have fear of the judgement that is to come and of those last waking moments when I cannot deny a wasted life. But they will come at their time, and it is not in my power to say whether that time is today or sixty years from now.'

She recommenced her grinding. 'That is perhaps for the best. Those who seek to have power over the time of their death waste the days of their living in worrying about it.'

'And were Patrick Davidson and Marion Arbuthnott amongst them?'

She ladled water from a barrel into a small pot hanging over the fire. She was very precise as to the number of ladles full, and did not answer me until she had finished. 'They wished for the power over life, and the knowledge of death.'

'I do not understand you.'

She sighed and at last sat down opposite me, on the other side of the fire, the simmering pot between us. She looked directly into my eyes, did not blink.

'Alexander Seaton. I knew you before you were born, before you were of this world. I knew you before your father knew you. Your mother came to me as many others have done – it was the doctor's wife that took her.'

'Jaffray's?' I interrupted.

'Aye, Jaffray's. She had been here to me before, Jaffray's wife. In a desperation that I could save her bairns, give her some compound, some infusion, some charm even, that they should live. But it was beyond my power or knowledge, as it was of her husband's, to effect such a thing. We fed her carrots to promote conception, had her drink decoctions of salted sage juice to stave off the miscarriage, and gave her savin. She took the wild, stinking arrach to cure her womb. She even slept with an empty cradle at her bedside, although her husband did not like this – he feared it was charming. And still they died, every one, scarce afore they had drawn breath. And then she took your mother here.'

'Why?' I asked. 'Was she too in fear of losing a child?'

She spat to the side and looked at me again. 'No, she was in fear of having one. You.'

All sound stopped in my ears, and in the middle of its roar, I knew what was coming next. I had no wish to hear it from this hag. I uttered the words myself. 'She wanted something from you to help her cast me from her womb.'

She nodded slowly, evidently taking little pleasure in the conversation.

'But what you gave her failed, just as what you gave the doctor's wife to save her bairns failed.'

'No,' she replied, emotionless, 'it did not, for I gave her nothing. Do not misunderstand me, Mr Seaton. There are many ways to help a woman rid herself of a child – it is not difficult. Many women have come to me in distress with the same request and I have helped them, but not all, and your mother was one whom I refused.'

The crone pulled back the lattice screen a moment, and the fog seeped into her dwelling. Nothing of the outer world could be seen. Inside the cavern, all save the fire and the pot now boiling above it was silent and still. I had returned to the place where the fact of my life had been decided. Jaffray had known what I would learn here, and that was why he had tried to stop me.

'Why did you refuse her?'

She stopped watching me and returned to her pot. 'Because I knew she would regret it. She did not truly want it. She wanted her life to be other than what it was and it could not be if she was tied to you. It was your father, or his world, she did not want. She wanted back to her own place, and her own like, but she could not go with you, so she sought to lose you, to dissolve the thing that would bind her here. I did not let her. There are choices that a woman must live with, and your mother had to live with hers. To the end of her days. It was not spite on my part, mind, but I knew she did not really want it. She could have effected the thing herself, if she had truly had her heart in it. There were many things she could have done, many things she could have taken. She could have taken dog's mercury, or the wild carrot. She could have drunk a strong tincture of tansy, or wallflowers, or juniper berries. She could have used nutmeg; it is known.'

'My mother would not have known of such things,' I said.

She smiled a bitter smile. 'You think not? I think she had such knowledge: she knew of the darkness. The doctor's wife could not see it though; she had thought your mother wished to be taken here for help with conceiving a child, not losing one. The deceit was great – a great and cruel betrayal. I have not known many women who could have trampled in that way over the heartbreak of a friend. But God has his reasons, although I cannot fathom Him.'

'His reasons?' My senses had been obliterated by the shock that my mother had not wanted me to draw breath, and I was not really following the crone now.

'Aye. His reasons. For blessing the one and torturing the other.' She looked up at me with keen eyes. 'For it is a torture, you know, to have the love within you for a child that will not be conceived, or if so, not born living. I have known many women who are mothers in their hearts, in their souls, but who never yet conceived or bore the child they carried within them. I have known women go through life with a broken heart for the loss of a tiny scrap of humanity that was all the world to them. They say Jaffray's wife, and the provost's wife too, Helen, the first one, died young because they were worn out with the constant burden of the children they carried and lost. They didn't: they died of despair.' She breathed a deep sigh. 'There is a despair that leads to distraction. The last time I saw Helen Black she was fearful, on the edge of losing her mind through grief, in such desperation for a living child as if she could go on no more without it. And yet there have been many more, like your mother, who came to me that I might cast off the bairn within them. But one woman at the edge of her wits does not see what another suffers.' She looked into memories in the flames. 'It was a warm autumn day they came, I remember. But their journey homeward must have been cold as December, your mother full of her resentments and regrets, and the doctor's wife abandoned to her devastation.'

These were not the women I remembered. 'You are wrong,' I said. 'They were friends. They even brought me here one day, I am sure of it.'

Something nearly approaching a smile crossed the old woman's lips, and there were images in her eyes. 'Aye, they did bring you. The coldness between them passed when you were born, for your mother took you to her heart with joy the moment she saw you. She recoiled from the knowledge of what she had almost done. She was filled with remorse. Elizabeth, the doctor's wife, could not carry hatreds against other of God's creatures, and so they were reconciled. They brought you here on your sixth birthday, that I might see what I was to be thanked for. That is how I knew you, when I found you last year, stumbling in your delirium on the road from Sandend. You are still all your mother's son.'

I almost laughed. 'But that there were twenty years between those times.'

She stirred her pot and looked up at me. 'Had it been forty I would have known you. You have the same eyes, and the same soul. A man cannot change his soul.'

'But he can lose it,' I said.

She narrowed her eyes quizzically. 'Are you turned papist, then?'

'No,' I was emphatic, 'never that.'

She sniffed, tiring of this line of conversation. I myself did not wish to pursue it: she had been leading me further away from what I wanted to know. 'What did you mean,' I began cautiously, 'when you said Marion Arbuthnott and Patrick Davidson sought the power over life and the knowledge of death?' I was fearful now, sitting here in this cavern, surrounded by herbs and plants and animal skins. In my head, the cries of the witchmongers began to sound.

She asked me once more, 'You are not on the baillie's business?'

I repeated that I was not.

'Nor yet the minister's?'

'We have no minister now, in Banff.'

'Indeed?'

'Since ...' I hesitated, unwilling to speak in this place of witchcraft.

'Since they burnt that poor girl for a witch,' she said.

I lowered my head. 'Yes. Robert Guild will never preach in Banff again.'

She spat again. 'Well, since you are here for neither Kirk nor council, I will tell you. The girl was with child. The bairn was his – her father's apprentice. They came to me at first to ask for some compound or practice that might help her carry the bairn a few weeks longer – beyond its term. They wished to marry, but they knew that before they had the banns up her belly would be swelling and their secret known. They did not wish that

252

shame on the bairn's name, or the humiliation for themselves of sitting before the kirk on the stool for all the hypocrites to rail at. Also, I think the girl did not wish to disappoint her father. She did not say so, but I have seen it many times, and the look was in her eyes that I have seen on many others.'

The horror of it came cold on me. This was what Jaffray had known; this the secret of the dead that he had kept in the face of all my questioning. And he had had to watch, helpless, as the mob had taken her dead body from his house and added barbarity to barbarity. A mother had been murdered and within her her child, and it had been burned in her womb. I did not know how I would face the lyikwake Arbuthnott intended for his daughter. The thing had been macabre enough without this.

My voice was hoarse. 'Were you able to help them?' I asked.

The crone shook her head. She indicated with a sweep of her hand the shelves of bottles and jars behind her. 'My skill is in cutting short a woman's time, or when it comes to it, assisting a living child into the arms of a living mother, when God so grants it. For the prolonging of a pregnancy I can do little, save to tell a woman to eat well and avoid toilsome labours. I explained this to them. She was much downcast, he agitated. I told them there had been many come to me in a worse case than they; that they should take their punishment and know that it would pass. I told them of those who have come to me in desperate straits – even of his own aunt, who had near lost her wits in fear and gone about like a thing haunted by the end of her life over the loss of all her children.' She stirred her pot thoughtfully. 'Aye, haunted she was indeed by them.' She did not linger long in her reverie. 'And so they left. And then the next thing I knew, the boy was dead by an unknown hand.' She paused again for thought, before adding very matter-of-fact, 'It may have been her father.'

I made no response to this, for it was a distraction from the path my mind was now taking. 'Marion Arbuthnott came to see you again, did she not?'

'Aye,' she responded warily, 'she did.'

'What did she come for the second time?'

She looked at me carefully, assessing me. For a moment I feared she might lie, try to tell me that the girl had come for some charm or compound to rid her of her fatherless child. But something set in the crone's face. A decision, a resolution. She would trust me. 'She came to ask me about a flower.'

'*Colchicum mortis.*'

She nodded slowly. 'Aye, that. She wanted to know if I knew of it. I have some little knowledge of it, of its nature and properties, but I have never seen nor used it, or known anyone who has. This I told her, and she was greatly disappointed. I told her to ask her father, but she said she could not risk that.' She stopped. 'Or did she say risk him? I cannot remember.'

I knew why: Marion Arbuthnott knew that knowledge of this evil was almost as deadly as the poison of the plant itself. It was the knowledge that had made her fear for Charles Thom and a conviction that had been proven correct by her own death. I persisted, nonetheless. 'Did she tell you why she wanted to know about this plant?'

'It took much to draw it out from her, for she was a close, strange girl, and frightened. But she told me in the end. The lad, she said, had been quiet, preoccupied, all their journey back to Banff. He had scarcely spoken two words on the long road home. But, as they had crested the Gallowhill and begun their descent into the town, he had stopped dead, as if struck by a vision. And then he had said quietly those two words. *Colchicum mortis.* He had repeated them, and then had said no more, but that he must leave her, for he had urgent business to attend to. She had seen him only once more, at her father's table the next night. He had eaten nothing and appeared agitated still, excited almost, but it was a dark sort of excitement. She told me she had a presentiment of evil.' The crone shrugged. 'And maybe she had; she was a sensitive child, and knowing. Anyhow, the boy had told her he had some business on hand that night, and she was not to ask him of it, or seek to follow him. The next morning he was dead.' The woman's tale told, she lifted her pot and set it in a dark recess to cool.

There was no more to be had from her, and I stood up and began to pull on my cloak. She looked up.

'Where are you going?'

'I am returning to Banff,' I said. 'I must before dark. There is much I must attend to.'

She smiled. 'You will not get back to Banff this night. The fog will not lift till the morning. You would be lost in five minutes and dead in ten.' It was not an opinion, but a statement of fact. She lit a small lamp and set it by me. Then she went to a chest in some dark recess of the cavern and brought out a slim volume, old and well read. 'This is my only book, save the Bible. You may entertain yourself with it if you wish. I do not seek company, and I have spoken more these last two weeks than I would wish to in half a year.' She brought me also a bowl of mussels and a hunk of bread. It was the last exchange we had for many hours.

I pulled the lamp closer to me and opened the book at the title page: *The Poems of William Dunbar*. Dunbar. An unexpected warmth spread through me, a memory of childhood evenings by the fire, listening to my father, the day's toils over, telling stories of his youth, of his journeying with the laird of Delgatie. Those were the nights he would sing the old ballads or say the poems. Those had been the magical nights, when my mother too had been young again and had remembered why she had loved him. For me, it was not the great adventures overseas, nor the ballads of romance, but those poems in our own Scots tongue, written by a court clerk dead a hundred years, that had allowed me to glimpse for a brief hour the humanity of my own father. I had not looked at or listened to one of Dunbar's poems since the day they told me he was dead. I feared almost to open the book further, for what memory I would find there. I laid the volume down and settled back on the furs and skins beneath me, hoping for sleep. None came. The silence of the sea outside was more terrifying than all the fury of its rages. The crone was oblivious to it. Some powders she had been grinding she now put in a glass jar and was adding distilled water, drop by drop. She would sniff at it every so often, then mutter to herself before adding some other powder.

I had learnt what I had come to learn from her, and had no wish to tarry longer in this place, but her advice was good: there could be no sense in attempting to reach Banff before morning. There was much I could have done in these futile hours, in any other place but this. I had no idea what hour of the day or night it was. I gave over trying to sleep and opened the volume once more, this time having the courage to turn the pages further.

The crone had finished her work and had gone about some necessary business in a place she had shown to me deep into the back of the cave, and I was still reading, lost in another time, my father's voice resonant in my ear. Even after she had put out the lamp and laid herself out to sleep on her trestle bed, the words echoed in my mind through the darkness from fifteen, twenty years ago. The ballads, the lusty drinking songs, the comic ditties on court life, all had come to life again in my head, and had brought warmth to me. But now, in the darkness of this cavern, with the haar seeping through the silent black, my father's sonorous voice at last spoke the words that had ended all those evenings, and sent me to my sleep in fear: *timor mortis conturbat me*. The fear of death disquiets me. It was the only certainty I had now to hold on to: the certainty of death. And the knowledge of death was everywhere in this place where three times now I had been accorded life. I prayed for sleep, for peace, and, many hours into the night, it came.

I was awakened by a blast of fresh air on my face. My eyes sought in vain the familiar objects of my own chamber in the schoolhouse until I remembered where I was. The crone had gone outside. I followed the passage of light to the cave entrance and pushed back the partition myself. Sunlight pierced my eyes. The haar had lifted. A clear, fine spring day spread out the beauty of the firth before me. With little conversation, the old woman busied herself about making some breakfast, and while I ate she worked once more at her potions. As I finished my porridge and rose to gather my few things she turned. 'Wait. It is not quite ready.' Without further explanation, she went back to her work, and spent some minutes checking on jars and bottles, finally selecting two small vessels into which she poured different liquids from the concoctions she had been making the previous night. She handed me the bottles. 'This,' she said, indicating the one containing a murky, yellowish treacle, 'you are to give to Baillie Buchan. It is the remedy he seeks.' I opened my mouth to say something but she silenced me. 'You know all you need to. Give it to him.' The other bottle contained a clear, almost blue tonic. 'This you will take for yourself. One spoonful at night. You will sleep more easy, and the dreams will not bother you.'

'Did I speak my dreams last night? Did I call out?' Sometimes lately, I had woken in the night at the sound of my own cry.

'I know your dreams of old,' she said, 'and have banished them before.'

And it was because of some preparation such as this, I guessed, that I remembered nothing of my last stay here, less than one year ago. 'I have no money,' I said.

'I look for none,' she replied. 'Take them, and do as I say. May God go with you.' As I stepped out of the cavern she spoke to me for the last time. It was as if she had been considering whether to tell me or not. 'The girl, Marion Arbuthnott, asked me if I knew what the flower looked like, this flower that you seek. As I told you, and her, I have never seen it, but I saw a picture of it once in an old herbal, under poisons. I was able to describe it to her, for she had a good knowledge of plants and their parts, and she pictured it well. She knew it from somewhere; she had seen it. When she left here, I have a mind she was going to seek it out.'

'She found it,' I said, 'and it killed her.'

The old woman nodded. 'I feared it might, in some fashion. I believe that you too have in mind to find it. Take care that you do not follow her too soon down death's dark passageway.' She turned away from me and retreated into the shadows of her dwelling. I left the cavern gladly and set out for home.

It seemed a shorter journey back to Banff than that I had made yesterday. Such was my purpose I scarcely noticed the miles disappear behind me. It was not yet noon when I headed the Gallow Hill and saw set out before me the old burgh. As I descended the road into town I could see before me those blue flowers, just as Marion Arbuthnott had done, falling, falling. I could almost touch them.

FOURTEEN

The Lykewake

The door of my chamber had only just closed behind me when I heard the voice.

'Hello, Alexander.' I spun round and saw him sitting there, in the dim light in the corner of the room: Thomas Stewart. 'You have been gone a long time.'

'Not so long, really,' I said, removing my hat but staying standing. 'I had not expected a visitor.'

Though he smiled, his face was troubled. 'You will be weary after your journey, but I must speak with you now. It would have been better if I had spoken before.' There had been a strange silent watchfulness in the town as I had made my way down through it; those whose eye I had caught had not held my look, but had quickly turned away. And now I felt unaccountably frightened to see the notary sitting there in my room. The fire had not been lit for two days and all was coldness and emptiness.

'Ask me what you will, Thomas,' I said.

He shifted uneasily in his seat. 'I am here on a matter of formality, Alexander, and I wish you to understand that it is the office and not the man who sits before you here. It is the only safeguard for friendships that I know.' I understood, now. I understood who it was that the messenger had been despatched to by the watch on my return to the burgh by the Boyndie gate less than an hour ago, and I understood that this visit augured nothing good for me. He shifted again on the bench and at length got up and began to pace the room. 'I have come to ask you questions, yes, but to caution you too.'

'To caution me?'

'Yes.' He stopped pacing and stood halfway down the room, facing me. 'It is rumoured throughout the town that you went yesterday to Findlater and to Darkwater, and that you passed the night in the dwelling of the wise woman, the crone there. Is there truth in this?"

'From whose mouth have you had it?'

'From one that is not to be doubted.'

'Then you know that it is true,' I said.

'I had hoped it might not be,' he said quietly. And then he turned on me with exasperation. 'Why must you court controversy, Alexander? Have you any idea of the dangers you expose yourself to?'

'What? By visiting an old midwife, and sheltering a night in her cave from the fog? Would it have been better for me to have hazarded my life in the haar on the cliff tops?'

'It would have been better for you not to have gone at all,' he said with some vehemence.

'Thomas,' I said, 'she is not a witch, but an old woman who tired of this world and its fancies and furies.'

'Do you think it matters, Alexander, whether she indulges in the black arts or does not? In the minds of some of the townsfolk she is already condemned as a servant of Lucifer, and you by your association with her. Be she utterly without blemish, once that idea is firmly fixed in the minds of the people there will be nothing to save her, or you. The witch-hunt has broken out of the south-west and has spread to Fife. What happened here was not the end of it, only the start.' He looked at me for a moment, making a decision. 'Though Jaffray would never say, there are those who believe you spent your,' he searched for words, 'your lost days, last year, in the care of the crone.'

'Then they are right,' I said, 'though I remember nothing of it.'

'And why should that be, Alexander, if not that she cast some charm upon you, to make you forget? How then can you know what you had done, or been, those lost days?'

'I was a man, Thomas, just a man. Not bound then to God or the Devil, but to my own self, and it is that that she tried to help me forget. Her charm failed me, I think.'

'Then I am sorry for it. But do nothing further to kindle their suspicions.'

'Nor their fires?' I asked.

'No,' he replied grimly, 'nor their fires.' He was silent for a moment, but I knew he had more to say. He cleared his throat, still more uncomfortable than before. 'I think, and I hope I may be wrong in this, and that you will forgive me for it, but I think you have it in mind to seek out for yourself the killer in our midst.'

'You are not wrong.'

'Can I ask your reasoning?'

I thought of Patrick Davidson, not on that last night of his life, when he had made the desperate appeal to me that I had chosen not to hear, but in all the time before that, all the weeks he had been in Banff before his death. I had never sought out his company in all that time. I had avoided it, and would have done even had Jaffray not been away in the South. The truth, which I had determinedly turned my face from these last few days and weeks was that the arrival of Patrick Davidson had discomfited me; for he had been what I should have aspired to be. Neither high nor base born, he had been educated and travelled far afield in pursuit of his education and his passions, proper passions. He had pursued a calling many thought beneath him for his love of it. He had been happy, kindly, well lettered and well loved. In another life, in another world, at another time, like Charles Thom, how gladly I would have called him friend. But that life and time and world had gone long before Patrick Davidson ever returned to the place of his childhood. And so I turned my face from him. To the end, I had turned from him. I was determined to be able to face him now, if not in this life, then in the next. How could I make Thomas Stewart understand this?

I could not, and I did not try. Instead, I told him what had once been a part of the truth. 'When Charles Thom was charged and imprisoned over this murder, Jaffray and I swore we would not rest until we had him freed. Well, he is freed now, and that is enough for the doctor – he has concerns enough in the world – but I am too far in to come out now.'

The notary did not like what he heard. He began to speak slowly, deliberately. 'Alexander, I must counsel you to leave off from this task. There are snares everywhere in this business. If you are not caught by cries of witchcraft, you may well be taken as a plotter and a spy.'

'A spy? How so?'

'The townsfolk may well hold Marion Arbuthnott to have been a witch, and Patrick Davidson to have been a victim of her craft, but I think it much more like he was a spy, and she his willing helper, for it is certain if he was not involved in the one it was the other.'

'You are wrong,' I said. 'He did love her.'

He looked at me sceptically, puzzled as to how I had come by such assurance. He evidently did not have the time to waste on such matters. 'Whether he loved the girl or not is of little moment. What should concern you is that by meddling too far in his affairs you might well find yourself tainted by them.'

'Is it the office or the man who tells me that?' I asked.

He replied firmly, quietly. 'It is both.'

I took flint and lit the tallow candle, for little light reached my chamber at this time of the day. I wanted to see the notary's face. 'Thomas, you yourself were amongst those who involved me in the matter of Patrick Davidson's maps. How else would I have known of their existence, or of fear of plots, other than those which are constantly with us? How can you now accuse me of something that you know was none of my doing?'

'I accuse you of nothing,' he said, 'but some of your encounters on your trip to Aberdeen were ill-advised.'

I could not follow him. 'In Aberdeen I lodged with an old friend, a re-spected lawyer, known in this town and in this house, and to you yourself.'

He nodded. 'William Cargill is a good man.'

I was no longer in the mood for platitudes. 'I achieved the purposes of my visit as far as the school here is concerned, and I fulfilled the commis-sions on which I was sent by this town. I cannot see where the fault is to be found in that. And if it is a question of George Jamesone, the artist, then you must refer to the provost, for I—'

He cut me short. 'It is not of the artist, or Principal Dun or Doctor Forbes or any of those citizens of whom I speak. You will not tell me, I hope, that you met with Matthew Lumsden on the business of this town?'

'Matthew Lumsden? What is Matthew Lumsden to do with this?'

'That is what I would have you tell me.' Here I saw we had reached the point of the interview.

Apprehension grew within me. 'Matthew Lumsden is my friend,' I said. 'He has been so for many years.'

261

'Matthew Lumsden is an adherent of the Marquis of Huntly. He has raised his head and spoken too loud and too often on matters he would have been wiser to keep to himself. His opinions are known and his religious adherence guessed at. Circumstanced as you are, he is a man whose company it would be better not to keep.'

I got up and walked over to the door; I opened it. 'He is a man who has not sold his honour for office. I will choose my own friends, Mr Notary.'

If the notary made any reply as he left, I did not hear it. As the door closed behind him, I felt I had lost a friend I had never properly valued, and I was sorry for it, but my words could not be retracted. My clothes were still damp from the journey back from Darkwater, my head was aching and I was beginning to shiver. I took the stopper from the bottle the crone had given me and drank down a mouthful of the bitter liquid. As I sank onto my bed, I realised, too late now, that Thomas Stewart should not have known my movements in Aberdeen at all.

The voice came to me as from a distant place. It entered my dreams and called me from them. *For without cause have they hid for me their net in a pit, which without cause they have digged for my soul.* Clear and pure, the voice came closer. It was joined by other voices, many voices, solemn, low, in unison, following the words exactly. The voices were marching on me, chanting. I stumbled from my bed, covered still in the warm damp of my clothes. *But in mine adversity they rejoiced, and gathered themselves together: yea, the abjects gathered themselves together against me, and I knew it not: they did tear me and ceased not.* Closer still came the voices. My eyes not properly opened, I felt my way from my chamber and out onto the top of the stairs. Four steps down, not yet fully out of my slumber, I pressed my face to the small window set deep in the outer turnpike wall. The crowd, for it was indeed a crowd, snaked from its tail, just clearing the kirkyard gate, by way of Low Shore and the western end of the kirk, round to its head at High Shore, where it would soon pass beneath, far beneath, my window. Behind the bier, she downcast and he defiant, walked the apothecary and his wife, and at the very head, as I had known he must be, was Charles Thom. His voice, always a gift from God, stood forth alone, reaching to the Heavens: *Lord, how long wilt thou look on? Rescue my soul from their destructions, my darling from the lions.* Alone, high above them and in a quiet voice, I took up the psalm, word for word, note for note, and joined with all those other voices in the commencement of the lyikwake of Marion Arbuthnott.

I had to find another stand of clothes – I could not go out in my night-shirt, yet I could scarcely remain like this. The warmth of my body from the bed had dissipated and the cold of the clothes cloyed at my every inch of skin. My other vestments, beaten in a tub just yesterday by the maid, hung yet before the kitchen fire, sending steam still to the ceilings and rolling back down the wall. I returned to my room and brought the key down from the mantelshelf where it had lain for nine months, disturbed only by the cleaning hand of Mistress Youngson or her maid. I crouched by the bed and dragged out the kist. The lock was stiff, but gave way at the third twist of the key in my hand. I opened the lid quietly, fearful, foolishly, that I should be discovered in the act. And yet in but half an hour I would stand before many who knew me in that which I now hesitated to move from its tomb. I lifted the papers first – why should I have kept my sermon? And there beneath, pristine, made from love and worn but once, were the night-black drapes of a man of God, the cloak and suit of fine English cloth, with the velvet collar, made up for me by Banff's finest tailor at the behest of all my kind friends here: Gilbert Grant and his wife, Jaffray, Charles, who had not two ha'pennies to rub together, and the parents of some of my scholars, who often had none. I had stood in my fine new clothing before the brethren at the Presbytery of Fordyce on that June night, and heard the laird of Delgatie pronounce my doom. Had I paid for them myself, the garments would have been long since consigned to the fire, but as I had not they had remained there, locked away in the kist beneath my bed, a hidden symbol of my fall. And tonight, in this town lost to its terror of a darkness it did not understand, gathering in a pagan farewell to a murdered girl and her unborn child, I would wear them again. It was almost fitting. I removed my sickly damp rags and began to dress.

The town bell had just tolled seven when I passed under the archway at the side of the apothecary's shop. The rhythmic chanting of the psalms and the tentacled aroma of roasting meats guided my steps. It was a mild evening, and the sun had not yet sunk beyond the mountains of the west. The sea was peaceful. Charles's voice seemed to guide the waves as they came surely to the shore, the people in unison taking up the line behind him, their voices rumbling away like the pebbles as the waves rolled them back to the sea. Many of the mourners had spilled out into the courtyard – although the women remained yet in the house. Unseen, as I thought, on my arrival, I scanned the faces of the people gathered there, some shifting slowly from one stance to another, some talking in low voices to their neighbours. I marvelled, but was in truth little surprised, at the hypocrisy of my townsmen – how many of them had gathered together not three hundred yards from here, but two nights ago, and watched the body burn of the girl they now mourned? As I began to pass amongst them, I noticed how few of any note were absent from this gathering. The guilds were there, those who were not locked away awaiting justice, their deans wearing the regalia of their office in honour of their fellow guildsman, the apothecary. Baxters, candlemakers, coopers, fleshers, shoemakers, dyers, weavers, hammermen. How resplendent, how strong had I seen my own father on many a night such as this. How my mother had hated the public appropriation of such private grief. She had not understood.

There was the baillie, watching. I was not greatly surprised to see him: despite his oft rehearsed condemnation of such 'popery' as the lyikwake, he was a man who liked to know his enemy. And there, not amongst the general throng, but alone in the shadows of the doorway to the apothecary's house, was the provost. My eye met his and he gave me the briefest of nods before retreating further back into the shadows, where a white wraith flitted behind him; Geleis Guild also had come to mourn her friend and helper. As I turned my gaze from the doorway I caught a glimpse, from the corner of my eye, of Jaffray. He was deep in conference with Thomas Stewart, and had evidently not seen me. I took a step towards them and the doctor looked up in my direction. I had not seen him since he had pleaded with me not to go to Darkwater. He raised a hand to acknowledge me, but the notary avoided my eye. Stung, I turned back towards the place the music was coming from.

My minister's garb cutting a path for me through my astonished neighbours, I made my way eventually towards the circle at the front of the throng, nearest to where the song schoolmaster and his scholars stood. Charles directed the boys in the old way, standing before them behind a makeshift lectern, turning the pages of the choirbook with one hand as he directed the boys behind him with the other. Away from the inn, away from Jaffray's, away from the kirk, he was a man transformed. The cares of his world and the confines of his duties lifted from him, he was at liberty, so seldom granted him, to enjoy fully and to offer to us his God-given gifts. The psalm he now took up was not, as the others had been, a monotone, stripped of all decoration and ornamentation, but something worthy of the gifts and training of a true musician. Voices of master and boys rose in magnificent polyphony, urging the Lord, for Marion Arbuthnott, to 'judge and avenge my cause'.

Baillie Buchan, whom I discovered a few feet away from me, did not move throughout the rendition of the whole piece, yet his face hardened in disapproval with every new proof of the virtuosity of my friend. He never once took his eyes from Charles though, and it was only as master and boys then set themselves in reports on the eighteenth psalm that he seemed to notice me. He said nothing, but moved slowly closer to me, evidently set on the guarding of either Charles or myself from escape.

In a moment he was at my shoulder. I was emboldened by the gradual dying of the light. 'The psalm is not to your taste, baillie?' I asked.

'The psalm is to my taste,' he said. 'The words of King David, cried out to our Lord, assured in the righteousness of his cause in a sinful world. But this playing upon it, this decoration and ostentation, born of the vanity of men, turns my stomach. What need has the psalmist of such perversions?'

'Surely, baillie, our music master's voice is a gift from God?'

He turned on me a look of frozen contempt for my words. 'Do you not recall the words of John Knox? Or is he out of favour with the great Episcopalians of the King's College?' There was the disdain in his voice of a man who made no compromise.

'I am no stranger to the works of John Knox,' I replied, 'and neither were my masters.' And indeed I recalled the words of the great Reformer, and their exposition as my classmates and I had debated the place of music in the worship of God. For the baillie, there was no debate.

He spoke quietly. 'He knew of the snares of the world waiting on all men, and warned against such as these. The schoolmaster's gifts should be applied to the edification of the people, not to the parading of his own vanity.' The vehemence of his words was almost beyond his strength to muster, and the baillie was overcome by the now familiar retching cough.

A spit with a hog roasting on it turned in one corner, near to the apothecary's well. Some ragged urchins were already gathering near it, ready to risk the wrath of the cook for the chance of a hot meal. I was hungry, and would gladly have sat down and eaten something myself, for I felt weak from hunger and fatigue. It was not time for eating though; the long trestle tables laid out in the courtyard were as yet empty of the delights that the women of Arbuthnott's kin had been preparing all day. The time of solemnity had not yet passed – that of gluttony and excess was still to come. My fine suit of English wool with its long cloak and collar were not sufficient to take the damp and cold from my bones. I began to feel shivery, and searched out a place beside the fire. Gladly would I have returned to my bed, for I had little time for lyikwakes and the superstitions they recalled, but I felt impelled to stay and see the night through.

The psalm the scholars were singing was finally brought to its dolorous end, and, with scarcely enough pause for breath, a new sound filled the air, a sweet and melancholic melody I knew well. One of the older boys had taken up his flute, while another played on the rebec, his bow calling a plaintive tune across the strings, and Charles began to sing out, no psalm now, but a mourning lover's air – 'I wish I was where Helen lies'. The women had come out of the house now. Some still stood on the backstairs, while others moved softly amongst the guests in the courtyard. And then, as from another place, the timeless notes of a clarsach joined with the flute and the rebec, matched to Charles's own voice. I turned my eyes to the source of the sound, for I knew Charles was no harpist. There, on a stool a little behind the musicians' dais, sat Ishbel, the doctor's girl, her fingers gently caressing the strings of the clarsach, as those of her people had done for centuries before. The instrument spoke the agony of lost love, of a life and of dreams departed, and for a few moments all other noise ceased. Charles himself fell silent. As the notes followed one another on the air, and the song came at last to its end, I saw that many in the crowd were now weeping. Marion Arbuthnott's moment had come. The doctor moved towards the girl, pride and love glowing in him. At the top of the forestairs, engulfed in her desolation, stood Marion's mother, her head buried in the shoulder of Mistress Youngson, whose eyes looked out on her own memories. Most of all though, it was the baillie that I noticed. He too was looking out, far from the place and time he now stood in, to an image of something long lost, long gone. I had never before seen such humanity in his face. Charles did not move, but watched Ishbel for many moments. His lips parted slightly and gradually came together again. A veil had been lifted from his eyes.

Once having composed himself, the doctor, with Ishbel firmly clamped in a father's embrace, called out, 'Come now, Charles, let us have something to lift our hearts.' Charles took a moment to come out of his spell, but smiling, took up his bow, called out a name to his players, who took up pipe, drum and tabor, and led them in a hearty harvest tune. The new sound was as a signal to mourners – guests and hosts both. Women bustled and boys ran up and down from the kitchen to the courtyard, and soon the trestles were filled with salvers, bowls and baskets of every sort of food imaginable: pies filled with pigeon, fish, rabbit; all manner of breads, pastries, puddings; custards, cakes, sweet meats of every description. The council and the session had proclaimed time and again against such feasting, and this indeed was more of a wedding banquet than a funeral feast, but for Marion Arbuthnott there would be no wedding and all that her anguished parents could now do for her, they would do.

The sun had gone at last, and its amber glow faded. Torches were lit in sconces about the courtyard walls, casting grotesque shadows of men, women and children in perverse celebration of the passage of a soul, two souls, into death. I tried not to look at them. I wanted to talk again with Thomas Stewart – it was not right that things should have been left between us as they had this afternoon, and it was for me to set things right with him. I stood up, my head setting inside my skull like molten lead as I did so, and began to cast around for some sight of the notary. There were too many people now, moving about alone or in groups, from fire, to table, to spit; I had no clear line of vision or access anywhere. I gradually pushed and jostled my way through them until I reached the place where I had seen the notary talking with Jaffray, but both were long gone now. The shivering of earlier now alternated with waves of intense heat throughout my body, culminating in the thumping of my head. I came to a bench and sat down again, fearful that my legs would buckle beneath me. Before I could breathe out my relief to be resting again, an arm shoved into my shoulder, almost knocking me from my seat. I looked round quickly but saw nothing save the ragged hem of a deftly retreating cloak. Lang Geordie's men had somehow got themselves here tonight, I was sure of it. It was not a night to sit in the dark corners, on the margins: safety lay in the heart of the crowd, and I forced myself to my feet again, and towards the busy tables. I could not tell if it was my own body that swayed, or those I pressed through, yet I knew my feet were not steady. I cursed the wise woman of Darkwater and her sleeping tonic, and my own stupidity in taking it not seven hours ago.

At last I found my way through the throng. I slipped onto a bench and had a platter of food – crackling pork, baked apple with cloves, a dark and peppery gravy and warm bread – pressed into my hand. It was Gilbert Grant who stood above me.

'Alexander, you look as if you might faint. Eat, my boy, eat. My wife tells me you have had nothing since you returned home to us this day. She bids you eat.' I accepted the plate and nodded my gratitude towards Mistress Youngson, who had taken over the duties of hostess from the grieving mother. A cup of warm, spiced wine was also handed to me, and as I ate and drank I began to recover myself somewhat. Gilbert Grant seemed content to eat in silence, looking up at me every now and then to make sure I did not flag. I was glad of it, for I was in no mood for conversation, even with this most gentle and genial of men. A reckoning was building in this place tonight that the music and the food and the drink and the dancing flames could not mask, and I was resolved to see it when it came. All around me I could sense a watching and a waiting.

Charles and his boys, the older and better players, embarked upon a *courante*, and some of the wealthier merchants, along with the landed folk, took up their wives and daughters and set forth to dance, mindful of their status and their dignity. I looked over to the baillie, who kept his place near the music master and the dais. His face was set as a stone; for the baillie, one dance, be it ever so graceful, was as much fuel for the Devil's fire as the wildest debauch. For myself, I had not seen dancing since that last Christmas at Delgatie, and I was drawn to watch as men and women moved with care in set steps towards each other, turned away, went back and took each other's hands again to move on in stately, mannered procession. All was propriety, all was order. The faces were as masks, but the eyes, the eyes always gave something away.

The dance came to an end, and before I had stepped back properly into the crowd, another had begun. Unwitting and unwilling, I found myself in a line of four men. Four women faced us, and before me was the pale and wasted form of Geleis Guild. I looked up to where the provost stood: he watched me, motionless. Was this a test? Was I to know that I was not to lay a hand upon this fragile, delicate ornament of his office and his place? I knew that well enough. The music began and I stepped forward and took the slender hand, for there was nothing to step back to. Geleis Guild looked straight ahead into nothing, as if she did not see me, and the dance progressed. No word, no acknowledgement of who I was, escaped her. I had not set eyes on her since that morning when we had brought the lifeless body of Patrick Davidson to her house. The double grief for her friend had almost washed all life from her. I wondered what decoction Jaffray had given her, for she looked as one who is already halfway to the next world. But then, as the dance neared its end, and we passed across one another for the last time, her mouth brushed my hair. The words took whatever strength was left to her. 'Do not fail them,' she breathed, and then her hand fell from mine and she had been folded back once again into the crowd. The provost no longer watched me – I could not see him – but the eyes of many others, of Dr Jaffray, of Thomas Stewart, of Baillie Buchan, all were on me now. I would have given much then to pass quietly as a stranger from the company. I stepped back towards the edges of the crowd and waited for it to envelop me.

From somewhere in the darkening gathering, over the aroma of the roasting meat and the pungent spices, over too the thick, warm stench of human sweat and dirt, a new sensation reached my nostrils and my mind. It was not the smoke from the spit-fire, or the bonfire made to warm us, nor yet from the tobacco of Virginia Jaffray so often railed against yet so much enjoyed, but sweet-smelling, of some other leaf dried and burned for the alteration of mind and spirit. It was reaching that time in the evening when such drugs would be smoked and others taken, their seeds crushed into drinks. The baillie and others of his ilk agonised over the danger to our souls from a few harmless songs and dances. How the Devil must have laughed at their simplicity, as he reached into our very minds and visions, with his pagan gifts from the New World. I wanted my wits about me tonight, and moved swiftly away from the source of the strange perfume, wondering at the words of the provost's wife. *Do not fail them.*

Some of the younger music scholars had been sent home, their promised penny in their hand to give to their mother, and the music and the dancing was becoming less stately. The doctor stepped up with Ishbel as the players struck up a popular measure. The cittern now came into play for the first time in the evening, and the tabor beat in perfect time to the small pipe over which Charles's fingers flew, his eyes smiling as Ishbel blushed to the doctor's exaggerated manners. For all that had occurred these last few days, and for all the dreadful sorrow that had occasioned this celebration, ten years had fallen from the doctor this night. The call went up for a lustier tune. I had avoided lyikwakes these many years past – students were banned from them in Aberdeen, but Archie had always made a hearty mourner. I knew that there came a point always when the authorities, in the shape of minister, session clerk, baillie or town serjeant, would call a halt to the festivities, in fear for the public morals and for order in the town. And this was the point at which they would have done so, at the point where the drinking surpassed the eating, when strange substances began to subvert the order of men's minds, and when good humour threatened to spill over into debauchery.

Tonight though, Banff was a town without minister or session clerk; the town serjeants and all their men needed every resource for the guarding of the prisoners dispersed over town. All the provost's care and attention was taken up this night on preventing the unravelling of his young wife's mind and the utter collapse of her spirit. There was only the baillie, but the baillie, like me, was waiting, watching for what was surely to come. After a hesitant glance at William Buchan, which drew no response, Charles took up his fiddle and let fly with the opening notes of the favourite, 'Gallua Tom'. The piccolo took up the challenge, and the two, with the tabor beating out their time and the cittern struggling to keep pace, flew against one another in speed and dexterity as in battle joined. The courtyard

became a mass of bodies, heaving, whirling, laughing, flinging one another across the floor. The flickering light of the torches played upon their
writhing forms, catching the glistening beads of sweat that trickled down
their foreheads and the glinting, shining, eager eyes, the lascivious, open
mouths.

And then, as the music reached its height and the dancers could scarcely
keep pace with the playing, there came looming, crashing into my view the
massive form of George Burnett, master stonemason, tormentor of Sarah
Forbes and father of her child. Being flung on his arm, a look of terror on
her face, was Ishbel. My stomach lurched. I stepped forward to grab the
girl, but they had gone whirling past and I was knocked and cursed out of
the way by oncoming dancers. Where was the doctor? I looked round but
could not see him. I looked after George Burnett and Ishbel but they had
been carried on the tide of the dance and I had no hope of reaching them
until they came back round to me. I caught a glimpse of the huge, gnarled
fingers on the girl's slender arm, and I thought of those same hands roughly
forcing Sarah Forbes. And yet she had not been crushed, she had not been
destroyed, and now she and her child would be safe in Aberdeen, away from
him. But Ishbel, no, Ishbel had not that strength. She would be crushed by
him like a flower beneath his feet, and it would kill the doctor. A crushed
flower, a broken, fallen, flower. And then I saw it, as the music threatened
to carry all with it in a whirlwind of madness and swirling bodies. As the
strange-scented smoke again snaked towards me I saw the flowers falling to
the floor, falling from an open hand, and I saw the face of the woman who
had once held them. She called to me through the music, through silence,
through time. Janet and Mary Dawson had heard it wrong, for Patrick
Davidson had not said 'James and the flowers' at all.

I began to push and crash my way through the crowd. The music was
now disjointed, discordant, and faltered to a stop as Charles Thom leapt
from the stage bellowing at George Burnett to leave off his hold on the girl.
On another night, at another time, I would have been there with him, but
now I could but commit him and Ishbel to God and to each other. There
was other work of the stonemason's I must see to tonight. A group of
tanners and dyers, laughing, drinking, blocked the entrance to the vennel
leading back out onto the street. Feeling sick, I tried to ask them to let me

pass, but the words fell disordered from my mouth. 'Falling down again, eh Mr Seaton?' Their laughter was less derision than amusement.

'I need to get past,' I said.

'Nor before you take a cup with us.' A voice I did not know was joined by a hand I could not rightly see. A cup was pressed on me, its contents burning with heat and spices. I drank quickly, but a dancer hurled from the floor slammed into my back and most of the warm liquid was spilled down my front. More laughter, and the craftsmen parted to let me by. I stumbled through the vennel and out into the open street, the noises of the lyikwake following me into the clear night. Men and women, shapes and shadows, emerged from corners, fell back against walls, slipped down dark pends and vennels, all having forgotten the business of the night, the burned and blackened corpse of a murdered girl.

Curses and shouting and noises of commotion followed me into the street; I turned around in time to see George Burnett, oaths flowing from his mouth, be bodily ejected from the apothecary's pend, Thomas Stewart behind him warning him not to come back. I slumped into a doorway to let the stonemason pass, swaying on unsteady feet, blood coursing from his nose. Charles had had the better of it and Ishbel would be all right, thank God. Burnett caught a glimpse of me just before he reached the door of the Market Inn. Uttering another curse he pushed through it, and the music from the lyikwake streamed into the night as the door banged shut behind him. I had scarcely the strength to stand now, and would have been no match for him, drunk though he was.

Over in the kirkyard all was dark and silent: no Dawson sisters now, or ever again, to call to me, or to give aid to a fallen stranger. Clouds passed from the face of the moon and the houses of the burgh stood like crooked sentinels in its light. The way was clear ahead of me and I did not have the option tonight of choosing any other. My throat was dry and beset by a raging thirst; only a supreme effort kept me from diverting my steps to the schoolhouse well, not so far away now. I forced one foot in front of the other, and somehow, nauseous, shivering, I began to drag myself along High Shore, and towards the Water Path. I glanced again at the kirkyard: bricks and mortar motionless for hundreds of years slowly began to shift and sway before my eyes. Headstones, large, small, flat, jagged to the ground, began to dance: I saw the headstones dance. Terror gripped me and I hastened my steps, but I too was swaying, hardly able to keep myself from falling over onto the swirling ground beneath my feet. The strains of music from the lyikwake followed me but lost their tune, became discordant and then a cacophony of screeching the further up the path I progressed. They were joined, I knew it, by a wailing that was not of this life or this world. I dared not look back again at the kirkyard.

The street narrowed as I ascended Water Path. The house frontages were narrower, the buildings closer together. Twisting alleyways ran off from the street into yards and backlands and emerged further on having met and crossed others. Any man – or woman – could shadow my path, to overtake me, without being seen by me from the street. Away from the heat and the clamour of the lyikwake, the intoxication of its sounds and aromas, of the music and the smoke, my mind was alive to all the terrors of the night. My throat burned in desperation for a drink, but to stop now, to turn back, would be death. I knew that. I could only look ahead, but nothing was as it should have been; nothing was as I knew it to be. Where there were two steps I saw four, moving away and coming closer together. Where I knew there to be only one door, I saw two, banging in unison in a wind that did not blow. I wanted to shut my eyes, to shut out these visions, and look ahead at the one vision I knew to be true, the vision of Helen's face. It stayed with me. I fixed the eye of my mind on hers and held her there as I forced myself on, as she led me on towards the end of her story. At last I reached my goal, just before the Water Path joined with the Castlegate, just before I came upon the high walls of the castle grounds. The breath and the eyes of the shadows were closer behind me now; I could feel their coldness on my skin. I turned, stumbling, into an opening in the half-crumbled wall to my left and found myself surrounded by the rubble and the foundations of the minister's new manse.

I had no lantern, torch or candle with me, and the great oaks and horse chestnut trees, just coming into bud as they were, let through only dappled partings of the moon's light. It was much darker here than it had been out on the street. The sound of the wind in the trees echoed that of the sea returning to the shore; noises of my fellow man from the town below were but a distant memory and murmur. This was a desolate place, too full of ghosts. Their fingers were in my hair. Shaking them loose I scrambled over stones and trenches to the area where, as Sarah Forbes had told me and as the notary's discussion with George Burnett had confirmed, the old garden had not yet been cleared. Helen's garden. There, in the far corner, beneath a wall, sheltered from the sea, the ground had scarce been disturbed; a chorus of deathly voices in my head whispered that this was the place. I stumbled over a branch and only just managed to right myself before my foot went into the trench. I cried out, but no sound came; my mouth, my tongue moved, but all in silence, powerless. No one would hear my cries: a just revenge for Patrick Davidson.

I forced myself up once more and my eye caught sight of something glinting in the moonlight. I moved closer. I had not been deceived – it was glass, thick, old, weather-worn glass. I stooped down, thinking at first it must be a window pane the builders had mislaid. But it was not a window pane, set though it was in what had once been a solid wooden frame. Mastering my flailing hands, I slid the frame along on reluctant runners and there, beneath, the palest of blue in the pale moonlight, I saw the beauty of death, the slender, delicate blooms of the *colchicum mortis*. I stretched out my hand in wonder towards it. A branch cracked that was not beneath my foot; the rasping cough filled my ears. I spun round in time to see the sharp-boned features of Baillie William Buchan's face bearing down on me, and the rock smashing towards my head.

FIFTEEN

Old Stories' Endings

The vast frame of Thomas Stewart barred the door. Iron bars filled a solitary window high above me. There was no furnishing to the room, other
than the trestle bed on which I lay. The walls and floor, both stone, were
bare of any covering. It was daylight, but I could not tell what time of
day it was: late morning, perhaps. I could not hear the sea. I tried to lift
my head, but the burning stone inside it brought it crashing down once
more upon the mattress. Thomas Stewart immediately shouted through
a grille in the door for a guard. A man appeared, a message was given
and the grille was slammed shut once more. Slowly, the notary turned
to me. He came closer, searching my face for further presence of life. I
opened my mouth in an attempt to speak, but little more than a croak
emerged. He dipped a cup into a basin of water by the side of the bed
and trickled some onto my lips. I swallowed, but the intense pain in my
head overwhelmed any relief I had hoped for. I tried again. 'The baillie?' I
asked.

'He is here.'

'And the provost?' I managed.

The notary shook his head. 'He has not been found. It was some time
before the baillie was able to raise the alarm, and by the time messages
were got to the town ports, Walter Watt was gone. He left by the Sandyhill
Gate, riding hard. The men on the watch did not challenge him, for who
would challenge the provost?'

One had, one man. Much of last night remained in some foggy recess of
my mind I could not yet reach, and yet one thing I did remember: William
Buchan had saved my life. I could see him still, lunging at the provost's
arm as Walter Watt aimed the sharp garden rock at my head. I could see
him still, being thrown back by the stronger man. And then I saw him rise

275

again, somehow, as Walter Watt lifted his hand a second time. Here my mind clouded over, and I could see no more.

'Is he badly hurt?' I asked.

'He is bruised about the face, and his hand is badly gashed – he will admit to nothing else – but he might have fared much worse against such an opponent, were it not for the merciful Providence of the storm.'

'The storm?'

'Aye. The storm of the night Patrick Davidson died ripped branches from trees throughout the country. It was one such branch the baillie managed to lift and bring down upon the neck of the provost before he could strike you again. The provost somehow righted himself before the baillie could, and fled, but William Buchan would not go after him until he had seen that you lived, and stemmed your bleeding.' He lowered his voice. 'He could never have caught him anyway; he could scarce walk by the time he reached us to raise the alarm. But the garden, Alexander – how did you know?'

I looked towards the water and he trickled some more into my mouth. Less pain this time, greater relief. I could answer truthfully, at last. 'Patrick Davidson told me.'

Before the notary could respond, the door behind him swung open slowly and there, between two guards, stood Baillie Buchan.

How could I put into words all that I had to say to him? I had scarcely the strength to speak, no more had he to hear. His face was sallower still, and his bones stood out as from a cold skull. 'Thank you,' I said.

He regarded me for a long hard minute and finally spoke. 'Let the thanks be unto God. He has revealed the truth, and you have been His instrument. He has preserved you for His work, and it will be my great blessing to see it completed.'

'When did you know?' I asked.

The baillie was taken by one of his coughing fits, and Thomas Stewart called for a chair to be brought.

William Buchan waved the chair away and kept to his feet. 'Eight years ago, I knew,' he said. 'And every day since, I have, on my knees, implored God that He would grant Helen justice in this world, as He himself will have judgement in the next.'

'But why did you wait so long? Why did you not speak out before now? If you have indeed spoken out yet?' I looked at Thomas Stewart, who by his eyes directed me back to the baillie.

'I had not the proof; I had only the certainty of my own heart, my own mind. I could not accuse a man of such a thing on those grounds – the Devil lays many snares for those who are not watchful of their own weaknesses, and I knew mine. I had to wait and watch these eight years, and he never put a foot wrong. Until two weeks ago, when he plunged himself once more into the acts of darkness and I knew his day was approaching. But still there was no proof, and strive though I might, and did, I could find none. But I prayed also; I prayed that the Lord might aid me in my striving. And He did, with the discovery of Patrick Davidson's maps; I knew then that I was to send for you. And when you came, and showed yourself not to have been corrupted by your failings, as men had thought; I knew that you were the man who could do what I could not. I had oftimes asked myself why God had given you such gifts, if they were only to be thrown away on the whim of your human failings. I had forgotten that our true calling is not always that which seems most likely to the eyes of men.'

'I am not called to be a searcher out of murderers,' I said coldly.

'No,' he replied, 'but a searcher for the truth. Even from your youngest days, I had marked you out as a searcher for the truth.'

From my youngest days. His words took me back three days to that bare chamber of his, to the kist that lay on the floor, to the notes I had read as he and Charles slept, of my sermon at Boyndie kirk. What great hopes he had had for my ministry, what thanks he had given for my gifts. And what a mockery I had made of his faith in me. Now, in this moment, he was telling me that what I had done, he had not: where I had given myself up as lost to God's plan in this world and His salvation in the next, he never had. I would never have believed that I could have felt warmth for William Buchan, or been desirous of being worthy of his praise, but I felt it now, humbled and honoured by the words of one I had so scorned.

He continued. 'From the moment the provost chose to entrust you with the maps, I knew you would go where I could not, ask what I could not, find what I could not. So I watched you, and I had you watched, and followed.'

277

Now I understood, all those times when I had felt myself to be watched, fancied I had heard footsteps but seen no man behind me when I turned. 'By Lang Geordie?'

For the first time in my life, I heard William Buchan laugh, a full, mirthful, delighted laugh. 'Lang Geordie?' he repeated, in disbelief. 'No, Mr Seaton, *I* at least do not consort with thieves and idle beggars.'

'Then who?'

'It was me, Alexander,' Thomas Stewart said softly, 'it was me.'

My mind struggled to open doors on the last few days, on things I had not understood. I had known I was watched, but had never had an inkling of by whom. In Aberdeen, on the road from Straloch, even ... 'You, Thomas, it was you who followed me to Darkwater?' I marvelled that the man had not stumbled to his death.

'No, it was not.' It was the baillie's voice. 'The notary could not be spared, and I feared you were getting too close, that the danger was too great. It was I who tracked your path to Darkwater. To the crone. She saw me, of course. But I knew she would not tell you. She has long been of my mind.'

The baillie and the witch? This was beyond my comprehension. But indeed she had seen him: the tonic she had given me that I had forgotten to give him, of Rosa Solis, Sun Dew, for his ravished lungs: how else could she have known? I looked at him. 'You could not have survived the night,' I said.

'The Lord watched over me,' he countered. 'I have often had cause to be at Findlater on business. Once I had seen you safely taken in by the woman, I sought out shelter with the keeper of the castle. At first light, when the worst of the haar had lifted, I was granted the trustiest of horses from their stable, and it brought me safe back to Banff well before you. I could not have left the burgh while Charles Thom was still in the tolbooth, for fear that he might have been killed before I returned, and so I sent the notary here to shadow and watch you. But with the music master free and in the safe protection of the doctor, I was able to watch over you for myself.' He was again taken by a convulsion of coughing, and this time he consented to take the seat pressed on him. He accepted a drink of water and waving away a second, turned to the notary. 'The doctor?'

'He has been alerted. He should be here within the hour.'

'Where are we?' I still had no notion of where I was, but was certain I was not in Banff.

'Inchdrewer. We are at Inchdrewer.' The majestic keep of the Ogilvies, perhaps four miles from Banff, surveying the countryside all around. The mere knowledge of it had terrified me as a boy, and in my childhood imaginings it had been home to the ogres of my mother's tales. The notary continued, 'The baillie and I agreed that it was safer to have you here, out of the town altogether, until at least the sheriff gets here. The doctor was hard put to permit it, but the burgh was not safe. Jaffray would have been here with you, but there are still fears for the music master, and so he agreed to stay in the town.'

'And Ishbel?'

'The girl is safe, and unsullied,' answered the baillie. 'And George Burnett will never lay his hand on a maiden of this burgh again. The new council and the new provost will not tolerate such a man in the bounds of Banff.'

'New council?' The council elections were not to be held until Martinmas, as they were every year.

The baillie was strengthened by the challenge. 'Half the present council are in the tolbooth or the laird of Banff's dungeon. The provost is fled. As soon as the sheriff is returned, a new council and provost will be elected. A godly magistrate will have the governance of our town, and the days of Babylon will be over.' But this was no crowing triumph of one man over an old enemy, of William Buchan over Walter Watt, for the baillie was looking over at Thomas Stewart. And the notary – soon, I realised, to be provost of Banff – simply looked at his feet and said, 'God's will be done.'

Into the silence came a rumble, then a thunder of hooves. Thomas Stewart ran to block the door and there was a shouting of guards through the castle. The baillie did not flinch at the commotion, but my mind, racing in a head that was pounding with every heartbeat, went straight to Walter Watt. Who was to say he had not gone for reinforcements? Who would take the word of a disgraced schoolmaster and an embittered baillie, known to have been set against him for years, against the upright, forthright, wealthy provost of Banff? The horses came closer, the shouting grew more urgent, and my mind coursed down avenues it had never before seen. Was Walter Watt Huntly's man? The maps of Patrick Davidson – might not his uncle have been the agency that called him to Banff? What had truly been in the letters to Gordon of Straloch? To Jamesone? But no; George Jamesone called me back to what I knew to be true: that this was not a matter of spies and maps and papist plots. This was a matter of a husband, his wife, a young man and some flowers, and by the mouths of the whores of Banff who thought they had heard 'James and the flowers', Patrick Davidson had told me it was at the very beginning. My apprehension faded as I heard the voice of James Jaffray corralling off the castle walls. Thomas Stewart had gone down to meet him.

'And he lives yet? He lives?'

The notary sought to calm the doctor. 'He is well, doctor; he speaks and understands and has taken a little water. He lives.'

'God be praised! I should never have permitted the journey.'

The baillie rose from his chair, dredging his chest for breath. 'There was little choice, Jaffray. In the confusion of the night, we had to get him to a place of surety.'

The doctor passed the baillie with never a look and arrived at my bedside. The strain on the kind face subsided. 'And so, Alexander Seaton. You have taken a bump on the head. Stealing apples from the manse garden at your age.'

Laughter hurt my head. 'There are no apples to be got in April, doctor. Did they teach you nothing of use in your medical studies?'

'Very little,' he smiled, 'very little.' He gently lifted some of the hair back from my forehead. Some strands had stuck in the drying blood of the wound and I winced as he tugged them free. He uttered a soft curse at himself. 'That should have been cut before I cleaned and stitched it. It is time this town had a new doctor; an old man in his cups working with a needle by candlelight! You could have lost your eye. What were you about, William Buchan? You should have had me thrown in the tolbooth long ago, and a decent sober young physician set in my place.'

The baillie laughed again through his wheezing. 'There is none can fill your place, James Jaffray, none. May the God that sent you back to us preserve you long for us.'

'Amen,' I said.

The doctor's eyes were filling and he looked away briskly from me. 'Aye, well, you will live. And I dare say a clout on the head may knock some sense into you, for nothing else will.'

I winced. 'I have had many a clout on the head before,' I said, 'but none has had such an aftermath as this. It is worse than the worst morning after a night's drinking. And I know it is not that, for I drank very little last night.'

Jaffray surveyed me gravely. 'You drank enough. A few mouthfuls more and you would have been dead.'

I laughed out loud, despite the pain it gave me. 'Doctor, I had but two cups of wine, the one of them spilt on the ground for the most part. I have drunk more with you at the inn while waiting on our dinner.'

'You should thank God for whoever knocked that second cup from your hand, Alexander, for the dregs of the poison were still in it when the notary picked it up from the ground.'

I looked at Thomas Stewart. 'I was behind you; I saw nothing but the hand that passed you the cup and then I saw you drop it. I would have been straight after you, had it not been for the fight that broke out on the dance floor. Whoever thought Charles Thom incapable of murder did not see him last night: it took four of us to pull him from George Burnett's throat. By the time the commotion was over you were gone from sight. The baillie bade me stay at the lyikwake while he went to look for you. When I found the cup lying on the ground I gave it to the doctor. We had had fears that your life might have been in danger.'

'And they were right,' said the doctor. 'The dregs of the belladonna were there in plenty.'

'Belladonna?' I asked stupidly.

'Aye, belladonna. It is still to be seen in your eyes. Your pupils are like plates. He wanted to make sure you were robbed of the power of speech before it killed you. Have you a thirst, Alexander?'

'It rages.'

'And what do you recall of events after you left the lyikwake?'

I closed my eyes and searched my memory for something. Fleeting glimpses of things came to me, a sensation of apprehension, but little else.

I tried again. This time there was something more, and apprehension was replaced by real fear. I looked to the doctor and swallowed hard. 'I think, it is hazy, you know, but I think at the kirkyard,' I hesitated, not knowing how the baillie would react to what I had to say.

'Go on,' said Jaffray.

I glanced at the baillie for a moment. 'I think I saw the dead walk.' I had expected thunderous rebuke, accusations of blasphemy, witchcraft, consorting with spirits, but none came. William Buchan merely looked at the doctor and the doctor nodded.

'The visions. You saw the visions. The belladonna brings on hallucinations. It is what the witches use to send them on their orgies of commune with the dead, to send them in their flights for Satan. It is fortunate for your mind and soul that the baillie came upon you when he did.'

'And for my body too,' I added. 'I do not think the provost had it in mind that I should live to tell his tale.'

'No,' agreed Jaffray. 'No more do I.' He went and murmured something to the notary who, nodding, sent one of the doorkeepers back down the stairs. The baillie had joined the doctor and the notary in conference, and for a moment none heeded me. I strained to hear their words, but could make out little. William Buchan asked Jaffray for news of the provost, but all I could hear by way of reply was 'Carnousie'. Carnousie. Nearer Turriff than Banff, yet away from the sea. If he wanted to get away, he should have gone by the sea. Some more instructions were relayed further down the castle and attention returned to me.

'Mr Seaton,' said the baillie, 'I doubt the doctor will permit you to be moved again for some days—'

'Indeed I will not,' interrupted Jaffray with some emphasis.

'And the notary and myself cannot tarry much longer from Banff. There is much to be attended to. Nevertheless, there is much I would know of you.'

'And perhaps tell me?'

He eyed me steadily for a moment. His mouth scarcely moved. 'Perhaps. But first, I would be grateful if you would tell me what you were telling the notary when I entered the room.'

My head was thumping more than ever, and again I tried to remember.

I looked to Thomas Stewart for help and he lifted paper from a shelf by the door and began to read. In my first moments of bleary consciousness, I had not noticed him writing it. 'When I asked you how you had known, you said that Patrick Davidson had told you.'

I remembered. A dead man had spoken to me, and I had listened, and heard, and understood at last, as I had not done while he lived. And so I told them, and as I spoke, the notary wrote. I told them, with shame, but honestly, of my staggering vision on the night of the murder, of the whores and of the man in the gutter. I told them of seeing Janet Dawson beaten from the burgh to the rhythm of the drum, and of her desperate words to me before she was torn away, Patrick Davidson's last words. Not 'James and the flowers' as she and her sister believed they had heard on that stormy, drink-fuelled night, from the lips of a vomiting, dying man, but 'Jamesone – the flowers'. George Jamesone and the flowers – the *colchicum mortis* – falling from the open hand of Patrick Davidson's aunt, dead eight years. As I had finally realised last night at the lyikwake, the painter's words had come back to me, 'You look, but you do not see.' Standing in the great hall of the provost's house, with the body of Patrick Davidson lying on a table beside me, I had seen a portrait hanging on the wall. It was a portrait of a man and a woman, a well-made man and his pale, grieving wife, flowers falling from her hand and lying crushed and lifeless at her feet. Their lost children, each a perfect promise of beauty in this life, of hope, that had slipped from her grasp. And around them, amongst the paraphernalia of their wealth, their attainments and their aspirations, hidden away in a dark corner, almost out of sight, was a lute, a lute with a broken string. Disharmony, a love that has been strained and snapped, the painter's vision of what he truly saw before him. Completed only a few weeks before Helen Black, the aunt of Patrick Davidson and first wife of Walter Watt, Provost of Banff, had died. The loved, beloved aunt; the aunt who had been almost a mother to him.

The grieving boy had left and studied and prospered in the world. And in that world he had pursued the love of botany, planted in him by the conversations at his uncle's fireside between Walter Watt and James Cargill, physician and great botanist. Had the provost not told us so himself? The boy had travelled, and the career in law, so dry, so lacking in the life and sun and water and air and colour and texture and fragrance that he truly loved, had gradually been pushed aside as he became more and more entranced by the world of science, of medicine, and above all, of plants. Patrick Davidson had known his calling: he would study the apothecary's art. And where else would he go to apprentice than the place of his happy boyhood, where the first stirring of that love for the minute perfections of God's creation had taken him? And so he had returned to Banff, and had been welcomed by the provost as a lost son, and taken to the heart of a new family. He had sat down to dine in his uncle's great hall, and let his eyes drift up to rest for a moment on the face of his dearly loved, long-dead aunt. But just for a moment, for then his eyes travelled further, to her hand and past her skirts to the floor and he saw what he should not have been able to see. He saw what had no godly cause to be in that painting, or in this town, or this land even. He saw the flowers whose only use, beautiful though they were, was the procuring of a death, her death. But he did not let himself make the connection, did not want to see it, until he went with Marion Arbuthnott to Darkwater.

'And what did he learn there? What did you learn there?' asked the baillie in a strange voice. He knew the answer but did not wish to know it.

There was no need for me to tell them of the child that Marion had been carrying – if they did not know it already, it was none of their concern. A vision of my own mother came to me, but I pushed it away. 'He learned,' I began, 'that his aunt, Helen, had gone to her in desperation, after all that Jaffray,' I looked at the doctor and with an incline of his head he urged me to go on, 'after all that Jaffray or any other could do to help her carry a child, living, to its delivery failed her.'

'There were many others who did the same,' said the doctor, softly. 'Would to God that he had given me the skill to effect that if nothing else.'

The expected reproof from the baillie did not come. He simply said, 'Continue, Mr Seaton.' We had yet to come to the point.

'They learned that eight years ago, Helen Black, from grief and fear, had almost reached the limits of her senses.'

The notary laid off his writing. 'Do you say she took her own life?'

I opened my mouth to answer, but the baillie was there before me, speaking quietly, as to himself. 'No, never that. It was taken from her.'

Thomas Stewart looked from one to the other of us. 'The crone told you this?'

I started to shake my head but the pain stilled me. 'No, she did not. But I think, I am almost certain, that the knowledge of his aunt's fear and desperation, so close to the time of her death, the same time at which the picture, with those flowers in it, was painted, convinced Patrick Davidson that his aunt had been poisoned.'

The notary turned to Jaffray. 'Doctor, how did she die?'

Into Jaffray's eyes came an image of eight years ago, and of two weeks ago, and of four days ago. His words were slow and deliberate, as the revelation came to him. 'She died quickly, and in agony, of a sudden vomiting through which she had not the strength to crawl. That is how it was described to me, for I came too late.'

'You were not there?' I asked.

He closed his eyes as realisation took him. 'I had been making my summer visit to Glenlivet, to the mountain people. I was away from Banff longer than I had planned to be, for on my journey back to the town I was waylaid perhaps twenty miles from home by Lang Geordie and his crew. They begged that I would treat their needs – and indeed they were many – before I returned to the burgh, for at that time they were not allowed to show their faces in the town. I was with them two days.' Jaffray lowered his voice and spoke almost to himself. 'And that was the only other time I saw Walter Watt shaken as he was two weeks ago. Both times I thought it was for grief.' He sat down on the end of the bed, his head in his hands. I could not lift my arm to comfort him.

'He has played too easily upon your goodness, doctor. Hold fast to the good you have done, not to the evil that was beyond your power to change.'

Jaffray looked up wearily at the baillie. 'And have you not spent your life in fighting evil, William Buchan?'

'It is my calling,' was the simple answer.

The notary put down his paper. 'There is something here that I do not understand. You are telling us, if I have the thing to rights, that Walter Watt murdered his first wife, poisoned her in fact, and that it was because his nephew discovered this and confronted him with the knowledge that he too was murdered?'

'Yes,' I said. 'That is what I believe.'

'But he loved Helen. He grieves for her yet; I know it, for I have seen it myself in his unguarded moments. I cannot believe that he could have killed her. Why would he ever have done such a thing? What did her grief over her children signify in this?'

There was a silence in the room. I could guess the answer, and I understood now that the other two knew it also. It was a cold, sharp answer, and across the room I saw it cut into old wounds. It was not for me to respond to Thomas Stewart. 'He killed her,' began the baillie, 'because she could not give him a dynasty. And so she knew it, and spent the last months of her life in terror and despair.' His voice fell away. 'He killed her because he did not love her enough.' There was a complete silence in the room, and through it the baillie's words echoed to a time and a place long past, and to a love long dead. His head fell forward on his chest and his shoulders heaved as he struggled for breath. The doctor went to him and kneeling before him grasped both his wrists in his own two hands, counting the breaths with him until the struggle subsided. I knew now who the *H.B.* was that had lovingly stitched the hanging on the baillie's wall, so many years ago. I cursed my stupidity that I had not realised it before.

The sound of horses and wheels on the bumpy track broke into the rhythm of the breathing and gradually thundered over it as the new arrivals came closer. A clatter of hooves in the courtyard was soon followed by a shout for the doctor, and assuring himself that the baillie's crisis was over, Jaffray got up and made for his next patients. I studied William Buchan, unnoticed, but what his thoughts were at that moment I could not tell. Thomas Stewart pulled up a chair at the side of my bed, and spoke in a low voice. 'Tell me again about these flowers you spoke of, and how they told Patrick Davidson of his uncle's crime.'

I tried to sit up a little, the better to get my breath, and to speak. 'You know the portrait of Walter Watt and Helen that hangs in the great hall of the provost's house?'

The notary nodded. 'I have often seen it, but never taken great notice of it.'

286

'In that painting, Helen is holding flowers in her hand – they are a symbol of her hopes, her children. But the flowers are falling from her hand, and many lie already crushed on the floor.'

'Her lost babies,' said the notary.

'Yes. Jamesone himself told me, if I had had the wit to listen properly. The point is, those flowers are not – or were not – grown in these parts. The laird of Banff tried many years ago and failed to cultivate them after bringing some specimens back from his travels abroad. But another did not fail. Walter Watt did not fail. And Walter Watt knew, probably from the mouth of James Cargill himself, that these plants were utterly lethal in all their parts. I believe he grew them at first for love of their beauty, and that is why they are there in the painting, as something beautiful. But when, sometime afterwards, he could no longer stand the strain of his wife's repeated losses of their children, when he came to realise that this woman, whom he is acknowledged to have loved, would bear him no heir, he took the roots of that same plant and poisoned her with them. He was safe until the day someone else came and looked upon that portrait and saw the flowers for what they were.'

'His own nephew,' said the notary, understanding now. 'And he never thought to take the painting down? He did not think discovery possible? Truly, the man's arrogance was monstrous.'

'Monstrous, yes, but I think also, in spite of all he had done, he loved her still. And just like Walter Watt himself, all that Patrick Davidson saw when he looked at that portrait was his beloved aunt's face. It was not until he had been to Darkwater, and considered the wise woman's words, that he questioned his aunt's state of mind before her death, and that led him back to the picture, painted in her last weeks on this earth, and the flowers that she held in her hand. I think he confronted his uncle with his suspicions, but where he intended to take the matter from that point, I do not know. Perhaps he did not know himself. In the end, it was immaterial: he died because of it.'

He pressed me further. 'How do you think the thing was brought about?'

'That I cannot tell you,' I said.

'Perhaps there is someone else who can,' murmured the baillie, who had been listening throughout. 'No matter, though. Continue, Mr Seaton.'

I reached for another sip of water which Thomas Stewart helped me to. 'I do not know that there is anything left I can tell you,' I said.

The notary, though, had more he would know. 'Do you think Patrick Davidson revealed his knowledge to Marion Arbuthnott?' His line of thought was logical; it was what Marion had feared and what Charles Thom had soon come to understand – that the possession of this knowledge would be as a death warrant to whoever came to own it.

'No,' I replied, 'I am certain he did not.'

'Why not?' asked the notary.

'Because she would not have kept on searching if he had.' It was the baillie who had spoken. He had got up from his chair and now began to pace the room. 'She would not have needed to continue searching for the truth of his death if she had known it already.'

He had said exactly what I had been thinking. 'That was why she went back to the wise woman of Darkwater after his death,' I said. 'Because she still did not know. The crone told me that. That Marion had gone back to her, asking about the *colchicum*, and she, the old woman, had been able to describe it to her. She had described to her the flower that, in the course of her duties as nursery maid to Geleis Guild, the girl must have seen, captured in oils on canvas, a dozen times a day. And now Marion is dead. She, too, must have confronted the provost.'

Again the baillie demurred. 'I do not think so. As soon as she returned from Darkwater she sent word by her father that she wished to see me. It was just after noon. The council had convened as a matter of urgency, to discuss the defence of the burgh in the event of foreign attack. The meeting was to be held in the utmost secrecy, and the town serjeant had been warned that it was not to be disturbed. It was almost five by the time we had finished with the business, and, fool that I was, instead of going directly to the apothecary's, I made my usual evening inspection of the tolbooth.' He was revisiting the scene in his mind. 'By the time I reached Arbuthnott's, the girl had gone. Her mother told me she had gone in a distracted state to meet with Geleis Guild shortly after sending me her note. She had returned later, in a worse case than she had left in, and would tell her mother nothing of the cause, but said only she must speak to me. A little after four, a messenger had arrived from the provost's house, requesting her to go there as a matter of urgency. Marion had set out immediately, and her mother never saw her alive again. She was found not two hours later by Geleis Guild in the castle grounds. Dead, dead.'

Images of a young woman gazing towards the waves from the height of the Elf Kirk, of the same woman softly singing to the children of Geleis Guild in the garden of the provost's house, of the same woman, dead and burning on a stake at the market cross of Banff filled my mind. At the last, they merged, horribly, with the indelible memory of Patrick Davidson lying, grass in his hands and his mouth, sprawled and dead across my desk in a pool of his own vomit.

This was not right. There was something that could not be right. 'It was Geleis Guild who found her?' I asked.

'Yes,' said the notary, 'and her children.'

And her children. She could not have done that, knowing what was to be found. And why, only last night at the lyikwake, had she urged me on in my searches?

The baillie interrupted my wonderings. 'Something puzzles you, Mr Seaton.'

'Aye, it does. It is Geleis Guild. I do not understand her. She is a woman distraught, and yet she must have joined with her husband in his murderous doings.'

'Why would you think that?' quizzed the baillie.

It was evident to me. 'Because I do not see how the provost could have been murdering Marion Arbuthnott while he was with you in the council chamber.'

Comprehension came over the baillie's face. 'But Walter Watt was not there. The nature of our discoveries about his nephew's activities caused some alarm amongst those few who knew of it, and it was adjudged best to keep the meeting a secret from the provost until such time as we had a clear knowledge and understanding of his nephew's activities and connections hereabouts. Walter Watt was not in the council chamber when Marion Arbuthnott died. To judge by the carriage of his wife these last days, I think it very unlikely she was an accomplice in his deeds.'

A soft voice drifted to us from the doorway. 'You are wrong, baillie, you are wrong.' And there, like a wraith from another world, stood Geleis Guild herself. Her pallor was complete, her eyes rimmed in red, then black, her hair loose and dull on her shoulders. She had the air of one further from the living than the dead. She could scarcely support herself in the doorway, and around her wrists were thick bands of linen, applied, as I later learned, a few hours ago by the doctor, in a desperate effort to stay the harm that she had determined to do herself.

Jaffray came in behind her. 'Take a seat, my dear; you are not well enough to be up yet.'

'It matters little,' she said, but nevertheless allowed herself to be led to a chair.

The baillie watched her, carefully, and with a strange curiosity on his face. 'I cannot fathom it, mistress. Indeed, I cannot believe it. Would you really have us believe that you were the willing companion of your husband's deed?'

'Not willing,' she said. 'No, never that.'

I saw it now, I thought. 'Nor witting, either?' I asked.

She looked over to me with a terrible desperation in her eyes, and made as if to speak but stopped, at a loss.

'Did you know what your husband was about, mistress?' asked the baillie.

She shook her head. 'Not at first. Not at all. I did not know all until Marion told me.' She looked down at her wrists and began to pick at the bandages, speaking almost absently as she did so. 'I should have realised long ago. Sometimes I think I should have wondered.' She trailed off, and then, having lost herself a few moments in her musing, she was recalled back to the present. 'I was little more than a girl when Helen died. In truth, I remember very little about her. She was a married woman, the wife of one of the magistrates with whom my brother, Robert, was keen to curry favour – for even then it could be seen that Walter would be a man of importance, and my brother liked to be counted amongst the men of importance. My brother had hopes that I might make an impression on Helen – become her companion, help her in the nursery – be to her in fact what Marion was to become to me. But Helen had her own friends – older women – like your mother,' she said, looking at me with an effort at kindness in her eyes.

'And as for the nursery – there was to be no nursery.' She paused and made herself leave off the picking at the bandages. 'When she died, my brother made a great show of sorrow, which I knew was not real. He would imagine himself perpetually required to give succour and counsel at Walter Watt's house, but I know Robert is an object of contempt to honourable and intelligent men, and such I could clearly perceive to be the case with Walter also. And yet, invitations came to us often from the magistrate, and soon I came to understand that it was not my brother's but my own company that Walter sought. I could not understand it, for he was deep, so deep in grief and love for his wife. He spoke little of her, but her face was always in his eyes, her name always ready to fall silent from his lips. I was not yet seventeen when it was agreed between him and Robert that we should marry, that I should take Helen's place.' She gave a small, humourless laugh. 'What a mockery! That I should take her place? He was kind to me, I can never deny that; he took pleasure – took his pleasure with me, and I came to love him beyond measure, and child after child though I bore him, I knew I would never take Helen's place. And so it went on, and by the grace of God, as I thought, our family thrived and Walter rose higher and higher in the burgh. I knew of no one better blessed, yet there was still a dark emptiness within him that I think was only truly filled when he looked at Helen's portrait. I thought she haunted him, and perhaps she did, and the memory of her tormented him.'

'And in all that time, mistress, you truly suspected nothing?'

'Nothing,' she said. 'And then Patrick came home. I must confess,' and here, for the first time, she allowed herself a real smile, 'I felt a little anxious at the prospect. He had come to visit us once before, but just for a few days, before he left for the continent, but this time he was coming to stay. For years, I had heard nothing but the praises of this boy – this young man as he was to be. To Walter he had been as a son. He had once said to me, before he could stop himself – for he was always careful not to hurt me – that if he could have had such a son, of Helen, he could have asked for nothing more. There was a joy in him when he heard Patrick was coming home that I had rarely seen, and I know he left Arbuthnott in little doubt as to how the boy was to be treated – it was impressed upon the apothecary what an honour it was for him to have and house such an apprentice.'

291

'And when the boy did return, how were things between them then?'

A light came into her eyes as she replied to the baillie. 'It was a thing lovely to behold. They were as father and son reunited. And in truth, for myself, I could not be jealous. Walter was so happy and so proud to show off his own little ones to Patrick who, he said, would be as a brother to them. And so it was. I have seldom met such a good, loving young man, and I know from Walter, and Arbuthnott – and indeed Marion – that he was greatly gifted. I had never seen my husband at such peace. That Patrick and Marion then became attached made it all the sweeter for me. There was true happiness in our household. It was our time of true happiness.'

I had known such a time. 'And then?' I said.

She looked at me directly and spoke bluntly. 'And then, it came to its end. Patrick was invited to take his dinner with Walter and with the doctor, who had just returned from Edinburgh, and who was very desirous to meet him.' The doctor, I could guess, had not been subtle in pressing for an invitation. 'Patrick had been that day with Marion out to Sandend, then onto Findlater and Darkwater, gathering plants as she told me. He did not go back to the apothecary's to wash or to change his clothing when they returned, but came directly here. A change had come over him – he was not his usual, easy self, but nervy and agitated. He was most desirous of seeing Walter privately before the doctor should arrive. I asked him to rest, or to take a little refreshment while he waited, but he would have none of it, and spent the whole time in gazing intently at the portrait on the wall – the one of Walter and Helen.'

'And did they have this private interview?' I asked.

'Yes,' she said. 'They did. I heard nothing of it – I was in the kitchens – but within half an hour of Walter arriving home, it was over – Patrick had left. Walter looked ill, shaken. He would have put off the doctor if he could have done. He would not tell me what was wrong or why Patrick had left, just that the boy had been upset, but he had managed to calm him and would speak with him the next day.'

'And was that the last you saw of the boy?' The baillie was watching her keenly.

She looked at her hands again and then directly at William Buchan. 'No,' she said, 'it was not.'

'He came to the house again?'

'I think so. That is,' she hesitated, unsure how to proceed. 'I did not see him come, but I saw him leave.'

'When was it?' asked the baillie.

She shook her head and began to weep.

'It was the night of the storm, was it not?' I said.

She nodded and then began to weep all the more uncontrollably. 'I had scarcely seen Walter all day. He had spent much of the morning in his business room and then the afternoon out and about in the town. He was drenched and muddy when he returned home. He said he wanted no supper, and was not to be disturbed in his work, although I heard him later go down to the kitchen where a pot of stew had been left on the hearth. I had much trouble with the children that evening – they were in such great fear of the storm. I was concerned about Walter, and sat at my needlework for as long as I could, but a little before ten, tiredness overwhelmed me and I decided to retire without having seen my husband. As I was mounting the back stairs, I saw a hooded figure come out of Walter's work room and leave the house by the side door, directly onto Water Path. I thought it was Patrick by the height and gait of him. I was so anxious to put right whatever had gone wrong with him and Walter, I threw a cloak around my shoulders and went out without even a lantern to try to overtake him. I had not expected the tempest outside to be so bad, and I made little headway in catching him up – the streets were near enough turned to rivers. I kept him in my sights, but then he started stumbling, falling, grabbing out at walls, banks, even the grass, it seemed to try to steady himself. I knew he was not drunk, because he had walked straight enough when he had left Walter's room and our house. I started to run, to go to his aid and then I saw . . .' She stopped, and bit her lip.

'You saw me, did you not?'

'Yes, Mr Seaton,' she said quietly, 'I saw you. I thought you would have helped him, but—'

'But I did not.' I could feel the eyes of the baillie and the notary on me, fast, now, and I could not look at either of them.

The baillie's mind was working quickly. 'And so you helped him to the schoolroom, in the hope that Mistress Youngson would hear and find him?'

'No,' she looked up, surprised, defensive even. 'Had I reached him, I would have helped him home – to the apothecary's, or to the doctor's if I could have managed it. Even to the schoolhouse, but I would have roused someone, wherever it might have been.'

'But you did not?' queried the baillie.

'No,' her voice was flat. 'I could not. As I watched Mr Seaton pass by, I saw two figures coming from the direction of the churchyard, and they saw me.'

'The Dawson sisters,' I said.

She nodded. 'They waited until you had turned into the schoolhouse pend and then went to him. They managed to lift him between them and drag him – somehow – after the way you had gone. They were gone from sight a few minutes and I waited – I thought they must have roused you. When they came out again, one of them looked towards where I stood. She turned again as they took the other fork up the path, as if to tell me all was well, that I could go back now. And so I did.'

Her head sank into her hands and I realised that someone else, for two weeks, had been carrying something of my guilt. 'There was little you could have done,' I offered her. 'You were not to know they had not alerted me. The fault is not yours.' My words did little to comfort her, if indeed they reached her at all.

The baillie gave her a moment, but there were still many questions to be answered, and every moment wasted was a moment more for Walter Watt to make good his flight. 'After all this,' he began, 'you still did not suspect your husband? Even when you heard how Patrick Davidson had died?'

She shook her head dumbly, her face puffy and blotched now. 'I was very scared, when the news of Patrick's death was brought to us the next morning, that his falling out with Walter might have something to do with it, in some manner or other. But then when I saw how Walter took the terrible news, how desolate it left him, I could not believe that he had had anything to do with it. And he did not want to talk to me about it; I could see that well enough.'

Yes, I remembered. Remembered how keen Walter Watt had been to shield his wife from us that morning when we had brought the dead body of Patrick Davidson on a bier to their home. I remembered how he had urged her away to the nursery early in that conference. And I remembered also how determined he had been, to begin with, to argue that I must have been with his nephew the night before. Only with the suggestions of Charles Thom as a worthy suspect for the murder had the provost lost interest in pressing my possible guilt.

'You told him, did you not, what you had seen, and by whom you had been seen? And you told him you had seen me?'

She looked at me, somewhat confused. 'I – yes, I did.' Unwilling, yes, but unwitting more so, she had consigned Janet and Mary Dawson to a perpetual banishment from this town; even, for Mary, from Scotland itself, warned off by the provost's henchman. And she would, but for the chance and ill-luck of Charles Thom, have consigned me to the hangman's noose. I was to have been her husband's scapegoat. But why then had he taken me into his confidence, entrusted me with the mission of the maps? I saw that my pride had set a trap for me. Once he had seen that the papers found in his nephew's room bore no account of Patrick Davidson's suspicions of him, the maps in themselves had mattered little to him. I had no doubt a report of my encounter with Janet Dawson as she had been beaten from the burgh bounds would have reached his ears. I had not been entrusted with some important mission on the burgh's behalf: I had been got out of the way.

The baillie had perhaps seen too many weeping women pleading ignorance of their husband's deeds, or perhaps his antipathy towards the Reverend Guild extended to his sister, but he certainly was not yet satisfied or finished with Geleis Guild. 'Do you have any knowledge of flowers, mistress, of the science of botany?'

'Why, no. Not more than is common for uses in the nursery and about the household, but in truth, even in that my knowledge was lacking, for with Marion to assist me, there was little need for me to look into such things myself.'

'But your husband had knowledge?' he persisted.

She shook her head slowly. 'I never knew it. He never once, in all the time I knew him, showed any interest in plants. Indeed, the garden of his first home, that he shared with Helen, had been a wondrous place, but it soon went to neglect after her death, and his housekeeper took over the growing of what was needful for the kitchens. He did not even seem to mind that Helen's Eden would be destroyed to make way for my brother's new manse.'

'Helen's Eden was destroyed long ago, mistress, and he the serpent.'

Geleis Guild had no answer to the baillie's words, and simply bit her lip, then said, 'It was only once Patrick returned, and they reminisced about their old days together, that I learned Walter had had a love of plants and flowers. I did not dwell long on the strangeness of it – I just thought it something too closely tied to Helen for him to think of without her.'

'It was, for it was what he used to kill her. The flowers that were to bring death to her, and to her nephew, and to Marion Arbuthnott, still grow in the garden of that house.'

'But Walter gifted the house and land to the kirk for my brother – and for all the ministers to follow. It was his great desire that the land be cleared for the new manse as soon as possible. He went often to check on the work, and was greatly frustrated by the delays occasioned by George Burnett's appearances before the session over his fornication with the servant girl.'

'The servant girl.' Said as if she had no name. In Sarah Forbes's position, how would Geleis Guild have fared? With less dignity, I told myself, and with no resilience at all.

The baillie's voice was cold. 'He wanted the evidence of his crime destroyed before the boy returned and saw it. But he could not bring himself to destroy it by his own hand, for fear that he would need it again. I think he wished the decision to be taken from him, and so they were still there, to be used in the killing of Patrick Davidson and then of Marion Arbuthnott.'

'Do not mistake me, baillie,' she said, suddenly strong, 'I do not doubt that it was his hand that killed them all, but I still do not understand it, for he loved Helen – loves her yet – and Patrick too.'

'And yet,' he replied, talking to her but looking at me, 'for some men, worldly ambition will fill the void left by what they imagine to be the greatest love. He did not truly love her at all.'

There was little comprehension in the young woman's eyes, and her bodily weakness was becoming more and more evident. The doctor had held his tongue longer than I would have thought possible, but he could hold it no longer. 'I must get this girl to her rest, baillie. You can take up your questioning again tomorrow.'

The baillie nodded his assent, but said, 'I must know one more thing, mistress. When did you finally understand what your husband was doing, and what he had done?'

She was standing now, leaning on the doctor's arm. 'When Marion came to me, to tell me what she knew. She wanted to warn me, to get the children away. But I did not believe her, and so I took her tales to Walter, who had me call her back, that he might reassure her, as he said. And I was touched,' she smiled bitterly, 'touched by his concern for her, for she looked truly ill. He left me with her and went himself to fetch her some broth from the kitchen. He spoke to her a few moments, kindly, gently, to calm her fears. He told me that he himself would see her safe home, but that first of all I should "bid the girl eat", and so I did, and sent her to her death.' The finality in the last words precluded any further questioning, and Jaffray took Geleis Guild away, to begin her own sentence of despair.

I was alone in the room now with William Buchan. 'You feared Marion might stumble on the truth and make it known, before there could be evidence or anything to protect her. That is why you strove so hard to keep everyone from her.'

'Aye,' he replied, 'to her own cost, and to theirs. If only the girl had told what she knew to me. Then I would have had him, and he could have done no further harm.'

'It was perhaps not God's will,' I said, no longer self-conscious at speaking of God's will with this man who strove daily to see and have it enacted on this earth.

'It was God's judgement on me, on my pride, on my carriage towards my fellow man, that she did not take her burden to me sooner. And I must look to it. I must look to it.' So saying, he got up from his chair, coughing, and without a backward glance to where I still lay, William Buchan, who last night had stayed the murderous hand of Walter Watt as it readied itself to crash down a second time on my forehead, left me to my thoughts.

EPILOGUE

August, 1626

William Cargill laughed as I tried to steady myself after clambering onto the boat.

'You would never have made a sailor, nor yet a merchant, Alexander.' No one else had noticed my awkwardness – it was of little interest to the shore porters that the black-cloaked man of learning could not balance himself aboard ship. The loading of the salmon barrels for Aberdeen had almost finished, and William and I took ourselves to the bow of the ship to keep out of the way of those that had work to do. We looked back at the town.

'It is not a bad sight, as such places go.'

'You have travelled more than I, William; you are the better qualified to judge.'

'Maybe, maybe so,' he said. 'But while I see fine buildings and poor hovels, you see the histories of those who inhabit them. I see the bricks and mortar; you see the fabric of the life.'

'And have often shut my eyes to it, and that gladly.' I looked up beyond the town, up towards the Sandyhill Gate, where a black smoke was rising and curling into the sky. The new provost, and the baillie, his health recovered now from the eight years of strain that he had very nearly succumbed to, had begun their work of cleansing the burgh: the codroche houses were ablaze. Few on the quayside cared to turn their gaze to the flames; there had been too many fires in this town. I wondered about the children, taken from their mothers and put to work in the salmon house, all to the service of God and the stability of the realm.

The last of the barrels was loaded, and there remained but one piece of

298

cargo before the ship could weigh anchor and set sail. I watched with some foreboding as the shore porters lashed ropes around my great oak chest and signalled for the men aboard to winch it up on their pulley. My life's worth of books was in that chest, with old notes, theses, sermons, and a fur rug pressed upon me last night by the doctor. Another, more flimsy kist carried my two changes of clothing, my winter cloak and old fur rug, and the pewter cup and plate that had come to me from my mother. Around my waist was the belt and great silver buckle that had been my father's last gift to me, and in the bundle at my feet one of Mistress Youngson's famed clootie dumplings. 'Mind you feed yourself – the college buttery is near enough bare, they tell me,' was all the old woman had said as she'd pressed it into my arms. Then she had straightened the collar of the fine suit I had not worn since Marion Arbuthnott's lyikwake some months before. 'And mind you do not disgrace us; I will know of it from Elizabeth if you do.' William had assured my old landlady that his wife would indeed keep her apprised of all my misadventures and misdemeanours.

In the pocket at my breast as the ropes were loosed and the vessel finally began to move away from the dock at Banff was the letter, the precious letter bearing the seal of the Marischal College in Aberdeen. My hand went to my pocket and felt for the hundredth time the fine vellum, and the hard wax of the seal. It had been delivered to Banff by none other than Robert Gordon of Straloch, sent by his master of Huntly to assure the new provost and council of Banff of his friendship and goodwill. And who would it have been more fitting to send on such a mission? For as I had passed my wakeful night in his house, Robert Gordon had sent his own young kinsmen through the dark night to Strathbogie to seek assurances from the marquis himself that he knew nothing of maps or invasions. But what was Huntly's word worth? Only time would tell. Patrick Davidson's maps, fine work that they were, were ashes now. And we would never know whether they had been, as Gilbert Grant always insisted they were, the blameless pursuit of a young man with a thirst to understand the world, or a God-given talent tainted and betrayed at the behest of the agents of Rome. Those secrets had gone with him to the grave.

Straloch had sought me out in my schoolroom, and had found me in the midst of explaining a passage of Buchanan to my scholars. The laird would not hear of me interrupting my lesson, and had sat quietly at the back of the room, now nodding, now noting a query, until I released the boys for lunch. But the letter he had then handed me was not of history, nor yet of politics or plots, but of philosophy, of logic, of rhetoric, and of mathematics. In short, it was an invitation from Patrick Dun, principal of the Marischal College in the new burgh of Aberdeen, to submit myself for trial before the principal, regents, magistrates and ministers of the new town for the vacant place of Regent of Philosophy in that college. The letter bore reference to recommendations of me from Dr John Forbes of Corse, from Bishop Patrick, his father, and from Robert Gordon of Straloch himself. At the end of Principal Dun's letter was a short note from Dr Forbes, a few words only, but they spoke from Philippians to my soul. 'He which hath begun a good work in you will perform it until the day of Jesus Christ.' As I read it and re-read it, chains and bounds snapped and fell away at my feet. After the laird had gone, I climbed the thirty-seven steps to my chamber and prayed as I had not prayed for almost a year; I prayed and knew I was heard. That night, I opened my books, grown dusty and threatened with damp from misuse and I began to read once more. And then, within two days of the arrival of Gordon of Straloch had come, hot on his heels, William Cargill, who knew all the business that passed in Aberdeen, often before it had passed. Such was his fear that I would still keep to my pit of self-pity that he dared not trust me to answer for myself and so had come to do it for me. How could I tell him that, within a moment of breaking the seal, I had known that I would accept this new call, and leave this place, with no mind ever to return?

Charles Thom was not there to bid me farewell, for he was returned to his post in the music school, and the baillie and his fellows kept a closer eye than ever on their young precentor, having learnt, at last, to look beyond a man's face to know his heart. There was no Jaffray there, either. He had wished me my farewells last night, over a bottle of the finest *uisge beatha* in his house. He had waxed long and hard at my ingratitude in leaving him now, in a household where his maid no longer cared whether he ate or starved, such was her anxiety for their new lodger. He had warned me of the fickleness of women, and the weakness of men, lamented the distance from Banff to Aberdeen and yet complained at my stubbornness at not taking ship for Europe, where a real career was still to be had. At the last he had told me he could not spare me the time to come down to the shore and see me off, for he was a busy man, and what was I to him but the ingrate stripling of an honourable hammerman and his lovely Irish wife. And he had held me close and called me son.

I looked towards the Gallow Hill, where but a month ago Walter Watt had been sent to meet his maker. He had been caught three days after his flight, his horse abandoned, trying to enter Aberdeen, alone, by night. It was thought he had been heading for the harbour, and a cargo ship bound for the Low Countries. He would never see them now.

And as I took my last look for many years at the burgh of my birth, my eye was drawn down to the shore side. A lone figure stood still amidst the hubbub of the harbour and watched until our vessel disappeared from sight. He stood there, unmoving, in the town where he had been born, grown up, fallen in love; the town where he had had to withdraw to the shadows and watch the girl he loved be given to a higher bidder, a man of greater means. He had had to see her suffering and loss, and see her buried, dead at that husband's hand. And he had had to wait eight years to see her have justice in this world. I raised my hand in silent farewell, understanding now, at last. It would be many a long day before I again came upon a man such as Baillie William Buchan.

GLOSSARY

backland	land to the rear of a burgess's house for growing foodstuffs, keeping animals, siting wells and middens
baillie	town magistrate, next in rank to provost in burgh hierarchy
besom	broom (stick)
burgess	privileged member of burgh society with land and institutionalised rights
burn	stream
cittern	guitar-like musical instrument
clarsach	celtic harp
codroche house	house of idle, slovenly people of low class and ill-repute
feu	right to the use of a property in return for a fixed yearly payment
furth of	away from; beyond the confines of
haar	sea mist
iron gad	iron bar to which prisoners' feet were shackled
kirk session	governing body of a parish, consisting of minister and elders, with spiritual authority, disciplinary powers and social welfare responsibilities
kist	chest
links	sandy, grassy ground near the shoreline
litster	dyer
lykewake	gathering at the night watch over someone who has died
mortcloth	cloth used to cover the bodies of the dead before burial

pend	an arched passageway
precentor	person who leads the congregation in psalm-singing
presbytery	church court/gathering made up of ministers from each parish in its area (superior to kirk session)
provost	civic head of burgh – equivalent to mayor
rebec	lute-shaped, violin-like instrument
regent	university teacher who took one class through the entire four years of their master of arts (philosophy) course. [verb: to regent]
tabor	small drum
tack	lease
toft	site of house; homestead
trials	a series of active tests for aspirants for the ministry
uisge beatha	whisky [Gaelic]
vague	to roam, wander
vennel	narrow alleyway or lane
wynd	narrow, winding alley

Note: 'Mistress Youngson'; 'Geleis Guild' etc. – Scottish women of the period did not take their husband's name on marriage, but kept their own.